RENEGADE CROWN

STAR BANDITS: UPRISING BOOK 6

JENNIFER M. EATON

Renegade Crown
Star Bandits: Uprising Book 6
© 2025 Jennifer M. Eaton

Published by Galactic Razor
Cover design: Covers by Julie
www.coversbyjulie.com

This book is dedicated to YOU.
Your commitment to saving the galaxy has not gone unnoticed.
You may now consider yourself an official Star Bandit.
Welcome to the crew.

CHAPTER 1
DANIA

DANIA STOOD on the command deck of Geron's cruiser and stared at the massive ship filling the monitors.

The *Oliganton*...the largest ship ever manufactured.

Under other circumstances, she'd see the arrival of the king as a thrill...a new challenge or the opportunity to discuss tactics with more hardened enforcers. Today, though, she could only see the megalith as a harbinger of doom, ready to swallow her and everyone she cared about whole.

Geron's father rarely left Kever space. Was he truly this angry with his son for not returning home when called?

"We're receiving a priority communication." The nav officer turned to Dania. "We're being boarded, General."

The former high prince's commander, Orion, stifled a snort, shifting his large frame. He probably looked forward to whatever punishment lay in store for her sponsor.

Dania wanted nothing more than to squelch Orion's over-inflated ego, but that would need to wait for a far more opportune time.

She turned back to her captain. "Notify Geron. I'll escort him to the hangar to meet his father."

Orion inclined his head, making the light shine through his silvery white hair. "I trust I can join you?"

Dania glared at him. "Fine."

After the high prince's recent death, Orion probably hoped to be absorbed by the highest-ranking Bane in the galaxy—meaning the king. Part of her wanted to lock him in the brig for his insolence. The more rational part of her was delighted at the thought of getting rid of him for good.

She stormed through the hall, Orion on her heels. If the king did absorb Orion, she needed to make sure that the commander transferred to the king's vessel immediately. He'd been a nuisance as the high prince's commander. If he actually spoke for the king, he would most likely make a play for control again.

That would only be if Orion saw the need, since Geron was most likely about to face his father's wrath.

A heaviness thickened her chest. Geron had—possibly for the first time in his life—done what many would consider the *right thing*. He'd placed the lives of dying enforcers in front of his own safety by defying his father's call to come home. It had been a selfless act.

That wouldn't matter, though, because defying the king never went well, no matter how good your reasons were for doing so.

As they approached Geron's rooms the door opened, and her sponsor exited, wearing a uniform with a red and bright-blue stripe on the left shoulder, a sign of his rank.

Geron rarely wore his royal insignia. He'd told her he found the stripe pompous and extraneous. The king, of course, disagreed.

His large form dwarfed his enforcers as he stepped into the hallway. His normally flawless green and blue complexion darkened, betraying both his anger and trepidation.

"Why is my father here?" Geron kept walking toward the main hangar, fastening the buttons on his sleeves.

If he'd wanted an answer, he would have waited for one. Dania assumed the question had been rhetorical, because they both knew the reason.

After the deaths of six of his siblings, Geron's brother Keza was now high prince, and Geron had been elevated to prime three, making him second in line for the throne.

Whether Geron liked it or not, he was no longer expendable.

Ignoring the king's order to return home would not be ignored, and now, the king was demonstrating a show of power to make a point. Dania hoped whatever punishment the king rendered would only be an admonishment. However, even the king's admonishments, she'd seen, could scar someone for life.

They moved into the hangar and Dania stood beside Geron as three large ships set down on the main guest landing pads. The *Star Renegade* remained parked just to the right of the royal ships. If Cal had been hoping for a distraction, this was certainly it. And with the hangar open, they wouldn't even have to blast their way out. They could just engage their engines and run.

This was the perfect time for them to make their escape. The *Star Renegade* was the least of Geron's problems, and no one even looked in the smuggling ship's direction. Cal would never get a better chance to get away.

But she knew he wouldn't take it. Dania and Alexander weren't on board, and Cal wouldn't leave without them. He certainly wouldn't leave without Dania.

When she'd first boarded the *Star Renegade*, she'd believed Cal's love for his crew was his greatest weakness. Now, she believed that more than ever. He had it in his power to save everyone on that ship, but instead, they sat there, giving up a once-in-a-millennia opportunity over the hope of saving two lives: hers and Alexander's.

It was inefficient and wrong. For the first time, she wished Geron had reabsorbed her, erasing her memory and making her a fully-powered enforcer again. If Cal no longer had hope, he would have done the right thing and escaped while he still had the chance.

The air shield screen flowed back over the ships until it hung over the hangar doors as they began to close.

Dania's second-in-command, Kile, stepped to her right, his massive frame instantly dwarfing her. Alexander took his place beside him, his long, silvery blond hair in juxtaposition to the commander's tightly cropped locks.

Their placement was the correct formation for an enforcer guard to greet the king, but she still wished Alexander stood directly beside her, rather than her commander.

The first two ships opened up. The third, the king's ship, remained sealed. His Illustriousness was known for taking his time. Dania always wondered if he simply enjoyed making a grand entrance. The man's ego truly had no bounds.

She flinched, wiping away the thoughts, even though they were true. With Geron's sudden elevation in rank, she'd be spending even more time in the king's royal presence. Dania needed to keep her focus and show respect at all times.

She looked longingly at the *Star Renegade* again as the hangar doors closed. That small, beaten-up ship had become her home. The crew had become her family, helping her to heal and become human again.

Dania had one wonderful night to remember with Cal. She wouldn't change it for the world, but she still wished he'd had the courage to leave her behind and save the others.

Male and female Kevers streamed from the two ships in royal house uniforms fitting their stations. A few uniforms were marred with black stains. Others were creased in the wrong places. Had the ship recently seen battle?

Geron shifted his weight from foot to foot as the officials fanned out on either side of the room. They each faced their prince, leaving a clear aisle between them leading to the last ship. The formation was meant to increase anticipation and call the most attention to the king.

Today, the effect was even more apparent. A small trickle of heat emanated from Geron's skin. The arrival of his father, especially with such a pompous display of pageantry, most likely meant Geron was in for a public admonishment.

This was nothing new. Geron had been in this situation before. This time, however, was the first time he'd be reprimanded for attempting to save lives. She hoped her sponsor would work to keep his ego in check and not use this public forum to tell his father exactly what he thought about him.

The last official took their place in the line of dignitaries. They each stood at attention and stared straight ahead in Geron's direction—looking far too much like an execution squad.

Many flinched as the doors to the king's ship opened.

The Counselor General, in full royal regalia with etched red gems fastened to a looped necklace over his perfectly placed uniform strode forward beside another blue-skinned

Kever man in a gray ambassador's uniform. They stopped about ten feet from Geron and stood at attention.

Geron tensed at the same moment Dania did. His father would wait a few moments to make sure all eyes were on him and then leave his ship.

She could feel her own distaste for the king simmering in her veins. She really needed to center herself and force herself to think clearly.

Alexander's voice exploded in her mind. *"Or…you are thinking clearly for the first time in your life."*

She looked past Kile to her friend. He kept his face forward, and no one outside the two of them would know he'd spoken to her.

His intrusions were normally admonishments, not shows of solidarity. He might be right, though. This was the first time she'd be in contact with Geron's father when her thoughts were not being controlled by her duty…by her *programming*. It was going to be like meeting the king for the first time.

Whether that was a good or a bad thing remained to be seen.

Someone in the back of the procession called out a word Dania didn't catch, and the entire royal procession dropped to one knee. The first row, including the Counselor General and the ambassador, touched their foreheads to the floor.

That was…*odd*. She couldn't recall the king ever requiring such reverence when he disembarked from a ship.

Geron strode forward, stopping a few steps in front of the Counselor General. "What is the meaning of this? Where is my father?"

The Counselor General's left hand shook on the floor. "Dead."

Several people behind Dania gasped. Her own lips parted. Had she heard that right?

Geron loomed over everyone. "What?"

"There was a full-scale attack on Keveron. Our military was scattered, protecting other planets. We didn't even see them coming until they were already on top of us."

Dania's gut clenched. That meant Geron was now the high prince. He'd been hiding from responsibility his whole life. And now, this?

The heat around Geron became blistering. "This is insane. There must be a mistake. Keza can't be king. He's not trained."

The ambassador and the Counselor General glanced at each other again.

The Counselor gulped. "Keza is not king. Your brother led the final line of defense when the Carteks arrived." He looked down. "The enemy hit us with wave after wave of ships. It seemed unending. Our planetary defenses were decimated within hours. We took it upon ourselves to evacuate everyone we could onto your father's ship."

Geron stepped back. "What are you saying?"

"There were no survivors. Every member of your family perished in the attack. You are the last living Bane. *You* are the king."

Dania worked to keep herself steady as others stumbled.

Orion's mouth fell open. He looked from the king's transport, to Geron, to the king's transport again.

Geron took a step back. "You're all mad. Is this some kind of twisted ruse? A test of resilience from my father? I can't be king. This is insanity."

The Counselor General stood slowly, holding up his palms. "I assure you, this is no game."

Fire erupted in Geron's hands. "This is not happening. How can my entire family be dead?"

The ambassador stood and pursed his lips, facing his counterpart. "I told you coming here is a waste of time." He pointed at Geron. "This one has never been worthy of his position. His father thought he was a waste of lineage, and he was right."

Geron roared, and the ambassador rose from his feet and flew across the hangar bay. He smashed into the wall with a sickening splat, blood shooting from his body on all sides before he burst into flames.

The Counselor dropped back to his knees and placed his forehead back to the ground. So did everyone else in the room, even those in the back rows.

What was left of the ambassador's body dripped down the wall and puddled on the floor as Geron watched, panting heavily.

Dania shook off her shock.

This couldn't be happening. He needed to gain control.

She placed her hand on Geron's arm. "Ada, I understand that this is a confusing time, but I think it would be a good idea not to execute your father's advisors. You may need to look to them for counsel."

A low growl rumbled up his throat. "I am angry."

"I understand, and I'm sure this is a shock. Would you like me to take care of things for you?"

Orion scoffed. "Of course he does. He's a simpleton, incapable of ruling. The ambassador was right, and he was just executed for telling the truth."

Geron spun on him, and Dania grabbed him again. "Orion is a commander with significant tactical training who has recently found himself without a sponsor. I suggest absorbing him at the next possible convenient time and utilizing his expertise."

"How dare you?" Orion growled.

Dania narrowed her eyes at him. "If you are looking for a fast execution, you will not get one here. As you like to keep reminding me, we're at war. We will need all available soldiers. Even you."

Geron rubbed the bridge of his nose, looking out over what was left of his father's governing body. He grimaced. "Get up. All of you. Stop groveling on the floor like animals begging for food."

The Counselor General folded his hands. "Sire, I know this is not the best time, but we need to discuss the state of the war."

Geron shook his head. "Not now."

"We must."

Heat surrounded Geron again. "I just found out my brothers, my sisters, my parents…are dead. And my home world has been decimated."

"I understand, sire, but we need to know if you intend to hold to your father's bonds."

Geron closed his eyes and formed several words but seemed to change his mind before saying each. "Can you give me a chance to process this?"

"I'm sorry, sire, but I cannot. The Carteks are assembling an attack force the likes of which we've never seen. One even greater than the force that decimated our world."

"What for? They already destroyed Keveron. Isn't that enough?"

"Apparently not, sire."

Geron rubbed the bridge of his nose again. "Fine. Where are they heading?"

The Counselor General glanced at Dania before lowering his eyes. "They're headed straight for Earth."

DANIA INCHED INTO THE OBSERVATORY, careful not to break Geron's concentration as he stared through the window at the continuing arrival of small civilian vessels that had answered the rendezvous call. For the past several days, the king's ship had been broadcasting on secure, encrypted channels, letting their people know where they could come to join those traveling under Geron's protection.

How much protection Dania would be able to provide the survivors should the Carteks attack, she wasn't sure, but her enforcers were sworn to defend Keveron, and they'd die in defense of the refugees, if needed.

For now, it didn't seem like that would be necessary, thank goodness.

The *Oliganton* had been monitoring the Cartek cloud heading for the Earthan Cradle for days. The data showed that, for the time being, the Carteks seemed to have no interest in the dregs of the Kever civilization. This gave Geron's people time to regroup. That didn't bode well for Earth, though.

Geron's large form shifted in front of the stars. "There's

no need to linger in doorways, Dania. I won't lash out at you."

She never thought that he would, but it would have been a valid concern for anyone else, after what had happened to the ambassador…who'd been the ambassador to Earth, she'd found out. Too bad those people no longer had anyone to lobby for them.

She sat beside her sponsor and looked out at the stars. "I remember you coming here anytime you needed to think."

Three ships, one badly damaged, drifted past the window.

Geron's lips thinned. "The stars used to give me peace. Now all these ships are a reminder of what we've lost."

That was a valid summation of their situation. However, it was probably not the best time to ask what he planned to do about it.

He drew in a deep breath and released it slowly. "I keep wondering if I'd gone home when my father summoned me, if I would have been able to make a difference." He turned to her. "What if my enforcers could have tipped the balance and saved Keveron?"

It was an interesting thought. Dwelling on what-ifs wasn't going to save any of the survivors though. "If Orion were here, he'd be reminding us that our enforcers, while formidable, are not military. Your instincts to stay away may have saved all of us."

"You are a highly competent general, Dania. One of the best, so I've heard. You are a work of art."

"If you do say so yourself."

His gaze remained lost among the ships circling them. "Too many said you didn't have what it took to be a general. I made sure you proved them wrong."

Dania looked out at the stars again. She wasn't sure what

to take from that bit of information. Maybe that was why Geron had been so hard on her and placed so many extra controls on her...because he didn't want anyone to question his decision. A female general wasn't unheard of, though. So why would anyone even question it?

Two more small ships passed the window—compact civilian vessels of a class she hadn't seen before. It seemed like more civilian ships arrived each day. Their numbers were few, when compared to the great civilization they'd left, but the numbers also seemed extraordinary, knowing these people were now her sponsor's responsibility.

She inched closer to him. "Do you know what you're going to do?"

Geron continued to stare at the circling ships. "There are a few systems in deeper space with uninhabited planets. Their ecosystems are sufficient to support life. I was thinking of starting over there."

"With no houses? No infrastructure?"

"I didn't say it would be easy." Geron massaged the back of his neck. "I have a few people working on plans. If it's possible, my scientists and engineers will find a way."

Worrying about their future was important. The Kever race needed a new home. There was another civilization in peril, though. "What about Earth?"

He shook his head. "I have enough problems with my own people to worry about. I still need to absorb all these enforcers, plus the new ones arriving daily. We've transferred half the Kever medical staff to my father's cruiser to increase production, but the smuggler's doctor says he may need even more supplies, and it's doubtful Themyscira will be willing to trade with us any longer." He massaged his temples. "It's too much to process and plan at the same time."

"You don't need to figure it out on your own. You have advisors."

"Yes, but the final decision is always mine. No matter what I do, people will die."

She'd said something similar to Peter once. It was one of the hard truths of being a leader.

While Geron had made life-and-death decisions when ordering the execution of criminals, his decisions had never affected the innocent populace.

Neither she nor Geron had ever dreamed he'd be responsible for Kever lives. Her sponsor was strong though, no matter what the aristocracy thought of him. The only question was: how long would it be before someone else tested his patience and ended up a bloody stain on a wall?

CHAPTER 3
CAL

CAL PACED the center of the *Star Renegade*'s lower Engineering deck while Doc, Ethan, and Rachel worked on repairs. He'd tried to help, but Cal's hands were shaking so badly while trying to tape the wiring that Ethan had threatened to kick him out.

Cal clenched and unclenched his fists as his hands still trembled slightly.

After everything else they'd already been through, now they needed to break away from not one military-grade cruiser, but also from the biggest cruiser Cal had ever seen. The *Oliganton* was a behemoth that defied reason. The ship was so big that it must have been built in outer space, with no intention of ever landing on a planet. There was no way anything that big could possibly break away from a planet's gravitational pull, let alone finding a place to land.

Cal dragged his fingers through his hair. Geron's ship had swallowed the *Star Renegade*, and they were still stuck in Geron's landing and cargo area with more than enough room for ships to come and go as they pleased. Cal had thought Geron's ship had been massive, but the king's ship was easily double in size. Who knew what kind of capability this new monster ship had?

The comm pinged, and Doc hit the button. "Friendly neighborhood Engineering department. How can we help you?"

Ty's voice filled the room. "Just giving my thirty-minute report. Nothing's changed. The Kevers keep coming and going, docking and taking off. I'm trying to pinpoint the intervals where they drop the shields to see if we can use it to our advantage."

Cal walked over to the comm. "I like the way you think. If there's anything you find, we need to come up with a plan and execute it right away." ...Before any more surprises showed up.

Ty's voice came through again. "Oh, and you'll be happy to hear a very lovely former general is walking up the cargo ramp as we speak."

Dania. Thank the stars!

"And on another good news note, her hair is still light brown and not moving. I think it's safe to say she's still playing for Team *Star Renegade*."

"Good to hear. Send her to Engineering."

"On it."

Rachel swiped back her long auburn hair as she helped Ethan tape off the last of the wiring inside a center panel while Cal continued to pace.

He'd been running from enforcers for years. He'd seen the Kevers' elite police force do things that had made his skin crawl, not to mention the nightmares that had plagued him since childhood after watching his father being executed for being at the wrong place at the wrong time.

He'd heard rumors of the insurmountable power of the

Banes, but standing on the bridge of the *Star Renegade*, help-less as they'd watched Prince Geron lose his temper made Cal's nightmares seem like a vacation.

Dania's infamous sponsor had murdered one of his own people in the blink of an eye. It didn't even look like he'd needed to grab hold of his powers like the enforcers did. It had been like flicking a finger to him.

That kind of power was an abomination. He'd known the Kevers were bad, but nothing had prepared him for this.

Cal tugged at the hair near his temples. "That prince is even worse than I thought."

"I don't know," Rachel said. "I always figured he was a big, overblown bully."

Cal lowered his hands. "He threw one of his own people against a wall and melted his body to nothing more than a smear of blood right in front of everyone."

Rachel shivered. "Okay, yeah, that was kinda gross."

Doc leaned against a control panel, crossing his arms over his gray T-shirt. "It was an existential show of strength, but also a lack of self-control, from what I saw. It was a pretty egregious error on his part that he'll probably have to make up for."

"I don't really give a damn what it looked like. I care about Dania and Alexander stuck out there with that loose cannon."

The doorway opened and Dania entered. Her gaze found Cal's and she ran to him.

Cal pulled her into his arms and knotted his fingers in her hair. Now more than ever, he never wanted her to leave the ship again.

He brushed the hair from her eyes. "Are you okay? Why were you gone for so long?"

"It's been a rough few days. Geron is king."

Cal's gut clenched. "Yeah, we heard."

"He's not taking it well."

"I think that guy he squashed would agree with you."

"That was unfortunate." She looked down. "I think now he understands he needs to keep control of his temper."

"Oh, *now* he understands? What normal sentient being doesn't understand that you can't just go around melting people and burning them alive?"

Ethan shrugged. "I'm thinking that guy was pretty much dead when he started burning."

Rachel wrinkled her nose. "Yeah, with that splat of blood, I doubt there was much left of his brain after..."

"*Rachel!*" Cal frowned at her.

"Geez, Ethan started it."

Cal rubbed his face. "We need to get out of here. Ty is watching for exit routes. The plan is still the same." He looked at Dania. "Can you get Alex back here?"

"I think so. He's trying to avoid Geron. For the time being, it should be easy for him to get away."

"What about you?"

"I'm expected to be on the command deck as much as possible, but Kile is more than capable of commanding in my stead. As long as we aren't attacked, I should be able to get away as needed." She lowered her eyes.

"What is it?"

"I don't know. So much has happened over the past few days. Maybe I'm having trouble processing it all."

Cal didn't like the sound of that. "You're still coming with us, right?"

She gazed into his eyes before she smiled. "Of course."

Cal's stomach clenched. He didn't like the way she'd paused before she'd answered.

Rachel crossed her arms. "I hate how you all talk about my Big Guy like he's just some random enforcer we don't care about."

Dania shook her head. "He's not the same person, Rachel. I thought you understood that the Kile you knew is gone."

"Hold on a minute." The overhead lighting made Ethan's coppery locks glow as he walked to his workstation. "I'm not so sure he's a lost cause."

Rachel followed him. "What do you mean?"

"I think he left himself messages from his past-self. Look at this." He opened a drawer and picked up one of several palm-sized data pads. "Remember these? Kile found one in the lounge a few weeks ago and threw it across the room after he'd read it."

"Yeah. So?" Rachel asked.

"Well, I keep a stock of these in Engineering so I can tape notes when I'm walking through the ship. I keep track of repairs that need to be done, and the occasional strokes of brilliance that I have, so I don't accidentally forget before I can act on it."

"Your point in all this?" Cal asked.

"Well, my point is that I've been finding these data pads all over the ship, hidden in strange places, just like where Kile found one in the lounge."

"Yeah, that was strange." Rachel shoved her hands in her pockets and hunched her shoulders. "He almost looked drawn to it, but he also seemed confused that he'd even known it was there."

"He sure did. And then when he read it, whatever it said ticked him off and he broke the screen."

Rachel hugged herself, her gaze locked on the drawer. "What do the rest of them say?"

"That's the mystery. I don't know." Ethan handed one to Dania

"Interesting." She turned the data pad over in her hand. "It looks like it has a bio lock."

"Can you open it?" Cal asked.

Dania shook her head. "No. If he calibrated it to his bio-sign, it's nearly foolproof."

Doc grabbed another data pad from the drawer. "I can try to crack it, if you want."

"No," Dania said.

Everyone looked at her.

She handed the pad back to Ethan. "You're thinking Kile left these scattered in the ship when he lived on the *Star Renegade*?"

"Well, yeah. The only other person who might have done it is Max, but he didn't seem to know anything about it. He had fun helping me find them, though."

Dania turned to the others. "Kile was close to needing a feeding in those final days. He was terrified he may be forced to take the artificial pathogens."

Doc scratched his head. "I'm not sure about that. I don't even think the option was on the table for him. He told me in no uncertain terms that he'd rather die."

She nodded. "If his pathogen degradation was anything like mine, he was starting to question things, even though he was still completely under Geron's control." She took the data pad from Doc. "These memos are probably a result of whatever was going through his mind at the time."

Doc looked at the drawer of haphazard supplies. "I'm not getting where you're going with this."

"Whatever he read on that data pad a few weeks ago made his fully-fed self very angry. Anything that would make a fully charged enforcer angry is probably something we'd see as a positive."

"What are you thinking?" Cal asked.

"I say we put them all back so he can find more of them."

Doc folded his arms. "Isn't it in our best interests *not* to make the mean version of Big Guy mad?"

Dania handed Ethan the second tablet. "In this case, I don't think so. Let's put them back where we found them and see what happens."

A deep heaviness spread through Cal's chest. "What if all these tablets are reminding him about how much he wants us dead?"

"You're all smugglers in his eyes. Trust me, that wouldn't make much of a difference. He wants you all dead either way."

CHAPTER 4
ALEXANDER

ALEXANDER PLACED his hand against the stark, pristine wall in the hallway of Geron's cruiser and took a deep breath. It wasn't too long ago that he'd looked forward to spending time with his sponsor. Deep down, he still *did* enjoy Geron's company, but at the same time, the current summons from his sponsor clawed at his soul. Alexander had managed to avoid situations conducive to feeding, but soon, he'd run out of excuses, and Geron would return him to his former self.

Bile rose in his throat. Being fed was something he wanted more than air, but that he also wanted to avoid, no matter the consequences. The warring battle raging between his body's base needs and his mind's will to survive was sometimes more than he could stand. He needed to keep his focus though, or he could lose everything.

Orion and the Counselor General walked through the hall in his direction. Alexander pulled himself away from the wall and followed. The commander narrowed his eyes at Alexander, no doubt noticing that he'd paused. Alexander needed to be more careful. He had to prove he could still be a dutiful soldier.

Enforcers never showed weakness, battling with broken bones at times, or even mortal wounds. He couldn't show that he was something *less* in any of their eyes, especially Orion. The longer Alexander could hold up the façade, the longer he'd be free. If anyone noticed him faltering, Geron would call him back into the fold.

Steadying himself, Alexander entered the meeting room alongside Orion and the Counselor General and took his place standing on the wall beside Kile, watching over their sponsor.

Geron sat at the head of the table, perusing his nails. His expression seemed more annoyed than interested. "I trust there was a reason to pull me away from the infirmary? I was saving lives."

The Counselor General lifted his chin, looking every bit as haughty as he had on Keveron when addressing an underling. "You were saving soldiers. They're expendable."

"Not when we've lost so many." Geron waved his hand dismissively. "I'm not here to argue with you. What do you want?"

"This is a topic of utmost importance to our culture and your sovereignty."

Geron flinched. He was used to being master of his own ship, but anything beyond that was new to him. He barely paid attention to his own safety outside his personal guard, acting in ways most considered reckless. Having to worry about others seemed to be an unwelcome development for him.

"What is it?" Geron asked.

"Our government is based on clear lines of power. All

levels of government work autonomously, but at the direction and whim of the king."

Geron sighed, leaning back. "Are you here to give me a childhood lesson in politics?"

Orion grimaced. "You spent so little time in your father's house, we thought it would be prudent."

Geron's temperature spiked by a quarter of a degree. Alexander wondered if Orion realized the only reason he was still alive was because Dania had deemed him valuable. Too many more outbursts and he'd end up like the Earthan ambassador.

Ada returned his attention to the Counselor General. "Are you going to make your point or continue to waste my time?"

The Counselor General seemed to consider his words carefully. "You are the last surviving Bane. You cannot allow your bloodlines to die."

Geron stood. "Did you actually call me here to tell me I should be spending my time breeding?"

"No, but I think we should be searching for a suitable mate with the ability to transfer primordial energy to your offspring. The actual breeding would only take a small amount of your time, which I understand is valuable, but we need to make sure the Bane bloodlines, and all the primordial energy they contain, carry on."

Geron rubbed his face. "You told me all Banes are dead but me."

"They are. We've done a census of incoming ships, and it appears you are still the only survivor."

"What about lower-class nobles? Certainly, one survived who can carry primordial energy."

"There are a few, but it seems all those with significant

enough strength to carry Bane blood fought to their deaths to defend Keveron.

The room heated point two degrees. The probably-intentional slight that Geron was the only one who *hadn't* defended Keveron hung in the air. Of course, if Geron had answered his father's call, they all might have been dead, too, and the people would have had no one to protect them.

Kile eased off the wall. "Ada, if I may speak?"

Geron waved him forward.

"In my time on board the *Star Renegade*, I studied many odd things about the ship, trying to discover why such an old, battered ship had been so hard to catch during the years."

"And?"

"Their navigator seems to have the ability to skip space over considerable distances. Not quite as far as a Bane, but with a similar aptitude."

Alexander's stomach clenched.

Both Kile and Geron looked at him.

"Did you just grasp your power?" Kile asked him.

Had he? Alexander's fingers tingled. His hair drifted lightly around his face.

He *had* grasped his power.

What had he intended to do? Certainly not use it against anyone in this room.

The power eased out of his fingers. He needed to control himself.

Alexander lowered his head. "Sorry, Ada. It was, possibly, excitement at the news." It wasn't quite a lie. Medically, excitement was a similar reaction to his body's innate need to find Alanna and hide her where none of them could find her.

The Counselor General scowled. "If she does hold power, she'd be an abomination. A half-breed that should be destroyed."

Geron held up his hand. "We're not destroying anyone, especially if they have primordial energy." He turned to Alexander. "If this human can harness the power, would it be reasonable that she'd be able to birth a child of Bane blood?"

Alexander gulped. Alanna's mother had done so, so there would be a good chance that Alanna could carry the Bane bloodline as well. His hands trembled, and he clenched his fists to hide his need to bolt from the room and find her. His mind whirled, looking for a solution…anything that would save Alanna from being used for no better reason than a heritage she wasn't even aware of.

He tried to press his lips together, to come up with a way to lie, but his sponsor had asked him a direct question. Not answering wasn't an option. "Yes, Ada. Statistically and biologically, her chances of producing a viable offspring are quite high, but…"

Geron tilted his head, waiting for Alexander to continue. "But what?"

That was an excellent question.

Because she belonged to Alexander? Because Alexander loved her? Because he couldn't stand the idea of anyone else touching her? Because she was a bright, thriving, ingenious woman worth more than being demoted to the rank of breeder stock…

Of course, none of this would have any meaning to Geron. If he needed her, he'd take her. What she wanted, or what Alexander wanted, would be of no consequence.

Still, the *Star Renegade* had plans of escaping. They could still execute those plans, rocketing Alanna as far away from

Geron as possible. Alexander just needed to give her more time to escape.

Alexander straightened. "I was thinking that the Counselor General was correct, that she already carries Bane blood, but it has been thinned. It may be better to keep looking among our own people to see if there is a better match. Most of the refugees have received medical care, so their blood is on file. We can search for the correct properties and then do a more direct analysis on any we find who may be a good match."

"That will take a considerable amount of time," the Counselor General said. "As heinous as it seems, it may be best to breed the human and have her gestating while we search for others."

Breed the human...

Gestating...

Alexander gritted his teeth, staving off the desire to execute the man for his lack of empathy. Lack of empathy wasn't a crime, though. But he very much wished it were.

"This is all ridiculous." Orion shook his head. "I cannot believe that we have to rest the future of our race and our culture on this simpleton." He pointed at Geron. "How could the greatest power in the galaxy have been reduced to this?"

Geron's jaw set before Orion flew from the center of the room and slammed against the wall. The deceased high prince's commander coughed but still managed to glare at Geron defiantly.

Ada sauntered toward the commander with all the confidence of a larger predator, which was exactly what he was. He put his hand on Orion's neck. "I will take for granted that your impudence is a byproduct of grief. My brother's death apparently affected his enforcers more deeply than the rest of us."

Orion's nostrils flared. "You felt no grief for your brother. You despised each other."

"True. Our opinions on how to live our lives differed significantly."

"The high prince was a good man. He was bound by duty. Bound by honor and loyalty to Keveron."

"And you think I'm none of these things."

"You are nothing like your brother. He would have been a great king."

"I agree, and I wish he were here. But he isn't." Geron leaned closer, his voice becoming menacing. "But I cannot have one of his former commanders undermining my efforts to save what little remains of our culture."

"Then kill me and get it over with. I don't want to live in an existence where our people have to bow to the likes of you."

Geron's lips thinned. "Still looking for that quick execution? Dania warned me you would."

Orion's eyes widened before he grimaced again. "She is even weaker than you are."

"Yes, but she is every bit the general I programmed—the general you *feared*, if my information is correct."

The startled flash in Orion's eyes gave him away before he was able to return to his practiced glare.

So, he *had* been threatened by Dania. Alexander supposed that wasn't a surprise. Dania had been a notable horror, her reputation known even by the Kevers she hadn't served.

"No matter your prejudices, Dania is a great leader." Geron lifted his hand and Orion's feet dangled from the floor. "It's going to be amusing, watching you cower at her feet."

Orion seemed to struggle, despite his inability to fight a power so much greater than his own. "I'd rather die."

"I believe you've already been reminded that dying is illegal."

Orion's eyes widened. "Then execute me for my crimes. I deserve it."

"I have a secret, Commander." Geron pulled him closer. "I'm not as foolish as I may seem."

The room heated as a flux of primordial energy swirled around Geron. Alexander moaned, relishing in the aftershock like a blanket of tingling bliss had fallen over him.

Orion screamed, his fists punching at Geron's back, his legs kicking, until his limbs fell lax. The energy pulsed, filling the room, the sweet essence of power coating everything.

Kile's head fell back. He closed his eyes and sighed.

Alexander's hair started to drift and his cells screamed, drinking in this slight tease of the infinite energy they'd been denied far too long.

Alanna was warm and wonderful and everything Alexander wanted, but *this* was the true meaning of power. She could only keep Alexander alive and partially charged. The infinite energy swirling through the air was what Alexander needed. What he *wanted*.

Orion fell to the floor at Geron's feet, and the Counselor General gaped at his new king.

Alexander shook his head as the primordial energy dissipated from the air. He blinked as his sight started to clear.

Of all that was right and good in the galaxy…had he really been drawn back so easily? Had the energy of Geron absorbing someone else been so powerful that Alexander's body had overpowered his mind, forgetting all he'd become over the past several months?

The answer was more than clear. He needed to get away as soon as possible. He needed to find Dania, drag her back to the *Star Renegade*, and get Alanna out of there before there was no more chance of escape.

Orion lay at Geron's feet, staring at the ceiling, blinking. It was odd that he didn't immediately stand at attention as the others had. He looked shocked, maybe processing the coding of a new sponsor.

Geron barely seemed winded as he narrowed his eyes at the Counselor General. "I would like a report on the number of people on the arriving ships, their professions, and their ages. It's time we made a plan to rebuild."

The Counselor General lifted his chin again. "And the smuggler's navigator?"

"She's not going anywhere. Follow Alexander's direction and check the blood ratings of the Kever refugees. If none of them suffice, the human hybrid will have to do."

DANIA HELD Cal's hand as Alanna sobbed on Alexander's shoulder. Rachel and Ethan stood on the other side of the *Star Renegade*'s lounge, both pale with lost looks on their faces. Christopher Columbus leaned against the wall to Ethan's left with his arms folded and a concerned expression on his unshaven face.

Cal tightened his grip on Dania's hand as Alanna wiped her tears and clung to Alexander. Dania had seen humans cry on many occasions, normally after begging for mercy she'd been unable to give. This time, though, her stomach clenched. Dread swept over her. She didn't want Alanna to cry. She wanted to fix this. She just didn't know how.

Peter and Ty stood near the food dispensers, exchanging wide-eyed glances. She understood their confusion. Alexander's news didn't make sense. Then again, in many ways, it did.

"This is ridiculous," Alanna said. "I'm not an alien. Just let them take a blood sample and prove it!"

Alexander looked down. His face was an odd mix of emotions. "I suspected some time ago that this was the reason you could skip space. I checked your DNA, and yes, it irrefutably links back to the Banes."

"How did you get my DNA?" She turned from him. "Never mind. Skies, why didn't you tell me?"

Dania frowned when her healer looked at the ground, not answering Alanna's question—probably because the real answer was quite telling.

"It's illegal for an enforcer to touch a Bane other than their sponsor." Dania's gaze carried to Alexander. "You knowingly broke the law."

He looked up. "By the time I'd found out, she was already acting as my sponsor. She'd been feeding me for months. I'm sorry for keeping it a secret, but I had to protect her."

"I understand." Dania would probably have done the same thing if it had been Cal. Thank goodness they'd both spent enough time away from Geron that they were able to consider the gray areas between right and wrong.

Alanna hugged herself—her puffy, red eyes trained on Alexander. "You should have told me."

"The knowledge would have put your life in danger. The Counselor General's first response was to call for your execution."

Alanna balked. "What?"

"The Banes think themselves exceptional. They are the only ones who've been able to harness infinite amounts of primordial energy. Other houses have tried, breeding above their ranks in an attempt to strengthen their bloodlines, but to no avail." Alexander looked down. "Humans are supposed to be weak. The Banes wouldn't like it if the information got out that a human could carry primordial energy."

A trickle of fear sizzled across Dania's chest. That was an eventuality she hadn't considered. Alanna probably wasn't the first child with Bane blood in their veins. Could there have been others who'd manifested primordial powers? It seemed unlikely, or she would have heard about it. Of course, the king had his own enforcers, and it was entirely possible any such children had been eliminated to erase any evidence of their existence. Or maybe, like in Kile's case, they'd actually been turned into enforcers themselves.

Alanna covered her face with her hands. "I never asked for any of this."

Alexander reached for her. "Alanna, you need to—"

She shoved him away. "Leave me alone."

"Why? This changes nothing between us."

"You took my DNA. You tested it without my permission and then you kept secrets from me, Alexander."

He gaped, leaning toward her. "To *protect* you."

"To protect me, or to protect yourself? And now what? Now they want to offer me up to a Kever. The very Kever we've been trying to hide Cal from. The Kever who just a few hours ago wanted me dead."

Ethan shrugged. "I guess he doesn't want you dead anymore. That's a bonus."

Alanna growled at the ceiling. "You're not helping, Ethan."

Rachel slapped him. "Yeah. That was cold."

Ethan raised his hands. "What did I say?"

Rachel turned back to Alanna. "He's kinda right, though."

She gaped at them. "Did both of you miss the part about *breeding?*"

"No one's breeding." Cal dragged his fingers through his tightly cropped dark hair. "Dania's right. We need to blow a hole in the prince's ship and run for it. Everything's ready, right? We're good to go?"

"Well, yeah," Ethan said. "We can't do a test run, so we're as ready as we'll ever be. We'll just need to have all hands prepped to scramble for repairs if anything catches fire."

"Heat and unintended combustion is a definite possibility," Peter said. "I'd like to do one more scan of the heat shielding. In this confined space, it's going to be like sitting in an oven when we start firing our weapons. If our hull starts to buckle, we may need to draw power we're depending on from elsewhere to keep ourselves from melting. I'd rather be prepared for nothing than caught with our pants down."

Cal's cheek ticked, like it always did when he tried to puzzle through something that might get them all killed. "How long do you need?"

"Maybe five hours?"

Cal stood. "You and Ethan get on that. I want to be racing through free space by this time tomorrow."

Dania massaged her temples. She wanted to get away just as much as the rest of them, but things had changed over the past several days. Geron wasn't just a wayward prince anymore. He had responsibilities that she wasn't sure he was capable of handling on his own.

Her sponsor needed help. He needed guidance. This was all starting to happen too fast for all of them, and Geron needed her now more than ever.

Kile was there for him, but her commander hadn't gained their sponsor's implicit trust as Dania had.

She took a deep breath, and her heart ached as she admitted the truth. "I'm afraid to leave Geron."

Cal spun on her. "What?"

"So much has happened. He's confused and he needs counsel. Everyone else wants to see him fail."

"So do we."

She pointed to her chest. "I don't. He has the power to fix this."

"Fix what?"

Dania held up her hands. "Everything. Have you forgotten that the Carteks are headed for Earth?"

Cal huffed out a breath. "Of course not, but right now I have to worry about what I *can* control, and that's saving my crew."

"I'm afraid of what will happen to him if I leave."

Cal stormed toward her. "Well, I'm afraid of what will happen if we stay. We all have death sentences hanging over our heads. You and Alex could be changed into monsters at any minute, and now this guy you both worship wants Alanna." Cal pointed a thumb at his chest. "I'm going to be the voice of reason here. We need to leave. Now."

"I'm with Cal on this one." Christopher Columbus pushed off the wall and walked toward them. Something metallic in the pockets of his military fatigues jingled with each step. "Staying here is asking to be executed. We need to get out of this hangar and find somewhere safe. Then we can assess our options."

The door opened and a chittering noise filled the room. Dania scanned the floor until a bushy tail appeared, and then the rest of Max turned a more visible gray. He sat on his hind legs and growled a few unintelligible words.

Rachel squatted beside him. "What is it, buddy?"

He pointed at the door, ran out, and came back, pulling two cracked data pads with his hind legs.

"More?" Ethan crouched beside the animal. "Wait. These have been smashed to smithereens. Where did you find these?"

Max growled and grumbled, waving his paws and pointing.

Ethan quirked a brow. "In the hall beside the med bay, and in lower Engineering?"

Cal cocked his head. "That's not what he said."

Rachel shrugged. "That's what it sounded like to me."

Ethan stood. "Even if I got it wrong, that's not the point." He picked up one of the data pads. "These are crushed, just like the last one Kile threw at the wall. I didn't even see the Big Guy come on the ship."

"Me neither," Ty said. "And I'm keeping a pretty good watch on who's coming and going."

Cal's face reddened. "Kile spent too much time on the *Star Renegade*, and we gave him too much latitude. He's proven too many times that he knows how to get around our security. We need to keep an eye on him, especially now. The last thing we want is to make our escape and then find out we've left with a fully-charged enforcer on board."

"I can't really keep him off the ship," Ty said.

"No, but we need to make sure we know when he's here."

Peter tapped on the computer panel on the wall. "I can keep a heart rate scan going. That's the only way I can think of to know about an intruder. I mean, Dania and Alex can project themselves through walls, so I'm sure the Big Guy can, too."

Rachel nodded. "He can. He definitely can."

Ethan snickered. "I bet there's a story behind that that the rest of us really don't want to know about."

"Enough." Cal pointed at Peter. "Heart rate scans are a good idea. And for the rest of you, don't leave the ship unless it's absolutely necessary. I don't want to worry about looking for anyone when it's time to go."

Alanna rubbed her shoulders like she was cold. "What if the prince calls for me?"

"Technically, he's a king now," Ethan said.

Alanna glowered at him. "Does that really matter?"

"You don't leave the ship for any reason. If he calls for you, we're gone." Cal turned, looking at the crew. "Make any final tweaks needed. We're blasting out of here tonight."

Tonight? "But…" Dania's throat went dry as everyone looked at her.

But what?

Was she about to say that she wanted to stay?

That wasn't true, but it also *was* true… The general inside her screamed to do her duty, while the logical side wanted to lock herself in her quarters on the *Star Renegade* until they were so far away that Geron would never find her again.

Cal's face was stony…harder than she'd ever seen him. "No one leaves. Especially you."

Her eyes started to burn, and she closed them. How could she make him understand? "I'm supposed to report to Geron's bridge in thirty minutes. If I don't go, they'll be suspicious." That was the truth, but it would also be time for her to…what? Give Geron a pep talk? Tell him he was worthy of leadership?

Dania gulped. She wasn't even sure Geron *was* worthy of leadership.

Ethan raised his hand like a schoolchild. "With our luck, if Dani gets off this ship, she'll come back with floating hair, glowing hands, and a whole lot of desire to kill us all. I think her leaving is a bad idea."

Alexander watched a ship landing outside the window. "She's safe for today. Geron absorbed Orion this morning and then returned to the med bay. He'll be too tired to bring her back to full strength." He turned to Cal. "And she's right —it would be very unlike her to miss bridge service. They will definitely come looking for her if she doesn't report. Keeping to our normal schedules is the safest plan."

Cal shook his head. "I don't like it."

Peter pursed his lips. "I don't like it, either, but I agree that they're watching her, waiting for any sign that she's not loyal. At this point, they can probably figure out the synthetic pathogens on their own. If there is even an inkling that Dania is Team *Star Renegade*, there's no doubt in my mind that His Royal Highness-ness will kill all of us to erase the competition."

"You're not making me feel better," Cal said.

"Good. You *should* be scared. We should all be scared. But not so scared that we do something foolhardy." Peter turned to Dania. "Do what you always do, to the letter, and then get back here. Don't do anything out of character, or they'll know."

He was right. Orion, especially, had been watching Dania's every move. Now that he was under Geron's control, his scrutiny might get worse because he now served the same sponsor that he thought she was planning to desert.

Cal walked over to her and placed a kiss on Dania's cheek. "I'd rather you stayed on the ship, but if you need to make an appearance on their bridge, do it, then keep your head down and get back here within five hours." His gaze carried over the crew. "We just spent our last day in this box, people. Do what you have to do to make this happen. I, for one, am more than ready to see the stars again."

CHAPTER 6
DANIA

THE CEILINGS SEEMED HIGHER in Geron's ship every time Dania left the *Star Renegade*. It was odd how quickly she grew accustomed to human surroundings. Geron's cruiser had been her home for so many years, though, and the stark, high walls were infinitely familiar. She couldn't imagine never seeing them again.

However, today, the farther she traversed into the ship, the more the hallways in the cruiser seemed to close in on her, as if they knew she was plotting escape. Part of her wanted to be caught, but the other part was ready to fight for her rights...rights she hadn't had since she'd been purchased by the Banes and turned into a monster.

She hesitated at the entrance to the command deck. While the cruiser had been her home, the command deck was her place of power...where she'd served Geron's will with the might of her small army and a galactic cruiser behind her. This might be the last time she entered the command center, and she wasn't sure if the burning in the back of her eyes was the start of tears of sorrow or relief.

She wiped her lashes, took a deep breath, and approached the entrance. As always, the door opened, reading her presence. She stepped through the threshold and frowned. Orion stood in the center of the main viewing screens, feet slightly apart and hands folded behind his back.

He stepped back and inclined his head to her before he announced, "General taking command."

She ground her teeth to keep from gaping as he settled himself against the wall to her left.

On the right of the room, Kile towered over the shoulder of a technician as they reviewed statistics scrolling across the screen.

She moved behind him. "Why was Orion in command?"

Kile glanced at Orion before returning his gaze to her. "Because he's an accomplished commander. I assumed you'd want him to lead now that he's tied to Geron."

He *assumed*? "You are my commander. Not him."

Kile shook his head. "These are dire times. Orion is battle-hardened and trained to protect the high prince."

"And you are trained to protect Geron."

"I was trained to protect a lesser prince with far less political value." He leaned toward her and whispered. "Dania, I'm trained to do what's right for our sponsor. Orion is better suited to protect a king."

She grabbed his arm, pulling him closer. "And I reiterate that *you* are trained to take care of Geron. And on top of that, I trust you."

Kile flinched, then straightened. A slight tremor of emotion whisked over him.

Was that…*pride*?

The emotion whisked away before he lowered his eyes. "Orion belongs to Geron now. You can trust him as well."

"Not like I trust you. You are my second, and you will remain that way. That's an order."

He sighed. "May I speak freely, General?"

"Of course."

"You have only had supplemental feedings since returning. It's entirely possible that this is an emotional response, rather than a tactical decision."

"You're right. It's absolutely an emotional response. Geron needs to be surrounded by his own now. These new enforcers belong to him, but they aren't part of who we are yet. Orion doesn't have the experience to make him part of our unit."

He narrowed his eyes, like that was a puzzling statement. If he had remembered more about living with the *Star Renegade* crew, he may have understood better.

She sighed. "You know Geron in ways that it will take Orion years to match. These new soldiers will serve Geron, but his core enforcers are those who will stand by his side. He needs our support even more than he needs any skills Orion may have."

"I hadn't considered that."

"Well, you should." Because Dania needed him to care for their sponsor once she was gone.

A surge of energy ghosted over her skin, and her body tingled, pulling her toward the entrance. She turned at the same time Orion and Kile did, and the door opened.

Geron strode into the room, staring at the screens. "Is there anything to report?"

For the past week, Geron had started his mornings in the infirmaries, absorbing enforcers, and stayed there until he'd been exhausted. What brought him here today?

"All is running per usual, Ada," Kile said. "We are waiting

for medical teams on the arriving ships to complete reports so we can finalize treatment plans for this evening and tomorrow, but those enforcers in dire need are already in our infirmaries waiting for…"

Geron held up his hand, silencing Kile. "That's not what I meant." He continued to stare at the screens, his eyes seeming to focus on one, then the next, like each image was a puzzle that needed to be figured out.

Dania moved closer. "Ada, what is it?"

His gaze moved on to another screen. "Something's wrong."

Captain Quaren tapped on his computer screen. "All systems are running at peak efficiency, sir."

Geron shook his head. "Something is definitely wrong."

Dania touched his arm. "Ada?"

He blinked, flicked a glance at her, then looked back to the screens. A sense of dread muddied the air about him— the same odd, fluxing energy she'd felt when he'd angered his brother three years ago and then played an intergalactic game of hiding behind small moons while his brother had searched for him, vowing to drag Geron home to face their father's wrath.

"What is it?" Dania asked.

His lips thinned. "Hate."

"Hate?"

He nodded. "Pure hate."

Geron shuddered, and Dania gasped. She'd never seen a deep visceral reaction like that from him. Even when he'd fought with his father or brother. What was this strange feeling that had affected him so deeply?

The security officer stood from her chair. "We're being scanned."

Captain Quaren strode to the security station, his deep blue skin standing out against his darker blue uniform. "By whom?"

"I don't know."

"Scans have signatures," the captain said. "Just decipher the code."

"There *is* no code."

Orion moved away from the wall. "It's the Carteks."

"This far from their border?" the captain asked.

Orion scoffed at him. "Have you not been informed of the massive blockade on sector Z8? The Carteks haven't kept to their borders in years."

Quaren looked at the ships moving in slow, circular formation around the cruiser.

Dania shook off her stupor. Why had she just been standing there? "We need to treat the scan as a threat until proven otherwise."

"I agree," Orion said. "Move the ships with the least military significance to the outer rings of the formation."

"What?" Dania gaped. "If this does prove to be a threat, they'll be annihilated."

"Better to lose insignificant ships until we can ascertain if our sponsor is in any danger."

She turned to Geron. "There are civilians on those passenger ships. Probably children."

Orion lifted his chin. "Geron is the last living Bane. We need to protect him at all costs."

Geron watched the ships on the screen. "Our planet was decimated. This fleet is all that's left of Keveron."

"We are enforcers." Dania moved beside him. "It is our duty to…"

Geron held up his hand. "Enough."

The dull hum of the computers filled the room while they watched the screens.

The same sense of foreboding pulsed in the air about Geron until he turned to Dania. "Pull all the ships into a tighter formation around us. Place the smaller ships with the least people in the outer rings."

The smaller ships...the civilian skippers...the private citizens who'd left their homes with nothing, placing their hopes and their lives on the slim chance they would find a Bane to protect them.

"But, Ada."

He glared at her. "Do it."

Her chest clenched as she lowered her eyes and nodded. These were the hard decisions she needed to get used to as she served their new king.

Captain Quaren stood next to the communications officer as they relayed the orders to the fleet.

Geron clawed at his temples. "It's getting closer."

Dania took one last look at the smaller ships, then closed her eyes. Geron had made a decision, and she really wasn't all that surprised he'd taken Orion's counsel. Geron had always placed himself first. His recent series of selfless acts had been an anomaly. She needed to come to terms with that. And, moreover, she needed to not concern herself with the smaller ships, if that was what Geron ordered.

She took slow, steady breaths as the ships outside changed formation, the skippers...both military and recreational...moved to the outer rings without question. They had to have known they were being sacrificed, but they took their orders and acted on them. She needed to do the same.

She set her feet apart and held her wrist behind her back.

"Navigator, check the flight patterns of the surrounding ships. Make sure they are tight, but not too close. We don't want accidents."

"No," Geron whispered, still looking at the screens. "Bring them closer."

Captain Quaren left the communications station. "Sir, they are already flying far closer than the capabilities of most of these pilots. It would be…"

Geron lowered his hands. "Closer!"

Dania moved back to Geron's side. "Ada?"

He finally met her gaze. "Orion is right. It *is* the Carteks. They've found us."

"We can't be sure of that."

He turned back to the screens. "I am."

Sweat beaded Dania's brow. If the Carteks *were* here, there was no way they could defend all the ships around them without more healthy enforcers.

Geron held out both his hands. A flicker of green, then blue light swirled at the end of his fingertips, then spread through the room. A blanket of blue-green energy swept over the ships and the command deck blurred. The floor rumbled beneath Dania's feet until the odd coloration winked out. Dania didn't need to check the readings to know that they'd skipped space.

"Checking location," the navigation officer said. "We are sixty-four *hestirins* from our previous location."

"That's not far enough," Orion said.

"I am aware of that." Geron looked to the Captain. "Are all ships accounted for?"

"The fleet is intact," the navigator said.

Geron held out his hands again. "Instruct them to keep as

tight a formation as possible." The green-blue hue once again filled the command deck and then swept over the fleet. When the floor stopped trembling the crew swept into action, calling off locations and statistics on the fleet.

"We're being scanned again," the security officer said. "This time, the signal is stronger."

Orion sneered at the screen. "They're following."

The room bathed in a blue-green sheen again, and when the regular lighting returned, Geron leaned over, holding his knees. His skin was tinged a dull gray.

"Ada." Dania grabbed his arm. "We need to get you to the infirmary."

Captain Quaren looked over the comm officer's shoulder. "We're being scanned again!"

Geron gritted his teeth, then looked at the ceiling. "Alexander, come."

Alexander? Why had he called for Alexander? Dania wasn't even sure where her healer was.

Geron balled his hands into fists and the blue-and-green veil shot out, through the walls and over the first several arcs of ships around them. The glow wavered, losing intensity.

Geron groaned, swaying, pressing out with both palms.

"The primordial energy is shrinking!" Captain Quaren shouted. "It's not getting around the outer band of ships!"

The glow shimmered before closing down, cutting through several of the ships in the last band. A passenger craft exploded in a flash of light as Geron propelled the fleet to another location. The light outside flickered, the energy struggling to hold together before the floor stopped rumbling.

The crew started calling off locations and damage reports.

A second ship exploded, and then a third detonated in a fiery ball before their oxygen burned out, leaving a mass of twisted metal behind.

Geron fell to his knees and then slammed to the floor before any of his enforcers were able to catch him.

CHAPTER 7
ALEXANDER

A DEEP ACHE sliced through Alexander's mind—a call he couldn't refuse. He reached out with his power, focused on his sponsor, and a flash of light surrounded him before Alexander appeared on the command deck.

Crew members scurried about, shouting at one another, while Orion crouched over Geron.

"Ada!" Dania bolted for their sponsor as a ship on one of the screens exploded.

Alexander grabbed her. "I have him. Stay in command."

She stared at Geron, pain in her eyes, before nodding and returning to Kile and Captain Quaren.

Orion sneered at him. "Are you going to do something, or just stand there? Aren't you a healer?"

Alexander took a steadying breath…more to stave off the panic of his fallen sponsor than to countermand the commander's quip. "What happened?"

"He skipped space four times."

Alexander nodded. From the hum of the ship, he'd say they'd skipped a considerable distance. He placed his palm on their sponsor's cheek. Geron's skin had lost its sheen, and the normal vibrant green-and-blue Kever coloring had dulled to a sickly gray.

"How could this have happened?" Orion asked. "He only skipped space."

Yes, but this time, he'd dragged hundreds of ships with him, and he'd done so after exhausting himself every day, giving his latent energy to others. Philosophers always speculated that the Bane power was limitless. Apparently, it wasn't.

Maybe this is why the rest of Geron's family had fallen in battle…the Carteks had swarmed, overwhelming with pure numbers, attacking constantly until the Banes, and their enforcers, had nothing left to give.

"He's out of energy," Alexander said.

Orion glared at him. "How can that be possible?"

It shouldn't be, yet it is. The high-ranking Banes had never been tested to such a capacity, and Geron had never been tested at all.

Alexander looked up at Orion. "He just fed you recently."

"Yes. Why?"

"He hasn't fed me in quite some time. I can rekindle his primordial energy, but I'll need to draw alternate power."

"How?"

It was the same principle as Alexander extracting the new primordial energy from Dania and returning it to Geron, but this would be on a much larger scale. In fact, Orion probably wouldn't be enough.

Alexander turned to Dania. "I need more of Geron's enforcers. It would be best to have those recently fed."

Which meant all the new enforcers, but that was fine.

Dania started shouting orders as Alexander placed his hands on Geron's collarbone.

Orion crouched beside him "What do you need me to do?"

"Put your hands on the back of my neck. No matter what happens, don't let go until I say it's okay. If you cannot comply with this directive, it is imperative that you ask for a replacement before breaking contact."

Orion moved behind him as Alexander reached out with his primordial energy and grabbed on to Orion's strength. Orion grunted, his hands twitching on Alexander's neck until warmth seeped through their connection. The sweet heat drifted through Alexander, out through his hands, and into Geron.

The door opened and closed and Orion started to sway.

Alexander kept his focus on extracting as much energy for Geron as he could, but Orion would soon fall. "Another needs to take his place."

"I'm here." Miguel moved his large, square frame beside him. "Tell me what to do."

"Place your hands on the back of my neck and don't let go."

Orion stumbled away as Miguel took his place. Alexander drew on the enforcer's energy until Miguel moaned and fell. Another took his place, then another, until there was a pile of groggy or sleeping enforcers around Geron. They would all be in need of a feeding after this, but they'd have to deal with that later.

Geron's breathing stabilized, but his skin still had a slightly gray hue. Geron groaned like he was in pain.

A lance ripped through Alexander's heart, and Dania and Kile appeared at his side.

"He's in pain," Kile said.

Obviously, they'd felt it, too.

The pain deepened as Alexander tightened his grip on Geron. "I'm going to give him the rest of my strength."

Kile pulled him back. "We need you to continue to treat him, and all those who've fallen. Take my power."

"You haven't fed recently, either."

"But I've had two full feedings since leaving Kirato, where you have had none. Take what you need."

Alexander studied the fine lines in Geron's lax face as Kile moved behind Alexander and placed his hands on his neck.

"We're clear!" Captain Quaren announced. "The scans have stopped. We're safe."

A few people cheered, but Alexander could sense the eyes of the crew on him. Concern for their new king thickened the air.

Dania stood. "I'll call for more enforcers."

Alexander concentrated on Kile's hands, poking at the primordial energy hiding beneath his commander's skin and then latching on, overpowering him and pulling it through their touch. Balling the new energy inside him, Alexander forced it through his hands and into Geron.

Ada moaned, and his eyes fluttered. He blinked, taking in his surroundings.

"He's awake." Alexander released Kile and the commander fell to one knee, panting as if he'd chased a criminal up a hill for three days.

Kile placed his hand on Alexander's shoulder. "Will he be all right?"

"I think so."

Geron sat up, his gaze flicking across the bridge. "Is the fleet safe?"

"Yes, Ada," Dania said. "The scans have stopped. You did it."

Geron stood slowly, accepting Kile's and Alexander's help. "Did we lose any ships?"

Dania grimaced. "A few."

Geron's gaze carried to the screens. "I remember explosions. What happened?"

Dania gulped. "It appears that the energy blanket you sent out to pull them with us closed on top of a few of the ships, crushing them."

Geron flinched. "How many?"

"Not many, Ada."

"How many?!" His voice boomed through the command deck, and several of the crew retreated a step.

Dania stood tall, channeling the general inside her. "Seven ships are lost."

Geron's gaze seemed glued to hers. "How many people?"

"Unfortunately, one of the ships was a passenger carrier. We lost thirty-eight Kevers."

Geron growled, clenching his hands.

Dania moved closer while everyone else backed away. "Ada, you saved thousands of lives. You need to focus on that."

He shoved her away, walking toward the door. "I am a Bane. I should have been able to save them all."

CHAPTER 8
DANIA

DANIA STEPPED AWAY from the command deck, leaving Alexander to tend to the drained enforcers. Kile, although tired, insisted he was still capable of commanding the fleet. Which was good, since so many enforcers now seemed to be as incapacitated as they had been when they'd first arrived.

She moved down the hall, barely needing to follow the pull to her sponsor. She knew where he'd be...where he always went to think.

The door to the observatory opened as she approached. At least he hadn't locked her out.

Geron sat by the massive windows looking out at the stars twinkling in the distance and the ships still huddled close. "Unless you have an important update, I prefer to be alone."

She took a step closer. "While I don't doubt that is true, I find it hard to believe that you would have allowed me to walk through the door if you really wanted to be alone."

"Wise, as usual, my Dania."

She sat beside him.

The air about her sponsor was cool, rather than pulsing with raw Bane power. Any other time he'd skipped space, he'd been in prime shape, not having used his primordial energy sometimes for months at a time. This time, he'd been drained probably more than any Kever had been drained of energy in modern times.

Most Banes accepted one enforcer into their ranks a year. It wasn't something Dania had given much thought to, but possibly it was to keep this from happening. Banes were known to be all-powerful, but in times like these, they'd all need to get used to the fact that their new king's strength had limits.

Geron looked down at his folded hands. "I don't have what it takes to be king."

"Why would you say that? You're a Bane."

"I've never been responsible for anything that could cost people their lives. At least not civilian lives."

"You saved a lot of lives today."

"I killed thirty-eight people."

"That wasn't your fault."

"It was!" His eyes were like daggers. "I killed them just as assuredly as if I'd placed my bare hands around their necks. I crushed their ships with my own power."

This was true, but he needed to look at the larger picture.

"Ada, you were tired. You knew there were risks, and I think that's why you made the tactical decision to place the smaller ships in the outer rings."

He looked back to his hands. "The first skip was simple. I thought I'd be able to save all of them."

She grabbed his hands. "Ada, you need to focus on the ones you *did* save. These people were as good as dead. They came to you for protection."

"And it cost them their lives."

"It cost a *small fraction of them* their lives. With small ships like that, they would certainly have died out there alone. You gave them a chance. You need to focus on the fact that over six hundred other ships are still huddled about you." She pointed out the window. "None of them blame you for what happened. These people have seen war up close. They are simply thankful to have somewhere to go."

He shook his head. "I'm not trained for this. I never wanted this kind of responsibility."

She squeezed his hands. "In Earthan culture, it's noted that some of the greatest leaders are those who never wanted to lead."

He looked at the ceiling. "That makes no sense."

"But it does. You despised your father and brother, and it wasn't just the way they treated you. You had a deep loathing for most of their rules."

"Everything my father deemed a law was decidedly self-serving."

"Now *you* have the power to change that."

He scoffed, shaking his head. "You're trying to make this sound like a good thing, but it doesn't change the fact that these people expect me to save them. I'm not a savior."

"Maybe not, but you could be. All they are looking for is safety. Someone to lead them and protect them."

"You are forgetting, once again, that I killed people—innocents—while I was trying to protect them. Some people are meant to rule. Others aren't." He looked out at the ships and stars again. "As my father always enjoyed pointing out... our designations had nothing to do with our ages. I was eighth for a reason. These people are clinging to me because of my last name—my heritage—but they are sorely mistaken." He looked at his hands again. "I'm not capable of helping anyone."

"I disagree. You sent food to Kirato when your father had deemed the colony a loss. You sent your enforcers to save Ephershia when your father ignored their plea for help. You've saved more lives than I think you realize."

"This is different."

"It's not. You need to understand, Ada, that just being here gives them peace and unity. Without you, they were small clusters alone in the stars. You brought them back together as a race again."

"For what purpose?"

"To start over."

He stared into her eyes, before he looked down. "I don't know how to do that for them."

"Of course you don't. None of us do." She released his hands. "The Kevers are strong. We'll figure this out."

"I wish I had the same faith in myself as you have."

Dania smiled. "You will."

CHAPTER 9

ALEXANDER

ALEXANDER HELD his hands over one of the newer enforcers in the infirmary, judging his remaining primordial energy. This one, like the others, would need a treatment of artificial pathogens. There were others in worse shape, though, so he'd let him sleep. There was no reason to wake him and leave him to deal with the suffering of—as Peter put it—the symptoms of withdrawal.

The enforcer in the next bed swung his legs over the side of the sleeping slab and sat, watching Alexander work on his patient. "How did you do it?" he asked.

"How did I review the patient's status?"

The enforcer shook his head. "No. How did you extract our power and put it back into our sponsor?"

Alexander turned to him. "Your name is Claris, right?"

Claris nodded.

"It's mostly instinct, I suppose. I saw there was a need, and I acted on it."

Claris narrowed his eyes. "It's more than that. I am trained as a healer as well. I can send my energy into another to heal them, but you acted as a conduit. That shouldn't be possible."

Orion eased off his own bed, rubbing his shoulder. "Alexander has always been renowned for his healing abilities."

"Which is fine, but reversing a gift of primordial energy shouldn't be possible." Claris looked back toward Alexander. "I have never seen anything like this. Olom was my previous sponsor, and there were times when I would have used such a skill, if I'd been able."

Alexander's gaze carried over the room. Olom was ranked higher than Geron, but he'd still been several levels away from the throne. How many others lying here were just like Alexander and had never expected their sponsor to be elevated any higher than they already had been?

Claris leaned on his knees, breaking his perfect, stiff enforcer posture. "My point is that even if I'd instinctually thought of drawing the energy from other enforcers, I couldn't have done it."

Couldn't…that was an interesting choice of words. That meant not simply that it would have been hard for him…he actually wouldn't have been able to do it. Which was strange, since his sponsor ranked higher than Geron, and Alexander had been without a full feeding from Geron in so long.

Orion glared at Claris. "We should be thankful he was able to help our sponsor after Geron had acted so rashly."

Rashly? If Orion's original disdain for their sponsor was showing through again, maybe Alexander had transferred too much energy back to Geron.

"He wasn't acting rashly," Alexander said. "He saved what was left of the Kever culture."

"At significant risk to himself. He is the last Bane. As

much as I detest saying this, he needs to start thinking about himself first again." Orion turned his back on them and walked out the door.

In many ways, he was right, but Alexander was glad Geron didn't feel that way. It would have been significantly safer for Geron to have left a certain number of ships behind in each jump. That would have slowed down the Carteks and left him with more energy to spare once they were safe. Of course, all those left behind would have been annihilated.

Their sponsor had made yet another uncharacteristically selfless decision, but Geron hadn't been trained for this kind of pressure. How long did these people have before Geron did exactly what Orion apparently expected him to do…leave behind the stragglers and save himself?

CHAPTER 10
CAL

CAL SAT in his chair on the *Star Renegade* bridge, leaning his elbow on the console and watching Kever technicians scurry past. Lately, it seemed like they had more to worry about than the old, beat-up smuggling ship they had trapped in their cargo hold. Which was fine with Cal.

Something big had happened, and all they knew was that the cruiser had jumped several times in a row. Cal had only asked Alanna to jump the ship that many times when they'd been running for their lives. Of course, the Banes could probably jump indefinitely. It still had to be hard, though, unless they'd left all the other ships behind.

Ty looked away from the hangar and seemed to notice something on his panel. "We just got a transmission."

"Really? I thought they'd blocked everything."

"They did." Ty pressed a few buttons. "It's addressed to you. It's from Earth."

"Earth? I don't know anyone from Earth."

Ty scrolled through something on the screen. "From the stamps, it looks like the comm officer on the command deck grabbed the transmission and then sent it to Kile."

"Kile?"

"You heard me right. Whatever it is, the Big Guy watched the entire transmission before releasing it to us."

Great. But what could it possibly be? Knowing Kile, it was something that would torture Cal for the rest of his life.

Ty glanced at him. "Cal, it's from your mom."

Ice chilled over Cal's skin. He used to talk to her once a week without fail. After Filluck Palogivan had died and Cal had taken the blame, he'd called her one last time from a secure line on a freighter to let her know he hadn't done it, and that he'd have to go dark for both their sakes. He hadn't spoken to her since.

But why was she calling, and why now? How had she even tracked him down? And why was she on Earth, of all places, where all hell was about to break loose?

Ty pressed a few buttons, and the message appeared on Cal's screen. He stood and tapped Cal's shoulder twice. "I'll give you a few moments alone, boss."

Cal didn't respond as Ty slipped out the door.

It had been years since Cal had talked to his mom. He remembered happier days, when she and his dad had taken him to museums or out into the fields before planting started.

Cal and his dad would fly drones together while his mom gathered some of the fresh herbs she and the other colonists planted along the edges of the main fields to get "good old-fashioned spices" for her home-cooked meals.

It was a simpler time. A happy time.

Until the enforcers had shown up and murdered his father for the unconscionable crime of walking his son home from the market.

For months, Cal had tried to find records of a crime, but

there were none. His father had been murdered for no reason by an automaton who'd stood there while Cal had sobbed, holding the bloody shell of a man who'd been laughing and joking with him only moments before.

Cal closed his eyes and sighed. Memories of his dad had flooded him no matter where he'd gone.

When Cal had been old enough and had decided to leave the planet where he'd been born, he'd asked his mother to go with him so they could start fresh somewhere else. She'd enjoyed those old family memories, though, and had felt like his dad had still been there with her in the small, tight-knit colony.

Cal didn't like it, but he had to respect her wishes while he left the planet looking for answers that he knew he'd never find.

But now she was on Earth. Why had she left their home after telling Cal she wanted to stay and have her ashes scattered in the forest with his dad's after her death?

His hands twitched over his console, and he gritted his teeth thinking that whatever his mom had to tell him, Kile already knew. But for some reason, the walking monstrosity had allowed the communication through to the *Star Renegade*.

Whatever the reason for that was, scared Cal more than whatever his mom might have to tell him.

He tapped the *play* button, and his mother's face appeared on the screen. She looked older, fine lines marring her eyes, and a streak of gray above her right eye. She'd never looked more beautiful.

"Oh, Cal, I really wish this were a two-way so I could see your face." His mother shifted her weight. "I got some great news today, and even though I know you said it would be dangerous to try to find you, I decided I'd try."

She smiled into the camera. "My new magistrate told me that you've been exonerated for the crime of murder by one of the members of the royal family themselves! How exciting!"

Cal wasn't really sure it was exciting, but if that made her happy, he'd redo everything that had gotten him here ten times over. She deserved some happiness in her life.

"As I'm sure you've figured out, I'm on Earth. We were evacuated three weeks ago. They tell me that we were lucky, that so many people weren't able to get out before the fighting started." She shifted her weight again. "I'm staying with my sister, back in our family home in Italy." She looked up and then to the left and right. "Oh, this brings back so many memories. I hope you get to see it someday. It's good to see where you come from."

Cal's stomach soured. That would probably never happen. There was an armada of countless ships pointed right at her. When this was over, there might not be much of Earth left.

He clawed at his hair. Why in the name of all that was good and right in the galaxy had they evacuated them to Earth?

Even if she were somewhere safer, the removal of the murder charge changed nothing. As Kile and Orion always loved to remind him, he was still wanted for smuggling and a myriad of other crimes. It was the safest to keep as far away from her as he could. The last thing he wanted was his mother facing the wrath of an enforcer if they fired a shot at Cal and missed.

She leaned closer to the screen. "If you can come to Earth, look up Regina and Marco Sangrini in Naples, Italy." She smiled again, tears in her eyes. "I'd love to introduce them to their nephew." She tapped a few keys. "I'm leaving a signature for you to reply, but I know you're busy." She blew a kiss at the screen. "Just come home, if you can."

Interesting that she'd said *come home* when there was a very good chance that his actual home planet was now occupied by the Carteks.

Cal sat back, his stomach roiling. Maybe they didn't know about the Cartek cloud?

No. That was ridiculous. They had to know. But maybe the government hadn't told the people? Were they worried there was nowhere left to send the civilians?

There had to be somewhere...*anywhere* safer than Earth. He'd let her know that. She could still get away.

He tapped the link to the signature log.

The *return message* field was blank, which meant the Big Guy had wanted Cal to get the message, but he'd made sure Cal couldn't respond.

Was that Kile's goal? To torture Cal, letting him know his mother was in the path of the Cartek storm, with no way to warn her? Was Kile out there on the cruiser, gloating over Cal's pain?

If not that, then why even let this through?

Cal rubbed his chin, considering the consecutive jumps the ship had made. If the cruiser had been running, they were maybe hiding. Any outbound communication would be a security risk. But then why grab this communication at all? Unless they'd grabbed it with normal reconnaissance days ago and just gotten around to listening to it.

The door opened and Ty stuck his head in. "Everything okay?"

"Yeah. My mom got evacuated to Earth. She's fine, thank goodness."

For now, at least.

"Good news is always a bonus." Ty pointed his thumb over his shoulder. "We have everyone in the lounge for that progress meeting you asked for. Do you want to put it off?"

Cal checked the time on his console. He'd been sitting there for over an hour already. "No need to cancel. We still need to get out of here."

And maybe, once they were free, he could look up his aunt and uncle in Italy and let them all know they needed to drop everything and board the first available ship off the planet.

Ty walked by Cal's side as they headed for the lounge. "You okay, boss?"

"Yeah. My mom's message just dredged up all those old, buried feelings about my dad." And unfortunately, now Cal was surrounded by those pearlescent uniforms that he'd been having nightmares about since the day his father had died.

The pirate captain Victor had been a first-rate jerk, but one thing he'd been right about was his initial reaction when he'd found out that the *Star Renegade* crew had been helping treat and save enforcers. Victor had wanted them all dead.

That may have been a bit extreme, but Cal agreed the galaxy would be a better place without them. There was simply no need to create a race of supercharged people with super-sized egos, only to set them loose in the guise of keeping the peace.

He tapped the pad and entered the lounge. "Okay, people, give me good news."

Ethan walked over to the table and took a chair. "The engines seem fine, overall. I can't test them, and I'm hoping they don't choke when we turn them on, but I'm as ready as I can get."

Ty sat in his normal place at the end of the table. "I've run all the tests Alanna threw at me. I'm like Ethan: I wish we could give it a test run, but I'm ready to go."

"Ethan and I double-checked all the wiring our pirate friends did, and everything looks solid." Chris folded his arms. "They were a bunch of pricks, but they were good mechanics. We finished the rest of the connections this morning."

Alanna took a deep breath and released it. "I looked at everything front, back, and sideways. This rewiring is unconventional, but it should work like a charm. When we turn on the engines, they're going to expel sixty times more power than they're supposed to. The cruiser is probably prepped for a ship accidentally exploding, but that would be force on all sides. This energy will be centered on one point." She pressed her palms on her thighs. "Alex agrees—in theory, of course—that concentrated energy of that magnitude will cut right through the hangar door."

Cal looked at Ethan. "This is all great, but can you make the switch back fast enough that we'll be able to power the ship up and leave after we blast a hole in it?"

His face twisted into a half-dozen different expressions before he puffed out a breath. "It's actually just a toggle we'll flip like an old-fashioned light switch. We blast a hole, I flip the switch, and then Ty does his magic to take us out of here."

Cal doubted it would be that easy.

Alanna shifted, biting her lower lip. "All we need is Alexander, Dania, and Doc back on board, and we can go."

That was a problem, though, since they hadn't heard from any of them in over a day. Their five-hour escape plan had been shot to hell once the cruiser had started jumping like they'd been running for their lives, and Cal still had no idea what they'd been running from.

Ty's comm band pinged. "It looks like Big Guy is walking up our cargo ramp."

"What does he want?" Cal headed for the door into the hallway. Kile was already walking down the main thoroughfare toward him, clutching what appeared to be one of Ethan's data pads.

Ty appeared at Cal's side. "What's up, Big Guy?"

Kile stopped inches from him. "You are an annoyance. You are far too conceited, even for a human, and you make irrational choices."

"Well, yeah, but tell me something I don't know."

Kile glared at Ty before turning his glaze to Cal. "You are insufficiently skilled to be a captain, yet these people flock to you. You utilize their skills to make up for your own shortcomings."

That was probably supposed to hurt, but by now, Cal was used to the Big Guy's bad attitude. "This is nothing *you* didn't already know."

Kile pushed past them and entered the lounge.

Rachel startled when she saw him, placing her hand at the base of her throat, but she managed to remain seated, wringing her hands.

Kile turned to Chris. "You're a pirate and a murderer. You don't belong here and are not a member of this crew."

Chris folded his arms again. "It's not like your shit don't stink, asshole."

Alanna elbowed him, drawing Kile's attention.

"You are a mystery, and probably the only member of this crew who won't be executed when this is done. From my time spent here, I will assume your pending pairing with my sponsor is not being received well by you or the crew, but you will soon see it for the opportunity that it is."

Like hell. Cal fisted his hands before relaxing them. It wasn't like he could punch the guy and live through it.

Ethan waved at the enforcer. "I'm still your favorite, right?"

Kile sneered at him. "You should be executed, simply due to your aptitude. Your skills make you far too dangerous to leave you alive as part of this crew."

Ethan's eyes widened. "I'm going to go over here and sit down and shut up for the first time in my life." He eased into a chair and stared at the tabletop.

Was Kile here just to reiterate how much he hated all of them?

Rachel stood, tears pooling in her lashes. "Why do you always have to come back here and be such a big jerk? Just get out if you don't have nothing nice to say to anybody."

Big Guy stared at the blank data pad in his hand as if there were words or pictures on the screen. His gaze carried across the room, but they seemed to scan over Rachel's head, instead of looking at her.

He looked down at the data pad again, before turning to Ethan and pointing to the wall to Ethan's left. "Did you make this repair to the wall?"

Ethan stood, easing away from the enforcer. "Umm, yeah, about a year ago. Why?"

"Is that metal overlay made from Titanium?" Kile placed the data pad on the table.

"Yeah. I know it's overkill, but we had a sheet on hand, and it fit over a hole in the wall. Why?"

Swirls of fire appeared in both of Kile's fists. He punched

with one fist, then the other, sending blasts of fire into the Titanium patch.

"Yo!" Ethan ducked, covering his head, even though the flames weren't aimed at him.

Heat erupted in the room as Kile blasted fire at the panel over and over until he dropped to his knees. The flames winked out and the room instantly cooled. Kile covered his face with his hands, and his shoulders shook like he might be sobbing.

Rachel inched toward him. "Big Guy?"

Cal grabbed her arm. "Don't go near him."

Ty picked up the data pad Kile had placed on the table. "You may want to belay that order, Captain."

He showed them the screen. It was a picture of Rachel with a broad smile, her head pressed up against Kile's. He looked significantly annoyed at her, but there was an odd glint in his eyes.

Amusement, maybe?

Ty swiped the screen, and another picture appeared. This one looked like Rachel had been holding the data pad over them while they'd lain in her bed.

"That's what he left all over the ship?" Alanna asked. "Pictures of him and Rachel?"

Ty nodded, swiping to another picture. "Big Guy knew that if he came back, that he'd be a different person. I guess he was sending himself a message from the grave."

Rachel shoved him. "Shut up. He ain't dead. He's right here."

"But why didn't he break this data pad like all the others?" Ethan asked.

Rachel hugged herself. "Doc told me once that the enforcers seem to get some of their emotions back after draining a lot of energy. Something must have happened on the ship." She looked at the partially melted Titanium. "Enough of a something to make him want to feel even more."

The Titanium plate glistened like it had been polished and slightly curved from the impact of so much heat. Maybe Kile knew if he'd used a little more energy, his memories might return.

Rachel kneeled beside him. "Big Guy, do you remember me now?"

He lowered his hands and looked at her for the first time. "No." He looked around the room. "I remember all of them, even the murderous pirate." He glanced at the data pad. "But it's like you weren't even on the ship."

Rachel pouted. "Well, I was."

Kile looked away. "So it would seem."

Alanna rubbed her shoulders like she had a chill. "Dania was always afraid that Geron would make her forget us all. Maybe he can be selective on who he makes people forget?"

Kile stood. "I need to return to my duties."

"Yo, Big Guy?" Ethan took a few steps toward him. "Do you still want to kill us all?"

"Of course. You're all criminals." Kile started walking toward the door. "But it will give me no pleasure."

A shiver ran down Cal's spine. Did that mean that killing *had* given him pleasure before? Were all those death machines programmed to enjoy murdering people?

Rachel pushed past Cal. "Wait!" Kile turned to her as she swiped back her hair, then held out her right hand. "Hi. My name is Rachel. Rachel Quirky. Pleased to meet you."

His gaze seemed to search her face. "You are a distraction. An encumbrance."

Rachel slipped her hands in her pockets. "Aww, I bet you say that to all the girls."

His eyes narrowed. "You are...*odd.*"

"Yeah, maybe." She tilted her head, blushing. "But trust me, you like odd."

His eyes narrowed again before he turned and left the room.

Rachel folded her hands and sighed, smiling.

What she had to smile about, Cal didn't know. What she was going through was Cal's worst nightmare...having Dania walk back onto the ship someday having no memory of who he was.

This was exactly why they needed to leave sooner rather than later.

Rachel bit her lower lip, looking pretty pleased with herself.

Hopefully, she wasn't going to be a problem when it was time for them to blast out of there, leaving the cruiser, the prince-turned-king, and even her precious Big Guy far behind.

CHAPTER 11
DANIA

DANIA SAT on Geron's left as the Counselor General went over statistics and numbers…two things Geron had avoided most his life. That morning, they'd rendezvous with two more smaller cruisers filled with both Kevers and the remainder, from what they could tell, of the higher-ranking Bane enforcers. The worst of the enforcers were sent to the infirmaries to get artificial pathogens, while those who could still walk and care for themselves came and offered their service to Geron. It would be interesting to see if they were still willing to serve when the time came to be absorbed by a new sponsor, or if their bodies would rebel and try to fight Geron off, as all the others had.

"News from the Earthan colonies is dire, sire," the Counselor General said. "We need to take stock of our forces and strategize the best way to defend the last of the free worlds."

Geron looked at him with tired eyes. "The last free worlds?"

"Earth, and the colonies in the central Earthan Cradle. At this time, the refugees are scattered, some heading to Trellus, some to a moon circling the gas giant, Jupiter, and the largest contingent has landed on or is heading for Earth itself."

Geron stared at him like he was speaking another language. "Why are you wasting my time with statistics about humans?"

The Counselor General gaped at him. "I know you registered some hesitation on the subject earlier, but now that things have settled, I thought you would see the wisdom in honoring your father's covenants."

"My father's covenants? The humans hated my father. They agreed to his terms because they had no other alternative, and they've regretted it ever since. They tried to break ties with Keveron four times since the treaty was signed, but my father refused." Geron turned away. "I think it's about time I gave them the freedom they so desperately desired."

The Counselor looked at Dania, then back to Geron. "Sir, they'll be slaughtered."

Geron closed his eyes, took a deep breath, then released it. "How many humans inhabit the Earthan Cradle?"

"Billions, sir. I can get you the exact numbers if you…"

Geron held up his palm. "How many Kevers are in the ships surrounding us?"

"At last count, eighty-seven-thousand six hundred and twenty-two."

"Eighty-seven thousand left of a galactic empire that has lasted over four thousand years." Geron folded his arms on the table. He seemed outwardly calm, but the air about him heated. "Stop telling me about the humans and start thinking of ways to save our own people. The Earthan Cradle is no longer our concern. We have our own more pressing difficulties to deal with."

"Sire, the Earthan Cradle may be the only way to save our people. We have nowhere else to go."

Geron slammed his fist on the table. "I will not send what's left of the Kever race in front of that cloud. This conversation is over."

The Counselor General's jaw dropped again, and he looked to Dania.

What he thought she could do, she wasn't sure, but she leaned closer to her sponsor. "Ada, maybe we should arrange a committee to discuss this?"

His lips twisted into a snarl. "What is a committee going to do? A committee is not going to change the fact that our people are on the brink of extinction."

"No, but I do think it's wise that we discuss our decisions with your father's former advisors. They are more attuned to looking at the larger political landscape."

"The only political landscape I care about is the one that saves my own people."

"An excellent declaration for a king." The Counselor General folded his hands on the edge of the table, doing a good job of appearing at ease, but his temperature spiked. "The unfortunate truth is that without Earth, we are alone in the galaxy. Do you think your father offered to protect them so many years ago out of the kindness of his heart?" He made a *pft* noise with his lips. "Even I'm not foolish enough to think that your father counted kindness as one of his virtues. Saving Earth was a tactical decision."

Geron reclined in his chair. "Tactical or not, I can't watch any more of my people die."

Dania placed her hand on his shoulder. "This is war, Ada. People will die. I wish there were a way around that, but I'm not sure that's possible."

"Are you advising me to take our remaining warships to Earth, leaving what's left of our race to fend for themselves?" He brushed her hand off his shoulder. "And you're worried about the *humans* being slaughtered?"

"I'm not saying that, Ada. I'm saying we should have an open discussion with advisors who have more experience in these kinds of decisions. They served your father and now they serve you, and not for their own good, but for the good of the Kever people. The decision, as always, will be in the hands of their king."

He stared at the ceiling, not answering.

"It cannot hurt to at least listen to them, Ada."

He shook his head. "It is wasting time in which I could be resting to regain my strength or absorbing more soldiers. As you keep pointing out, I need to rebuild the military to protect what's left of our people."

The Counselor General remained silent, but his eyes were imploring.

Dania looked back to Geron. "I suggest taking a short sabbatical, Ada, and then giving them an hour of your time. Listen to their positives and negatives and then make a decision on your own."

"Fine, but after that, I don't want to hear about Earth anymore."

The Counselor General stood and bowed. "Thank you, sire." He left the room, the door closing behind him.

Dania tapped the table with her finger. Cal will hate this idea but... "I think it would be a good idea to invite the smugglers to the discussion with the advisors as well."

Geron's eyes widened. "What?"

"As humans, I think they could provide a valuable perspective."

"The only person in the galaxy who hates me more than the Carteks is the smuggler captain."

"Exactly."

"You're making no sense."

"It makes perfect sense. This will give the advisors an idea of what humans are like. If they see the humans' distaste for the Kevers, they may reconsider an alliance with Earth as an option."

"Do you actually believe that?"

"If we can find a safe place for our people, then yes, I do. Most of them probably have no conception of how unhappy the humans are under Keveron's rule."

Moreover, although she wouldn't admit it out loud, this would give Cal a chance to understand how the stakes in the galaxy had changed. He wanted to leave. That was the right thing to do to save his crew.

For the rest of the humans, though, the sad truth was that there were few places in the galaxy left to hide. If no one faced the Carteks, they would swarm over the galaxy destroying anyone who might be or *could become* a threat.

With the survival of both Earth and the Kever refugees hanging in the balance, Geron needed her guidance now more than ever. Dania was one of the few people Geron listened to, and without her, there was a high chance that Geron would spend the rest of his inordinately long life running.

She'd still support Cal in wanting to leave, but she needed him to understand why she was staying behind. It wouldn't make it hurt any less for either of them, but this was the way it had to be.

Hopefully she could convince him to leave before Geron erased Cal from her memory forever.

THE MASSIVE CEILINGS of Geron's cruiser made Cal feel small as he took a seat next to Doc near the middle of a long, floating table twice the size of the one he'd sat at the day the *Star Renegade* had been swallowed by the blasted royal behemoth. He'd spent the last few days pulling his hair out, trying to figure out a way to contact Dania, Doc, and Alexander so he could get them back on the *Star Renegade*.

Now *Cal* was off-ship, too. But at least he'd hopefully find out what was going on, and now that he'd found Doc, with any luck, he could find Dani and Alex, too. Then they could finally get out of there and rid themselves of Geron Bane.

Four blue-and-green skinned Kever men sat on the opposite side of the table, all in blue robes so dark, they were almost black. Another Kever whose skin was more green than blue sat beside Cal, and a female Kever in long robes a few shades lighter blue than all the others sat beside Doc. The two sides of the table seemed to glare at each other, and Cal had to wonder if they'd seated him and Doc on the pariah side.

Everyone in the room stood when the door opened.

Geron's translator entered first, followed by a Kever man in a fancy uniform with insignias on his shoulder who stood behind the chair at the far end of the table near the door. Kile and Orion followed, walking to the far side of the room and joining the translator in standing against the back wall.

The new king entered next with Dania right beside him. She was back in that hideous white-opal uniform, but her hair was still dark, and she smiled when their eyes met.

Cal puffed out a relieved breath. At least she hadn't been turned back into a monomaniacal death machine yet.

Yet was a pretty big word in that statement. Every second they stayed there, both she and Alexander were in worse danger. He needed to get them all to safety.

"Keep a cool head, boss," Doc whispered.

Easy for him to say. He wasn't at risk of losing someone he loved.

Dania sat in the seat next to the green-skinned Kever on Cal's side of the table. She kept her gaze straight ahead and seemed to take careful breaths.

Geron took the seat at the end of the table on Dania's right. "Proceed."

Cal startled, hearing the first syllable in the Kever's harsh speech pattern, followed by the English translation forced into his head from the enforcer standing behind Geron. He'd known it would happen, but it was always disquieting to hear the enforcer's voice exploding in his mind.

Everyone sat, with the exception of the Kever man wearing the fancy uniform. "There is a massive cloud of Cartek ships heading into the Earthan Cradle."

Fancy-Guy's Kever words warbled, sounding like gibberish, but the voice Cal heard in his head sounded just like the translator's. He did his best to focus on the words, and not the fact that everyone in the room who spoke would have the same voice.

Fancy-Guy continued. "They've already decimated most of the worlds between Keveron and the outskirts of Earth's primary holdings."

Cal gripped the edge of the table at the same time Doc flinched. Alanna's home planet was on the edge of Kever space. Her family was now hidden on Europa, but knowing the Carteks had destroyed one of his own crew's birthplaces hit a little too close to home.

"It is our expectation that the Cartek cloud will overwhelm Earth's forces within eight days of their arrival in the center of the system."

"Eight days?" Cal's stomach sank. His mother was on Earth!

"Easy, boss," Doc whispered. "We're just here to listen for now."

Yeah, as glorified replacements for the melted former Earthan ambassador. Lucky them.

Fancy-Guy looked around the room. "They've destroyed all technology on the planets left behind, and we estimate that seventy-five percent of the populations of all the lost colonies are gone, with technology and infrastructure at a total loss."

Seventy-five percent? How could that be possible? And it sounded like they were leaving those people in the Dark Ages. Humanity hadn't lived without technology for hundreds of years. They'd have no idea how to grow their own food, let alone how to store it safely. It was as bad as leaving them to die.

Fancy-Guy continued, "With the patterns in the cloud advancing on Earth, we are expecting the Carteks are about to initiate their most decisive strike."

"Decisive?" Cal asked. "What does that mean?"

Doc covered his eyes, but Cal didn't care that they'd been warned to keep their mouths shut. He needed to know what was going on.

Fancy-Guy lowered his gaze. "It means that our statisticians believe they plan to do the same to Earth, if not worse."

Geron massaged the bridge of his thin, nearly bridgeless nose. "Why would they do that? They caused considerable damage to Earthan settlements before my father offered assistance, but nothing like you're describing."

Fancy-Guy shrugged. "Vengeance? We can't be sure, but their attacks have been merciless, as well as well calculated. They systematically split up your father's forces, attacking planets on opposite sides of the galaxy so they couldn't be overwhelmed by the might of Keveron."

The king laughed, shaking his head. "The might of Keveron?" He sat back in his chair, looking down.

Doc glanced at Cal, shifting his weight.

Cal didn't feel all that comfortable, either. There was an odd pressure in the room, but was it Geron's blasted primordial energy, or everyone's fear of his homicidal temper?

When His Royalness didn't elaborate, Fancy-Guy continued. "While communications are down, we believe we can create a web using existing satellites to create a rudimentary communication network that human technology will be able to read, but one that the Carteks would consider no better than static."

"You're not talking about Morse code, right?" Cal leaned on the table. "Because I doubt even anyone on Earth would pick up on that, especially if they're panicking with the Carteks heading their way."

"No. What our people are suggesting is more along the lines of ancient cellular communication devices. We believe the Carteks would discount the signal as no more menacing than the ancient television or radio waves still floating about the galaxy from Earth's earlier communications networks."

Cal shivered. It had been those very early communications networks and the satellites that short-sighted 'visionaries' had shot out into space with friendly messages for anyone who might find them that had brought the Carteks to Earth's doorstep the first time. Too bad those were mistakes that couldn't be undone.

"Communications are great, but they don't mean much if we don't have a plan to save Earth." Cal looked at Geron. "What are you going to do to help them?"

The king looked at his fingernails. "Nothing."

"Nothing?" Doc and Cal said at the same time.

The king glanced around the table. "I've thought about this extensively over the past few hours. My father made many promises to Earth, but in the end, fulfilling those promises led to the destruction of our own world. I won't be making the same mistakes."

Mistakes? Helping Earth had been one of the few things that his father had done right! How could he consider saving Earth a mistake?

Geron's gaze scanned his advisors. "We are going to take what's left of our people and search for a habitable world. I have my scientists searching for a wide range of compatible suns and planets with a high chance of being able to support our people. These planets will be added to the list of the options we already have, and we will choose from those with the most viable chance of success."

Cal stood. "You can't just leave Earth."

"I can do whatever I please." Geron shook his head like he was bored. "We relayed several communications to Earth letting them know we have freed them of the covenant. They are no longer beholden to Keveron."

"You can't just cut them off like that. You made them a promise."

"Earth's covenant was with my father. My father, as well as the military that backed him, are no longer in existence. I am choosing to save my own people."

"You're choosing to be a coward."

The advisors on the other side of the table gasped.

Dania's eyes widened, and she flicked a glance at Geron. She held up her hands like she might grab him, but she knew as well as Cal that she couldn't do anything if the king got mad enough.

That didn't mean Cal was going to back down and cower like the rest of these simpletons, though.

Doc's hand appeared on his arm. "A modicum of humility would probably be a good idea, boss."

Cal took a breath to calm himself. "Please, all I ask is that you give Earth a chance."

Geron looked at his fingernails again. "I can't do that and give my *own people* a chance. This is an unfortunate decision, but in the end, I have to do what's right for what's left of Keveron."

"Do you actually think the Carteks are going to stop with Earth? As long as you're alive, you'll be a threat. Your only real chance is to join forces with Earth's military and fight the Carteks now—together. Because I guarantee you the Carteks won't stop with Earth. They'll hunt you down. Your people will never be safe."

The king folded his hands on the edge of the table. "They

won't find us if we travel far enough. It will take time, but we will find a new world and start over."

Around the table, everyone shifted, glancing at each other nervously.

Cal gritted his teeth. There needed to be another way. "Earth would take your people in. Earth has everything you need. Infrastructure, power…you wouldn't have to completely start over. If we stand together, we can both thrive."

The green-skinned Kever sitting to Cal's right shook his head. "That, I unfortunately have to disagree with. Humanity doesn't blend with other cultures. They've pushed out native species on the planets they inhabit, carrying on traditions from the beginnings of their civilizations. We would always be outsiders to them and would be treated with disdain."

Cal slammed his fist on the table. "That's not true."

Green-Guy smirked. "If you believe that, you are a bigger fool than we've been told."

"Why is this man even here?" Fancy-Guy asked.

Dania stood. "He's here at my request, Counselor General. I wanted to give the humans a voice and help us understand humanity's stance on their relationships between Earth and Keveron."

"Look," Cal said. "The free people of Earth haven't been happy under Kever law. I admit that. We aren't used to living with such stringent rules."

"Says the lawbreaker," Green-Guy said.

"Yes, I *am* a lawbreaker—because half your previous king's laws hurt good people."

Orion stormed from the wall, his hands ablaze.

"Stop!" Geron held up his palm. "My administration will not now, nor ever, punish someone for speaking the truth."

The fire winked out in Orion's hands. He glared at Cal before returning to his place against the wall.

Green-Guy lifted his chin. "How are these words considered truth? Keveron's laws have always served the greater good."

"No, they haven't." Cal turned back to Geron. "And I think you noticed that, too, because you sent food to Kirato when you found out they'd been cut off from the trading routes."

The Counselor General shook his head. "Kirato was never cut off from the trading routes."

"Maybe not officially, but the traders never came all the same. Those people were starving, until your new king—who at the time was a lowly prince no one thought would amount to anything—stepped up and did the right thing."

They all looked at Geron.

Dania's sponsor tapped his thumb on the edge of the table. "I think some information has been left out of general communications among my people. In the time period we are discussing, my commander"—he gestured to Kile—"came back from a mission and informed me of the conditions on the planet Kirato." Geron looked up from his fingers. "I sent a message to my father, and I received a response that the colony had been deemed a loss due to its closeness to the Cartek border. He decreed that any aid would be a waste of supplies."

Cal gaped. Those supplies had been in a direct violation to the king's order?

Geron looked around the room. "Many Earthan colonies have been a problem, but not Kirato. They've always been quiet and accepting."

Maybe on the outside, but their people had the hearts of

tigers. Still, they were better at not causing trouble than most.

Geron continued. "It is my understanding that in the last few years, the colony on Kirato may have taken to questionable trade practices to stay alive, but that was probably due to their lack of Bane support, rather than their desire to break any laws. So I took it upon myself to help them."

Cal held out his hands. "You were willing to go against your father's orders because it was the right thing to do. All I ask is you do the same, now."

Geron's eyes narrowed. "You are asking me to risk my people."

"No. I'm asking you... No, I'm *begging you* to save mine. You have tons of ships out there, and I'm guessing you're adding to your enforcers every day. You have an army that the Carteks don't know about. Wield it now, when they're not expecting it."

The Kever woman in the light-blue robes shook her head. "The human overestimates our numbers."

Dania leaned across the table toward Geron. "While the Civic Advocate is correct about our current statistics, Cal makes a good point. There are hundreds of enforcers waiting to be added into your fold. If you pace yourself, you may be able to absorb greater numbers."

"I protest, General." Orion stepped away from the wall. "The process is weakening our new king. He nearly lost consciousness when he skipped space."

Dania straightened. "Only because he was dragging the fleet with him when he was already tired."

Doc raised his hand like he was in a classroom. "I have an idea that may help with that." He eased out of his seat. "They explained to me what happened when the fleet jumped, and I do agree that His Royal Highness-ness simply overdid it."

Geron rubbed his eyes. "Please stop wasting my time by telling me things I already know."

Doc walked around his chair and leaned on the back. "Okay, where I was going with this is: I've been talking to a few of your physicians, and we think that if we stop giving you a constant supply of enforcers on the verge of death that you'll be able to absorb more per day without weakening so quickly. You could probably take on a few dozen of the healthier enforcers right now and you'd be completely fine."

The king lowered his hand to the table. "But what about the ones who are dying?"

Doc looked down. "I do admit that the chances are high that we'll lose a few this way." He held up his hands. "Now, I know you won't like that, but the truth is that we're already losing some. If you think of it, the ones that you absorb early would eventually have become like the sicker ones. In this case, you'd be catching them before they get that far. And not as many will get that sick, so we may even have fewer casualties then we do now."

Geron tapped his fingers on the table, staring at nothing. "But you're not certain on this."

Doc grimaced. "No. It's just my hypothesis."

Geron shook his head and sighed.

Dania stood. "The doctor's idea has merit. If we're talking about full-on war, or even if we are simply talking about protecting our own, the more fully-fed enforcers we have, the better. This option will make us stronger, and you won't be incapacitated."

The king seemed to stare into space.

The room remained silent as Dania, Doc, then Cal eased back into their seats.

Geron twitched, looking at the exit, then closing his eyes and bringing his focus back to the table.

Cal half expected him to use that door—to run like the spoiled, little rich boy they all took him for. Each second of silence, though, gave him hope.

Would Geron end up just like his father and call Earth an acceptable loss, just like they'd done to Kirato, or would the new king step up and be the person Dania always claimed him to be?

Geron drummed his fingers on the table. "I would very much like to see more data about absorbing the stronger enforcers. As much as I hate the idea of choosing who lives and who dies, I think this may be a better course of action."

Doc nodded. "And we're not talking about death sentences. If you're absorbing more enforcers the natural way, I'll have more synthetics to spare. I can start treating the sickest of them today. They won't be as powerful as the enforcers with the real juice in them, but they won't die, and you can always do your thing with the real stuff later."

"Fine." Geron stood. "We're done here."

They were? Cal stood again. "What about Earth?"

Geron glared at him and started for the door. "I've already made my decision. I will not be forced to repeat myself."

CAL FOLLOWED Doc down the hall. "This is bull. Geron listens to you. You have to talk to him."

"I *did* talk to him. I just got him to pace himself so he can create an army."

"I'm not talking about that. I'm talking about Earth."

"So am I." Doc stopped and turned to Cal. "If you haven't noticed, His Royalness isn't taking to all of this very well. If there were someone else he could pass this crown off to, he'd do it, but there isn't anyone else. So we're stuck with him."

"Your point?"

"The king is not used to decisions any more complicated than what he wants for dessert on any given night. You're throwing too many things at him at one time. Hide his people, save the enforcers, save Earth... It's too much for him to wrap his head around."

"He's the king. He needs to get used to it."

"He *is* getting used to it. You're alive, aren't you? You spoke out against him several times in that room. Hell, I'm surprised Orion didn't snap and pass judgment even after the king told him to stand down."

"I assume there is a point you're trying to get to?"

"The prince—I mean, the king—is crashing under the pressure. He's tired and cranky. Let's give him one thing to think about at a time, and when things start to get a little better, then let's ask for a little more. The squeaky wheel gets the worm and all that."

"I'm not sure that's the saying. But what does it even mean?"

"It has something to do with a wagon, but that doesn't matter. Geron agreed to pace himself."

"How does that help Earth?"

"It helps Earth because while he's thinking that Earth is no longer his concern, he'll be building an army large enough to save the entire Earthan Cradle. I've spoken to some of these enforcers. They're hardcore soldiers. When they're juiced up, they're going to be the kind of unholy terrors that they used to make horror movies about."

"Again…how does this help Earth?"

"Because once His Royalness sees his army, he may be more inclined to 'wield it' as you so eloquently put it. Right now, he can't even fathom having that kind of power because his father cut him off from all this political stuff. I think if we time this right, we can save Earth."

Cal drew his eyebrows together. "You heard them. We only have eight days, and he's going to send us farther away to hide the fleet."

"He can't run and hide if we have to make one more stop for supplies." Doc smiled. "I won't even have to lie. We *are* going to start running out of supplies. That will keep us local a few more days."

"Will that be enough?"

"I don't know, but it's something."

Doc looked past Cal as Dania and Fallon walked toward them shoulder to shoulder, blocking the hall with their shiny, opal enforcer uniforms.

Fallon's waving, ghostlike hair made him seem taller than Cal had remembered. Then again, the last time Cal had seen Fallon was just before the enforcer's original sponsor, the recently-deceased high prince, had died, leaving both Fallon and Orion a mush of useless, blubbering enforcer mess.

That seemed like ages ago.

"Looks like Fallon is playing for Team Geron now."

Cal nodded. He wasn't sure if that was good news or bad news.

Fallon's nose flared slightly as he and Dania stopped, glancing at each of them.

"Continue to the infirmary," Dania said. "I'll join you in a moment."

Fallon quirked a brow at her, then Cal, before heading for the door.

"Looks like our boy Fallon kept his sunny disposition," Doc said.

Dania watched Fallon enter the infirmary. "He's a good soldier. I wish I could trust Orion as much as I trust him."

"Mr. Cranky Pants hasn't stepped in line yet?" Cal asked.

Dania shrugged. "Orion's in line, all right. He belongs to Geron now. Being absorbed doesn't make him any less pompous, though."

Cal stroked her arm with his fingertips. "I'm sure he and Kile will be more than capable of taking over when you're gone."

She sighed. "Maybe."

Doc pointed over his shoulder. "We were headed to the

infirmary. I wanted to check on our supplies since it looks like we're going to get an influx of patients."

Dania followed him toward the infirmary. "That's a good call. We need to get everything we need before we leave the system."

Cal frowned. Her inflection on the word *we* sounded a bit too much like she would be leaving with Geron.

He grabbed her arm. "Dania?"

She didn't meet his gaze. "I still have a lot to figure out, Cal. Geron…"

"Has plenty of other enforcers to take care of him."

Dania paled and looked over both shoulders. "We can't talk about this here."

She motioned to the door as Doc slipped inside.

A chill settled over Cal's skin. He wanted to stay in the hall and talk this through, but she was right. There were too many people watching her, waiting for a sign she'd changed sides. He needed to get her alone, sooner rather than later, though.

Cal followed Doc into the infirmary. Dania slipped in behind them, tapped the computer panel on the wall, and started scrolling through files.

As usual, beds lined the walls, and machines shook and blended solutions that Cal assumed were synthetic pathogen treatments.

An enforcer with long, silvery-white hair that lay flat on his shoulders spoke a few words in the Kever tongue to the physician. The enforcer rubbed a bandage on the inside of his arm before he turned and started walking toward the door.

Cal gasped and the air froze in his chest as the enforcer seemed to slip into slow motion. Despite the man's hair not moving on its own, the overhead lighting called out each individual strand, the opalescent tones looking just as menacing as it had when the dust in the road had kicked up about the enforcer over twenty years ago, after he'd executed a man for no reason and destroyed Cal's life forever.

Cal released the breath lodged in his throat and stepped in the way of the enforcer, stopping the larger man's gait. "You killed my father."

The enforcer narrowed his eyes. "That's entirely possible. I've executed many criminals."

"My father was *not* a criminal. He was a good man."

The enforcer looked bored. "If he was executed, I assure you he was a criminal."

"He didn't do anything. I was there. You cut him down for no reason."

Dania left the computer and moved to Cal's side. She frowned, glancing between the two of them.

The enforcer tilted his head, his expression blank. "Recently?"

Cal flinched and took a step back. "No. It was in the Gratugan trading center. I was twelve."

The enforcer raised his right brow. "I've only been to Gratuga once. I executed four men that day. I assure you, they were all guilty."

"No way. You came out of nowhere. You cut him down for nothing."

The enforcer sighed. "What was your father's name?"

"Luis Espinoza. He was a farmer."

Dania's brow furrowed as she inched closer to Cal.

"I do recall that name." The enforcer looked to the side, like he was trying to remember. "Yes. I remember. I assure you, his sentence was warranted."

"Then what was his crime?"

The enforcer folded his hands. "Would you truly like to know, or would you rather live out your life believing your father was the person you remembered him to be?"

"Cal." Dania touched his arm.

Cal shrugged her off. "There's no way my father committed a crime."

Even if he *had* done something wrong, most of the things enforcers considered crimes were minor infractions. If his father had done something wrong, there was no way that he'd deserved execution.

Heat coursed through Cal's veins. "You ruined my life that day. How do you live with yourself?"

The enforcer tilted his head to the other side. "I live with myself by considering that all things happen for a reason...a reason that is not always apparent at the time."

"A reason? What reason could you have to cut down a man who had a family? Who had a wife who needed him...a son who loved him more than breathing?"

"You are Calvin Espinoza, are you not?"

Cal lifted his chin. "Yes, I am." He wasn't afraid of this monster. He wasn't afraid of any of them. Not anymore.

The enforcer placed his hand on his chest and bowed. "Thank you."

Cal startled. "For what?"

"It is my understanding you are aware that enforcers, when they begin to drain down their power and need to be charged, have the ability to ponder what they've done to uphold the law." He looked down before returning his gaze to Cal. "This is not always a pleasant time." He rolled his arm like it hurt. "When we are not fully charged with primordial energy, it is sometimes difficult to deal with memories of our past."

Did the guy want Cal to feel sorry for him? If he did, he had another thing coming.

"There are times when I have particularly vivid memories, like watching a twelve-year-old boy, covered in his father's blood, sobbing…and I deal with them by telling myself that there is a good reason all things happen, and you just proved me right."

Was he serious? "No good came out of that day, I assure you."

The enforcer's eyes narrowed again. "I disagree. That boy covered in blood turned into one of the most renowned smugglers in the galaxy—a man who was willing to break the law in order to feed a colony that our previous king cut off and left for dead." He nodded at Dania and started walking toward the door. "Thank you, Mr. Espinoza, for letting me know that at least one of the less agreeable things I was forced to do saved thousands of lives."

Dania headed after him. "Corin, wait!"

Cal gaped until well after the door had closed behind them.

His mind was…*blank*, like a swirling void had taken over. His chest tightened, but it wasn't in anger, hatred, or fear.

Doc inched beside him. "You okay, boss?"

Cal looked down. "Honestly, I don't know."

The door opened, and Dania re-entered. She motioned Cal to the side and tapped on a panel, before a sheen of white light encircled them.

Her eyes seemed on the verge of tears. "Why didn't you tell me an enforcer had killed your father?"

Fallon glared at them through the shield.

Cal ground his teeth, wishing that exchange hadn't happened in such a public place.

He turned back to Dania. "It didn't seem important."

"You've been carrying that burden since you were a child, and you didn't think it was important?"

Cal blew out a sigh. "Would it have changed anything? We were working at gaining your trust. Then, once we had it, and you started to become a member of the crew, I didn't want to put that wedge between us. Anyway, by that time, you weren't an enforcer anymore."

Dania looked through the shimmering screen of light, to all the faces looking right at them.

She pursed her lips and turned back to him. "I'll always be an enforcer, Cal."

"Not like the others. You care. You have a soul."

"It seems Corin does, too."

Corin...the man who'd killed his father. So, the demon from his nightmares finally had a name.

She folded her arms. "We all have souls, and we all have too many regrets, Cal. I found Kile drawing once. He made pictures of people he'd passed judgement on."

A burning ball lodged in Cal's throat. "That's kind of sick."

"No, he did it to heal. To remember. Enforcers are all human under their programming. You need to remember that."

Cal rubbed his face. "This is too much to process. That enforcer has always been a specter to me. Now finding him... getting a name...and all of that on top of my mother being on Earth."

She lowered her eyes. "Do you want to know what your father did?"

Cal gaped. "Corin told you?"

Dania nodded.

All these years, Cal had always wondered...but deep down, he knew his father had been a kind, generous man who'd loved him and his mother. Nothing else mattered.

"I don't need to know. It wouldn't change the fact that he's gone."

She squeezed his arm. "He'd be proud of you."

Cal ground his teeth again, fighting off the burning behind his eyes as he headed for the door. "I really hope so."

CHAPTER 14
ALEXANDER

ALEXANDER PICKED up a flask from the heating station and handed it to Peter. "Do you really need as many supplies as you requisitioned Geron for?"

The doctor took the flask. "With treating all these near-death enforcers, yes, I do. We've been okay with the influx over the past several days, but the supplies I have won't last for much longer."

Alexander looked over the filled beds in the infirmary. "Thankfully, the numbers you're treating are small compared to the new enforcers he's taking on every day."

A few months ago, he would have been horrified by the quantity of enforcers so close to death, but Geron had taken to absorbing the stronger enforcers with surprising, concentrated focus.

"Yeah, he's actually turning more than we thought he'd be capable of. It's like he's getting stronger every time."

A machine pinged, and Alexander grabbed another flask and checked the clarity up against the light. "When are you planning to re-petition for Geron's intervention to help Earth?"

"Cal told you, huh?"

"He didn't have to. It just makes sense." Alexander lowered the flask, not meeting the doctor's gaze.

"What's wrong?"

Alexander raised his eyes. "You are playing a game with Geron, but he's playing a game right back. He has no intention of letting Dania or me go. Haven't you noticed that she and I are never in the same place at the same time? He's purposely keeping us apart."

"Why?"

"Because he's not a fool. He knows you want to escape."

"Don't you mean *we* want to escape?"

Alexander spun one of the flasks so the labels all faced in the same direction. "I don't think escape is an option anymore. There's too much at risk."

Peter's eyes narrowed. "What do you mean?"

Across the room, Bob—the enforcer Geron hadn't absorbed because they couldn't determine who his sponsor had been—stumbled and grabbed on to a bed.

Doc ran over to him. "What happened?"

Bob held his stomach. "I feel odd."

"Can you elaborate on that a little?" Doc pulled a small medical instrument out of his coat pocket.

"I feel a tugging in my gut. Like someone has tied a rope to my navel and is pulling on it."

"Huh." Peter ran the scanner over Bob. "I don't see anything out of the ordinary."

Alexander moved his palm around the enforcer. "Your primordial energy is low, as expected, but I sense no illness."

Peter laughed, waving his medical instrument. "These little doo-hickeys tell me all that without the magic mojo."

"Indeed." Alexander looked back to Bob. "How strong is the pull?"

"Strong enough that I feel like following it."

Following it…like an incessant need to go to a certain place. Alexander closed his eyes, considering the constant tug in his own gut.

Bob, whose name was not actually *Bob*, had been injured in battle and had lost his memory. His sponsor could have been anyone…and Bob was the only enforcer whom no one had seen fall in excruciating pain after their sponsor had died.

Peter slipped the scanner back into his pocket. "Do you have a hypothesis?"

Alexander frowned. "Yes, but it would be unlikely, especially if this sensation just started today."

Bob groaned, holding his stomach.

Peter placed his hand on the enforcer's forehead. "Is it getting worse?"

"No." Bob blinked and rubbed the back of his neck. "It just stopped. It was strange, like flipping a switch."

Alexander narrowed his eyes. "Or the rope suddenly being cut?"

Bob lowered his hand. "Yes, exactly like that."

If it was like a rope being cut, then it *could be* the least-likely scenario. In fact, that made the least-likely scenario the most likely. And if that were true, that could change everything.

He grabbed Bob's arm. "Come with me."

"Where are we going?"

"We need to talk to Dania."

DANIA ENTERED THE OBSERVATORY, expecting to find Geron on the lounger, staring out at the stars. Instead, he stood with stiff posture, hands folded behind his back, watching the ships fly past with what appeared to be pointed concentration.

She took a step forward. "You called for me, Ada?"

He didn't meet her gaze. "My advisors are getting increasingly insistent that I breed. They've found no other suitable mates that can carry the Bane bloodline."

Dania's heart clenched. That left Alanna as his only choice.

He turned to her. "I feel your trepidation. This is why enforcers should not engage in friendships. They are a liability."

"No one in the *Star Renegade* crew is a liability. If anything, they make me stronger."

He glared at her. "We shall see."

A deep chill settled over her skin. Geron seemed strong and healthy. He could take her back at any time. The question was: why hadn't he done so?

He turned back to the window, and his silence pressed against her skin. Had he expected her to lobby for Alanna's release? Was he waiting for her to respond?

Geron shifted his weight. "I've sent most of my long-time enforcers and the strongest of my new enforcers out and scattered them in the ships circling us."

What did that have to do with Alanna?

Knowing Geron, the two topics were worlds apart. Then again, they could also be having the same conversation, and the connection wouldn't make itself known until the end.

Dania approached the window. A myriad of larger passenger ships drifted casually past, while smaller skippers wove in and out of their paths, and others hung in space just behind the larger ships, being pulled along in their wake. She wasn't aware of any new arrivals, but it still seemed like more ships than yesterday. "Which ships are the enforcers in?"

Geron folded his arms and turned to her. "That is what I'd like you to tell me."

Dania looked out the window again. No ship was flying any differently than they had been for weeks. How was she supposed to know?

Her stomach clenched. Her sponsor wasn't asking her to *look*. He was asking her to *feel*. When she looked out at those ships, she felt nothing but worry and fear. Probably the same emotions Geron had felt since the fleet arrived.

Should she admit that she couldn't sense the enforcers? She certainly couldn't lie.

"This is not unexpected, my Dania. Let's move on to more important things." He looked back out the window. "Make all the ships with enforcers inside them change directions."

"Ada?"

"Link my enforcers and have them do my bidding. They are perfectly capable of relaying my orders or taking over those ships if the captains refuse to comply." He turned back to her. "Link them. Make them a part of us. Make them an extension of my own hands."

He was testing her, seeing how effective a tool she could be with her limited power.

Dania's heart rate increased, and she steadied her breathing to control it, even though he would have already registered her fear the second the emotion had taken hold. Geron was many things the advisors thought he was, but he'd never been a fool.

Still, he'd given her an order, and she needed to comply. She looked out at the ships and concentrated on each one, searching for a sparkle of primordial energy that she could grab on to, overcome, and bend to her will. But each ship continued to drift in perfect formation.

Geron sighed. "Dania DuBane would have had those ships flying in elaborate formations, just to prove that she could."

"Ada, I'm sorry."

He held up his hand, stopping her. "I am well aware that Alexander removed your shunt but then didn't replace it." He looked out the window again. "I thought of ordering it reinserted, but I decided to allow your request to hold on to your memories."

He'd allowed this? "Thank you, Ada."

He looked back at her. "I've brought most of my enforcers back to full power."

He had? "Kile?"

"Kile has been recently fed, but as soon as I notice signs of wavering, I'll care for him."

"Shivana?"

"Why are you concerned with these two?"

She parted her lips. "Kile is my commander. Shivana is a pilot with great aptitude. A general should always be aware of the status of their tools."

All three of those statements were true, even if not her main concern.

Geron pointed out the window. "If this fleet falls under attack, all these enforcers will be useless to me."

"They're hardly useless. They are each lethal in their own right."

"But they are disjointed and accustomed to following the direction of different commanders, different generals, and different Banes." He walked away from the window with his hands held behind his back and looking at the floor. "I've had my people analyze how a race as historically insignificant as the Carteks could overpower the most advanced military in the galaxy." He looked back at her. "Their attacks seemed random, and they hit what we thought were insignificant worlds. But they were far from insignificant."

"Some of the colonies were small, less than a thousand inhabitants. It appeared they were searching for easy conquests."

"No. They were attacking planets that were far from each other."

"I don't understand."

"They forced my father to separate our military. The Carteks hid their numbers until our cruisers arrived, and then they attacked."

Dania lowered her gaze. "Divide and conquer."

"Indeed." He walked back to the window. "I will learn from my father's mistakes. This military will never be divided. I now have more enforcers than all my brothers and sisters combined. I have an army at my fingertips the likes of which this galaxy has never seen, but I am missing the most important element." He turned back to her. "My general."

Dania's chest tightened. He was right. The enforcers had been considered unstoppable because, once linked, they were a single mind. Dania could simply think the word *punch*, and a single enforcer seven spans away, or all of them, if she chose, would punch. She could see through their eyes and read their thoughts like her own, keeping them part of her but at the same time separate. For their adversaries, it was like fighting a single foe with dozens of lethal arms.

Now, Geron had hundreds of these arms. Throughout history, each enforcer had been compared to the equal of hundreds of common soldiers, if not more. This army he had created could easily be unstoppable...with a general to link them.

Geron had always scoffed at his brothers and sisters for having multiple generals. He'd never understood why they would take the years required to create each of them when, in his opinion, they only needed one.

Now, he finally seemed to understand why.

In battle, people die. If one general fell, they had another to immediately take their place. Geron only had one general —and no time to create another. He was at war, and his greatest asset, at the moment, was unable to efficiently command his army.

"I sense your understanding of the situation. I have given you the opportunity to experience all the meaningless human interactions you wanted, Dania. It's now time for you to take your place."

Her eyes filled with tears. The struggle inside her began anew...the excitement of being brought back to power, fighting against the deep, dreadful loss of losing her friends —of losing *Cal*.

"I know you've grown disgustingly fond of the smuggler. I will not lecture you again on the incompatibility of enforcers and outside relationships, but I have also been considering your petition to keep your memories."

"You have?"

"I am not the monster your smuggler thinks I am, Dania."

"I never thought that."

Which was true. No matter what Cal had said about Geron, her love and devotion to her sponsor always rose to the surface. She dearly wished she could have both, but she knew that was impossible.

She lowered her eyes. "I always tried to explain to them that you are a good Kever, which is not the same as being a good human being."

He took a step toward her and ran the back of his hand down her cheek. The energy sparked against her skin, stronger than she'd felt in quite some time. Apparently, Peter's plan of pacing had worked. But that meant he no longer had any issue with bringing both her and Alexander back into the fold.

"While I don't care what the smuggler thinks, I do care about you."

"Ada?"

His lips thinned slightly. "While your relationship with that human is an inconvenience, I will not ignore that it exists, and that until you are brought back to strength, it has meaning to you."

Why was he telling her this?

"Therefore, I am giving you a final day to enjoy whatever it is you do with the repugnant smuggler. Tomorrow, you'll take your place at my side. If I am going to be king, I need to protect my people, and I can't do that without a general."

Dania tried to hide her shock, although she knew he could probably feel it.

"I am going to return Alexander to full strength after we speak. You may take the rest of this day to your own menial designs. Report to me in the morning.

Dania cringed. He obviously didn't know about Alexander and Alanna. Alexander would have had to keep that a tight secret, and Geron had probably never seen the two of them alone, or he would have sensed it.

Possibly, if she were tactful, she could give Alexander a few last moments as well.

"Alexander has also made friends among the crew. I'm sure he would appreciate some time with them before returning."

Geron's eyes narrowed. "Has Alexander been involved with the smuggler's doctor?"

Peter? No, but that was certainly a safer consideration than Alexander's illegal relationship with a woman with Bane blood.

"Alexander and the doctor are closer than most." Which wasn't a lie, thank goodness.

Geron grimaced. "Fine. Tell Alexander he can return to the smuggling ship for the night and report back in the morning. You, Dania, will bring the smuggler captain back to your own quarters on my cruiser."

On the cruiser? "Our rooms on the *Star Renegade* would be much more comfortable for a human, Ada."

Geron tilted his head back and laughed, an unusual sound containing only a spattering of mirth. "You have been spending far too long with the smugglers, Dania. I'm not a fool. My advisors tell me there is no way a ship with engines disabled can escape. However, Kile assures me that we have left the *Star Renegade* crew to their own devices for far too long."

A soil ball formed in Dania's gut. "Ada?"

"By now, the captain has most likely figured out an escape plan that probably won't work, but he will no doubt try. I imagine that he is only waiting for both you and Alexander to be on board, which is why I've purposely made sure neither of you could board that ship at the same time.

Dania widened her eyes. He'd known all along?

"I am being more than amicable in this situation, Dania. Spend a final night with your smuggler and then end this fantasy. I tire of being patient with you."

She nodded. She was actually surprised he'd been patient at all. There was a time when Geron would have made the decision that she should come home, and he would have reached out for her without comment or discussion, doing with her what he pleased.

That was her place in his life. She was a tool. A weapon. A piece of his arsenal and nothing more. Yes, he cared for her on a deeper level, but when the stars fell into alignment, the simple truth was that she wasn't much more than a highly valued possession.

Her stomach clenched. Not too long ago, she'd been a person. Someone with hopes and dreams. Geron was right, though. That had only been a fantasy.

A swirl of warm, caring energy flooded her, and both she and Geron turned to the door before it opened and Alexander walked through, with Bob behind him.

Alexander inclined his head to Dania, then turned to Geron. "I apologize for the intrusion, but Bob's sponsor called him back."

"What?" Geron and Dania said at the same time.

Bob eased forward. "It's true." He held his stomach. "The link opened temporarily and then stopped."

"What does that mean?" Geron asked.

"It sounds to me like they're hiding," Alexander said. "They're repressing their own power so the Carteks can't find them, just like we are doing by lowering our power to be harder to scan."

Geron frowned. "Then why call their enforcers for a moment, and then stop?"

"Because an enforcer would understand that call," Dania said. "No matter how far away I was from you, Ada, I always knew what direction you were in, even when we were lost in uncharted space. If I wanted to find you, I could simply keep moving in that direction."

Geron turned to Bob. "Can you feel the pull now? Do you know which direction your sponsor is?"

"I don't feel it anymore, but I can clearly tell you that they pulled me from that direction." He pointed to the left.

Geron looked at the computer station Bob had pointed to as if it held not only new possibilities, but new terrors as well.

Either way, the ebbs and flows of the universe had suddenly changed. Geron would not have been able to feed Bob if his sponsor hadn't shared the same bloodline.

That meant somewhere out there was another living Bane.

CHAPTER 16

DANIA

DANIA HELD the back of the captain's chair on Geron's command deck as the primordial energy surging through the room blurred her vision. The ship jolted slightly before stars twinkled in the view screens again.

Bob stood a few paces away, shivering with sweat beading on his forehead.

The call to one's sponsor could be strong. This, Dania knew better than most.

Geron stood in the center of the observation area with his hands clasped behind his back and his head high as their crew ascertained their new location and scanned for any possible threats.

Skipping the fleet for the third time that day with what appeared to be relative ease was a definitive sign of Geron's newfound strength. He hadn't tired, despite growing his army of enforcers exponentially. Trusting the human doctor, it seemed, had been the right choice.

Bob's brow furrowed, and he held his midriff. "We've gone too far."

Geron looked down at him. "Explain."

"The pull is no longer in this direction. It's behind us."

Dania released the back of the captain's chair. "That makes sense. We've been skipping space blindly, heading in one direction. Now we know his sponsor is somewhere between here and our last location."

Captain Quaren stood at attention before Geron. "I suggest that we use engine power from here on out to make sure we don't overshoot our target again. We also don't want to materialize in front of a mass of Cartek ships."

"Agreed."

"All about," Captain Quaren announced. "Engines at fifty-five percent."

Geron looked back to Bob. "Is the pull stronger now?"

"Most definitely."

Dania called up a map of the sector and sent the image to the main screens. "We are just outside the borders of Trellan space."

"Scanning the area around the planets," the nav officer said.

The map disappeared, showing a live feed of Trellis, where a small contingent of Cartek ships was spaced in a balanced orbit around the planet.

"That's it," Bob whispered.

"Are you sure?" Dania asked.

"Every cell in my body is screaming to go there." He winced, taking a step back. "It's gone again. They stopped calling."

Dania placed her hand on his shoulder. "You've done your part. Thank you." She turned to Geron. "I suggest we retire to the presentation room to review the data."

"Agreed." Ada strode from the room with his translator, Theon, trailing close behind.

The royal advisors and key enforcers followed.

"Any orders?" Captain Quaren asked.

"Hold our position and keep the fleet out of scanning range." Dania considered the enemy ships circling the planet. "I doubt we will be out here long."

Geron was already seated at the head of the oblong, floating presentation table when Dania arrived in the room known as the *war chamber* in most ships, but one that had been used mostly for recreation before today.

Theon stood behind Geron with his hands behind his back, waiting to be of service, which was strange, since everyone in the room spoke the same language.

Kile stood a few feet behind their sponsor, tapping on a computer panel. He glanced at Dania and quirked a brow at her, making her think that she should know what he had been doing. She wished she could read his thoughts as easily as she could read Alexander's.

The Counselor General arrived last, taking a seat next to Geron.

"Begin," Geron said.

Orion walked toward the side of the table, and the wall came to life with a feed of the ships around Trellis. "Place an overlay showing native ships."

The nav officer typed on a screen in the table. "There are no signs of the Earthan colonists."

Orion folded his arms. "It is probable that the humans evacuated long ago, or they were eradicated."

Dania shuddered. Trellis was one of the colonies Geron's advisors had probably been referring to when saying that humans didn't blend well with the native flora and fauna. They'd thought the Trellan cave boars were extinct due to human hunters, until the *Star Renegade* crew had found a pregnant female on display as an expensive focal point in an eccentric millionaire's zoo. Dania had been unconscious at the time, but they'd later brought the cave boar back home, here, to Trellis. The pregnant mother had been released far away from the colony, where she'd been greeted by dozens more not-quite-extinct boars probably hiding from the humans who'd been hunting them.

They'd also picked up their latest passenger on that excursion, although no one but Rachel even knew Max had been on board for several months after leaving the planet.

Despite knowing what the colonists had done to the native inhabitants of Trellis, she didn't wish anyone to be forced from their home, or worse, euthanized for being on a planet another species desired.

"There appear to be only fifteen ships defending the planet," Orion said. "We should be able to easily cut through their defenses and liberate whoever is on the surface."

The door opened, and Alexander entered, followed by Cal.

Dania perked up when their eyes met, and relief filled Cal's face. She wished he didn't have to worry about her every day. But she supposed his nightmares would soon come true, and he could move on to worrying about his crew —and hopefully forget her.

The door started to close behind Cal, then bounced back like it had hit something. Cal glanced behind him, his eyes wide, before he turned forward again.

"Why is this human here?" the Counselor General asked.

Cal glared at him, following Alexander to where they took two of the few remaining empty seats at the table.

"I called for the smuggler captain." Kile turned from the screens. "This human has a history of sneaking into places unnoticed and extracting those confined there."

Dania wasn't quite sure anyone would consider the extraction of Alexander from the eccentric governor's mansion *unnoticed*, but she was glad Cal could be a part of the planning.

"This is still a smuggler, sire." The Counselor General turned to Geron. "This is highly irregular."

"These are uncertain times, Counselor. Both of my commanders spent a considerable amount of time on the smuggling ship, and they agreed the human's input may be helpful."

Dania frowned. *Both* his commanders? That meant Orion had given Cal a vote of confidence as well?

Cal leaned his arm on the table. "Alexander already filled me in on what's going on. Are we sure there are no colonists left on the planet?"

Orion pointed to a simulation of ships moving on the screen. "According to this new information, all registered inhabitants scanned into one of the people carriers that were bound for Earth. There are between twenty and thirty Carteks on the surface, plus those in orbit."

"That's not much of an invasion party," Cal said.

"There are no more humans left in this quadrant to defend the planet against. They probably deemed it more valuable to send resources elsewhere." Orion pointed at the screen again. "We cannot ascertain if they are even aware Bob's sponsor is there, which may be why whoever is hiding has been calling for help in short bursts that could only be felt by an enforcer and are probably undetectable to the Carteks."

The Counselor General faced Bob. "Are you certain your sponsor is on Trellis?"

"Now that we are this close, there is no doubt."

"And you still don't know who your sponsor is?"

Bob shook his head, then turned to Geron. "I would tell you if I knew, sir."

The Counselor General made a *pft* sound. "I find it hard to believe he can't remember something as important as who sponsors him."

"The brain is an intricate system," Alexander said. "Not even I can heal many brain injuries."

"The number of Carteks on and around the planet are not a concern," Orion said. We can obliterate them easily, with little chance of any harm coming to Bob's sponsor if they are inside the satellite station, as we believe."

Dania sat back in her chair. "I disagree. Any show of force will be met in kind. The Carteks will fight us."

"I thought that was why the smuggler was here," the Counselor General said.

Dania sighed. "Cal's skills aside, at the moment, we are still moving through the galaxy undetected. No matter how many ships we send to Trellis, the chances are at least one will be discovered. It is statistically impossible to annihilate all of them simultaneously. All it will take is one transmission and the Carteks will know where we are."

Geron cocked his head. "Are you suggesting we don't liberate Bob's sponsor?"

She gaped. "No, of course not. But we need to seriously consider how to eradicate those in the air, and those on the ground at the same time."

"Those in the sky will be simple," Dania said. "Our enforcers can project themselves around those ships and dismantle their communications systems before they even know we are there."

"Can you do the same for those on the surface?" Cal asked.

Geron leered at Cal. "It would be simple, after I give my general a full feeding."

Cal shot to his feet. "Whoa, whoa, whoa…that's not necessary." He looked left and right, as if looking for another answer.

Dania wanted to run to his arms and console him, letting him know it was okay, that she'd already made her decision. But she knew that truth would be nearly impossible for him to accept.

Cal's eyes widened. "I have an idea that may work even better."

Geron folded his hands across his chest. "I'm listening."

"If this were me, I'd be looking for a way to take them out that wouldn't have them sounding an alarm."

"And how would we do that?"

"We can use the planet against them." Cal looked around the table. "We need the smallest ship you have. Something that wouldn't be detectable."

Orion scoffed. "*Everything* is detectible."

"We have a Cartek cloak on the *Star Renegade*."

"The *Star Renegade* is not leaving our cargo hold, Mr. Espinoza," Geron said. "Try again."

Cal closed his eyes and took a deep breath before holding out his hands about three feet apart. "I need to deliver a package to the planet about this big."

Orion folded his arms. "The only thing that small is a drone, or a bomb, both of which would be detected, and they would sound an alarm."

Cal dragged his fingers through his hair. Dania wished she knew what he was thinking, because she might be able to help him. His gaze kept trailing back to her, and she had to wonder…did he really have an idea, or was he killing time, hoping to find any answer that didn't involve Dania being drawn back into the enforcers, again.

His eyes widened. "But if you're thinking of sending enforcers out there to disable their ships, does that mean *they* won't be detected?"

"As far as we know, Cartek systems are calibrated to detect all known materials used in ships. They have not been able to detect enforcers."

Which was why the king had been so successful in driving the Carteks out of Earth's holdings the first time. The king had been the attacker at the time, though. The king's defensive strategies, they'd all found out, hadn't been as effective.

Cal turned to Alexander. "When we were back on Kirato, you jumped out of the ship and hung in midair like you were flying to fend off that crashing cruiser. If you're talking about sending enforcers to project themselves out there and take out those ships, could you deliver a small package to the planet the same way?"

"In my current condition? Maybe. I'm not sure."

Cal turned to the table. "What about another enforcer? Someone already completely juiced up?"

The Counselor General pounded on the table. "Mr. Espinoza, make your point. What are you proposing?"

Cal swallowed deeply. "I propose hitting them in a way they have no possible way to prepare for." He pushed out his chair and looked at the floor before addressing the group again. "Like I said, we use the planet against them, and they won't even know we're there."

"Meaning?" the Counselor General asked.

Cal turned to the middle of the table. "Ladies and gentlemen, I'd like to introduce you to Max."

The center of the table seemed to lose focus, and a fluffy, gray tail appeared, followed by a fur-coated back, four legs, and then Max's head. The creature sat on his haunches and waved at Dania. She laughed and waved back.

Geron narrowed his eyes, leaning forward. "What is that?"

"This is our secret weapon. A member of the indigenous population of Trellis."

"How is that animal going to help?"

Cal leaned on the edge of the table. "Max, I'm sorry for volunteering you before asking, but I know how good you are in a fight, and I figured you'd be willing to help."

Max nodded.

"If we get you to the planet, can you talk your people into being part of a coordinated attack?"

Max ran in circles three times before sitting at full attention like an excited child waiting to hear the rules of a new game.

"Would this work?" the Counselor General asked.

Orion stared at Max like he was a puzzle yet to be figured out. "Yes, I think it would work. They would think they were being attacked by wild animals. There would be no reason to sound an alarm farther than their own ships surrounding the planet."

"And by the time they do that, the ships in the air won't be able to get their call. The enforcers will take out the Carteks in the air, and the natives will take out the ones on the planet."

Max waved his hands, growling a few words at Cal, and then continuing the sentence facing Geron.

Cal leaned forward, tilting his head as if trying to decipher the gibberish, before turning to Geron. "Max wants to make sure that his people won't be hunted anymore in exchange for their help. Is that right, buddy?"

Max nodded again before garbling a few more animated sentences to Geron, waving his paws for emphasis.

The energy around Geron twinkled with amusement as he studied the creature. "Counselor General, please make an official log that there is an indigenous population of intelligent life on Trellis that has a claim to the planet. Any further colonization must be approved by the crown and agreed to by the native inhabitants." He looked back to Max. "Will that suffice?"

Max ran in circles again. Dania had to appreciate the creature's enthusiasm.

Orion approached the table. "I volunteer to bring the rodent to the surface."

Max spun and hissed at him before winking out of existence.

Geron smirked. "I do believe our new friend is not amicable with that solution." The king stood and walked around the table to where Cal and Alexander sat. He scanned the empty table. "Is our new friend still here?"

Max shook and his color returned.

"Fascinating," one of the advisors said.

Geron gestured to Alexander. "Can I trust that you are more comfortable with Alexander transporting you to the surface?"

Max looked at Alexander, then back to Geron before nodding.

Alexander gazed up at his sponsor. "But, Ada, I'm not sure if I'm strong enough to…"

Geron grabbed the back of Alexander's neck.

Dania shot to her feet. "Alexander!"

Alexander whimpered, gaping, his eyes fixed on nothing as his hair instantly took flight.

Cal stood and shoved Geron. "Let him go!"

Orion appeared at Cal's side and pulled him back. "Touch the king again and I will execute you now, despite your reprieve."

Dania dug her fingers into her hair. "Ada, you promised."

The king looked in her direction and then released Alexander, keeping eye contact with her as he strode back to her side and took his seat.

Dania eased down beside him, but her gaze remained glued to Alexander as he slumped in his seat, staring at the ceiling. Geron had promised to give them both one more day with the *Star Renegade* crew. How could he have taken that promise so lightly?

She turned to him. "Ada?" She hoped her voice encompassed her pain, because there was nothing left to say.

Geron flicked a glance at her before looking back at Alexander.

Her friend moaned, panting. His eyes darted about but didn't seem to focus on anything.

"Alexander?" Geron called across the table.

Alexander jolted to attention. His eyes had returned to an icy blue. His hair floated about him in gentle, moving waves.

Geron continued. "Do you now have enough power to ferry the creature to the surface?"

"He won't," Orion said. "You didn't make contact long enough."

"Alexander is different. He doesn't take as long to feed as others."

Orion frowned. "What? Why?"

"That is none of your concern."

Orion bowed and backed off. "Of course, Ada."

Geron returned his attention to Alexander. "I asked you a question."

Alexander's panting deepened. "Ada." He grabbed the arms of his chair. "Why did you stop feeding me? Can't you see I'm depleted?"

Geron's cheeks darkened slightly. "Do you have enough energy to ferry the creature to the surface?"

Alexander grabbed his temples. "Yes, but I need more. Ada, please!"

He lowered his hands and remained seated but leaned as far as he could toward Geron. His chest rose and fell, his eyes dilating with what appeared to be intoxicated anticipation.

Had Dania looked so desperate, so needy, so *hungry* after a feeding?

Alexander reached for Geron. "Ada, please."

Geron turned away. "You will take the creature to the surface. You will return after a successful mission, and then I will give you a full feeding."

"Why not now?" Alexander asked. "Please!"

Cal gaped, his face paler than Dania had ever seen him.

He stared at Alexander like he'd become a desperate, needy demon. In many ways, he was right.

Geron stood. "I made your general a promise that I intend to keep. Be assured, Alexander, that when you return, you will both take your places at my side."

Tears flooded Dania's eyes. Alexander had been autonomous, a person with hopes and dreams, with a woman he loved waiting for him back on the *Star Renegade*. In a brief flash of Geron's power, he'd devolved back into the perfect soldier.

Could Dania really do this? Could she walk back to Geron and give up all she'd learned? Could she really live her life never waking up in Cal's arms again?

Geron's gaze latched on to hers, and she shivered. There was a challenge in his eyes, a possessiveness that made her want to run.

Alexander flopped back to this seat, panting again, smiling, probably dreaming of the exhilaration of a full hit of primordial energy racing through his veins.

Dania understood. She craved the same thing.

Yet her stomach roiled, seeing her best friend reduced to a begging, pleading... What word had Peter used?

Junkie.

That was exactly what they both were, but even though she saw it for what it truly was, she knew there was nothing she could do to stop Geron from turning her back into the general she had once been.

CAL STORMED down the hallway with Kile as an escort. This whole thing was ridiculous. He'd thought he'd had a good idea, but he'd never meant to offer up Alexander to Geron as a consolation prize.

Alex had been nearly normal one minute, and the next, he'd been a heaving, sloppy mess. Cal couldn't believe he'd lost a member of his crew so easily. But now he was even more determined to get Dania off that death ship as soon as possible.

"You need to calm down," Kile said.

"Like hell I do."

Kile grabbed him, stopping his gait. "You've been invited to the command deck to observe and give counsel as necessary. I suggest you treat that as the gift it is and erase whatever ridiculous ideas that are going through your head."

Heat coursed through his veins. Kile was one of *them*. He always had been. Yet at times, like this, he seemed almost human.

"How can you stand it?" Cal asked. "How can you stand looking at Alexander all…"

"Filled with exhilaration? Enjoying the flow of power seeping through his tissues, making him stronger and more lethal than any human could ever comprehend?" Kile smiled. "It made me look forward to my next feeding."

"I don't get you. You threw fireballs at a wall for ten minutes hoping to remember Rachel and then started sobbing when you realized your memory had been erased. You obviously aren't okay with this."

"Whatever was erased was not intrinsic to my duties. In fact, those memories would probably have been a distraction."

"Oh, I guarantee you, Rachel was the kind of distraction that you enjoyed, my friend."

The commander looked down. "So it would seem."

"I don't understand why you're not pissed about this. Your old self obviously wasn't okay with it, or you wouldn't have left all those data pads for your new self to find later."

He grimaced. "I did seem to think it would be important that I was aware of her."

"Maybe it was because you were happy—and not the kind of happy that comes from having alien pathogens forced into your system. I'm talking about the kind of happy where you hold someone in your arms, and they are the most important thing in the universe. Like the kind of happiness where you would do anything for them."

"Like rashly shooting a member of the royal family, knowing you'd instantly be executed for it?"

Cal lifted his chin. "Yes."

Kile held up his palm and the weapon tucked in Cal's boot scraped across Cal's shin and flew into Kile's hand.

Cal stumbled to the wall and grabbed his leg as Kile held

up the gun. The air around his hand blurred before metal dripped through his fingers and puddled on the floor.

Cal released his leg. "I always knew you'd betray us."

"Indeed." Kile shook the remainder of the metal from his hand. "You need to learn to look at the bigger picture, Mr. Espinoza."

"And what bigger picture is that?"

"You sacrificed yourself, becoming a smuggler in order to help bring supplies to people who helped you when you were in need."

"Yeah, so?"

"Then you understand the simple philosophy that the needs of one person are not more important than the needs of billions."

"What are you getting at?"

"The Kever world is decimated. Chances are we will never be able to embrace the same comfort or intricate culture and arts we used to enjoy. This fleet around us is the last of our race."

"This is not new information."

"You should not be so trite, Mr. Espinoza. Because humanity is on the brink of a similar precipice."

"What does this have to do with Dania?"

"If you know Dania as well as you claim to, you'd already know the answer to that question."

Kile continued to the command deck, and Cal hesitated before catching up to him. Part of him wanted to ask for an explanation, but the wiser part knew that Kile was right.

Earth needed Dania.

Cal's mom needed Dania.

But Cal's heart yearned for another solution.

He'd always managed to find a way out of bad situations. This should be no different.

Although deep down, he knew it was.

He needed to face the fact that Dania would do what she thought was the best for the people, even if that meant giving up herself, but the thought of living without her scared him more than any impending war.

———

Cal stepped foot on the command deck right behind Kile. The dozens of screens on the far wall each held a small picture of space, combining into a larger tapestry as a whole, making it look very much like a multi-paned window.

He moved beside Dania. "Are you all right?"

She nodded but didn't meet his gaze. There was a slight sheen to her eyes, like she may have recently been crying. It had to be hard for her, seeing Alexander degrade like that.

"I know it's not the best time, but if you ever want to talk about it…"

"There's nothing to talk about, Cal."

Cal flinched like he'd been punched in the chest. Did she blame him for the loss of her friend?

The doors opened, and Geron entered. His skin was a deeper blue, more like the color he'd been when he'd first arrived, before he'd started making all those new enforcers into pieces of his property. Too bad there hadn't been a way to free them, rather than passing them from one slave master to another.

Geron glanced at Cal before walking past him and moving closer to the screens. The long-haired enforcer who did all of

Geron's translating settled along the far wall like a piece of furniture, ready to be pulled out as needed.

Dania moved beside her star-forsaken sponsor. "Alexander and Max are already on the surface. The rest of our people are in the smallest ships we could find. They are skipping between moons and satellites, using the natural surroundings to cover their approach."

Geron watched the movement of red and blue dots on the monitors. "An interesting idea."

She looked at Cal, beaming. No doubt she'd gotten that idea from hiding in bushes and finding hidden panels in walls. When you needed stealth, you worked with what you had. It was certainly a much different approach than the enforcers' normal modus operandi of showing up in mass and obliterating everything in sight.

Dania pointed at the dots on the screen. "Once they're as close as they can get without detection, they will project themselves from their ships and begin the operation."

Cal frowned. "When we last saw the boars, they'd moved pretty far away from the colony. How can we be sure we've given Alexander enough time to convince them and then rally his troops?"

Geron gave Cal a bored glance. "I'll know."

"As will I." Dania leaned over the captain's shoulder and touched a point on his screen.

Cal should have figured as much. He'd caught Dania and Alexander staring at each other a lot. Many times, it seemed like they could have conversations without speaking. He thought it was just intuition, like the kind a brother and sister sometimes have after living so long together. But maybe it was something else entirely.

Dania straightened. "Alexander is moving into position."

Geron walked to the center of the room. "Deploy the enforcers."

Three different people started tapping on screens.

"Our enforcers have left their ships," the captain announced.

Now they'd just have to wait and hope for the best, he supposed.

"What do we do if things go wrong?" Cal asked.

They all glanced at him, then brought their attention back to the screen. That probably meant that he wouldn't like plan B.

Dania stood at the front of the room, studying the screens and occasionally directing changes to their headings and camera angles.

She looked up from one of the monitors. "The last of the Cartek ships are no longer transmitting communications."

Wow, that was fast. Would those enforcers now destroy those ships?

A flash lit up a section of space over the planet.

"One of the ships is fighting back," the nav officer said.

That probably wasn't good.

The deck was silent as everyone hyper-focused on the screens. To Cal, it looked like any other day over Trellis.

The glow around the last Cartek ship abated.

"Target neutralized," the comm officer said.

"Excellent." Dania's face turned blank, maybe relaying the information to Alexander, before she continued her rounds, checking the different stations.

Many times, on the *Star Renegade*, she'd looked lost, like she'd been confused or hadn't known what to do. Here, she looked at home. Like she belonged. If she could only stay herself and still be in command, she could thrive here. But

Cal had a painful suspicion that Kile had been trying to tell him that freedom, for an enforcer, was only a dream.

Dania's attention darted back to the planet. Her expression blanked again, like her thoughts were miles away, before she turned to Geron. "Alexander is about to engage on the ground."

CHAPTER 18
ALEXANDER

ALEXANDER CROUCHED in the tall grass on the outskirts of what had once been a thriving trade colony. The houses they'd passed as they'd approached had been deserted. Several had looked like they'd been despoiled by the Cartek invaders, but it was hard to ascertain if anything had been looted.

The grass beside Alexander shifted, and Max's face appeared hovering over the ground.

Alexander squinted, barely making out the creature's foxlike form as he blended in with his natural habitat. After seeing so many of the creatures up close, he found each had distinct markings when they weren't blending with their environment. Max's ears had darker tips than the others, while a few of the other creatures had white spots on their chests or tails. And the garbling and barking was definitely a distinct language understood by the whole, even the boars.

"Does everyone understand what needs to be done?"

Max nodded as he looked over his fuzzy shoulder at the crouching army of large, muscular boars, animals standing over forty inches tall with thick, bristly, blackish-brown fur and elongated snouts with sharp, finger-long teeth jutting out from their lips. The two in the front dug their four-inch claws into the dirt, as if preparing to pounce.

There would be an equal number of creatures like Max: intelligent, furry beings with an incredible ability to camouflage by mimicking their surroundings. With the boars' strength and the mimics' stealth and dexterity, it was easy to see why the colonists feared the native wildlife so much.

Out beyond the reeds, the Carteks moved about the trading port, which was not much more than a level, metal surface made for landing small ships. Their bodies were mostly covered with thin layers of shiny membrane. Foggy gas emanated around each creature, most likely humidity being pumped under the membrane to keep their cephalopod bodies damp while also increasing the humidity so the Carteks could breathe in this dry climate.

Max's tiny claws sunk into the grass as he peeked through the reeds. His nose twitched and his heart rate increased.

Alexander needed to unleash this pack before their adrenaline led them to do something that would cost them the element of surprise.

He curled his fingers, and heat filled his hands, readying his power to be unleashed.

"Ready?" Alexander whispered.

The animals shifted behind him, some of the boars stomping their feet.

"Go!"

The reeds parted like dozens of ghosts pushed them out of the way as the mimics advanced. The hot breath of one of the boars steamed up Alexander's neck as the larger, less-clandestine beasts hung in wait for their wave of the attack.

Down on the platform, the Carteks continued working on

their ships or adjusting machinery, oblivious to the army about to trample them.

One Cartek stopped working, looking around the platform like it may have heard something. Even though Alexander knew the mimics would be weaving in and out of the machinery, taking positions, he could still see nothing. Likewise, the Carteks remained woefully unaware of the impending assault.

Silence hung over the area as the other Carteks turned, looking at each other through the translucent drapes with their tentacle-like legs dangling out from beneath them. They probably sensed something was off—possibly a slight, unfamiliar scent or miniscule sounds of paws on the pavement. Hopefully, by the time the Carteks figured it out, it would be too late.

On the far side of the landing site, a Cartek shrieked as five long claw slices shredded his protective membrane. The alien invader twisted and spun as a thick fog of the creature's life-giving humidity billowed around him. His shrill cry filled the area as the injured Cartek ran toward the building.

Alexander drew on his primordial energy and stood, holding out hands filled with swirling, blue fire. "Now!"

The boars behind him roared, stampeding through the reeds toward the platform.

One of the Carteks in the back spun a stationary weapon as Alexander and Max's army bore down on them. As the enemy readied to fire, Alexander raised his palm and the Cartek flew back from the controls.

Another weapon fired and a glowing yellow bolt targeted Alexander. He raised a shield around himself, and the energy scattered over him.

Across the landing area, Max and his mimics seemed to

appear out of nowhere, ripping through the breathing apparatuses, leaving the occupying force racing for the building and into a line of snarling, stomping boars. Alexander threw a fireball, setting the boxes near the entrance aflame, funneling any retreating Carteks away from the building.

The boars roared, trampling any invaders in their paths and biting through their cloaks. The Carteks screamed, their voices the same pitch as an ion engine igniting too close to the surface.

As their companions struggled, several of the Carteks fell back and clustered behind a weapons array and started fighting.

The air to the left of the battle flashed and Dania appeared. Another flash lit up the right of the battle and Kile rolled away, a boar just missing him.

What were they doing there?

Dania raced toward Alexander, glowing. A Cartek ran for her, but she didn't seem to notice, her focus still centered on Alexander.

A boar rushed toward the Cartek, but the squid shot some sort of gun, and the animal slid to a stop a few feet away.

Alexander called up a burst of energy and the Cartek exploded in flames, the weapon falling to the ground.

Dania's expression turned feral.

"What's wrong?" Alexander pressed the words into her mind, but she kept running.

If she was so desperate, why didn't she project herself directly to him?

Two boars spun and charged her. Alexander's chest tightened. They'd been told any non-native being on the ground, other than him, was a threat.

If attacked, Dania would slaughter the boars without giving it a thought. They'd already suffered casualties. They couldn't lose any more to mistaken identity.

Alexander sent out a burst of power, pushing the boars back as a ray of laser energy shot from Dania's arm directly at Alexander.

He ducked, holding up a shield as the ray sprayed over him…not primordial energy…some sort of particle beam.

Kile got off the ground and raced for him. "That's not Dania!"

Alexander balked as another beam of energy flared over his shielding. He let his shield fall and pressed out a burst of air, tossing Dania to her back.

The real Dania would have shrugged off that attack and then made Alexander feel her sting. He sent another burst of energy, and Dania jumped to her feet. She hissed, her opal uniform fading to blue, then black, then gray before returning to the glistening enforcer white.

"Get back, you fool!" Kile skirted an attacking boar.

Alexander sent another shove of air, and Dania stumbled. The air about her shimmered, showing her tentacled feet before her boots returned.

Alexander roared at his own foolishness, calling up a ball of white heat and throwing it toward her. Had that actually been Dania, that bolt wouldn't have done more than burn her if it got through her formidable defenses. To anyone else but an enforcer, it was certain death.

Dania burst into flames. She shrieked, the sound like a water lance cutting through iron before the façade dropped and flailing tentacles whipped about, covered in flames. The Cartek fell to the ground, floundering on the tarmac until it went still.

Kile made it to Alexander's side, huffing like the run had exerted him.

"Thank you for your assistance." Alexander held up his fist and three Carteks exploded in flames.

He'd let himself be distracted. That wouldn't happen again.

"Of course. I'm always happy to assist you, my brother." Kile grimaced at the burning corpse and the carnage of boars trampling Carteks on the far side of the landing platform.

The indigenous soldiers barked and growled and Kile twitched, almost like a shiver, as the mimics sliced through the Cartek breathing apparatuses.

He must have needed a feeding.

The commander flexed and unflexed his hands, preparing to draw on his primordial energy. "Track forward. I will watch your rear."

Alexander refocused his energy shield toward the front. Letting it fall, only to throw volleys of power at Carteks getting the better of the indigenous rebels. The enemy was falling quickly, but not as fast as he'd anticipated.

The Cartek ploy had taken him off guard. Dania would have called him with her mind had there been any change in plan. He should have realized this. Alexander was lucky Kile had been there.

But why *was* Kile there?

And had he really referred to Alexander as his *brother*?

Hearing a click behind him, Alexander refocused his strength into his hands and spun, but Kile had already fired a red flare of light directly at Alexander. The particles curled around Alexander's shield, gaining access before he'd covered himself.

His skin seared as he looked past the swirling energy into

a cold, lifeless stare, and a long, cylindrical weapon no competent enforcer would ever have to wield.

The light burned Alexander's eyes, and he lost his focus, falling to one knee as the skin on his hands started to bubble.

Kile's stolen form snickered, the sound cutting through Alexander's eardrums as the creature raised the weapon again. Alexander tried to lift his arm, but it felt like it weighed more than a carbon infuser. He gritted his teeth, trying to call up strength that wouldn't come as the barrel of the weapon pointed at his face.

Kile's double shimmered as it flinched, losing its aim as a barking sound carried over the crackling particles around Alexander. Kile spun like he was trying to dislodge something from his shoulder when a ten-inch tear sliced though him from his eye to the base of his neck.

Kile howled, a screeching, raspy sound, before the façade flickered out, leaving several squid-like arms fighting with a snarling, scratching mimic with black-tipped ears biting at his face.

One of the tentacles flared out, punching Max in the head. The mimic hissed, clawing at the tentacle, but another arm reared up behind him. The Cartek wrapped its tentacle around Max's throat. The mimic's eyes widened before the Cartek threw Max to the ground, where he landed with a dull *thump*.

Pain exploded up Alexander's arm as he raised his hand, pulsing energy from his fingertips and widening the hole in the Cartek's breathing apparatus.

Steam and a fetid heat hissed into the air as the creature sprinted for the structure in the center of the battle. Alexander struggled to his feet and raised his hand, but a pair of boars knocked the Cartek to the ground and gored the creature before Alexander could fire.

Bolts of energy shot from the cannon, slicing through several of the boars.

Alexander's skin ached as he pressed out his power toward the planetary defense station. One of the gun turrets melted. The next warped, but Alexander fell to his knees again as the third turret focused on him.

His sight wavered and the glow in his hands winked out. He fell and the weapon fired over his head just as two mimics appeared, clawing at the gun's wires until the cables hung loose.

Alexander's sight grew dim, and he pulled himself past the charred remains of the Cartek that had been Kile.

The enemy had played Alexander better than he ever could have imagined. Back when the Cartek cloud had attacked Ephershia, the enemy had stolen the *Star Renegade*'s medical records. Alexander, Kile, and Dania had all been treated by Peter. Apparently, those scans were all the enemy had needed to fabricate the likenesses of two people Alexander trusted implicitly.

Dust and grime caked into the open sores on Alexander's hands as he pulled himself past the Cartek to the foxlike creature lying in the grass.

Max was still breathing but had a thick, weeping cut at the base of his neck and oozing sores around his throat. Groaning under the strain, Alexander placed his hand over the wounds and pushed healing energy through the creature's fur until Alexander's sight began to spin.

The world became a kaleidoscope. Alexander blinked hard and dropped to his shoulder as Max's nose began to wiggle, and his ears twitched.

Alexander fell onto his back. "You need to make sure none of the enemy made it into the building."

Max's large, expressive eyes appeared over Alexander's face. He garbled something as he wiggled his nose.

"I can't help anymore. I need to heal myself."

The small creature placed his paw on Alexander's forehead, just like a human would. Another mimic appeared and Max growled a few words to him before the second creature scampered off.

Max watched the last few Carteks fall before he curled up in the crook of Alexander's shoulder.

"You don't need to protect me. I'm an enforcer."

Max snorted.

Was that incredulity?

Max cooed when Alexander ran his fingers through the creature's hair. His presence was oddly soothing. Now he understood why Rachel had allowed the creature to hide in her room for so long.

Alexander closed his eyes and sent a healing charge to the blisters on his hands and then through his body.

Max lifted his head, checking his surroundings before laying his chin on Alexander's chest.

Alexander's own foolishness had left him under the protection of a creature a fraction of his size. The real Kile would never let Alexander forget this, if he found out.

Max purred beside him. Hopefully, no one would need to know but them.

A SWATH of relief flowed over Dania as the panic flowing through her bond with Alexander relaxed.

Geron turned from the screen. "It's done. Alexander has eradicated the Cartek threat on the planet." He started walking toward the door. "Prepare my transport. I'm going to the surface."

Dania's eyes widened. "Ada, that may not be prudent."

"The planet is secure. I'm going."

The Counselor General caught up with him. "At least let us discuss this."

"There is nothing to discuss."

Dania sprinted ahead and stopped in front of her sponsor. "Ada, it will take some time to prepare your ship. Perhaps it would calm your advisors' fears if you spoke with them."

Geron's cheeks darkened again. "Why would I care about their fears? There is a Bane on that Planet. One of my kin."

Dania shook her head, looking for the right words to change his mind. He'd absorbed enforcers who had belonged to each of his brothers and sisters. They'd all fallen ill after their links to their sponsors had been severed. How could she make him understand how unlikely it was for one of his actual siblings to be out there?

Geron pushed past her. "Alexander told us the threat has been neutralized. I'm going."

"Ada, it would be useless to stand outside your ship waiting. Would taking a few moments to speak to your advisors be that much of an inconvenience?"

Geron glared at the Counselor General before returning his attention to Dania. "They annoy me."

"I believe they annoyed your father, too. He rarely listened to them, so I've been told."

The Counselor General nodded. "He was known to ignore us most of the time. A few of us did mention that thinning our military was a bad idea."

That was an interesting bit of information she'd been unaware of.

"Fine. I will take your counsel." Geron continued walking to the door. "But prepare my ship. I want to be on the surface within an hour."

The Counselor General pounded his fist on the table in the long ancillary meeting space, a risky action on the best of days, but decidedly unwise when emotions were heavily charged in the room.

The politician leaned on the edge of the table. "What if we're walking into a trap? The Carteks could be waiting inside the station to ambush us. It is ridiculous to even consider allowing our king to risk himself."

Geron rubbed his temple. "The Carteks are not inside the station."

"How do you know?" the Counselor General asked.

Dania eased back, taking a similar relaxed pose as that of her sponsor. "Because Bob received another call just moments ago. You cannot replicate the call of a sponsor." Dania looked at the advisors seated at the table. "It is a link instilled in each enforcer when they are absorbed. It is distinct and only capable of being detected by those in each sponsor's fold. If the Carteks tried to replicate it, more of us would feel it. Bob is the only one who feels the call."

The Counselor General wrung his hands. "How can we be sure whoever it is isn't a captive? The Carteks could be forcing them to call their enforcers back to ambush whoever answers."

Geron continued to rub his brow. "They are not."

"How can you be sure?"

"Simply—"

A jolt of adrenaline lanced Dania's spine. She jumped from her seat, her hands splayed, ready to filet anyone who...

Around the room, the other enforcers moved away from the wall. Twenty more had manifested in the room, surrounding Geron, some with balls of fire at the ready.

Geron waved them away. "As you were."

The newly arrived enforcers winked out, and the others eased back to the walls where they'd been.

A deep calm settled over Dania, and she eased back to her own seat.

Geron leaned on the edge of the table. "You do not fully understand the link between a sponsor and their enforcers. If I were being forced to call my enforcers home, I would do so. But at the same time, my enforcers would be aware that I was under duress. They would come for me, fully charged and prepared to obliterate everyone standing between me and them." Geron glanced at Bob. "I assure you, his sponsor is not in any immediate danger, and they are also being wise to slowly draw their enforcers back so as not to call attention to themselves." Geron stood. "I tire of this conversation. I want to know who is down there."

———

Scraps of garbage and abandoned crates lay scattered on the landing pad. The lighting in the small observation station was just bright enough to see, which made it harder for Dania, but Geron's gaze carried across the platform and down the hall. In these conditions, he could no doubt see better than any of his contingent of enforcers surrounding him.

Bob moved ahead. "I'm here." His voice echoed in the hollow cavity.

Silence answered him, and he looked over his shoulder to Dania.

"Can you sense any of your people?" she asked.

He shook his head. "No."

"I sense a shroud." Geron took a few steps forward.

"A shroud?"

"A slight, latent tingle in the air. When we were children, we could sense each other. It made it easier to find our siblings, but it was much harder to remain hidden if we didn't want to be found. We all learned a game called *shroud*, where we would pull our energy into ourselves, thus hiding. It was a game at first, to see how long it took us to find each other without using our main sense, but when we got older, we found it had other uses." He started walking. "I very much want to know who is hiding."

"Geron?" A soft voice filled the chamber before a young Kever female in a long, soiled white dress stepped into the hall. She covered her mouth with her hand before lowering it. "Geron! It *is* you!" She sprinted toward him as three enforcers popped into existence around her until she jumped into the king's arms.

"Kalina." Geron tentatively held her, looking at Dania from over the young Kever girl's head.

Dania had only met Kalina once, when her father had been negotiating her betrothal to Geron's youngest brother. That had been just under two years ago, and the girl had barely been old enough to be presented at the royal house.

Geron leaned back, holding her at a more respectable distance. "Where is my brother?"

She blanched. "I think he's gone. Two of his enforcers were with me, and they fell to their knees, screaming." She wiped tears from her eyes. "We couldn't help them. They died soon after."

Geron's cheek twitched. He'd obviously hoped to find a member of his family, not a lost and frightened child.

Kalina turned to Bob. "Esidian, we thought you were lost." She hugged him.

Bob returned the gesture, but he frowned.

"What's wrong?" She held his head in both her hands. "Do you need to be fed?"

"Geron fed me. I'm fine for now."

But he obviously still had no recollection of her.

She petted his hair. "Well, you're back where you belong now." She turned back to Geron. "And even more importantly, we've found a prince." She beamed, clasping her hands. "They told me I was the last one. They wanted me to take the crown, but I'm barely a Bane."

Dania startled. She may have been barely a Bane *of note*, but she was still a full-blooded Kever with Bane heritage. She'd been betrothed to Geron's brother, which meant she was a suitable match for the Bane bloodline.

Dania released a relief-filled sigh, maybe the first since they'd earmarked Alanna for breeding. Alanna had only been a last resort. No one had thought she was perfect, but she was all they had. Now, there was another. Alanna would no longer be considered an option. That, at least, was a small respite Dania could take into her final hours of humanity.

"How many people do you have with you?" Geron asked.

"Nineteen. My three enforcers, four now with Esidian back, and the other passengers of the transport I was traveling on when the fighting started." She shook her head. "They've been treating me like a queen, asking me questions and expecting me to have answers. I'm so glad you're here."

Geron nodded, then lowered his eyes. He'd no doubt had the same hope she had, that they'd find someone on the surface of this planet who could have taken over his place as king so the people could start looking to someone else for answers.

That hope was now lost.

GERON STORMED off the docking platform and into the cruiser, heading down the hallway in the direction of his private suites and the observatory. Kalina watched him go with her head held high and her expression stoic. She was probably more happy to be on a large ship and under the care of a Bane again than anything else. Other emotions might come into play once the advisors let her know that she'd be expected to birth a new royal line, but that was none of Dania's concern.

As the advisors met Kalina and walked her to the halls on the left, possibly to the infirmary, Dania headed down the hall after Geron.

A swirl of heated, confused, and possibly disappointed energy loomed over her sponsor. She needed to be there for him to remind him that he was worthy of the crown being forced on him. And, if she was lucky, she'd also be able to steer him back into doing all he could for the humans.

Dania slipped into the observatory to find him already looking out at the stars. A shadow fell across his face as his father's massive cruiser moved past, making everything in its presence seem insignificant.

Geron looked down and shivered.

Dania moved to his side. "It was an exciting day today."

"I suppose."

"You were hoping to find one of your brothers or sisters, weren't you?"

Geron looked down. "Is it wrong not to want this power? Not to want all these people entrusting me with their lives?"

"You've always had enforcers to care for."

"That's nothing like this."

"True, but there has to be some comfort in knowing you're no longer the last Bane."

He shook his head. "Kalina is a child. She's barely old enough to breed and already the Counselor General is suggesting she sleep in my quarters." He puffed out a breath, looking at the ceiling. "She was to be my youngest brother's mate."

"I know." Geron was the only Bane who hadn't been mated or, like this youngest brother, at least matched for breeding. She wasn't sure if that had been by design, convenience, or Geron's refusal to commit.

Dania looked out at the stars. "Today was a triumph, though. Our enforcers were victorious."

"Against the world's smallest occupying army, and we won because of a pack of wild dogs."

"Not dogs, Ada. They are sentient, four-legged intelligent life. Life that you declared protected." She sat beside him. "You protected a race that your father overlooked just because they were different from him."

He sighed. "Is this going to be another lecture about how much better I am than my father?"

"No. I think you already know that you're better."

He smirked, then returned his gaze to the stars. "He was far stronger than I am."

"Strength doesn't always make a great man."

He puffed out a mirthless laugh. "What did you come here to discuss, Dania? You are wasting your last hours where you could have been with your *human* plaything."

Ada pressed his lips together. He'd never be able to appreciate Cal, even if Cal had been the one who came up with the plan to have Max help save Kalina.

"I'm not here to talk about Cal."

"I find that hard to believe. Tomorrow, you'll be made whole. You are hoping I will let them go."

"I never expected you to let them go. Not freely, at least." But hopefully, Cal would still be able to get away.

Maybe she could convince Cal to take Alexander with him, since he'd already be on the ship. Her friends could hide on a beautiful green planet, just like they'd always planned. Of course, this meant that Cal would have to agree to leave her behind.

"Then tell me what is so important that you are willing to give up the last few hours of this odd, little fantasy."

She held herself steady, not allowing him to rattle her. "Earth."

"I already told you, my people are more important."

"Of course they are. But that is exactly why you should protect Earth."

"Nothing has changed since our last conversation on the subject."

"The entire galaxy has changed. When you made this decision you were tired and sick. Now you are strong, and you have, as you put it, the greatest army this galaxy has ever known at your fingertips."

"Your point?"

"You now have it in your power to save the Earthan Cradle."

"I have it in my power to protect my own people. My father was unable to protect them, and I swore to them I would succeed where my father failed."

"Your father's biggest failure was the Carteks. The enemy spent years studying your father and his military and then they used that information against him. You are an unknown, and you proved today that you were able to best them."

"That was just a handful of Carteks."

"And we disabled them with far less than a handful of enforcers." She took his hands in hers. "Ada, you know what the Carteks are like. Your advisors are correct. They will never stop coming until the last Kever is dead." She looked into his eyes. "The Carteks are probably counting on either your fear, or your ego. They will expect you to run, and they would never expect you to band with a race your father considered below them."

He narrowed his eyes. "What are you suggesting?"

"Don't just defend Earth. Join them. Fight alongside them. Blend this massive military with theirs and destroy the invaders. Do what your father was unable to do."

"Once again, I reiterate that this foolishness will put what's left of the Kever race at risk. I won't leave them, and I refuse to make the same mistakes my father made. I will not split up our military so we can be picked off by a larger, coordinated force."

She squeezed his much-larger hands. "Ada, if we join Earth's forces, we may have a chance of defeating the

Carteks, but alone, both our cultures could be obliterated. Deep down, you know that. There is nowhere in this galaxy far enough that the Carteks won't find us. We need to stand against them now, when they least expect it."

He looked out at the ships. "You want me to order these people to war?"

"No. I want you to request that all ships able to fight volunteer to fight with us. The weakest ships we can hide or send them away from the fighting."

"Without escort?"

That probably wasn't the best plan. "We can send half to Earth, and half into space. That way, statistically, some of them will survive no matter the outcome. But if we all run, Ada, as soon as Earth falls, the Carteks will come for us. You know it's true."

Geron watched a small civilian craft pass close to the window. "I don't know how to wage war, Dania."

She stood. "That's why you have me."

CHAPTER 21
CAL

CAL HELD Alanna as she wept on his shoulder. On the other side of the phantom floating table, in the same meeting room Geron had pulled Doc and Cal into the day they'd decided to go to Themyscira for supplies, Alexander stood motionless. His eyes were a glassy, ice blue. His skin was paler than it had been when he'd first stepped on board the *Star Renegade*, and his hair drifted about like he was floating in space.

Even worse, he looked at them both like they were rats in an alley that needed to be exterminated.

Max curled around Cal's leg, holding on to his calf and staring at Alexander. Cal wasn't sure the little guy completely understood what had happened to their enforcer friend. Seeing Alex so blank, especially around Alanna, had to be jarring.

Alexander had stuck to his end of the bargain and brought Max to the planet and back in one of those crazy, airtight enforcer bubbles that allowed them to pop into space without dying.

Cal half-expected the little guy to have stayed on the

planet. His own kind was there...beings he could talk to without waving his hands or typing into a data pad. He wasn't even sure how he'd been able to convince Alexander to bring him home.

The door opened and Dania and Kile bounded into the room. Dania's smile would have been welcome, if Alanna hadn't still been sobbing.

"I have amazing news!" Dania skidded to a stop and the smile disappeared from her face when she saw Alanna. "What's wrong?"

Alanna lifted her face from Cal's shoulder and pointed at Alex. "He's gone."

"He's not gone," Kile said. "He's only partially fed."

Cal cringed. "If that's partial, what the hell would a full feeding do?"

Alexander lifted his chin. "I assure you, Commander, despite not being fully charged, I'm still capable of doing my duty."

"I never had a doubt." Kile pursed his lips. "What were your orders?"

"To deliver the animal back to the captain of the *Star Renegade* and await further direction from my general."

So he'd just stood there, staring at them for the past five minutes?

Kile looked Alexander over, then swiped his palm across a panel in the wall. A sheen cast over them, like a thin curtain had been placed between them and Alexander.

"What's this?" Alanna asked.

"It's a privacy screen," Dania said. "No one can hear anything outside the shield." She looked at Alexander through the curtain. "The more pertinent question is: why?"

Kile's lips thinned as his gaze drew to Alexander. "You

gave me a beating once, Dania. You made me fight for my life."

"You deserved it."

Kile smirked. "I never questioned your orders again." He turned to her. "In your current condition, you are unable to do that for Alexander." He held out his hand to Alex. "Do I have your permission, General?"

She lifted a brow. "You want to fight Alexander? Are you seeking an early death?"

"I will trust that you will keep him from killing me."

She glanced at Alexander before she stepped back. "Proceed."

Wait. What? Cal strode toward her. "What's going on?"

"Let's give them space." Dania pulled Alanna and Cal to the other side of the room.

"What's he going to do?" Alanna asked.

Dania placed herself between the humans and Alexander and Kile. "Geron gave Alexander permission to spend one last night on the *Star Renegade*, but we need to give him the chance to enjoy it."

Cal opened his mouth to question, but the veil around them disappeared, and Kile shoved Alexander, drawing the enforcer's soulless, icy-blue stare. Kile shoved him again before fireballs formed in the commander's hands.

"What is he doing?" Alanna asked.

Kile punched his fists toward Alexander, and two fireballs left his hands, throttling toward Alexander.

Alexander held up his arm, forming a shield. The room heated as fire licked up and over the thin wall of primordial energy until it closed around him. The fire turned from yellow to red, and Alexander advanced on Kile.

The larger man took a step back, then another, until he

was backed into the corner. Alexander continued to advance until Kile was lost behind a wall of red flames.

Dania's brow furrowed. "Alexander, stop!"

The fire winked out and the room cooled. Alexander turned, lancing Dania with that ghostly, ice-blue gaze. "He attacked me unprovoked, General. He must…"

Kile pushed away from the wall, hitting Alexander again with a barrage of licking yellow flames. Alexander held up another shield and advanced on Kile again, but the flames seemed less intent, and after a third barrage from Kile, Alexander's flames winked out.

The healer opened and closed his hands, panting, and then frowned at Kile. "What's come over you? Don't you realize I could have ended your life?"

Kile breathed heavily. "I'd like you to turn around and identify the humans standing behind you."

Alexander spun, his eyes still inhumanly blue.

He blinked twice. "Alanna!" He winked out and then reappeared in front of her, taking her into his arms.

Cal gaped at Kile. "What'd you do?"

"I helped extract enough power that he could feel again."

Alexander's hair still floated, and his skin was just as pale as ever. He still looked like a walking death machine.

"I get that. But why?"

Dania hugged Cal's arm. "Like I said, Geron promised us one last night. Alexander couldn't have that unless he was able to feel emotions again."

Cal eased away from her. "What do you mean *one last night*?"

"Geron has granted Alexander and me an unprecedented gift." Her expression softened. "He is allowing each of us one last night with the people we care about."

A chill settled over him. "Before what?"

She lowered her gaze. "You know what."

Heat flashed through Cal. "Like hell. You're not going back."

"I have to."

"No, you don't. He gave you permission, so let's get on the *Star Renegade* right now. We can blast out of here and never look back."

Kile folded his arms. "You do realize I'm standing right here."

"You can come too." Cal's heart rattled in his chest. "I know you don't remember Rachel, but believe me, you thought she was worth every aggravating moment. Come with us, Kile. Doc can help cure you. We'll all be free."

"Cal, that's not possible." Dania grabbed his hands. "I was coming here to tell you that Geron changed his mind. He's going to try to save the Earthan Cradle."

A wave of relief swept over Cal, but it wasn't enough to squelch the need to get Dania and Alexander away from the Kevers.

"That's amazing news, but that changes nothing. We can still leave. Three less enforcers won't make a difference."

"Yes, it will. I'm Geron's general. He needs me to command his army."

"Like hell he does. He has plenty of enforcers now. He can find himself another general."

"It's not that simple. Generals are grown and programmed over years. The ability to link enforcers is not something easily achieved."

"There has to be another general out there."

Dania shook her head. "I was hoping so, too, but there

isn't. It appears that they were all killed defending their sponsors."

Cal's breathing became erratic. "Well, he can't have you."

Her gaze cut through him. "I think we both knew this time would come."

A million weights coated in sharp glass pressed into Cal's chest. "No. You told me you didn't want this."

"I've been trapped between my two lives for far too long, but I need to take into consideration that my life is not worth the number of lives that could be lost if I don't return." She took a step closer. "Cal, I can help save Earth."

The glass cut deeper as he pulled her into his arms. He knew everything she said was true. He knew that his mom had a better chance to survive with Dania in command. But something inside him cracked in two, and he wasn't sure he could survive it.

He buried his face in her hair. "I can't give you up."

"I wish there were another way."

There was always another way. She was just probably not capable of seeing it.

"Okay. I have to respect your decision." Cal grabbed her hands. "Let's get back to the *Star Renegade*. I don't want to waste a moment."

"I can't."

"What?"

"Geron was quite specific about his orders. Alexander may go back to the *Star Renegade*, but if I want to be alone with you, it will be in my quarters here, on the cruiser."

"Why?"

"Because Geron is not a fool," Kile said. "If you have them both on your ship, you will try to escape."

The Big Guy was right, but all Cal wanted was more time

to figure out something…*anything*…that might allow Dania to come out of this with her humanity intact.

Cal dragged his fingers through his hair and growled at the ceiling. "You can't just expect me to do nothing."

Kile started walking toward the door. "Mr. Espinoza, as I've explained to you many times, you don't have a choice."

Cal gritted his teeth. There was always a choice. Someway, somehow, he was going to figure out how to save Earth without sacrificing Dania.

CHAPTER 22
ALANNA

ALANNA PACED the floor in her quarters while Alexander leaned against the door with his ankles crossed.

"This is ridiculous." She stopped and faced him. "There has to be another way."

"You know there isn't."

"No, I don't. Are you telling me that you *want* to go back to him?"

He shook his head slowly. "What I want, and what I must do, are two very different things."

"They don't have to be."

"In this case, they are."

She hugged herself. "Do you love him more than me?"

"It's not like that at all." He looked down. "You are part of my soul. Geron is part of who I am. He made me."

Could he even hear himself? "He stole you from your parents and made you into a monster."

Alex closed his eyes. "No matter how you choose to look at it, I cannot change that I am programmed to be a part of him. I'm an intricate component of a machine."

"That machine has been running fine without you."

"True, but any machine works best when it is finely tuned, and all parts are working to capacity."

She held her chest, and a sob broke free. "I can't deal with this. I feel like you're willingly walking to your death."

"It's not death."

"It might as well be if he erases who you are."

"It's not certain that he will erase my memories. Kile remembers most of the crew."

"But not Rachel."

He lowered his eyes. "No."

"And that doesn't bother you?"

"Yes, of course it does. And I'm actually thrilled that Kile decided to be uncharacteristically kind and help me burn down my power so I could spend my last few hours with you."

"Then let's use these hours to our advantage." Alanna's heart raced. "Help me get Dania and Cal back here so we can all escape together."

"No."

She dug her fingers into her hair. "Don't you want to be free?"

"Yes, more than anything. But I also *need* to perform the duties I was created for. No matter how much I want to live the life you've shown me, I am unable to put anyone but Geron first."

Alanna's shoulder slumped as she puffed out a breath. "I can't believe there's no possible way out of this. Please at least try to help me find a way."

Alexander took her hands in his. "I can't expect anyone but an enforcer to comprehend what Dania and I are going through." He placed her hand on his heart. "This ache inside me is unlike any injury I've received in battle. But it doesn't change the fact that my sponsor is about to go to war, and he needs me. I cannot say *no* to him, and in this instant, I would still go to him, even if I had a choice."

"Why?"

"Because Geron, maybe for the first time in his life, is knowingly heading into danger, and he's doing it for the right reasons. The Carteks are prepped to obliterate all cultures in this sector but their own. Geron is taking a stand, and I'm going to be there with him."

"Why do you have to be so noble?"

He pulled her into his arms. "I have a few hours left. I'd rather not spend them fighting."

She nodded into his chest. "I'm sorry. It's hard not to fight for someone I love. It's just who I am."

He brushed away her tears with his thumbs and kissed her. "I wouldn't have you any other way."

CAL STEPPED into Dania's quarters and the door slid closed behind him so fast, it could have cut him in half. The lighting rose slowly, revealing stark, metallic gray walls, a pristine metal desk with a large touchpad monitor over it, a long metal slab that may have been a couch, and a door in the rear.

"I love what you've done with the place."

Dania shook her head. "It's horrible. I never realized how sterile it was. It's so...blank."

Blank... Very much like an enforcer. "If you hate it so much, why do you want to stay here?"

Tears blurred her vision as she turned to him. "Cal, these are our last hours together. Please don't argue with me."

Her tears hit him like a pile driver to the gut. "I'm not arguing. I'm trying to understand."

She closed her eyes and swallowed deeply. "I don't want to stay. I want to sneak back to the *Star Renegade*. I want to play in your kitchen and make really bad food that the crew will pretend to love. I want to learn nav as good as Alanna, and how to fly the ship as good as you and Ty. I want to play ancient games and laugh with my friends and spend every night in your arms."

"Then do it!"

"It would be wrong. Don't you understand?" She dragged her fingers through her hair. "The Carteks decimated Kever's military because they were arrogant. Each Bane thought themselves unbeatable. None of them expected anyone to figure out that if they just kept attacking long enough, the enforcers, and finally the sponsor, would get too weak to defend themselves. Once the Carteks figured that out, they used the Banes' own arrogance against them."

"What does this have to do with you?"

"Geron's enforcers are strong, but they are just as disjointed as the king's forces were. The Carteks will be able to easily split them apart."

"No way. There're too many of them."

"Let me try to explain." She looked around the room before tapping on a wall. A panel slid to the side, and she pulled out an old-fashioned paper book. "Alanna gave me this. She thought it would give me comfort." She handed it to Cal.

He ran his fingers over the cover. "*A Tale of Two Cities.* Yeah, this seems to be a favorite of hers." But what did an old novel have to do with enforcers?

He handed the book back to her.

She opened the cover and held up a page. "Imagine this page was an enforcer. If you were to punch this page, you'd make a hole in it easily."

"Yeah, so?"

She closed the book and held it up. "If those weaker pages are bound together, they are nearly impossible to punch a hole through."

That made sense, but what was she getting at?

"Geron's enforcers are now the largest military force Keveron has ever seen." She spun the book and showed him the spine. "I am the binding that makes them unstoppable." She opened the book again. "Without me, they are just an assembly of pages. Each important—but meaningless, unless joined with the rest." She placed the book on the metal desk. "Geron is going to throw all his might at the forces threatening Earth. I can win this for him. This is the only chance humanity has."

"You don't know that."

She reached up and touched his face. "I *do* know that. And I think you do, too. If it were Kile, wouldn't you be lobbying for him to take his place at Geron's side?"

"Of course. Because he's not you... And I hate him."

She laughed and pulled him into a hug. She was warm and soft and everything he wanted. How had this woman, who'd been a monster when they'd first met, become the most important thing in his life?

He closed his eyes as a ball lodged in his throat. "My mother is on Earth. Her colony was evacuated. They were supposed to be safe there."

Dania looked up at him. "Your mother?"

"Yeah. She's tough. Stern. A real stickler for the rules. You'd love her."

"She sounds lovely. You told me once about her recipes, but you never spoke more about her."

"Probably because I was afraid of your reaction if you found out what happened to my father." He lowered his eyes. "I should have told you everything. I'm sorry."

She looked down. "I understand."

"When I took the blame for Filluck Palogivan's murder, I

purposely went dark to protect her. I hadn't talked to her in years. But now she's back in the sector where she was born, in a place called Italy."

"Is it nice there?"

"I've never been to Earth."

She hugged him again. "I'd love to meet your mother."

But that wasn't going to happen. Either Dania was about to be erased, or Earth was about to be obliterated. Cal could have Dania at his side forever, or billions of people, including possibly his mother, would die.

It should have been an obvious choice, but instead, it was the hardest choice of his life.

Maybe the galaxy was better off that it wasn't Cal's choice to make—because he wasn't strong enough to do the right thing.

DANIA STOOD outside the doors of the ancillary meeting room with Alexander at her side. She'd hoped for a calm, quiet evening with Cal. She'd wanted to pretend it was any other night, and not their last time together. Their evening had been far from calm, though. She supposed with Cal's overprotective nature, she shouldn't have expected the evening to go any other way.

Her heart clenched. At least they'd had one more night in each other's arms. She'd hold on to that memory as long as she could.

Alexander seemed to study the markings on the door. "I'm going to guess Cal is no happier about this than Alanna is."

"I don't know what I expected him to say or do. I think I just wanted him to understand."

"I think they do understand. They just feel helpless. They are in mourning before there is even anything to mourn."

"They're both fighters. They're not used to..." To what? Giving in? Allowing themselves to be subjugated by another?

"Are you all right?"

She hugged her midriff. "I understand all the arguments he gave me. Most, I even agreed with. But in the end, it came down to the fact that Geron needs me. I not only *have to* be at his side, but I want to be. I wish I didn't have to give up my past life, but I will because it's the right thing to do."

"I came to the same conclusion." He grasped her hand and kissed it. "Are you ready?"

"I suppose so."

She took a step toward the doorway, and it opened.

The Civic Advocate stood on the far side of the hovering table, while Geron stood with his hands folded behind his back, staring at the simulated window projecting images of the ships outside.

The Civic Advocate pulled at the edges of her light-blue dress, glancing at Dania before returning her attention to Geron. "This is foolishness. We should take what's left of our people and run. You told me you would protect them."

The king's cheek ticked like he was losing patience with her. "I intend to protect them, but I also intend to fulfill my father's covenants and protect Earth as well."

"Those two missions are in opposition to each other. If we don't want to become extinct, we need to think of our own kind."

Geron rubbed his eyes. "And allow the humans to become extinct?"

"If necessary, yes. It's natural order. The strongest will survive."

He lowered his hand and sighed. "Interesting that you say the strongest will survive when you are advising me to run and hide."

Dania stepped forward. "We are reporting as requested, Ada. I'm here to take my place at your side."

The Civic Advocate made a *pft* sound. "It won't be enough." She looked at Geron. "You wasted a perfectly good general, and now you want to go into battle with a healer?"

What was that supposed to mean?

Dania took another step closer. "I am standing right here, ready to take my place."

The Civic Advocate shook her head. "That's the problem. You're not strong enough to do what needs to be done."

Geron turned from the false-window. "Enough. Dania has surpassed everyone's expectations, even my own."

"Surpassing expectations won't be enough if you are planning to take on the Carteks. You'll need a full-blooded general, and you wasted yours."

Dania frowned. "I am not wasted. I'm here ready to do my duty."

The Civic Advocate made a *pft* sound again. "I'm not talking about you. I'm talking about him." She pointed to Alexander.

Heat erupted around Geron. "I. Said. Enough."

The Civic Advocate lowered her eyes. "Please forgive, sire, but I'm trying to make sure you understand my concern. You cannot place the future of Keveron in the hands of a healer."

Dania's hands formed fists, and she wished she already had her power back so she could put this woman in her place. "Alexander is more than capable of doing the duties assigned to him."

The Civic Advocate huffed at the ceiling. "I don't doubt that for a moment—because he was never supposed to be a healer."

Alexander tilted his head to the side, looking from Geron to the politician and back again.

The Civic Advocate turned back to Geron. "I don't doubt that she's lethal. I've seen what she can do. But let's harness her to protect our people, rather than expecting her to do something she's incapable of."

Alexander continued to look between them, appearing just as confused as she was.

Geron closed his eyes. The energy about him swirled and abated, a mass of confusion and general uncertainty.

Dania took a step closer to Geron. "Ada, what is she talking about?"

The Civic Advocate lifted her chin. "I served his father, the king. I was there when he found out what Geron had done. He was furious."

Geron looked over his shoulder. "My father's omnipresent disdain for me is no longer our concern."

Dania frowned, wondering if maybe it *should be* a concern.

She turned to the Civic Advocate. "Which infraction are you referencing?"

The Civic Advocate smirked. "You were never meant to be his general." She pointed to Alexander. "He was."

Dania blinked, staring at her.

She couldn't have heard that right.

But then again, it made sense. Dania had struggled in her training. She'd fought hard, and many had said she wasn't worthy. She'd always thought they'd been concerned about her size or that she was a woman, and she'd worked harder, gotten colder, and done everything she could to make her sponsor proud.

And she'd succeeded. At least, she'd thought she had.

Alexander eased forward. "Ada, is this true?"

Geron rubbed his face, then lowered his hands. "It doesn't matter. Dania is my general."

Alexander gaped, glancing at Dania, then back to their sponsor. "But why?"

"I couldn't do that to you." Geron placed his palm on Alexander's cheek. "You were so beautiful, even then. I couldn't imagine you covered in blood."

"But…" Alexander held his forehead. "I'm compelled to help people, not destroy."

"I faced challenges with both of you. For you, I added a love for life to counteract the bloodlust my father had instilled inside you. I was quite proud of that. You were an excellent healer, but when needed, you were a fierce warrior."

Dania shuddered. While she'd been on the *Star Renegade*, Alexander had singlehandedly taken on over a dozen Cartek ships attacking the colony on Opanus. Kile had called it a *bloodbath*. Alexander hadn't left any Cartek survivors. His base military programming must have fed off the desire to save the colonists, making him nearly unstoppable.

She'd always wondered why he'd healed so quickly after he'd woken up on the *Star Renegade*. Yes, he'd siphoned some energy from Alanna. They both had. But Alexander had been simply stronger to begin with.

Alexander continued to look at the floor as if the long, narrow tiles would explain the missing pieces of his life.

"It's not that great of a puzzle to figure out, Alexander." Geron gripped his shoulders. "When the time for programming came, I administered the military codes to Dania, and the healer training to you. My father never knew until it was too late." Geron stroked Alexander's hair. "I saved you."

Dania gaped. He *saved* him?

If he'd saved Alexander, what had he done to her?

Alexander's brow furrowed. "But if Dania was meant to be a healer, she would have had heightened empathy. In order to make her a general, you would have..." He closed his eyes and sighed.

Geron took a step back. "I placed the shunt in her to control the healer programming my father had inserted before she'd come to me. It didn't work as well as we hoped, so I modified it to erase emotional extremes."

Dania flinched. "What?"

"You were going to be executing people, Dania. I didn't want you feeling pain. When you were fully charged, you felt nothing. You did what you needed to do without remorse. It worked wonderfully. You were ruthless." He pursed his lips. "Unfortunately, once your primordial energy had depleted, it seemed to allow an initial emotional response but then deleted it to avoid long-term trauma."

Dania took a staggered breath. "It deleted everything that made me happy."

"Not everything," Alexander whispered. "Only the extremes."

Cal... It had erased her most intimate moments with Cal —the few times where she'd felt free enough to truly express her humanity.

The Civic Advocate pointed at Alexander. "The issue is that he can't be reprogrammed."

Alexander furrowed his brow. "That's not true. If my base programming is there, I could still be converted."

Dania's stomach flipped, and she crossed her arms over her stomach to thwart the nausea. "Alexander, you don't want this."

"I would, if it freed you. You weren't meant for this. Your brain is…" He shook his head. "Your mind knows what it's done. I don't know how you're even sane."

"According to our scientists, it would take five months to insert the programming, and years to train you on how to use it," the Civic Advocate said.

"We don't have that long." Geron looked at the false-window again. "The Cartek cloud is already in the Earthan Cradle. It's gaining in intensity. If I'm going to face them, it has to be now."

The Civic Advocate folded her hands, allowing her long, blue sleeves to cover her fingers. "I reiterate that no matter our numbers, this weakens us. Saving your own people is still the most viable option."

Geron turned, taking in Dania's gaze. "What are your thoughts, Dania?"

Abandon Earth, or give the Kevers a running start? Either way, people would die. As Kile had once told her, she'd been a beautiful horror. She'd overcome whatever had made her seem less in their eyes and exceeded their expectations, becoming a general to be feared.

She could be the same once again.

Dania straightened. "I say we take a stand. The Carteks have a great deal of intelligence on the Banes. They never came for you because you were not a threat. That's probably why they aren't seeking you out now. They expect you to run. They won't expect a cruiser and hundreds of linked soldiers to skip space and appear right in front of them. We'll have the element of surprise."

"But will we have strength?" the Civic Advocate asked.

Geron glared at her. "I tire of your lack of support."

"I meant no disrespect, sire." The Kever woman bowed.

"It was a genuine question. My station requires me to advise the king on what's best for our people. All I ask is that you consider the reality of our situation. If we face the Carteks, can we link our soldiers? Can you truly say we'll have a high chance of success?"

Geron turned to Dania. "We shall see."

CHAPTER 25
CAL

CAL STARED AT THE STERILE, metal walls, clutching the hard, metal bed slab below him. Geron had called for Dania less than an hour ago, and they'd barely had a few moments to say goodbye before she was gone.

She was already so blasted loyal to that prince. She could function perfectly well without being erased. Why couldn't he see that?

The door opened and Kile loomed in the doorway.

Cal stood. "Dania isn't here."

"Do you think I don't know that?" Kile held his hand out to the doorway. "You've been summoned by the king."

Probably for a tidy execution. His mind whirled with possible ways to fool the commander and escape. Deep within the halls of the Kever cruiser, though, and without any weapons, there wasn't much he could do except comply.

Cal walked toward the hall and looked left, hearing boot stomps.

"Cal!"

Alanna ran to him, her eyes red and puffy. Behind her,

Rachel quickened her pace, with Shivana's massive form filling the hallway behind them.

Alanna threw her arms around Cal. "I couldn't talk Alex out of it."

Cal hugged her. "Yeah. I didn't have luck with Dania, either."

Rachel reached them. "Hi, Cally." She glanced at Kile, then looked down. "Sorry about Dani."

Cal's gut clenched. Part of him was still in denial, like if he blocked everything about this horrible situation out, then it wouldn't be true. He wished it could be that easy.

Doc, Ty, and Ethan walked up, being led by Hendry, one of the enforcers who'd accepted Doc's artificial pathogens back on the *Star Renegade*.

The enforcer kept his eyes down.

"Where's Chris?" Cal asked.

Kile turned and started walking to the right. "The pirate is no longer your concern."

"Wait. What? Why?" Cal caught up with him.

"Christopher Columbus is a known pirate and murderer who has his own crimes to atone for."

"Atone for?" Sweat beaded Cal's brow. "Chris is a good man. If you were capable of seeing the good in any of us, you should be willing to see the good in him."

"The council called for Christopher Columbus's execution moments before they called for you."

The chill in Cal's veins turned to ice. "Does that mean he's already dead?"

Kile quickened his pace. "You should be worried about yourself and your crew, Mr. Espinoza."

A deep hole hollowed Cal's gut. Chris wasn't a model citizen, but he'd been a good friend. Hell, Cal would be dead ten times over if it hadn't been for Chris.

Cal closed his eyes and shook his head. He should have insisted Chris leave the *Star Renegade* the first chance they'd had. Then he'd still be alive.

A painful ball built in his throat, and he slowed his pace until his crew was walking beside him.

"Do we have a plan, boss?" Ethan asked.

Cal looked back at the massive woman walking beside Alanna and Rachel. "Do you think your girlfriend will let us go?"

Shivana glanced down at them, her expression as stony as Kile's.

Ethan's lips pursed. "No."

"Then there's nothing we can do."

Kile led them through several hallways that felt like walking in circles before stopping in front of a set of tall, metal doors that opened when he stepped toward them.

They entered a massive chamber with windows lining the outer walls from the floor to the ceiling.

"Whoa," Ethan whispered.

"This is the observatory." Kile walked to an interior metal wall and stood facing them with his hands folded. "We have been instructed to wait here."

Shivana stood beside Kile, taking on a similar pose. Their opalescent uniforms sparkled in the overhead lights, standing out from the stark, metal surface.

Hendry glanced at each member of the crew, his face a mix of conflicting emotions. His hair was still darker than the others.

Apparently, Doc's Pathogen treatments were still working

enough to keep him strong, or Geron would have relieved Hendry of all those inconvenient emotions.

The enforcer locked gazes with Cal before he looked down and exited the room.

Cal wished he knew what the enforcer had been thinking. Then again, maybe he was better off not knowing.

The high ceilings loomed above, making Cal feel small, despite the constant sensation of the walls closing in. Ethan and Ty drew to the windows like star flies, while Doc remained beside him.

"This is a pretty big place," Doc said.

"Yeah, I noticed that."

Alanna rubbed her shoulder like she had a chill. "Where do you think Alex and Dania are?"

They both glanced at her, and she looked down. Cal guessed she was also having trouble dealing with their new reality.

Across the room, Shivana looked straight ahead, as if studying the wall opposite her. Kile remained oddly silent, staring at Rachel.

"You could say something, you know." Rachel folded her arms, but he continued to stare, like she was a puzzle, or, more likely, the missing piece of a puzzle.

Ethan stuck his nose close to the massive, glass wall and rapped his knuckles on it. "How thick do you think this is? It's so clear."

Ty squinted at the glass. "It has to be thick enough to take a beating, or this would be the first location an enemy would hit if the ship were attacked."

"Nah." Ethan pointed up. "That looks like a shielding apparatus. I bet it slams down like a window shade the second anyone smells trouble."

"The two of you stop. Just stop." Alanna pulled at her hair. "Don't you care that Dania and Alexander are somewhere getting…" She covered her face with her hands. "I just can't take this anymore."

Ty and Ethan glanced at each other. Ethan lowered his eyes, then Ty shoved his hands in his pockets and whispered something that sounded like, "Sorry."

Cal held out his arm to Alanna, and she pressed her cheek to his chest. He wanted to tell her it would be okay, but that was obviously a lie.

Doc rubbed her back, then lowered his eyes. He understood as well as Cal what was at stake. Not only were the people they loved and cared about most-likely already gone, but the crew probably hadn't been escorted there to celebrate Alexander and Dania's return.

Cal wished he could get one final message back to his mom. He wanted her to know that he'd done the best he could with his life. That even though he was a criminal in the eyes of the Banes, that he had broken laws for the right reasons and hopefully saved lives along the way.

He'd take that knowledge with him while taking his last breaths. He was a good person, despite what the galaxy had thrown at him.

The doors opened and a stream of tall, blue- and green-skinned Kevers entered the room. Many wore the same long robes and metal insignias as the advisor-people had when the king's ship first arrived. Hopefully, none of them would get burned alive and melted this time.

The Kevers scattered around the outskirts of the observatory in a solemn procession, until Geron stepped through the door, followed by his translator and Miguel, the enforcer whom Kile had shot on the *Star Renegade* and blamed Ethan for.

Stars, that seemed like years ago.

Behind them came the Counselor General, the Kever woman in the light-blue robes from the council meeting, the Kever princess they'd saved, and then Dania and Alexander.

Cal sucked in a breath and held it until Dania smiled at him.

She…*smiled!*

Geron walked to the center of the room. "I have officially decided to stand between the Cartek cloud and Earth."

The Kever princess cheered and clapped, then stopped when she realized no one else followed suit. She pouted, her eyes darting about the room.

Geron continued. "Some think this foolish, and I've taken all counsel on the matter, but I believe that the Carteks won't stop at Earth. There are many planets where we may be able to settle and start over, but none will be safe unless we eradicate this threat once and for all." He looked around the room, as if gauging their reactions. "Then, and only then, will we rest and resettle, possibly even rebuilding Keveron. Those decisions, however, are for a later date. Today, we will convene as a solidified front and plan our strategy. Once our people are safe, we will talk about rebuilding, and not before. Is that clear?"

Dania approached the window. "All the civilian ships have departed?"

"Yes," the Kever woman in the light-blue dress said. "All remaining ships, per your direction, are manned by enforcer soldiers, or by volunteers. All those who expressed a desire to defend the civilian ships were assigned to escort the passenger ships to an undisclosed location." She looked at Geron. "One I dearly hope is quite secure."

"It is, because I'm the only one who knows where they are going. They will be as safe as I can make them in this climate." Geron turned to Shivana. "One thing left to do."

The king held up his hand to Shivana.

She walked to him and bowed. "Yes, Ada."

Geron wrapped his arm around her neck and pulled her head into his shoulder.

"Shiv?" Ethan whispered.

Shivana's feet left the ground, and she seemed to hover before her head tilted back and she moaned.

"This is not happening," Ethan whispered. "This is *not* happening."

Rachel placed her arm around his shoulder. "I got you."

Ethan shook his head. His lips parted as his skin grew pale.

A shimmer of yellow light floated about Shivana before Geron released her.

Ethan cursed under his breath as Shivana's feet touched the ground. Her hair floated about like she was in zero-G, and she nodded as the king whispered into her ear.

That woman had been on their ship, eaten at their table, and despite her rigid enforcer exterior, she did seem to have a tender side. Maybe that was why Geron had given her a boost. Maybe she'd started to seem too soft for the battle ahead.

Ethan's cheeks turned crimson, and he closed his eyes, probably realizing whatever odd relationship he'd had with the enforcer woman was now over.

Cal supposed that was the risk all of them had taken

when they'd opened their hearts to people who were owned by someone else.

Dania pressed her lips together tightly, then looked at Cal. Her hands trembled, and she made fists out of them. She'd seemed so sure of herself last night.

Now that the time had come, could she possibly have changed her mind?

Shivana bowed and left the room, not even looking in Ethan's direction.

Alexander slipped his hand into Dania's, and she broke Cal's gaze to look into her friend's eyes. The two of them always seemed to have entire conversations just by looking at each other. This one looked filled with far too many goodbyes for Cal to handle.

Geron held out his hand again. "Alexander."

Alex gulped and let Dania go.

Alanna broke a sob before covering her mouth. Doc wrapped his arms around her and she muffled her cries against his shoulder. Alex's cheek ticked and he seemed to struggle to keep his gaze straight ahead. Maybe he was afraid he'd change his mind if he looked Alanna in the eyes again.

Geron flicked a glance in Alanna's direction before he waved Alexander closer.

Alex's hair drifted in long, ghostly waves. He already looked fully charged to Cal. Why did he need more? Couldn't the enforcers just live their lives *lethal* instead of *exponentially murderous*?

Geron pulled Alexander to him and gripped him tightly, just like he'd done with Shivana.

"No. Please, no," Alanna whispered.

A flash of white-and-yellow light lit up the deck. Alexander moaned and his head lolled back. The air about him blurred, like the heat rising from a campfire. The movement of Alexander's hair heightened, and he panted as Geron set him back on the floor.

The drumming of the ship's engines tingled through the decking, buzzing in the silence, shadowed only by the pulsing throb beating against Cal's temples.

Alex stood ghostly still, his gaze fixed on nothing.

Dania blanched, and Cal's chest clenched as his fingers trembled.

Her eyes told him everything he needed to know.

Alexander was gone, probably for good, this time.

CHAPTER 26

DANIA

DANIA'S SKIN tingled as Geron whispered into Alexander's ear. Her cells screamed for the power coursing through her sponsor's veins, while her mind checked the location of the exit, trying to find a means of escape.

She closed her eyes, wanting to fulfill all her needs, but there was no way for both of her identities to coexist.

Geron lifted his left hand and Alanna slid across the floor into the center of the room. "This human seemed overly emotional when I fed you, Alexander. Did you have a relationship with her?"

A chill settled in Dania's chest.

Alexander blinked. He seemed to look over Alanna, rather than *at* her. "It was the best of times. It was the worst of times."

Dania's eyes widened. That phrase was from a book Alanna had read to him when he'd been recovering in the med bay on the *Star Renegade*. Could he possibly...*remember*?

Geron frowned. "What does that mean?"

Alexander shook his head, like clearing a fog. "This

woman is a member of the *Star Renegade* crew. I lived on the ship. I had daily interactions with all of them."

Geron seemed to consider this answer before he pointed at Alanna. "This woman is part of a smuggler crew and is wanted for thievery and larceny. Execute her swiftly."

"No!" Dania screamed.

A sphere of fire appeared in Alexander's hand. A line of enforcers held the *Star Renegade* crew back as Alexander threw the ball of flames. Alanna cried out, holding up her hands as the fire exploded over her like a molten faucet.

"Stop." Geron's voice boomed through the room. "I still need this one for breeding."

Alexander closed his hand, and the flames engulfing Alanna dripped down and puddled to the floor before winking out.

Alanna stood in the center of a charred circle on the floor, sobbing. She grabbed her chest and fell to her knees as the barely perceptible shield of primordial energy encircling her winked out.

Dania gaped. The only one in the room powerful enough to stop a direct volley from Alexander was Geron.

"Still as lethal as you are beautiful." Geron cupped Alexander's cheek. "I missed you immensely." Alexander bowed slightly and stepped aside.

Kalina placed trembling fingers over her mouth but held her tongue. Dania wondered if she'd even seen primordial energy wielded as a weapon, or if she could comprehend the horribly painful death those flames would have caused.

Alanna sidled back on all fours before getting up on her feet and bolting into Peter's arms. Her sobs echoed through the deck.

The doctor hugged her. "That wasn't Alex. You gotta get that in your head, girl. He'd never hurt you."

A vein in Cal's neck pulsed and his face flushed red.

Dania didn't have to read his mind to know what he was thinking.

What her sponsor had done seemed overly cruel, but in Geron's mind, he was probably making sure Alexander was back under his control. It was odd, though, that he'd let Alanna live, despite the fact that she was one of only two known females who could foster the Bane bloodline.

Geron had said, though, that he never wanted to see Alexander covered in blood.

It didn't seem like anyone worried about seeing *Dania* coated in blood, though.

A chill settled over her. When she'd asked to have the shunt removed, she'd said that she'd wanted to feel pain. Nothing would hurt more than watching Cal suffer or watching her friends die.

Dania closed her eyes, wishing herself to anywhere in the galaxy but in that chamber. This wasn't a nightmare she could wake up from, though.

Alexander strode forward and yanked Alanna from Peter's arms.

"Let me go!" Alanna pulled against him as he dragged her across the room.

Alexander, of course, didn't respond.

Miguel, Kile, and two other enforcers pushed the remaining humans into a tight circle.

"Dania." Geron held out his hand to her.

Dania flinched. Geron intended to prove her strength and allegiance in one swift show of power.

The crew, with the exception of Alanna, were now nothing more than an annoyance to him.

This had always been her worst fear. She'd known it had been unavoidable. The crew had sealed their fates the moment Ty and Ethan had placed Palian steel handcuffs around her wrists.

A deep dread settled over her as sweat dampened her brow.

Her hands started to tremble, and her heartbeat drummed in her ears.

It was foolish to have believed she could escape who she was. She belonged to someone else, and now her friends would pay the price for trying to free her.

"Dania." Geron's eyes narrowed as he repeated her name.

Her breath hitched as she took a step toward him, then stepped back. "You're going to ask me to execute them."

"There are laws, Dania. Those laws are in place to stop the galaxy from falling into anarchy."

"I'm not saying that they didn't break laws. I'm saying that they broke those laws for the right reasons. You even admitted that it was wrong of your father to cut off the colony of Kirato. You took it upon yourself to send food, even when your father said it would be a waste of resources."

He pursed his lips. "Your point?"

She pointed at the crew. "These people also took it upon themselves to feed the same colonists. Granted, they did not have your wealth to buy the supplies themselves, but they did what they could, placing themselves in danger to do the right thing."

"They stole to get that food."

"On occasion, yes. But that colony would have died without them. I saw the deplorable conditions with my own eyes, Ada. Even Kile agreed to go back and tell you what was happening there."

"This is nothing I do not know, Dania."

"Then take into consideration that the wealthy people they stole from were indifferent to their losses. They simply ordered a fresh shipment. The *Star Renegade* was nothing more than an inconvenience for them, while it was a lifeline for Kirato." She took a step toward him. "You despised your father's totalitarianism. You are now king. You have the power to make this galaxy a better place."

"I refuse to let anyone starve, Dania. Not if it's within my power to help them."

"And I'm asking you to realize that the people standing here, accused, did no different. None of them would have stolen if they didn't have to."

He seemed to contemplate that before turning to Kile. "Your assessment?"

Kile's gaze scanned the crew. "They are a deplorable lot guilty of many crimes, but I do attest that their crimes were never for personal gain. Even the doctor who is still wanted for murder was trying to save a child whom human medicine had been unable to help."

Geron turned to Dania. "What would you have me do?"

Alanna pulled against Alexander's hold.

Ethan shifted his weight, his eyes darting about.

Ty had his hands in his pockets, facing the floor while Rachel stood beside him, her cheeks wet with tears as she looked at Kile.

Cal stood with his arms at his sides, staring right at Dania.

His gaze was imploring. There was no doubt that he'd die to save the people standing behind him, but Dania would do everything in her power to keep that from happening.

She turned back to Geron. "I ask that you show mercy, Ada. I ask that you realize these people were in an impossible situation and did what they had to do to save others."

He closed his eyes and turned away. "You ask too much."

"Promise that you will not execute them for what they have done, and I will come to you willingly. I will fight at your side until your enemies are annihilated."

"You will come to me either way."

"Yes, but in one way you will have my respect. I will be fighting for a leader I believe in, not just the sponsor controlling me."

Geron stared into her eyes, his gaze as pointed and focused as ever.

Her sponsor didn't like to be questioned. He preferred a fast finish to his problems without chance of later complications. This request went against who he was as a person.

He was probably equally annoyed about how weak this probably made Dania seem. But the soul crying out inside her was more human than Kever, and until that humanity was gone, she would do everything in her power to help her friends.

Geron's lips twisted in disgust. "Very well."

He turned to the Counselor General. "Make an official record that Calvin Espinoza and the five people on his crew are exonerated of all their past crimes."

Orion stepped forward. "Ada, this is highly irregular and unnecessary. They have already been rightfully convicted of their crimes."

"Yes, they have, and I've made a decision to change that

ruling." He turned to the Counselor General. "Make it official."

The Counselor General shifted his weight before tapping on a data pad. "It's done."

Dania clutched her chest as a sob simmered just below the surface.

She looked at Kile. "Are you compelled to execute Calvin Espinoza?"

The commander closed his eyes, then opened them. "No, Calvin Espinoza has not committed a crime."

She turned to Orion. "Would you execute this crew if you had the chance?"

"I do not like any of them, but no, they have not committed a crime."

Dania covered her face with both hands, and the sob broke free.

Geron's brow wrinkled. "Why are you crying? This is what you wanted."

"Yes, Ada, it is." She choked out another sob. "Thank you for being the good Kever I always believed you to be."

He shook his head. "I neither understand nor enjoy human emotions. I will alleviate you of this pain now." He held out his hand to her.

She met Cal's gaze.

His face contorted, expressing more emotions than she could count. She knew him well enough to know that he was looking for a final way out of this, but there was none. Their time together was over, and she'd done all she could for him.

CHAPTER 27

CAL

CAL'S BREATH hitched as Geron waved Dania to him. Her cheeks were still wet with tears as she looked at Cal.

She mouthed the words "I love you," and Cal's heart ripped from his chest as she turned and started walking toward her sponsor.

"Wait!" Cal reached for her, but an enforcer grabbed him from behind. "You don't have to do this!"

Dania looked back at Cal. She opened her lips to speak.

"Enough!" Geron held out his palm and Dania flew into his arms.

The room seemed to spin, and Cal hissed through his teeth as the air about them grew hazy and an immense heat filled the room.

Cal's heartbeat drummed in his head. This couldn't be the end. They'd come so far!

Doc breathed heavily beside him.

Ethan repeated the words, "Not cool," over and over.

Ty remained at Cal's side, their shoulders touching.

Alanna sniffed, tears streaming from her eyes.

These were the people Cal loved. The people he'd

depended on for years. They were safe, if Geron remained true to his word, but at the moment, nothing else mattered than the woman limp in Geron's arms, sacrificing herself for what she believed was the greater good.

If he only had more time, maybe they could have come up with another way. He could have saved her. With each passing second, though, all his dreams of a future with Dania drifted away like star flies chasing an ion engine.

The last of the color in Dania's hair faded to silvery white as the strands took flight, drifting as if she were hanging in space. Her head lolled back and she moaned. Her lips were dark pink and shiny, standing out against skin that had paled almost to the white hue of her opalescent uniform.

Geron leaned away, groaning deeply with closed eyes. Dania swayed as if she were in a trance. The blasted Kever held her and whispered into her ear.

An odd emptiness settled in Cal's gut, deeper than the moment on Europa Nine when he'd told that child to run, knowing full well that Cal would be charged with a murder he hadn't committed.

This time, though, adrenaline couldn't cover the deep-seeded dread spreading through his body. There was nowhere to run and no possible way to hide from the haunting vision of a fully-charged general taking demonic possession of the woman he loved.

Geron stepped back and Dania stood in the center of the room. Blank. Lifeless.

She looked like a full-sized marionette, or a robot that had yet to receive its programming.

There was no smile, no warmth, no drive to better herself or learn what it was to be human.

No desire to cook. To create. To make mistakes and learn from them. To foster friendships. To love and be loved.

She was a shell…lost in the very hell she'd worked so hard to escape.

Geron lifted his right hand, and Dania did the same, their movements in perfect coordination. The Kever tilted his head, and Dania tilted hers.

Bile rose in Cal's throat. She'd wanted to be free. To be her own person. But now she was being completely controlled by another. Slavery and bondage was illegal, deemed a heinous crime by the previous king. How could any law-abiding Kever look at this as okay?

The king looked over the assembly. "I had planned on demonstrating Dania's power by eradicating the smugglers, but since that is no longer an option I'm willing to entertain, we'll provide an example on a smaller scale." He held his hand out to the door. "Hendry, bring me the pirate."

Cal balked. *The pirate?* Chris?

The door opened, and Hendry entered. He held his head low as he approached the king.

Geron's eyes narrowed. "You were instructed to bring the pirate."

The enforcer slowly raised his eyes. "He's gone, sir."

Cal puffed out a nearly-silent laugh.

Geron's nose flared. "Gone?"

"Yes, sir. I…"

Dania roared, flying through the air as a fiery blade appeared in her hand. She swiped the molten razor at Hendry's head before landing on her feet between him and her sponsor.

Silence fell over the room as Hendry fell to his knees first and then to his hands. He held himself prostrate as blood streamed from his face, pooling on the floor. It barely looked like he was breathing.

Geron grimaced. "Remove him."

Miguel strode to the front of the room, grabbed Hendry by the shoulder, and dragged him out—leaving a trail of blood behind them.

Geron seemed to wait until the door closed. "As you can see, she still channels my anger without hesitation. Our general has returned."

The congregation applauded. The Kever princess stared at them all with her brow furrowed and her lips parted before a smile appeared on her face, and she clapped as well.

Cal gaped, his gaze carrying along the trail of blood leading to the door. Dania had cared about Hendry and had been thrilled when he'd started to regain his humanity. Yet she'd struck without a second thought.

How Chris had squirmed out of the enforcers' grip, Cal didn't know. But Chris's penchant for disappearing had once again saved his friend's life.

As the applause died down, the Kever woman in the light-blue dress whispered something into the Counselor General's ear.

He nodded, then handed his data pad to the attendant standing next to him.

"The Civic Advocate has concerns the general may be damaged from the artificial treatments inflicted on her by the humans." The Counselor General folded his hands. "Can we confirm that she will be able to do what needs to be done?"

Geron cupped Dania's cheek and whispered into her ear again before stepping back. Dania stretched her neck from the left to the right and then looked at Kile. She held up her right hand, and Kile did the same. She held up her left hand, and Kile followed suit. Then she held both her hands over her head. Across the room, every enforcer did the same, and swirling balls of white flames appeared between their palms.

The Kever princess giggled and clapped her hands. Like before, she stopped when no one else joined her. She glanced around the room, wide-eyed, before her posture slackened, and she eased closer to the wall.

Dania's fire extinguished, and the balls of fire swirling between the enforcers' hands winked out at the same moment.

"Parlor tricks." The Civil Advocate tugged on the light blue sleeves of her robes. "Your general can control her immediate subordinates, but will that win us a war?"

Geron gestured to the window. "Dania?"

Dania turned slightly toward her sponsor. Her eyes were light like ice. Emotionless. Soulless. Was there anything left of her in there, or had Geron erased it all?

Geron folded his arms. "I think, in many ways, all of my father's advisors underestimated me, as did my father himself." He looked around the room. "You all thought me a fool. You thought I was traveling to remote sectors of the galaxy to avoid responsibilities." He shrugged. "In some ways, that was true. However, I was not spending my time idly. I consider myself an artist. I like beautiful things, but I also appreciate power. And one thing I appreciate more than power is proving my father wrong." He stepped behind Dania. "They don't believe you can save them, my Dania. Prove them wrong."

Dania cocked her head in an almost robotic fashion, still looking out the window. "Alexander."

White light flashed around Alexander and Alanna. The

healer disappeared and instantly re-appeared at Dania's side. His hand slipped into hers.

Alanna blinked, her eyes wide, before she stumbled back to Doc.

Geron's gaze carried over the assembly. "Everyone told me I couldn't do what I wanted to do, so, of course, I proved them wrong. Alexander was originally engineered to be a general, this is true. Everyone said I was wasting his power by turning him into a healer. But if you understand the laws of primordial energy, true power can never be wasted. It can only be repurposed and stored, waiting to be tapped."

He strolled behind Alexander and Dania, strutting like a cat.

Alex's and Dania's hair swirled around their heads, in sync, like they were in a duplicated breeze.

Outside, the ships began to move. First to the right. Then to the left. Up. Then down. Then they formed rows. And the top row moved to the left, the bottom row moved to the right.

Ten of the ships clustered and throttled toward the window. The Kevers screamed, ducking, before the ships stopped inches from the thick glass.

Cal's hands trembled. He'd seen enforcers do incredible things. Unthinkable things… But this was on another level entirely.

"Release them," Geron said.

The ships outside drifted back into their standard positions around the cruiser.

Geron smirked at the shocked faces in the room. "I linked them when they were children. They can communicate more efficiently than any other enforcers, and with Dania's healer coding, she is able to tap into Alexander's power. So, as you see, instead of weakening them, I built on their base programming and made them both stronger. Together..." He pointed to the window. "I believe the results are plain."

"Does she have that kind of control over all of them?" the Counselor General asked.

Enforcers started appearing in the room. Three, then ten, then twenty materialized from nothing.

"Stop!" Geron held up a hand. "I believe our point has been made."

The enforcers winked out in the same way they'd arrived.

"I did this simply to alleviate some of your fears. I know many of you don't think fondly of me, but I assure you, I am a Bane, and I intend to succeed where my father failed." Geron's gaze lanced the Civil Advocate. "From this point forward, any negative discussions about my abilities or those of my enforcers shall be considered insolence and will be dealt with in the realm of the law."

The Kever woman bowed, trembling slightly. The other advisors glanced at each other, their blue and green skin growing sallow.

"I will not have dissention in my ranks in any way. I have made a decision to make a stand. Here." Geron pointed at the deck. "Some of you wanted me to run and hide, but I agree with my general. Now is the best time to strike back, when the Carteks don't expect it. Their tactics, while significantly more successful than they have been in the past, still hold true to their past patterns. They expect to swarm over the center of the Earthan Cradle and overwhelm the humans with sheer numbers. Once that is done, they'll turn to the last known threat in the galaxy. Me." He walked to the window and looked out. "Running from the Carteks and preparing for a defensive stance would be misguided from a tactical standpoint." He looked back over his shoulder. "I do not care as much about Earth as I do about the Kevers. Therefore, my decisions will be more focused on the goal: stopping the Carteks before they retarget their fury against what remains of our people." He turned to Dania. "I want the Cartek threat eliminated. Do whatever you have to do."

Dania bowed. "Yes, Ada." She left the room with Alexander, Kile, and Orion following her.

"She didn't even look at us," Ty whispered.

Cal's lips thinned. "Yeah, I noticed that."

Alanna held her midriff, clearly still trying to hold back tears.

Rachel put her arm around her shoulder. "I got you, girl."

Alanna accepted the hug, but tears still welled in her lashes.

Cal understood. There was a hole in his own chest, and he took short, staggered breaths trying to keep it from getting larger. A numbness settled over him, and he welcomed it. He wasn't sure he'd be able to stay sane if he were still capable of feeling.

Doc sighed, looking at Alanna. "Let's get anything we left in our rooms downstairs and get back to the *Star Renegade*. I think we need a little bit of normalness to get our heads together."

Normal would be good, but Cal wasn't sure anything would ever be normal again.

CHAPTER 28
ALANNA

ALANNA STEPPED INTO THE SMALL, square room the Kevers had given her to stay in while Cal and Rachel had gone to Themyscira to get supplies for Doc. That seemed like a lifetime ago. The walls in the room seemed closer, stark and lifeless. Her small bag sat on the edge of the metal bed slab, unopened. She'd been worried about Cal and Rachel at the time, but deep down, she'd never expected to be in that room long.

She sat on the slab and the cold metal seeped through her pants and chilled her skin. A hum vibrated in the air around her, pressing in and making it hard to breathe. She knew it was all in her head, though.

The room had been silent earlier. It wasn't that the air had changed. *She* had changed. Part of her was missing.

Alanna wiped her eyes with the heels of her hands.

The vision of that massive Kever holding the man she loved, and Alex's lifeless, ice-blue eyes focusing on her like a target—soulless—as he threw a killing bolt of power at her...

That hadn't been him...not the Alex she loved.

He'd been nothing more than an extension of Geron's

arms...like a gun. The Kever had just pulled the trigger, and Alexander had done what he'd been created to do.

Was the Alex she loved still inside the enforcer? Had he been watching, screaming, begging Geron not to hurt her? Was he just as helpless as the rest of them?

Or was he simply gone? Was the real Alex dead, and the enforcer who'd taken hold of his body happy to be finally set free, ready to eliminate all law-breakers?

She closed her eyes. It may have been easier if his body had died, too. She never imagined herself wishing anyone dead, especially someone who'd meant so much to her. However, seeing someone with Alex's face but no capacity for love or mercy was a whole new level of cruelty.

"Hey." Ethan stood in the open doorway. "I just came from Cal. He's...umm..." He shook his head. "I guess you can imagine how he is." He looked down the hall, then grabbed the doorframe. "How're you doing?"

She shook her head, pressing her lips together.

"Yeah, I kinda figured." He let go of the doorframe. "May I come in?"

She nodded, holding her breath to keep herself from crying again.

He sat beside her. "Wow. Your room is just as elegantly decorated as mine was. These Kevers really know how to entertain their guests."

Alanna puffed out a laugh, then pressed her lips together again. How could she laugh when Alexander and Dania were gone?

"Do you need any help getting your stuff?"

She almost laughed again. She'd only grabbed her emergency kit...a toothbrush, a protein bar, a bottle of water...

And she'd stuffed a book inside it as she'd left. She could certainly carry it herself.

He put his arm around her shoulder. "This sucks. I get it."

No. He didn't. He hated Alexander.

Ethan did care about Dania, but she wasn't his best friend. And he didn't love her like Cal did. He had no idea what it was like.

Ethan sighed. "I know I said some mean things about Alex early on, and I'm kinda regretting them. I hope you believe that I never wanted this to happen."

Alanna took a settling breath. Ethan had said this day would be inevitable. He'd said Alex would always be an enforcer.

And he'd been right. She should have listened to him.

Heck, she should have listened to *herself*. Why had she let herself fall so hard for someone who didn't have the power to make his own choices?

She'd been burned so hard in the past. She should have known better. But here she was, broken and mentally bleeding.

Again.

Ethan lowered his eyes. "I get it if you never want to talk to me again."

Alanna jolted. "I never said that." She wiped her palms on her thighs. "This isn't your fault any more than it's my fault or Dania's fault or Alex's fault." She wiped her face. "I'm not even sure that it's Geron's fault."

"What do you mean?"

She stared at the floor. "Dania and Alex are tools. We all knew that. And I don't think any of us can say that we don't want Geron to try to save Earth. I just wish there would have been another way that he could have done that without taking our friends away from us."

"Yeah, it was pretty disturbing watching Shivana walk away from His Big, Tall, and Blue-ness looking so blank. Well, blank-er. I know she was never bright and bubbly, but she'd never been robotic like that."

Shivana?

Alanna gaped. "Wait. You really had a thing for her?"

"Well, I guess it was nothing like what you had with Alex. I mean, Shivana and I got to know each other while we were doing the repairs. One thing led to another and..." He held up both his hands. "As you know, I *am* pretty irresistible."

"But she's huge. She's almost scarier than Kile."

Ethan shrugged. "That just made it all the more fun."

"Did you...love her?"

"I don't know. I mean, I liked her. She respected me for my knowledge, I think, and it was fun spending time with someone who was just as into engine parts as I was." Ethan nudged her. "It was almost as much fun as hanging with my bestie."

He considered Alanna his best friend?

She leaned on his shoulder. "I love you. You know that?"

"As I've said..."

"You're pretty irresistible. I know, I know."

He laughed. "Hey. I know you and I are never going to be a thing. And I'm good with that. But that doesn't mean I'm not going to protect you and stick up for you and do all those big-brotherly things that you might find annoying."

"Like warning me that one day, my boyfriend will probably try to kill me?"

He looked at the ceiling. "Again, I'm wishing I never said that, but yeah. And I hope you'd warn me, too. Not that it would stop me from doing anything reckless and irresponsible."

"Like sleeping with an enforcer three times your size?"

"Exactly, because that was way too much fun." He put his arm around her again. "No one had ever accused me of being responsible and thinking things through. I love living life. I like taking chances. Sometimes it bites me in the rear, but sometimes it's good. The truth is, though, that now I have something in my life that I never had before." He chewed the inside of his cheek, as if thinking it over. "I have a family who will be there to catch me if I fall. To tell me I've been a jerk but not throw me out an airlock because of it. To support me while I find out who *Ethan* really is." He squeezed her again. "And I want to be that same person for all of you, even if I don't do all that good a job of it sometimes."

She hugged him back. "You do a great job."

"Thanks, Mom."

Ty walked to the edge of the doorframe and knocked three times. "You all okay?"

Alanna wiped her eyes and straightened. "Yeah. I'm good. As good as I'm going to be, I guess." She stood and grabbed her bag. "Let's go home."

Ethan walked out the door with them. "I gotta go grab my stuff still."

"You need help?" Ty asked.

"Nah. I got it here myself." He glanced at Alanna, then back to Ty. "Why don't you walk Alanna back to the ship? But don't *act like* you're walking her back to the ship. Because, you know, she doesn't need an escort or anything. Because she could totally kick anyone's ass if she wanted to."

Alanna pushed her bag into the crook of her arm. "Okay, let's not start overcompensating, guys."

Ty put his arm around her shoulder. "I got her."

His arm actually seemed to ground her as they walked down the hall. As much as Ethan was right and she didn't need an escort, she also really didn't want to be alone.

What if she walked into Alexander? What if she had to look into those cold, icy eyes again?

She didn't think she could bear it, and she couldn't wait to get back into the safe, warm halls of the *Star Renegade* again. She just hoped, after all that had happened, that they really would be safe. Because even though Geron had erased all their crimes, they would never really be safe until they were off this ship.

CAL SPEED-WALKED through the halls of the cruiser—doing his best to look like he *wasn't* speed-walking. Everything that had just happened was almost too much to process.

He was excited that Geron would try to save Earth... Scared to death to be stuck on the command ship that intended to face that cloud... And his chest seemed to shrink a little more, knowing the woman he loved was gone forever.

He looked up and followed the yellow dots on the wall that would steer him in the direction of the hangar.

It was strange, no longer being considered a criminal. The enforcers he passed in the hallway didn't sneer at him or twist their noses like he smelled bad. He was also allowed to move through the hallways alone, now that no one was worried that they might try to escape.

He walked through the hangar door. Several ships lined the area in front of the energy field, preparing to leave. Many of the officials who'd attended the reinstatement of Geron's general were boarding those ships, preparing to return to wherever their home-base ships were. Cal wondered, if he asked for clearance, if they would just let the *Star Renegade* leave, too.

A hand wrapped around Cal's mouth and a thick arm grabbed his chest, pulling him into a corner several yards behind the *Star Renegade*.

Cal struggled, trying to get free. *Now what?*

"Shhh. It's me," Chris Columbus whispered in his ear. "You good?"

Cal nodded, and Chris released him.

Cal gaped at him. "How the hell aren't you in a prison cell, or worse, dead?"

Chris looked over each shoulder. "I thought I was screwed, too. But our big, blue host forgot that Hendry is jacked up on Doc's artificial space voodoo, still."

Cal furrowed his brow. "What are you talking about?"

"Hendry forgot to lock my cell. That couldn't have been an accident. The only thing I can think of is that no one expressly ordered him to lock the door."

Enforcers and their technicalities. At least this time, it had gone in their favor, even if Hendry had nearly lost his head over it.

Cal huffed a laugh. "You are luckier than a star fly in an ion explosion."

"Not yet, I'm not. But I will be in about ten minutes." Chris pointed to a small, personal transport parked along the edge of the ships preparing to leave. "That skipper isn't assigned to anyone. My plan is to be on it when these ships start leaving. I'll just scoot out the door and be gone before anyone notices I took a ship."

"That's risky."

"Of course it is. I'm counting on most of their resources being assigned to planning Earth's defense. They don't have time to track me down, and even if they did, one thing I'm great at is disappearing." Chris gave Cal a friendly punch in the arm. "I can fit two people in there. Come with me."

"What?"

"I know you'll have to leave the crew, but they can manage on their own. Ty can fly them out of here if His Big-Blueness decides to let them go." Chris pointed at Cal. "You, though, are problematical. Princey-poo might still decide to kill you just to avoid future complications."

Cal rubbed his face. "Yeah, I'd kinda wondered about that."

Chris gripped his arm. "Then come with me. It will be like old times."

Cal looked out over the hangar, and his eyes drew to the cargo ramp of the *Star Renegade*. That ship, and the people onboard, had become everything to him.

Chris nudged him. "Hey, you need to wrap your head around the fact that Dania is gone. Even if they save Earth, she's not going to be there waiting for you." He pointed at the skipper with his thumb. "This is our chance to get out while we still can and start fresh, no matter what happens with Earth."

Cal sighed. In another life, Chris's offer might have been tempting. The banged-up smuggling ship parked to their right was one of the few places in the galaxy where he felt safe. But would the *Star Renegade* still be home, with ghosts of the woman he loved hovering around every corner?

The skipper craft closest to the energy shield hovered and then drifted through the shimmering canopy and shot into space.

"That's my cue," Chris said. "Are you with me?"

Cal looked back at the *Star Renegade*. The answer was

simple. His family was there, and ghosts or no ghosts, that was where he belonged.

"I'm staying, but you go. You're still up for execution. This chance might not come again for you."

"It might not come again for you, either."

"I know, but we'll figure it out, like we always do."

Another ship drifted through the shield.

"All right, brother." Chris pulled him into a hug. "I really hope I get to see you again when this is all over."

Call tapped his friend's back. "Yeah, me, too."

Chris released him and backed away. "Good luck, buddy."

He ducked behind the crates and Cal headed for the *Star Renegade*.

It would have been smart to go with Chris. The guy did have a penchant for escaping tight spaces. But so did the *Star Renegade*. Cal just needed to get his crew together, talk through their new situation, and decide what to do.

Usually, Cal had some idea where he'd guide them, but everything was still too new, too fresh in his head. He needed time to digest it all.

To mourn.

But, unfortunately, the mourning part would probably have to wait.

Chris reached the skipper and slipped inside as Cal stepped onto the *Star Renegade*'s cargo ramp. By the time Cal had reached the top, Chris's skipper was hovering, and when the next ship in line drifted toward the curtain, Chris gunned the engines, making it out first.

Cal smiled. That was a pirate exit if he'd ever seen one.

"Good luck, my friend."

Now he needed to get his own crew out of there.

CHAPTER 30
ETHAN

ETHAN THREW the last of the small engine components into the box while Doc leaned against the doorframe of his temporary quarters in the Kever cruiser.

"You do realize that we were only supposed to be sleeping here for a night, right? Why'd you bring engine components?"

Ethan threw the last one in the box. "Hey, a guy's gotta have things to do. I didn't want to die of boredom."

A wall of opalescent white stepped behind Doc.

"Shiv?" Ethan asked.

Doc stepped aside so the enforcer could enter. "I am called 'Shivana.'"

Ethan shoved his hands in his pockets. "It's okay. It's just us. We don't have to be all formal-like."

Her lips thinned. "Geron has requested you meet him in the lounge."

Ethan stepped back. "Just me?"

"You and the doctor."

Ethan glanced at Doc. "Umm, he remembers that he gave all of us pardons, right?"

"He has no problems with his memory, if that is what you are asking." She grabbed Ethan's arm. "Come. We cannot leave him waiting."

"Okay, okay, I'm coming. No reason to drag me."

Shivana brought them back upstairs to the same room where His Royal Highness-ness had turned Dania and Alex —and even Shivana, apparently—back into robotic enforcers.

The room was now empty, though, with the exception of the big, bluish-green royal guy himself, seated on a long, wide metal shelf in front of the window that looked like a very uncomfortable couch. The massive window was incredibly clear. The glass had to be over three feet thick, yet it was flawless. The manufacturing facilities for the parts to these cruisers alone must have been immense. Ethan would love to take a tour of one some day.

Shivana stood at attention. "The human doctor and the human engineer, as requested, Ada."

Human. Huh. Ethan supposed that was an upgrade from the smuggler doctor and the smuggler engineer. Getting exonerated by a recently crowned king seemed to have its privileges.

"Thank you, Shivana. You may leave them."

She quirked a brow in that adorable way she did when she was surprised. "You want me to leave you alone with them, Ada?"

"They are not a threat. You may go."

"Of course, Ada." She bowed and slipped through the door.

Doc inched toward the window. "Can we trust that we're not here to be executed? Because that certainly would bring down my blood pressure."

The king's body shifted like he'd inhaled deeply, then let it out slowly. "You will not be executed today."

Ethan raised a hand. "Could we maybe not be executed any day? Because I gotta tell you, that would be the best thing for *my* blood pressure."

His Royalness kept looking out the window. Ethan didn't blame him. It was a heck of a view. Sitting there on the bench —as uncomfortable as it looked—had to feel like floating in space.

"I require council," the king said.

"Don't you have a counselor-guy?" Ethan asked.

"I do, but they have predetermined misconceptions about myself and my family. They both fear me and disrespect me at the same time."

Ethan sat on the bench next to him. "Well, you gotta admit that they have a reason for being nervous around you. You *did* melt one of their buddies. I mean, that was pretty badass, if I'm being honest, but it was also pretty gross."

The king cocked his head. "*Bad-ass?*"

Ethan held up his pointer finger. "Not to be confused with ass-hole. Ass-hole is bad. Bad-ass is cool."

"*Cool?*"

"Yeah, like, good. Well, good in a bad way. Well, no, melting the guy wasn't good, but just knowing that you *could do that* is pretty badass, you know what I mean?"

Doc walked up and placed his hand over Ethan's mouth. "Ethan means that you're really strong and aren't afraid to use your power."

Geron frowned. "And that is *bad-ass?*"

"Yes, but I doubt we're really here for a lesson in Ethan-isms." Doc took his hand off Ethan's mouth. "Why are you looking for counsel from us?"

"As I said, the others have preconceived opinions. The two of you are neutral in the matter, and other than Dania, you are the only ones I can trust to give me honest, unfettered opinions."

Ethan cracked his knuckles. "Well, I'm your guy. I'm full of opinions."

"How is Dania, by the way?" Doc asked.

"She is fine," Geron said. "Completely healed. She is making battle plans with Orion and Kile."

Doc glanced at Ethan. Judging by the look on his face, *completely healed* was a bad thing. Like an *asshole*-bad thing, not a *badass*-bad thing.

Ethan leaned closer to the glass. It was sooo clear! He'd love to get his hands on the engineering specifications for the equipment that...

Doc nudged him and Ethan blinked, turning back to the king. *Oh, yeah...counsel. King. Opinions.*

"What can we do for you?" Doc asked.

"My people have been going over the files in my father's ship. A few interesting things have been brought to my attention." His Highness-ness looked out at the stars again. "There were many locked files. I've started reading some and have found them disturbingly enlightening."

Doc folded his arms. "I bet. Politics can't always be fun."

"One of my enforcers pointed out that a seal used in the royal documents matched the signature of a file sent to me by Dania." He turned back to them. "It was the file that proved that your captain didn't kill Filluck Palogivan."

"So it *was* a royal seal?" Doc asked.

Geron nodded. "What's worse is the same seal was used to lock several other files from before Filluck's death. Filluck was not the person I thought he was, but apparently, neither was my brother."

Doc lowered his arms. "Your brother? Which one?"

"The high prince. The one so many people were looking forward to taking power."

"Could he maybe have been trying to protect you?" Ethan asked. "You know, brotherly love and all?"

"My brother disliked me profusely. If anything, he would have called me home to personally show me all of this to cause me pain." Geron ran his hand along the bench he sat on. "I don't want to believe my brother was actually involved, but all evidence shows that he at least knew about it." He looked down. "And did nothing to stop it."

Doc shrugged. "Well, I hate to admit it, but Earth had their share of crooked politicians, too. Sometimes people in power do bad things. Not everyone is above corruption."

Geron stood. "But the king—the high prince—*should be* above corruption. That is their duty and their place in the galaxy. They are there for one reason: to keep the galaxy in order. To protect those who have requested protection. Not to send children into slavery. Not to..." He shook his head and looked out the window again. "I have suspicions that my brother is the cause of the current strife with the Carteks."

"How so?" Doc asked.

"There is evidence that my brother didn't heed the Cartek treaty. He crossed the zone into Cartek space and..." His Highness-ness took a deep breath and held it. "I wouldn't have believed it, but there were images locked with my brother's royal seal." He lowered his head. "I have no reason to believe they'd been altered." He looked out at the stars again. "My advisors said the Carteks had been acting vengefully. Now I believe they were right. The Carteks destroyed the Earthan colonies with no less mercy than my brother showed them. My brother obliterated entire worlds. He murdered innocents by the thousands and then took photos like trophies. He looked like he was...*enjoying himself.*"

Ethan's stomach turned. None of them ever really liked Kevers, but this was a new level of ick.

"One Cartek general, by the name of Rgrythei, vowed to destroy anything ever touched by a Bane." Geron looked down. "Not long after, our enforcers started disappearing, and I believe you both know how the rest of this played out."

Heck yeah. They'd all been in the thick of it.

Geron turned to them. "I thought I knew my brother. I was not fond of him. I may have even been jealous of him. But I believed him incapable of wrongdoing, let alone these levels of crime. I was one of the people who thought he would be a better king than my father. I was sorely wrong."

Doc held up his pointer-finger like he was raising his hand. "I'd just like to make sure you remember that you promised not to execute us, because this sounds like the kind of information that you wouldn't want anyone to know."

"You are correct. I cannot discuss this with my normal advisors. Tarnishing the reputation of my family would benefit no one. I simply..."

"Didn't want to be the only one who knew?" Doc gave him a sad smile.

Geron rubbed his eyes. "It might be that simple. But I also appreciate guidance from those who understand the information as I understand it. My brother and father hated me. I was the cause of most of that hate. I actually enjoyed inciting their anger. I thought them above reproach, so I was reproachable myself. But despite what many of my advisors think of me, I never abused my power in a way that would hurt anyone."

Yeah, anyone but his enforcers.

But it would probably be a pretty good idea not to shove that little bit of reality down the guy's big, blue throat, yet.

Ethan stood. "You know, my family didn't like me much, either. My dad told me over and over that I wasn't worth the price of the food on my plate, and that I'd never amount to anything. Granted, I made some really bad choices back then, but I was looking to him for advice on how to make things right...for hope." He pursed his lips. "Instead, he said fate would catch up with me one day, and there was nothing anyone could do to stop it."

A ship passed close outside the window. People moved about inside, but they were too far away to see what they were doing.

Ethan continued. "I guess my point is that maybe fate caught up with your family. Maybe this is the galaxy re-aligning and making things right."

"What does that mean?" Geron asked.

"Well, maybe fate decided you were the better prince. Maybe the galaxy realized that you might be the right person to rule."

Geron shook his head. "I know nothing about ruling. I'm not used to worrying about anyone other than myself."

"I get that. I was the same way. Everyone told me I was trash, so guess what? I was trash. Then I couldn't take it anymore, and I ran. And guess what happened? I was still trash. I did all the same irresponsible things that got me in trouble all my life. And then one day, I happened to be working on a ship to pay off a gambling debt when someone came looking for a piece of my hide, and the captain decided to blast out of there to avoid a fight, with me still onboard. That ship was the *Star Renegade*, and let me tell you, that was the luckiest day of my life. All of a sudden, I could start over."

"As a smuggler."

"Yes, but I was smuggling for good. I was feeding kids who couldn't feed themselves. I turned my life around and became someone I'm proud of."

A skipper headed toward the window before cutting downward, probably heading for the hangars.

"I know I already told you this before, but I'll tell you again." Ethan pointed at Geron's chest. "You can become your own man, too. The reason you'll make a good king is because you don't want to be one. Now it's your job to be the best king you can, and don't let corruption in like your brother did. Prove to all of us that you aren't the asshole we all think you are."

"*Ethan!*" Doc hissed.

The king narrowed his eyes. "You think I'm an ass-hole? Like my father?"

"Yeah, well, your dad was probably a bigger asshole, but yeah. We all hated you, but maybe hated you a little less when we found out you decided to try to help Earth, but then we hated you again when you stole our friends."

Geron's lips thinned. "If you are referring to Dania and Alexander, I restored them to health. They were dying."

"They weren't dying. They were living for the first time in their lives. And if you don't want to become the same level of asshole as your father, you need to step back and realize what you did to them was wrong."

Doc nudged him. "Ethan, you're pushing it."

Ethan shook his head. "He's not going to execute me for

telling him the truth. He brought us here because everyone else is afraid of him. He knows you and I aren't afraid of telling it like it is. He wants actual advice, not political pandering."

The king turned back to the window. "I need Dania and Alexander. I cannot face the Carteks without them."

"I get that. But maybe, when this is all over, you could consider letting them go? And Shivana too?"

Geron furrowed his brow. "Shivana?"

Ethan leaned toward him. "Yeah. And maybe even Kile, too. He knows you erased Rachel. That guy is so dedicated to you that he doesn't even seem to care. But when you let them, your enforcers have lives. That's not a bad thing."

"It is when they are going to war. They cannot be distracted when I need them."

"They're not distracted. Dania came back to you, didn't she? She walked right back into your arms, even though she knew you'd erase everything that she'd become. I don't know if you force that dedication or if it's real, but either way, it's there. What you are doing to them is just as bad as your buddy Filluck selling those kids into slavery."

Geron bore down on him. "My enforcers are not slaves."

"I have to agree with Ethan on this one." Doc moved between them. "They *are* slaves, and in many ways it's even worse than slavery. You steal who they are. You *changed* who they were."

Geron pointed his thumb at his chest. "I made them better."

"But they didn't have a choice. They still don't have choices. How is that any better than slavery?"

A low hiss filled the room, and the king closed his eyes. "I no longer need your counsel. This conversation is over."

Ethan frowned. "Why, because you don't like hearing the truth? Isn't that why you asked us here?"

"You may leave."

Doc pulled on Ethan's arm. "Come on. I think we've overstayed our welcome."

Ethan looked over his shoulder before passing through the door. "Would you at least consider letting them go when this is over?"

A wall of air hit them, shoving them from the room before the door sealed shut.

"He didn't answer," Ethan said.

"Yeah, he seems to do that a lot."

"Do you think that's a good kind of not answering, or the bad kind of not answering?"

"I don't think he's even capable of comprehending that what he's done is wrong. In his eyes, they're better off."

"They're not."

"You know that. I know that. But I don't think he'll ever agree."

CHAPTER 31

CAL

CAL LEFT his bedroom on the *Star Renegade* feeling just as tired as he had when he'd put his head down. Every time he closed his eyes, he saw Dania beside him, smiling. They'd come so far. They could have run and made it to safety if they'd just had a little more time.

Deep down, he knew she probably would have stayed, though. Either by fabricated sense of duty to that star-forsaken prince-turned-king, or her own personal commitment to do the right thing, their relationship had been destined to fail before it had even started.

Cal knew that a life with Dania had never been a sure thing, but he'd gotten good at beating the odds throughout the years. He'd hoped this time would have been the same.

He tapped the control panel for the lounge. Rachel, Alanna, Doc, and Ethan sat at the table and looked up as he entered.

Ty walked toward him, holding a data pad. "I checked all the security feeds. Chris is still labeled missing. As long as he's still free, he might be able to make it back to us."

Doc shook his head. "They have to be watching our perimeter. They'll grab him the moment he shows his face."

"That's why I want to move the ship closer to the wall. We just need to convince them that we need a refueling cell."

Cal paused, startled. He'd collapsed in bed when he'd boarded, and he hadn't even realized the rest of the crew didn't know. "Chris is gone. He jumped on a skipper in true pirate style and slipped out with the dignitaries. He's probably halfway to Z8 by now."

Ty looked at his data pad, twisting his lips. "Okay, then. So much for my master plan."

"Your master plan was filled with holes, anyway," Ethan said. "It never would have worked."

Cal rubbed his eyes. "I'm sorry. I should have told you all."

Ty tossed the data pad on the table. "It's not like we're all not a little distracted." He sat. "So, what's our new game plan? Do we just leave?"

Alanna hugged herself. "Are we giving up on Dania and Alexander?"

Rachel straightened. "And Kile, too. Don't forget the Big Guy."

Ethan reclined in his chair. "I feel like I should vote for Shiv, too, but I think we all need to be realistic here. Alex almost killed Alanna. Heck, he *would have* killed her if the Blue Guy hadn't put a shield around her...which—we all have to admit—was uncharacteristically nice of him. We can't assume that His Royal Highness-ness will keep being nice."

"He's right," Doc said. "He has a real princess, but he said he still needed Alanna for breeding. Apparently, one baby-maker isn't enough."

Alanna hugged herself again.

"Sorry, sweetie, but we need to consider worst-case scenarios, the least of which is not the fact that he could have Dania, Alexander, or even the Big Guy kill us at any moment just as a test of their loyalty."

"Doc's right." Ty raised his hand. "I vote for getting out of here."

Alanna placed her hand on the table. "You'd just leave them all?"

"I don't want to leave them, but I'm going to be the realist here and think for the rest of you." Ty pointed at his chest. "I'm going to be the selfish one and say all of you are more important to me than anyone else. I get that some of you were mixed up with the enforcers, but that's over. We have to go back to the way it always has been on the *Star Renegade*. We have to look out for each other." A tone sounded, and Ty looked at his arm band. "Aww, crap. Now what?"

The door opened, and Hendry entered. He smiled in a stiff, enforcer-like way, the movement lifting a light-red scar on his left cheek running from just below his eye to the start of his neck. "I trust I'm not interrupting some nefarious plot concocted by our former convicted smuggler guests?"

Ty stood. "How did you get this far without setting off my alarms?"

Hendry tilted his head. "I'm an enforcer." He turned to Cal. "General Dania DuBane requests your presence in the war room."

Cal folded his arms. "Why?"

"I would never question my general."

"Maybe you should."

"Why? It would change nothing. I would still be required

to bring you to her." He turned to Peter. "She requested your doctor as well."

Doc's lips parted. "May I ask if we are all still off the execution list? Geron said we're all in the clear."

"You have all been exonerated of your past crimes. Such an order has never been given before, but it is my understanding that this cannot be undone. Therefore, as long as you don't commit another crime, you are guests on this ship."

Cal gaped at Doc, then back to Hendry. "Does that mean we can leave whenever we want?"

"You would need to get clearance."

"How likely are we to get that clearance?" Ty asked.

"At this moment? I would think that highly unlikely."

Cal sighed. "Then we're not guests."

"Your doctor is still required for his expertise in artificial treatments, but he is still our guest." Hendry held his hand out to the door. "Now, I do not care to leave my general waiting."

"Fine." Cal walked through the exit with Hendry and Doc following as they walked down the ramp to the cargo bay.

Doc caught up to Hendry. "Your face is healing nicely."

The enforcer touched his cheek, frowning before lowering his hand. "My general was merciful."

Cal stopped walking. "Like hell she was. I thought you were dead."

"Yet I am still alive. As I said, she was merciful."

Cal steadied himself, realizing this was the same woman whom he used to laugh with, cook with, sleep with. The woman he loved hadn't been Dania DuBane, though. Cal's Dania was gone.

He shook it off, re-focusing on the *now*. "Chris escaping

wasn't your fault. You did your duty. I'm sure you put him in the cell, just like Geron asked."

"I could have left him more secure while I did so." Hendry looked down. "I *should have* left him more secure."

"But you didn't," Cal said, "because you didn't want to see him executed."

"I *should have* wanted to see him executed. He validly committed crimes. I do agree with Geron freeing all of you. Frankly, that was a relief. But Christopher Columbus?"

"But you still let him go."

Hendry lifted his chin. "I did no such thing."

"Okay, sorry. You accidentally forgot to lock the door."

"Yes." Hendry touched his face again. "She gave me a painful reminder that I need to anticipate the next command and not be so focused on the exact task given me." He lowered his hand. "Thankfully, Dania allowed Alexander to heal me, but trust me, I will be thinking over my orders very carefully from here on out."

Cal closed his eyes. It was hard to believe that the sweet, thoughtful woman he'd grown to love would be capable of nearly cutting a person's head off.

They started walking again.

"I'm sorry you got hurt," Cal said. "You're a good guy."

"I would certainly like to think so."

"Thanks for what you did for Chris."

Hendry stopped at the base of the ramp. "I do still enjoy my temporary autonomy. I've done my best to avoid King Geron, but I will eventually be fed. Once I do, my choices will be limited again, as well as my ability to enjoy my own thoughts." He placed his palm on his cheek. "This was a small price to pay to help the people who helped me, even if any freedom you gave me will be short-lived."

"Chris was never really one of us, though," Doc said.

"I realize that, but he is your captain's friend. In my mind, that means there must be something of value in him. I don't believe that no criminal is beyond rehabilitation. Some, possibly, but not all."

That was a very interesting admission that probably had everything to do with artificial pathogens and nothing to do with his enforcer training. As long as Doc was able to keep Hendry on artificials, it seemed like they had an ally. Those days were numbered, though, just like Dania's and Alexander's had been.

Cal moved closer to Hendry. "You might like to know that Chris got away. He stole a skipper and slipped out with the dignitaries."

Hendry stopped abruptly and narrowed his eyes at Cal.

A slight smile spread across his lips, before he returned to a more rigid, stony countenance. "I trust you had nothing to do with that, Mr. Espinoza. Helping a criminal would be a crime."

Cal held up his hands. "Believe me, Christopher Columbus doesn't need help from anyone."

The slight smile returned. "So it would seem."

They continued down the hall and into the cruiser. There were more people mulling about the massive ship than there had been the first time Cal had been escorted from the *Star Renegade*. Cal wasn't sure if that was all the additional people from the surrounding vessels, or because all of a sudden, these people, who were used to working on what had basically been a pleasure cruiser, were now serving on a command ship of a war-bound king.

It was a little strange that Geron hadn't switched his command center to his father's cruiser. The ship was stronger and safer, just from the sheer mass of it. Then again, if Cal had the chance to move to a bigger, sleeker ship, he'd probably stay on the *Star Renegade*. Sometimes, home could provide the safest feeling of all.

Hendry approached a large, metal door and tapped on the control pad. Within, over a dozen enforcers either sat at a floating table, looking over the screen on the surface, or stood about the room.

On the other side of the table, General Dania DuBane's white-opal uniform glinted in the overhead lighting as she strolled in front of a large, artificial window showing the fleet outside. Her hair floated about her in long, moving waves, like she was under water. Her hands were clasped behind her back as she passed rows and rows of ships outside. Cal had never seen so many transports clinging to a larger ship before. War changed many things, he supposed.

Hendry stepped forward. "Calvin Espinoza and Peter Sanders, as requested, General."

Dania turned, her lifeless, crystal-blue eyes lancing him. "Good. Now leave."

Hendry bowed, glanced at Cal, then slipped out the door.

Kile moved away from the wall beside the large screen and approached Cal. "My general thought you would be able to give counsel since you had done significant research on the Cartek cloud that threatened Ephershia." He scanned the room, looking at no one in particular. "Many didn't want you here, but I convinced them that your loyalties, while maybe not to our sponsor, were strong with Earth, and that you would do all you could to help save the planet that birthed your ancestors."

Cal folded his arms. "You got that right."

It wasn't just that Earth was humanity's native world.

This star-forsaken war had sent his mother fleeing back home to Italy—a little ancient colony on Earth. She'd gone there because she'd thought she would be safe, and now Earth was the Cartek's new primary target for obliteration.

Cal's chest clenched as Dania's hair continued to swirl through the air as if it were alive. The demonic enforcer standing before him was her, and it was also not her at all.

His stomach soured, and he returned his gaze to her commander. "I don't like your sponsor, but what's done can't be undone. I think we can all put that behind us and focus on saving innocent lives."

"I agree. Thank you for being more level-headed than Orion believed you'd be." Kile flicked a glance in Dania's direction. "However, I would caution you not to speak out against Geron. Our sponsor has given your doctor and your engineer a reprieve on insolence for some reason, but that does not extend to their captain. You would be ill-advised not to think that most of the enforcers in this chamber are waiting for you to commit a crime. Especially Orion."

On the other side of the room, Orion watched a monitor while another enforcer pointed at dots on the screen. He turned and sneered at Cal before returning his attention to their task.

"Thanks for the tip." Cal moved closer and spoke softly. "Can I trust you need a feeding?"

Kile narrowed his eyes. "Do not confuse needing a feeding with disloyalty to my sponsor or my general."

Cal held up his hands. "Never crossed my mind."

Dania approached the table and looked over the shoulder of an enforcer Cal hadn't seen before. She didn't bother looking up, but maybe it was better that way. It saved Cal the pain of looking into the eyes of a stranger within the face of the woman he loved.

"My advisors seem to have a maddening difference of opinion on the estimation of the Carteks' numbers," Dania said. "My commander suggested you could give valuable input based on your recent research."

She tapped on the table. A second later, the wall-sized screen behind her faded to black and then changed to one of the images Cal remembered from their own database on the *Star Renegade*.

"Where did you get that?" Cal asked.

"From your ship. However, your encryption is slowing down even my most proficient personnel."

Cal bet it was. Ty may have been a hothead and took more chances than necessary, but his hacking skills were legendary. They weren't getting deeper access to those documents unless Ty okayed it.

Normally, Cal would be hellbent on keeping the enforcers out of his files. In this case, though, Cal agreed with the unspoken request hanging in the air. They needed access to anything in the *Star Renegade* database that could help defeat the Carteks.

Cal turned to Orion. "I trust you can still tap into the comms on my ship at will?"

"Of course."

"I need to speak with Ty."

The commander walked to the far side of the room and waved his hand over a screen in the wall.

Ty's voice filled the room. "Umm...hello?"

Cal approached the screen. "It's Cal. I'm in the middle of a room filled with enforcers."

"Roger that. Keeping my mouth shut."

Cal looked at the larger screen and checked the code on the bottom of the image. "I need you to send the decryption code for image 14J65K. Also decrypt any information we had on the Cartek cloud and release it to Kile."

Doc spoke to the comm. "And, Ty, I've noticed that you've gotten a little sloppy with your filing. Maybe you should make good use of your downtime to clean things up a bit?"

"Roger that, Doc. I wouldn't want to be known for messy files. My mama taught me better."

Clean things up a bit was a discreet way to say 'change all the encryption and make it hacker-proof again.' Which was a really good call. *My mama taught me better* was probably code for 'hell yeah, I'm changing the passcodes as soon as I get off the call.'

Cal wanted to give the enforcers enough information to help Earth, but having one decryption code might be enough for the enforcers to hack into the entire ship. It was bad enough they'd once shut down the *Star Renegade*'s engines and had an irrevocable link into the comms. He didn't want the enforcers getting into anything else, or—even worse— reminding Dania and Orion that they hadn't taken away the *Star Renegade*'s engines again after their run to Themyscira.

Ty's voice came over the comm. "Okay, the file is all set. Come and get it, Big Guy."

Kile tapped on the panel. "Downloading."

Doc clapped his hands and rubbed them together. "In the meantime, what information do you have on the cloud headed for Earth?"

The picture on the screen changed to an image of Mars. The left of the mottled, coppery red planet was aglow with stars, as it should have been. The right of the image, though, where the asteroid belt should have been visible, was a murky, dark gray, like a large swath of space had been erased, or partially blurred.

Kile pointed at the screen. "Our people are estimating nearly a thousand Cartek warships of varying sizes. Most are smaller vessels in the range of our skippers, but they're equally deadly."

Doc walked up to the screen. "What are you basing that information on? This image was taken pretty wide. We were almost on top of the cloud when we were analyzing."

"We're using data from previous encounters. All ships engaged with the Carteks were sending data back to the former king for processing. Our analysts took reports on the numbers and related those numbers to the darkness of the cloud." He pointed at the screen. "These dark points in the cloud are the larger ships. The smaller ships are on the outside of the cloud. We assume this is due to their maneuverability."

Doc scratched his chin. "Yeah, maybe. But something doesn't look quite right to me."

Orion stormed forward. "Our best people have analyzed this data. This was the very data fed to our king."

Cal frowned. "Wait a minute. *Fed to your king?* As in the previous king? The one who's dead? Are you all seriously going off the same data that got most of the royal family killed?"

Orion bore down on Cal, his hair taking flight.

Doc stepped between them. "Since I'm the lucky one with an insolence reprieve, let me interject a little here." He turned to Dania. "With your permission, General?"

Her hair was the only thing that moved other than her eyes as she scanned the room. "This is why the humans are here. Proceed."

The humans…not Cal and Doc. Did she have *any* memory of them?

Doc released a breath. "Cal makes a good point, and I think you all need to take a step back and listen to people before you start getting unnecessarily defensive."

The enforcers shifted their weight, looking like snakes ready to strike.

Doc held up his palms. "Now, I've heard things about your previous king, and they may be right and they may be wrong…but in my educated opinion, I think he grossly underestimated his opponents, and it cost the Kever race their planet. And no one in this room can tell me I'm wrong about that. Because if I were, we wouldn't be in this position right now."

Orion folded his arms. "Tell us something we don't know."

Doc looked back at the screen. "When the Banes liberated the Earthan Cradle, they attacked the Carteks and annihilated them in one wide sweep. Face it. You obliterated them. They didn't see it coming, and they fell back." Doc tapped his fingertips together, looking at the floor like he was working things out. "The Carteks disappeared for years. We all thought we'd defeated them forever. But that's where we underestimated them. They weren't just licking their wounds. They were regrouping. They analyzed what went wrong, and they learned from it."

Orion sneered. "They learned that the Banes were the dominant force in the galaxy."

Cal guffawed, and Doc made a stop sign with his hand. Cal pressed his lips together. He needed to keep a cooler head or he was going to get thrown out for his own safety.

These people all needed to get over their enforcer egos, though, and face reality.

Doc lowered his palm. "My friend is laughing because you all know that statement is no longer true. The molecular waves in the galaxy have turned, and not in your favor."

Orion grimaced. "Your points are not helpful. We are here to devise a plan to change that."

"You're right," Doc said. "But we can't change that until we do exactly what the Carteks did." He pointed at the screen. "They studied what went wrong. They weren't simply worried about your numbers. They knew that the enforcers were stronger soldier for soldier than anything they could throw at you."

Orion took a step and pointed at the screen. "So how, in your educated opinion, did they decimate the strongest military in the galaxy?"

"Easy," Cal said. "They took emotion out of the equation."

"*Emotion?*" Kile asked.

"They didn't get pissed off and strike back without a plan."

"Cal's right." Doc continued to watch the ships on the screen. "The Carteks, from what I can tell, aren't a pleasant bunch. They're probably just as arrogant as all of you."

The room heated.

"Doc?" Cal inched closer to him.

Dania held up her hand, and the temperature cooled.

"Proceed." She glanced around the room. "And remember we are here to listen. The *Star Renegade* is one of the few ships to have avoided being destroyed by the Carteks. Keep that in mind."

Surviving their last run-in with a Cartek cloud hadn't had

anything to do with their intel at the time. There had been luck involved. Not to mention that the Carteks had run for their lives when the high prince had shown up out of nowhere.

Still, thanks to Doc's quick thinking, the *Star Renegade* had more detailed imagery of a Cartek cloud than the long-range images the enforcers were working from.

Doc gulped as the enforcers around them glared. "The Carteks were probably pretty darn pissed and embarrassed at how quickly you all pushed them out of the Earthan Cradle. But like Cal said, instead of being foolish and regrouping and attacking again, they stepped back and watched. They probably combed through the data on the few battles that they'd almost won, looking for reasons why some battles had been better fought than others."

"They realized that the enforcers were superior." Dania leaned on the table. "So they partnered with the pirates to capture as many of us as possible."

Doc pointed at her. "Exactly. And in doing so, they were testing their hypothesis without putting themselves at risk. They didn't care if the pirates died."

Where was Doc going with this. What *hypotheses*?

Doc started pacing again. "At first, they started targeting younger enforcers, perfecting their techniques. Then the pirates started going after bigger prizes. The pirates, as well as the Carteks, figured out that if they separated even the strongest of enforcers from the pack"—he pointed at Alexander—"that the enforcer would weaken themselves. There may be a high body count to reach their end-goal, but the Carteks found out, from the tenaciousness of the pirates, that the all-powerful enforcers would eventually get tired."

Dania cocked her head, making her hair sway in the opposite direction. Those freakishly cold eyes looked so barren. "When the Carteks destroyed Keveron, the king's enforcers were not spread out. They were together, defending him like a solid unit."

"Whoa there, little lady. Let's not jump ahead in the lesson. We're learning, just like the Carteks. One step at a time."

She narrowed her eyes at him.

Doc held up his palms again. "I mean, let's back up a bit and not jump to the end of the story. May I continue?"

Dania continued to glare. "Proceed."

She wanted answers, probably so she could throw all the might of the last living Bane at whatever answer Doc came up with. Cal had a bad feeling it wasn't going to be that easy, though.

Doc lowered his hands. "Yes, the king had all his enforcers on Keveron. But remember, the Carteks didn't start with the king." Kever words flashed across the screens as Doc walked past them. "They did the same thing to the royal family that they did to the individual enforcers. They knew that if they attacked Keveron head-on, that they would be dealing with every single Bane, and every enforcer under them all at the same time. They learned the first time that facing the full might of the Banes was a losing proposition." Doc tapped his fingers to his lips, his eyes fixed on nothing. "So they made it look like they were desperate. They attacked planets far from the Bane home world."

Doc paced to the end of the room, then turned back. A habit he'd probably learned from Cal.

"By then, the king had learned that sending one enforcer wouldn't work." Doc pointed at Alexander. "We temporarily lost our boy Alex that way."

"My name is Alexander," Alex said.

Doc inclined his head. "You are absolutely right. Please forgive my human faux pas." Doc started pacing again. "As I was saying, instead of sending one or even a few enforcers, the former king sent one of his daughters to make a statement. She was supposed to hit them over the head with a striking show of force. They probably thought the Carteks would run back to their own space and leave us alone for another few decades." His eyes scanned the enforcers. "But when the princess got there, she wasn't just facing the small number of Cartek ships that the planet had reported. The enemy hid their numbers. They probably kept hitting her and her enforcers over and over again, wave after wave of fresh troops, probably at huge sacrifice to their own ships. But eventually, she got tired."

"But they kept her alive," Dania said.

"Yeah. Again, they were probably experimenting, hoping another one of her siblings would come for her. But the high prince...he didn't fall for the bait. He sent Orion."

Doc tapped his fingers on his lips again, working through things.

"I always wondered where the Carteks were that day on the tank. The pirates certainly weren't strong enough to hold Zindiria, even if she was tired." Doc pointed at Orion. "I bet that if your high prince had gone on his own to find her, an even larger Cartek force would have fallen on him. When we showed up instead, they decided to blow up the tank and try to get rid of a few enforcers for their efforts. They didn't attack because that may have revealed their numbers, and the king would have realized they'd set a trap." Doc shook his head. "So they just systematically went back to attacking planets far away from each other. It's genius, if you think about it. They knew the Kevers were overconfident and thought that one Bane could easily take out a small band of Carteks. The king fell for it...sending his children and their enforcers to the far sides of the galaxy, splitting them up, and all of them were too far from help once the Carteks fell on them in mass." Doc turned to Dania. "Don't you see? All these years, they've been building the perfect army of countless ships and pilots. They knew what kind of technology we had to travel and scan for intruders, so they built new tech that got around anything we had. By the time they'd split up the Banes for those final coordinated attacks, the Carteks had an insurmountable armada behind them. They probably just kept coming and coming until each one of the Bane kids was exhausted. The only enforcers who survived were the ones they'd left behind on Keveron or on other ships in different parts of the galaxy." He pointed around the room. "You all were probably bummed that you were left behind for local law enforcement or other boring assignments, rather than fighting alongside your sponsors, but it saved your lives. If you'd been with them, you would have fought to exhaustion, too."

Dania shifted her weight from one foot to the other. "Many of these things Geron's analysts already suspected, but the tactical side, how they systematically removed the strongest of the Banes was...*brilliant*." Dania's light-blue eyes looked at several pictures of Bane cruisers flashing across the surface of the hovering table. "Once the reserves had been eliminated, they went after the high prince."

Doc watched the ships projected on the screen. "And I bet that force was larger than anything any of you had seen before, but it wasn't everything they had in reserves. They knew the high prince was an even bigger obstacle than the king. They took him out, and then they hit Keveron with everything they had."

The Counselor General paled to match his lighter-blue, fancy shirt and slipped into a seat at the table. "There were so many ships, we couldn't even see the stars. They just kept coming. The king called for the evacuation of the civilians before the fighting even started." He shook his head. "The enforcers tried to shield our escape, but only a fraction of the ships made it to deep space.

Dania folded her arms. "Tactically, it was a stronger move on the Carteks' part to let them go. The civilians could be hunted down and eradicated once the enforcers were dealt with."

"And I bet that's still what they plan on doing." Doc looked at the Counselor General. "You were probably right to tell Geron to save the people, because they'll be hunted down if we don't stop them."

Fancy-Guy quirked a brow. "And how do you propose to do that, knowing that the Carteks apparently know what we are going to do before we do it?"

"That's where you got it wrong. They don't know what we're going to do. They expect Geron to be just as obnoxiously self-centered as his father. They expect him to either run, which, I'd wager, is what their data on him says he'll do, or they'll expect him to come at them in a rage of fury."

The Counselor General frowned. "But isn't that what we've been planning? Standing between the Cartek cloud and Earth?"

"Yes, but they expect us to act like we're invulnerable. They're expecting raw Bane ego. We need to do what the Carteks did. We need to learn from our mistakes."

"And how do we do that and still save Earth?"

Dania looked at the screen again. "The human is right. They may assume that Geron will run, but they will be prepared if he does not." She turned back to Doc. "They probably have intelligence that tells them the number of enforcers he had before the war. No Bane in generations has taken on the responsibility of someone else's enforcers. Even if they thought Geron charitable, they would postulate he wouldn't take more than five. Possibly ten. No Bane in history has done what our sponsor has done."

Doc clapped his hands. "I'm with you, girl. They have no idea that the largest army of enforcers on record is aimed at them right now."

Orion pounded his fist on the table. "A decisive strike head-on, like I've been advising. We'll take them apart before they even realize what they're up against."

"Whoa there, my large friend." Doc held up his palms. "I do appreciate the enthusiasm, but let's also learn from what they did to us. They'll expect us to hit them with everything we have. Now, I'm not saying to divide our forces, because that's what got the Banes in trouble the first time. But I think we need to analyze that cloud with every bit of data at our fingertips and come up with a tactical plan."

Dania turned to the screens again. "We are estimating nearly a thousand ships in that cloud. Do you think there is another cloud lying in wait?"

"I doubt it. Again, they probably expect Geron to run. They'll also expect that if he doesn't run, he might realize how overpowered he is and *then* run anyway. They probably have people analyzing psychological studies on him. Your Illustrious Highness-ness doesn't have a very heroic reputation. From what I surmise from news feeds, he's managed to avoid anything one might consider a battle for his entire life."

She rubbed her chin. "He does tend to react emotionally. That's one of the reasons he is not here. I told him I would let him know what I decide."

"So what do you think?" Doc asked.

Interesting that he'd stopped postulating now, after laying everything out in front of them. Frankly, Cal hadn't even considered their situation with that much granularity. If he knew Doc, all of that had just popped into his big brain in the moment. Figuring things out was Doc's superpower. War tactics probably weren't in his skillset unless he looked at it as a puzzle and had to connect the pieces in the best way for the desired outcome.

Dania was supposed to be a tactician, though. Maybe the only one of Geron's original enforcers, except for maybe Kile, with any military training. Orion, obviously, was voting for the typical full-throttle smash-and-burn enforcer approach. Doc seemed to want something a little more moderate. Cal had no idea what to do.

The interesting question was, if Dania were to make the wrong choice, and Doc couldn't see the pattern, or the pieces fitting into the puzzle correctly, would Doc have the guts to tell her? And if he did, would she listen?

Dania continued to consider the screen. "I believe everything you said is correct. Our former king, despite any good intentions, made poor decisions that led to Keveron's annihilation."

The enforcers shifted their weight, some casting nervous glances at each other.

Doc shook his head. "Dania's right, and I know none of you like the idea of saying anything bad about the guy, but we can't ignore the facts. The former king's ego was a prime motivator to the fall of your empire. It sucks. I get that. But we need to own up to it now and do everything in our power to support your new ruler. We need to make sure he doesn't make the same mistakes."

Orion folded his arms again. "You are speaking in circles and not providing any actionable data."

Dania considered the cloud again. "I disagree. He provided a great deal of actionable data. I was aware that our forces had been thinned. I hadn't considered that this had been part of a calculated attack. The colonies they threatened never seemed to have military value. Their attacks made no sense. But it was never about the value of the planet. Rather, it was the location, and the ability to lure anyone who tried to help to their deaths."

"So what do we learn from this?" Orion asked. "Do you expect *us* to lure them to *their* deaths?"

"We need more analysis." Dania turned from the screen. "But yes, ideally, that is exactly what I'm going to do."

Orion opened his mouth but then closed it and looked down.

Cal wished he'd had the courage to say whatever he'd been about to say, because a few minutes ago, they'd said there were almost a thousand ships in that cloud.

Doc walked closer to the screen. "I'll need to see the most up-to-date imagery of the cloud. We can't form a solid plan unless we know the numbers."

The Counselor General sighed. "I already told you the number. It's insurmountable."

Dania's hair whipped about, making her seem taller. "A thousand ships is a large annoyance. We will suffer signifi-cant casualties. But it is far from insurmountable."

Cal wondered what the general thought a large number of casualties were, and if Cal's Dania was inside, screaming that any casualties were too many.

Cal wanted—stars, he *needed*—to believe the woman he loved was still hiding behind those cold, pale-blue eyes, but at the same time, he hoped she wasn't suffering, suffocated inside while her body moved of its own accord.

Doc tapped his fingers against his lips, looking at the screen. "I don't know about the numbers your people came up with. These patterns are a lot more congested than what we saw last time."

"I do not see patterns in this chaos. Even in the cloud that threatened Ephershia, I only saw blank space." Dania moved closer to Doc. "Help me to see what you see."

Good. She still trusted Doc. Hopefully, Peter had some concrete facts to back all this, and he wasn't making things up. Not that he'd ever done that, but half the time, the man talked circles around what Cal's brain was capable of comprehending.

"Can you call up the images that Ty decrypted?" Doc asked.

A new image appeared on the screen.

Doc said "skip" four times and the image changed over and over. "Wait. Go back."

The image flipped back one.

Doc's eyes narrowed. "Huh."

"What do you see?" Dania moved beside him.

He pointed at the screen. "See these light patches and dark patches?"

"Yes." She glanced at him as if waiting for an explanation.

Doc wiped his mouth with his palm. "That can't be right."

Cal's stomach sank, and he inched closer to the screen. "Those dark patches are where they hid their numbers."

"Yeah." Doc leaned closer and whispered, "You were paying attention?"

"Of course." Cal didn't always understand, but he at least paid attention. This one part he had understood, though. "What are you thinking?"

"Can I see the latest image of the cloud next to this one?"

The original image appeared to the right of Ty's image. The image on the left had seemed black when they'd first seen it, but compared to this new image, it looked gray. But if the darker patches were the higher concentrations of ships, that meant...

"We've got a problem," Doc said. "I don't think we're looking at under a thousand ships. I think we're looking at *tens of thousands*." He pointed at several places on the screen. "Each one of those dark patches could be at least nine hundred ships."

And there were at least fourteen dark patches, and those were only the ones visible from this vantage point.

The sound seemed to suck from the room. Orion's lips dropped into a gape before he pressed them together. All eyes seemed fixed on Dania before she turned from the screen. "This makes no difference. We always knew we'd be outnumbered."

"There's outnumbered, and there's impossible odds," the Counselor General said.

Dania bore down on him. "Your negativity is becoming an annoyance, Counselor General. I highly suggest you realign your thinking."

His lips formed an 'O'. "But I'm here to counsel. I need to be the voice of reason."

"The time for negotiation is over. Our sponsor has made a decision. We will stand between this cloud and Earth. We can fight here, with the addition of whatever meager forces the Earthans can provide, or we can wait for the Carteks to obliterate Earth and then hunt us down. Either option may lead to our deaths. Geron has made the only choice where two races have the possibility of surviving. If anyone in this room does not support that decision, I would be happy to wake the king and you can tell him yourself."

She scanned the room. Many enforcers met her gaze straight on, some nodding. Others lowered their eyes.

"That's what I thought. The next person who even *whispers* a thought contrary to our king's decision will be considered insolent and punished appropriately. If any of you would like to leave, you may get on a skipper and go now."

She glared at the Counselor General. He stared at the table, not meeting her gaze.

Dania smirked, walking back to the screen. "I want to see the most recent analysis of our firepower, as well as the capabilities of all the volunteers who chose to fight at Geron's side." Her gaze carried over the room. "Losing this war is not an option. The Carteks are in for an unprecedented surprise."

CHAPTER 32
CAL

THE WALLS SEEMED to press in on Cal as he walked through the *Star Renegade*'s halls. His footfalls seemed to echo along with Doc's, the sound making the ship seem ominously empty.

"You okay with this plan?" Doc asked.

"No. But it's not like I have a choice."

"Dani did give everyone the opportunity to leave if they didn't want to fight. We can still run."

Cal stopped walking. "Is that what you think I should do?"

"What *I* think you should do? No. Not at all. I think you should fight. I'd be lying, though, if I didn't admit that I *want you* to run. I'm scared."

"Yeah. Me, too." And not so much for himself anymore. He was worried about his friends.

He tapped on the panel beside the entrance to the lounge and the door opened.

Ty and Ethan stood from the table, while Rachel and Alanna sprang for the door.

"What's happened?" Alanna asked.

"Yeah, Cally," Rachel said. "You don't look so good."

Cal dragged his fingers through his hair. "Dania is going to command the fleet from the *Star Renegade*."

"*What?*" They all asked at the same time.

"Is she okay?" Alanna hugged her own shoulders. "Is she still herself?"

"Not from what we could tell. Her hair is nearly white and floating, her skin is pale, and she barely even looked at us." Recounting all those details hurt a little more than Cal wanted to admit. "She said the cruiser's viewscreens could only show her images of the battle immediately around them. She wants to be able to slide in and out of the fray so she can see more of what's going on."

Ty's cheeks paled. "That would put the *Star Renegade* right in the thick of battle."

"She gave us the same option Geron gave to the civilians in the fleet. We can go and take cover if we want."

"But not with the *Star Renegade*," Ethan said.

"The *Star Renegade* isn't negotiable. It's part of her battle plan."

"No way," Ty said. "No one is flying my baby but me."

Cal turned to Ty. "She admitted that you are a good pilot and said if you wanted to stay, you'd be welcome."

Ty puffed out a breath. "Well, I'm certainly not going to leave my girl to get manhandled by an enforcer."

"Does that mean you're staying?"

"Hell yeah. And I'm going to take a wild guess and say you are, too."

"Of course." Cal wasn't too keen to leave the *Star Renegade* in the hands of enforcers, either. If he were being honest with himself, he also hoped that maybe once they got Dania away from the others, she might tell him that she was fine, that she was just acting like an enforcer to gain the others' trust.

He knew that was just a fantasy, though. She couldn't fake the color of her eyes. She couldn't fabricate the way her hair floated even without a breeze. She was gone.

"I'm staying, too." Doc shrugged. "I don't really have anywhere else to go."

Cal turned to Alanna, Rachel, and Ethan. "I know you all have family. If you want to stay on the cruiser, or see if you can catch a civilian ride, I wouldn't blame you."

"And miss all the fun?" Ethan said. "Besides. You're going to need the engines running at peak efficiency. And I don't want anyone playing in my engine room any more that Ty wants someone else piloting."

Alanna shifted nervously in her seat. "I don't want to be in the middle of a fight, but I don't want to be alone when all this is going on. I love you all. You're my family."

Rachel gulped. "Even me? I know I haven't been part of the crew long."

Alanna placed her arm around her. "Of course!"

Rachel smiled, releasing her breath with a *whoosh*.

She may have been a late addition to the crew and had come on board in possibly the strangest of ways...sneaking on board and stowing away to be with Kile. But Rachel had learned to pull her weight, and the ship would feel empty without her, or without any of them.

Rachel turned to Cal. "I'm not sure what I can do that everyone else isn't already good at. But I'm here to help out however I can."

The air at her feet blurred, and Max's head and upper body materialized, as if floating above the floor. He waved his paws and gave a high-pitched bark before tilting his snout and folding his tiny arms.

Cal dragged his fingers through his hair again. "I appreciate all the support, but I don't want any of you feeling obligated. Dania isn't the kind of general who is going to hang back, where it's safe. If we join this fight, there's no guarantee we'll come home in one piece."

"That's exactly why we're not leaving," Ty said. "The *Star Renegade* needs her crew, not a bunch of Kevers who don't know her like we do."

Ethan laughed. "Yeah, besides, all our modifications would just scare them."

The weight of the galaxy lightened a bit as Cal looked about the room. At the same time, the weight of all their lives dragged him into a pit. "Are you all sure about this?"

"Hey, this is our home," Ty said. "The *Renegade* has the best chance of getting out of this in one piece if we stick with her." He ran his hands along the wall. "She's a good girl, and if this is her last flight, I don't want her to be alone."

Rachel raised her hand slowly. "Can I vote for this *not* being her last flight?"

"That's the plan." Cal moved to the center of the room. "And Ty's right. The *Renegade* is as much a part of our family as everyone in this room. We stick with her, and she'll be here for us. It's the best way to get out of this in one piece."

"So, when does all this happen?" Rachel asked.

Ty pointed out the window. "Looks like right now."

Dania, Alexander, Kile, and Orion walked toward the base of the *Star Renegade*.

"I hope all four of them don't expect to fit on the bridge."

Cal's cheek ticked. There wasn't enough room on the ship

for Kile's and Orion's egos, let alone all four of the enforcers cramped in a space with only three already-occupied chairs.

Doc tapped Cal's back. "I'll stay in the med bay. I can watch things from there and let you know if I see anything interesting."

"Thanks. Let's keep interior comms from the bridge open throughout the ship so everyone knows what's going on."

"Good call," Ethan said. "I can try to keep a step ahead of you." He waved Rachel toward the door. "You can hang with me in Engineering if you want. I may be able to use a second pair of hands."

She saluted, smiling brightly. "You got it!"

Max materialized beside her feet and copied a similar salute.

Three sets of hands in Engineering, or claws, in Max's case, was probably a good call. That was possibly the only place on the ship where extra bodies could actually help.

Dania stopped a few yards from the *Star Renegade* and spoke to her enforcers, her hair swirling about her head and glinting in the lights. After a few moments, Kile and Orion bowed and walked back into Geron's cruiser, while Dania and Alexander headed up the ramp.

Cal took a steadying breath. "We should get to the bridge. My guess is she'll want to leave right away."

"Don't you think they'll want to get settled back into their rooms?" Alanna asked.

"Honestly, I doubt they even remember living here."

Her eyes saddened. Cal hadn't meant to sound so sharp, but they all needed to get used to the idea that Dania and Alexander were gone.

The enforcers were already heading down the hall when Ty, Doc, and Alanna entered the bridge.

Cal greeted his former crew members at the door. "I didn't expect both of you."

Dania's icy eyes seemed devoid of life. "Alexander is intrinsic to the success of the operation. He will remain at my side."

"Understood." Cal held out his hand, motioning them to enter. Luckily, they both took standing positions, allowing Cal to take his seat at the captain's station. "I guess we can pull a few mobile chairs up here for the two of you."

Dania looked out the window. "That is unnecessary. Standing keeps you engaged. You may pilot the ship out of the hangar. I have already given you clearance to depart."

"Yes, ma'am." Ty flicked a glance at Cal. His lips pursed before his hands moved over the controls and the ship rose from the decking.

They spun once and the air shield sparkled before they broke through the shimmering, blue energy veil that kept the oxygen from getting sucked out of the cruiser when ships passed through.

Ty piloted them up and over the trail of ships circling the cruiser. Half of them appeared to be rebuilt hobby ships. Others were shiny, new pleasure vessels drifting aside dented and blast-stained skippers.

This was a ragtag fleet if Cal had ever seen one. They didn't have numbers on their side, but they did have the will to survive. Both the humans and the Kevers knew this was the last stand. They were fighting for their right to exist.

Cal shuddered as the king's cruiser came into view, dwarfing Geron's ship, which had seemed like a monstrosity when it had first appeared. The *Oliganton* made Geron's cruiser look not much larger than a small passenger transport. Cal still couldn't fathom how anything that large could fly, even through weightless space.

Dozens of smaller ships formed a line, exiting the massive cruiser and heading to Geron's ship. Another line left Geron's cruiser, heading back to the megalith.

"Huh." Alanna squinted at the screen. "The ships leaving the *Oliganton* are stuffed tight with people. The ones returning are empty." She turned to Dania. "Are they evacuating?"

"Only necessary military personnel are staying on board. All others are being re-assigned."

Cal watched the two lines of ships, looking very much like the ants his mother had described on Earth, following tightly one behind the other in a line to get to their destination and back. It was suddenly obvious why Geron hadn't changed ships. That thing was impossible to hide. It was like flying around in the galaxy saying, *'Hey, I'm important, come shoot at me!'*

Of course, a ship that size probably had enough firepower behind it to ward off most attacks. That was why the military personnel were remaining behind. They were most-likely going to use the *Oliganton* as a battering ram, maybe hoping to distract or cut through the Carteks. They might lose the megalith in the process, but it would be unexpected, which was what Dania and Doc agreed was a necessary tactic when dealing with an alien race that always seemed two steps ahead of them.

Ty maneuvered them up through the ships and hovered above Geron's cruiser.

"Well done, pilot." Dania stood behind him. "Continue to follow orders and you may remain at your station. Fail to follow orders, and you will be expediently replaced with an enforcer who *will* follow orders."

Ty snorted. "Wow, you sound a lot like Orion all of a sudden. Loosen up, Dani."

The room heated slightly, and her hair billowed around her.

Ty glanced up at her and snickered. "Or not. I guess either way works for me, Your General-ness."

Cal wished he could be as lighthearted about the situation. This was the same woman he'd held. Kissed. Loved.

Dania was standing right there. He could see her. Yet she was still more than a million miles away. She was there, but not there. Alive, but also dead. He wasn't sure he could stand being in the same room with her much longer.

He needed to focus on the goal. His mother was on Earth, and billions of other innocent people were counting on him.

General Dania DuBane was a ruthless tactician, and all her thirst for blood was now aimed at the Carteks. He needed to embrace that and be thankful for it. There would be time to mourn the woman he loved later.

The general looked at Alanna. "Navigator, you also control communications?"

"Comms? Yeah. I'm your girl, sir. Umm, ma'am...or, General."

Dania narrowed her eyes. "'General' will suffice. Open a secure comm to ship B8."

Alanna frowned at her and then scanned the screen. She usually controlled the comms for incoming transmissions, or when there was a single ship to focus on. Cal couldn't recall a time she'd tried to pluck a certain ship out of dozens circling them.

Dania growled and looked over Alanna's shoulder, pointing at the screen. "That one."

"That one. Got it." She tapped on her screens. "Here we go."

Kile's voice filled the bridge. "Yes, General."

"Slight change in plans. I want half your ships to fly in front of the *Star Renegade*. The other half scatter on all sides and behind."

"That will make it look like we are trying to protect you, General. It will call attention to your ship."

"Exactly."

"Yes, General." The comm cut out.

Two dozen ships floated into view ahead of them. That meant that there were a similar number of ships moving behind them.

"That's all we're taking with us?" Cal asked.

"Hiding our numbers," Dania announced. "Your doctor's idea. Fear not, Captain Espinoza, there are more than enough ready to come to our aid if needed."

Sure, but would they get there in time?

Hopefully, they wouldn't need to get too close. They were starting with reconnaissance. The Carteks would know they were there. They just needed to get a few really good pictures of the Cartek cloud to try to gauge the enemy's actual numbers and then get out of there.

Dania held her hands behind her back, standing behind Ty. "Proceed."

The small armada made a steady burn to get deeper into the Earthan Cradle and then cut their engines and basically floated into the area between Earth and the cloud. It appeared they were trying to sneak in, but that was by design. They wanted the Carteks to believe they were inept, but they knew they were being watched very closely.

Just beyond Earth's immediate galactic border, the Cartek cloud loomed in space, completely blocking out the other planets and stars. The gray-black cloud swirled and flexed around darker, nearly-black patches. It was like facing a void, knowing that mass of swirling nothingness, at any moment, could become a shrieking, many-armed monster bent on their destruction.

"Keep those cameras snapping pictures," Cal whispered.

"On it, boss," Alanna said.

The onboard comm pinged from the med bay, and Doc's voice filled the room. "I'm not liking all those really big dark patches."

Cal wasn't liking them, either. The cloud spread higher and wider than any blockade they'd seen, and they still had no idea how deep it was. They had to be ready for anything, and by anything, that meant more attacking ships than any of them could possibly imagine.

In many ways, this battle had been inevitable, but now that they were facing it, Cal still couldn't believe he was there. He'd wanted to keep his people out of danger, and now they were at the brink of the largest battle in humanity's history. And the *Star Renegade* had a front-row seat.

Whether they wanted it or not.

CHAPTER 33
DANIA

THE SLIGHT, unsteady hum running through the floor of the small smuggling ship seemed oddly familiar, like a visit home after a long absence. She'd lived there for some time, but it had never truly been home. How she ever could have convinced herself she'd been happy in such a confined, degraded space was beyond her comprehension. It seemed that the doctor's abominable concoctions had done their job, poisoning her mind. She wouldn't allow that to happen again.

The human captain glanced over his shoulder at her for the eleventh time since she'd stepped onto the bridge. He seemed expectant, or possibly hopeful. If he was looking for a sign of weakness, he wouldn't find it. She was on board the *Star Renegade* for a singular purpose: to eradicate the threat to Geron and what was left of the Kever race. Those were her orders, and she'd see it done, no matter the cost.

"Comm coming in from Earth," Alanna said.

Dania was surprised the planet hadn't contacted them sooner. "Let it through."

"Thank the stars!" the voice on the line said. "We thought

we'd be alone. We haven't heard from the king in weeks. We've taken on so many refugees, and then the cloud kept getting closer."

Dania understood their trepidation. The Carteks had been plowing through the colonies nearly undeterred since the high prince had been lost. With so much going wrong in the galaxy, Earth may not have even realized that Keveron had fallen.

"This is General Dania DuBane, commanding the fleet from the *Star Renegade*. You are now under the protection of Geron Bane. Please send us your numbers and capabilities. Your military will be blended with our own."

"Understood, General. Sending stats now."

Alexander walked to the nav station and looked at the woman's screen. "They are only offering 2,876 ships, and only 732 are defense class."

"It's not unexpected." Dania reviewed the makes and models of the ships.

"But only 2,876 ships to protect their entire planet?"

Dania glanced at him. "Do we have that many more?"

"I suppose not, but Earth hasn't been decimated like we have. Certainly, they can spare more ships."

Alexander tapped the comm over the navigator's shoulder. She closed her eyes, like his closeness bothered her in some way.

Alexander called in to the comm. "Earth, confirm your numbers. Include your reserves."

"All the sectors are trying to call in civilian ships, and we're calling reserves and retired military. We just don't have a lot of combat-worthy ships. We'll send you new numbers when we have them."

One of the benefits of the king's protection was the

reduction of planetary defense spending. Earth was supposed to place that extra funding into the arts and education. Now, it seemed, they'd left themselves unable to defend themselves in a time of need.

Captain Espinoza looked over his shoulder again. "Those people are protecting their home. They'll fight with more heart than the Carteks are bargaining for, I guarantee it."

Dania nodded. "I'm counting on that." Hopefully, though, the sheer number of Carteks wouldn't cut through the planet's defenses too quickly. "Split the Earthan squadrons into ten segments under Orion's command. Send two out on the front lines."

Espinoza stood. "You're sending the humans to engage first? They'll be slaughtered."

"*Someone* has to engage first. I'd rather lose humans than enforcers."

Espinoza grimaced, then looked away. Even he had to understand the validity of that plan. She'd need every enforcer available when the main wave of Carteks struck. Sacrificing the weakest first was the most logical course of action.

The humans didn't argue their orders. They separated and blended into their new commands, and the last two groups headed out to engage the Carteks. The small ships shot wave after wave of artillery at the massive wall of skewed space, but the blast sparks scattered across the surface of the cloud, flashing with bright light but not doing any damage.

"They're slowing down," the navigator said. "In fact, I think the cloud is hovering. It's not moving forward anymore."

Dania grasped her hands behind her back. "Excellent."

"How is that excellent?" Ty asked from the pilot station

on her right. "Wouldn't it be better if they broke formation so we can fight them?"

An obvious question.

"All in good time. We'll continue to taunt them. They'll break ranks eventually."

A larger explosion lit up the stars before winking out.

"It looks like we destroyed a Cartek ship on the lower third of the cloud," Alanna said. "Our ships finally got through their shielding."

Dania reset her footing. "Good. We'll take them out one at a time if we have to."

Concern furrowed across the captain's brow as he glanced at her again. His temperature spiked, as did that of the pilot and navigator.

Alexander stood tall, scanning the ships heading toward the cloud. His thoughts were jumbled and mixed. He understood his duty to be at her side, more so now that they both understood she may need to draw on his power before this fight was over, but she could tell he'd rather be out there among the pilots.

Whether that would be to destroy—or to keep others from being destroyed—was the question.

"Something's happening," the navigator said.

Seven long, murky points formed at the base of the Cartek cloud, like they'd suddenly lost cohesiveness and started to drip. The points pinched and detached from the whole, becoming sharp, conical warships.

Dania surveyed her front line. "Prepare for attack!"

"Yeah, no shit, lady," one of the human pilots said over the comm.

Dania smirked at their lack of decorum. Under other circumstances, she would have admonished him, but in this case, she was glad that they'd been paying attention. When working with pilots who were not her own, she never knew what to expect.

"Stay in tight formation," Dania directed. "Don't give them holes to weave through."

When the Carteks scattered, the human ships scattered.

The *Star Renegade* banked right suddenly.

Dania grabbed the back of the pilot's chair to steady herself. "What are you doing?"

"We got pinged." Ty shivered. "I could feel it. I got the heebie-jeebies all over."

"Confirmed," Alanna said. "Here comes another one."

"On it." Ty banked down. "That one was faster. Feels like they're trailing us."

"Always trust your instincts," Alanna said. "It looks like they're throwing a tracking beam at us."

"I guess they figured out where the commands are coming from."

Also, not completely unexpected, being that she was forced to use standard communication with the non-enforcer pilots. This was why she'd wanted to command from a more maneuverable ship. "Don't allow them to scan us. The less information they have on who is aboard, the better."

The pilot pursed his lips at her. "I'm not a fool." He returned his gaze forward. "The real Dania knew that."

Indeed, she did, but she'd also learned never to take things for granted when dealing with a human.

This time, when Ty spiraled from the tracking beam, she called a slight trickle of power to keep herself stationary.

The Cartek cone-fighters burned their engines, hitting the human and enforcer pilots straight on. The enforcers shouted commands, but the humans spiraled up and over the Carteks.

One human craft exploded. Then another. A third lost their engines and hung in space before a Cartek banked over them, firing the killing shot.

Espinoza stood. "They're being annihilated. Do something!"

Dania folded her arms. "I *did* do something. I ordered them to stay in tight formation. They did not comply."

Ty gaped at her. "So you're not going to help them?"

"No."

The young pilot's hand eased toward the controls.

"I'm perfectly capable of replacing you at the helm, pilot," Alex reminded him.

The human eased his hand back. "My name's Ty. You used to know that." He pointed to the captain. "That's Cal, and that's Alanna over there."

Alanna waved her fingers, but her eyes seemed sad.

"We used to all be friends." Ty tapped a flashing yellow light three times. "I'm kinda missing you both more than I expected. The new yous are jerks."

A very human, but not completely unexpected reaction. Dania had lived on this ship and formed extraneous relationships with the crew. Those relationships were now secondary and unnecessary. These people needed to realize this and follow orders, like any others under her command.

Outside, the remaining human ships returned to the cluster, and the groups hit the Cartek cones with a pointed and coordinated attack. All but one Cartek ship exploded. The last backed off and raced toward the cloud, where it was reabsorbed like a droplet of water into a pond.

"Excellent," Dania said.

"Excellent?" Espinoza, stood. "We lost a lot of good people out there."

"Yes, but the other human pilots saw what happened to those who didn't follow orders. Their sacrifices were not needless if it improves the cohesion of the whole."

"Cohesion of the whole?"

Ty grabbed Espinoza's arm, pulling him back into his seat. "Easy, boss. I hate it, too, but she has a point."

Good. If the pilot could see reason, hopefully, the others would as well. War meant casualties, and Dania knew all too well that those losses were only the beginning. She didn't have time to save those who couldn't follow direction, and the more ships they had under her control when the cloud finally dissipated, the better.

The *Star Renegade* throttled through the friendly ships and then banked down to get behind them again.

Ty leaned his body to the right, anticipating G-forces that didn't actually materialize in space. "The bad guys may not have scanned us yet, but that's not for lack of trying."

Espinoza's muscles tensed as he held on to his armrests. "They're probably still pissed at me for not handing over the enforcers after they cut that ridiculously one-sided deal."

One-sided, but understandable. The Carteks had threatened to crush the *Star Renegade*, and everyone inside, if Espinoza didn't surrender Dania, Kile, and Alexander to them. The captain hadn't had a choice but to agree, and then he'd done everything in his power to avoid making good on that arrangement.

Dania would have acted no differently; however, she would have been compelled to arrest the Carteks involved, since the deal had been illegal in the first place.

Three more needles shot out of the cloud, and when their

engine trails dissipated, three small conical ships appeared to engage the remaining humans and the enforcers.

Three... Just three.

What games were the Carteks playing? Why send out so few ships?

Another small explosion erupted near Orion's ship as a Cartek cone blew up. The commander's shield lowered by a quarter of a percent.

Dania chilled. Those ships were probably drones. They were sacrificing their unmanned crafts to lower the shields on the leaders before the main attack.

Her lips thinned. It was an excellent strategy. She wished she'd thought of it.

"Pull away from the cloud and regroup," she said to the screen.

"We can eradicate the remaining ships," Orion's voice answered.

"Negative. Fall back and regroup."

"But..."

Dania called on her power, overtaking Orion's mind. She seeded her belief that they were slowly breaking down his shield and repeated the order to return. The ships instantly complied, the humans trailing close behind them.

She blinked, dropping the link. Orion's insolence would need to be dealt with. It was right for Geron to keep the commander's military training intact, but Dania very much looked forward to giving Orion an attitude adjustment once this battle was won.

For now, though, she needed to reserve her strength. She didn't want to risk weakening too soon, which would force her to tap into Alexander's power. This battle wasn't going to be over quickly, and they needed to be ready for anything.

The Cartek ships fired their engines and chased down Orion and the ships under his command. Dania gritted her teeth. Orion probably wouldn't be able to resist firing on them, even though it would slow them down.

She understood his tenacity, but she needed him regrouped with the others to show a more united front. In order to make that happen, they needed to clear his path.

Dania pointed past Ty's shoulder. "Shoot those Cartek cones. Give our ships the space they need."

"Yes, ma'am." Ty rolled the *Star Renegade* up and over the retreating ships, spraying fire down on the drones. Three consecutive explosions lit up and winked out so quickly, she might have missed it had she blinked.

"They're scanning us again!" Alanna shouted. "From the right, Ty."

"I'm on it!" Ty banked the ship left, and down, then back up again, as the beam of light shot out of the cloud, following them before it winked out.

They'd only engaged for eight point nine seconds. They could have held the scan longer, but it seemed the enemy was watching their own power usage as well.

Ty released a relieved breath, and his temperature lowered zero point two degrees as the *Star Renegade* circled back to the retreating ships. "They sure are jonesing for the *Renegade*."

Yes, they certainly were. But were they looking for the leader, as she'd originally thought, or was Espinoza correct, and they were seeking retribution for a broken agreement?

"The cloud is advancing again," Alanna said. "At this rate, they'll be within Earth's defensive zone in one hour."

One hour certainly wasn't enough time. She needed to slow their advance and make them disperse so her pilots had some actual living targets to shoot at.

At one time, it had seemed that the Carteks' sole focus had been destroying Keveron.

Now that force was aimed at Earth: the next-biggest prize in the galaxy. If she wanted to distract them, her only viable option was to offer the Carteks something that they possibly wanted more than Earth.

But there was nothing left. They'd already decimated Keveron, and Earth stood before them, pruned and exposed, ready to be conquered.

Ty spun them around another scanning beam. The man flew the ship like an extension of his own arms. It was true that Alexander could have taken over the ship, but Dania doubted even Alexander would be able to pilot the *Star Renegade* as well.

Another beam of light shot from the cloud, cutting them off.

"Whoa!" Ty spiraled the ship, managing to miss both beams.

"I think I'm gonna puke," Alanna said.

"Sorry!" But judging by the smile reflecting in the screen, the pilot was far from sorry. He seemed to be...*enjoying himself*.

"Keep your eyes open," Espinoza said. "They're being relentless."

That they were. Far more relentless than she would have expected. The Carteks had to know Geron's cruiser was on the edge of the battle, and the king's cruiser was prepped, ready for her call. These were far more valuable targets, so why all this interest in the *Star Renegade*? Yes, the limits of the Earthan communications systems would make it obvious that commands were coming from this ship, but this excessive attention seemed personal.

She glanced at the back of the captain's head. Maybe it *was* personal. The Carteks were used to getting what they wanted. Espinoza had denied them that. True, obtaining high-level enforcers would have been more beneficial to their plans *before* Keveron had fallen, but maybe that wasn't the point.

If the Carteks were still incensed over the *Star Renegade* not complying with their agreement, maybe she could use that egotistical flaw against them, the same way the Carteks had exploited the ego of an overly-confident king.

She focused her mind and searched out the officers manning the weapons on the *Oliganton*. After implanting her orders, she released the connection, and before she took her next breath, a pulse shot through the galaxy.

The *Star Renegade's* overhead lights flickered and then went out. The screens went blank.

"What the hell?" Espinoza swiped his hands over his controls. His ship, as Dania expected, didn't respond. "Did we lose power?"

"We got hit." Alanna turned toward Dania. "The shot came from the *Oliganton*."

Dania kept her eyes on the screen. The Cartek cloud shimmered, then waved, now looking more fluid than solid.

*Yes...*that had gotten their attention.

"You don't look surprised." Espinoza stood. "What are you doing?"

She flicked a glance at him before returning her attention to the cloud. "Giving them what they want."

He slid his chair aside, advancing on her. "And what is that, exactly?"

"The *Star Renegade*."

THE DANIA CAL had known never would have even considered sacrificing the *Star Renegade*, let alone leaving her friends vulnerable like this.

Then again, this same, new Dania had thrown those human pilots to the front lines, leaving them to die needlessly. She didn't care that most of those pilots had been civilians who'd never dreamed of going to war. They'd just been regular people trying to do the right thing, hoping to make a difference.

There'd been a time when he'd thought that maybe a cold, calculating automaton would be what they needed to destroy the even larger beast bearing down on them.

He never dreamed she'd dangle the very ship she stood inside as bait, though.

Alanna looked up from her screen. "The cloud is advancing again."

And Dania had left them dead in space.

But why? She and Alexander would be obliterated, too.

"Kile." Dania's voice was soft but stern, spoken as if her commander had been standing in the room.

Then she looked at Alexander. His eyes widened, and his lips parted slightly before he nodded.

Wait a minute…they *could* hear each other's thoughts? Cal had often wondered, but now that it was basically confirmed, he couldn't stand being left in the dark on his own bridge.

He took a step toward them. "What's going on?" When Dania didn't answer, Cal grabbed her arm. "Hey. Don't ignore me. You can't just…"

His palm heated like her skin had gone ablaze beneath her uniform. A slight, yellow light flashed around her, and then she was gone. Alexander winked out a second later.

Alanna shot up from her chair. "Where did they go?"

Ty puffed a mirthless laugh. "I'll give you two guesses, and the second one doesn't count."

Cal turned to the front viewscreen.

Dania and Alexander hung in space between the *Star Renegade* and the Cartek cloud. Their hands were out to their sides, in a similar posture to when Dania had first woken from her enforcer stupor and had protected Cal's crew from her sponsor.

But why disable the *Star Renegade* and then defend it?

A flash of yellow light flared on Dania's right, and Kile appeared beside her.

The cloud shimmered and bulged, looking like it wanted to break apart but thought better of it. Balls of blue and purple fire appeared in all three enforcers' hands, the flames lapping and swirling as if they'd been fueled by actual oxygen, before the enforcers punched, sending the bursts into the cloud. The glowing fireballs penetrated the shield, forming small, black holes in the thick Cartek exterior, but it simply wasn't enough against something so big.

Long points shot out of the cloud, looking like ancient pens or Doc's styluses before the tails dissipated and they morphed into the Cartek versions of skippers—no doubt more highly modified and deadly skippers than they were used to. They bore down on the enforcers and the space between the cloud and the *Star Renegade* alighted with artillery and primordial energy, swallowing the enforcers in a gleaming ball of light.

Alanna gasped, holding her hand over her mouth. "Can they survive that?"

Cal scowled. That *thing* out there wasn't Dania. At least not anymore. "I'm more worried about our own hides."

Ty frantically toyed with the controls. "Why'd she leave us stranded?"

Cal tested his own controls. "It makes no sense. The whole reason she'd wanted to command from the *Star Renegade* was maneuverability. Now we're sitting ducks."

The glow dimmed as a blast of artillery bounced off Kile's shield bubble and slammed into the *Star Renegade*. The ship shook and then took another hit. Three more Cartek skippers approached and shot right past the enforcers, hitting the *Star Renegade* head-on.

So, maybe the enforcers *weren't* the targets. The *Star Renegade* was.

Or maybe Rgrythei really was still holding a grudge. After all, the three enforcers hanging in space were the very enforcers whom he'd been bartering the *Star Renegade*'s crew's lives for. Maybe Rgrythei saw a way to get his prizes, maybe retrieve some of his pride, and get back at Cal for wriggling out of their agreement.

Cal would have been fine with that in a fair fight. But Dania had left them without a way to fight back.

Another flash of light skidded over their hull.

Cal hit the comm. "Ethan, we need to get our engines running. We're going to get smashed out here." There was no answer. *Dammit!*

The door opened a few inches, then opened a little more. The edges of a pry bar poked through the opening before Doc slid inside.

"Lovely weather we've been having," Doc said before sprinting to the engineering panel and inserting a portable drive into the interface. The panel came alive.

"We have power?" Cal asked.

"Just comms and a few instruments." Doc tapped on the panel. "Ethan, can you hear me?"

"Damn! It actually worked!" Ethan's voice rang through the speaker.

"Exactly as you said it would," Doc said. "Be careful, though. People are going to mistake you for a real engineer."

"I *am* the competent one."

Cal swiped back his hair. "All right, people. I'd love some ideas. We're going to get fried like yesterday's breakfast if we stay out here."

"I'm sorry," Ethan said. "I thought I plugged all the holes in our systems. I don't know how they disabled us with a single shot."

"It's not your fault. Kile lived here for more than long enough to find flaws that we never would have even thought of looking for. Let's focus on *the now*. How do we fix this?" The ship shook again.

Outside, Dania's and Alexander's long, glinting silvery-opal hair floated about in zero-G. Kile's hair was probably floating as well, but it was too short to see at this distance.

All three of them punched balls of fire at the oncoming ships, firing blow after lethal blow at the Carteks.

It certainly looked like they were defending the *Star Renegade*. None of it made sense. If there was some sort of master plan, at least she could have shared with the bait before she'd offered them up for slaughter.

Alanna stood. "Is Dania's bubble getting duller?"

Cal squinted, shielding his eyes from the flashing lights. It was entirely possible. All three of them were expelling an excessive amount of primordial energy. And all they were doing was keeping the onslaught of ships coming out of that cloud away from the *Star Renegade*.

Kile threw a blast, and it fizzled before it reached the ship it had been aimed at. Were they all getting tired? Wasn't this the very thing Dania had just warned Orion about?

Dania held out both her hands, and a blinding flash engulfed her before snapping back at the attacking ships. The last three Cartek skippers exploded.

"Damn, that was badass," Ty whispered.

It certainly had been. Was she just flexing her muscles? Showing them what they were up against?

Or was she showing off for Geron, demonstrating that she was just as strong as she'd ever been? Her bubble flickered and she spun, looking back at the *Star Renegade*. Her eyes were soft, maybe slightly lost and scared.

"Dania?" Cal whispered.

Doc tapped on his screen. "We got hundreds of Bane ships lining up behind us."

"The cloud is slowing down again," Alanna said. "Could the enforcers have done that much damage?"

"Maybe." Doc pointed to the screen, where bright explosions lit up a small area of the cloud. "She's concentrating the attack here. It must sting if they're slowing down. They'll either have to recalibrate to make that section stronger or break apart for a full-on attack."

"Breaking them apart is what she wants," Cal said. But then why not hit them like that sooner? And still, why knock out power on the *Star Renegade*? Did she think Cal would run if she wasn't on board?

Dania threw several more bolts of light into the same area the ships were firing on. A hole seemed to open, but they weren't doing enough damage. She spun back toward the *Star Renegade* and her gaze hardened before the space around her wavered.

The *Star Renegade* jolted like it had been hit from behind by a ship twice its size. Cal held on to the edges of his station as they careened away from the Bane ships, past the enforcers, and headed straight for the Cartek cloud.

"What the hell?" Ty waved his hands over the controls, trying to stop their momentum, but it was fruitless until they stopped with a sudden jolt, like hitting a wall.

That had been too calculated a start and stop. Dania had moved them to the front on purpose. "What is she doing?"

"Dangling us like bait." Doc gaped, looking at the screen. "She threw us close enough to tempt them, but not close enough to capture us unless they send out enough ships to snatch us and fend off the enforcers and Banes at the same time."

"Why would she do that?" Cal asked.

"She's trying to make them disperse." Doc puffed out a breath. "It actually makes sense. The Carteks have been tracking us like crazy. They can't get closer with those ships pummeling them, so they either need to change their advance strategy or they'll have to disperse to come get us.

"But they can sure as the blazes hit us with a missile!"

The Cartek cloud shimmered and the black points broke apart. Ships started shooting off in different directions. The massive cloud disseminated, breaking into thousands of pinpricks of light.

No, not light... Ships... Thousands and thousands of ships.

"It worked!" Doc said.

Sure. Great. But several of them started heading straight for the *Star Renegade*.

DANIA WATCHED the cloud dissipate with immense satisfaction. She'd kept her enforcers back, hiding their true numbers. Not only had she stopped their advance, but the enemy was now vulnerable, and she'd use all the power of her sponsor to annihilate them.

A ship came from the right and a bolt of energy sliced inches from her face. The Carteks spread more quickly than she'd anticipated, but no matter. They were separated, without their massive cloud shield protecting them. That was all she needed to devour them one at a time.

The light beside her dulled, and she checked over her shoulder. Kile hung lax in space, a burn across his cheek. The blast must have gotten through his shield, but then he'd used the last of his power to seal the bubble before he'd passed out.

It was a cowardly gesture. He could have used his last breath to destroy another ship before he'd fallen useless.

Alexander floated toward him. *"I can heal him."*

"No." Dania looked past him to the throng of incoming ships. *"Leave him. Our focus is on the battle."*

All soldiers were expendable. Alexander should have known this. Survivors would be collected and healed afterward. Saving the injured only put the others in danger. Once an enforcer fell, they were a weakness that needed to be ignored for the greater good.

But were they? Kile had been one of the first enforcers to hold her hand. He'd taught her so much.

Until she'd become the strong one. Until she'd taken the place of power she deserved.

But he'd supported her, even when others hadn't.

He'd challenged her authority. He'd always been a problem.

But his challenges always made her stronger. He wasn't above placing himself at risk to make her a better general.

Irrelevant. She called on her power and drew in the first rank of ships lying in wait. She'd crush the Carteks one wave at a time.

A ship exploded in the distance. Not a Cartek ship, but one of her own.

Who had been in that ship? Had she known them?

She blinked, her eyes focusing on a Cartek skipper baring down on Kile's lax body, weapons aglow. Behind both, the *Star Renegade* hung limp in space as an unfathomable amount of ships circled them.

Inconsequential. Both Kile and the Star Renegade had done their part in disseminating the cloud.

But these were people she cared about. People who loved her. And she'd left them to die!

She had to. She needed to save Earth.

But not at any cost. Life was valuable. All life. People were not pawns to be used and thrown away for a cause.

Yes, they were.

No, they weren't.

Dania held her head and screamed.

She needed to obey orders. She needed to do everything in her power to save Earth.

Three large Cartek ships throttled smaller friendly targets. Dania raised her hands and the largest of the enemy ships exploded, careening into a second. The Earthan defenders swarmed over the third.

Her gut clenched.

But why? She should have been exhilarated.

A spike of pain carried over her bond, and she spun toward Kile. His uniform was burned through on his right side while Shivana engaged the Cartek who'd attacked him.

Kile's resonance grew weaker.

Alexander threw a blast at an oncoming ship. *"Let me help him!"*

She shouldn't allow it. All soldiers knew their place.

But she was no longer the cold, calculating general of the past.

She spun toward Alexander. "Save Kile!"

"I have him!" Alexander winked out and reappeared next to Kile. He wrapped himself around the commander, and they both disappeared in a flash of yellow light.

A blast lit up the side of the *Star Renegade*.

She'd left them their shields, but they wouldn't last forever. Kile was safe. Now she needed to do everything in her power to save her friends—without sacrificing Earth.

CAL'S STOMACH sank as the Carteks surrounded them.

So, this was it? The last chapter in the life of the *Star Renegade*.

He supposed it was inevitable, but part of him had still clung to the hope of growing old and dying on a small farm beside a river, away from interplanetary intrigue, space battles, and princes. It didn't seem like all that much to ask for.

A flash of light lit up the bridge, and Dania appeared. She grabbed on to the back of Ty's chair and clung to it, panting heavily and looking through the main viewscreen.

Her eyes were wild. Panicked.

And was that…*confusion?*

She muttered something under her breath. The air about her grew hazy.

"Cal!" Alanna shouted. "Geron's cruiser just fired on us again!"

"What?"

The ship jolted, and the overhead lights flickered on.

Cal looked up at the lights, gaping. "Do we have power?"

"Hell yeah!" Ethan said over the comm. "Full engines, baby!"

"Get us out of here!"

They were already banking up and over the oncoming ships, but when they passed those, more took their place.

The enforcer ships outside broke ranks, swirling up and around the other ships like the humans had.

Dania grunted, holding her temples and gnashing her teeth.

Doc placed his hand on her back. "What's wrong?"

She shook her head. "Why am I here? Why did I come back to this ship?" She grabbed on to the back of Ty's chair again. "This makes no sense. Nothing makes sense."

Doc ran a silver light over her forehead. "Stay with me, sweetie. Are you okay?"

"Did you just call me *sweetie?*" Dania straightened and glared at him, then her eyes widened and she thrust her fist toward the main viewing screen.

"Whoa!" Ty banked right as two ships throttling toward them crashed into each other and exploded.

One of the human ships flew toward a Cartek, guns blazing, but a Cartek ship shot from overhead, and the human ship broke apart. Just beyond, another Kever ship exploded. They were all flying like first-year cadets. Cal supposed facing insurmountable odds could do that to you.

Dania grabbed her temples again. "I can't control them," she whispered. "I've lost the link."

Three human ships cut away from the others and left the fight, heading back toward Earth at full throttle. Two Cartek ships gave chase. Five more friendly ships exploded in nearly consecutive blasts.

"This *is not* going well!" Ty spun them again as three more human ships cut from the battle and ran.

Dania dragged her fingers through her floating hair. "What are they doing?"

Cal added power to their shields. "It looks like they're panicking."

Alanna held her palm over her earpiece. "There's a comm coming through whether we like it or not."

Geron appeared on the side of the screen. "Dania, what's going on?"

"Something's wrong. I lost them. I can't control them." She pressed her palms against her temples. "I can't even feel them."

Geron's image rocked like the prince's cruiser had been hit. "I'm coming."

Cal jarred upright. "Wait. What? Coming? Coming where?"

A blue light flashed around them, and the king appeared on the bridge. His head nearly grazed the ceiling.

Dania's face turned crimson as she continued to hold her head. "I'm sorry. I'm so sorry."

Geron hissed before grabbing her and pulling her into his arms. He tucked his nose into the crook of her neck, and the temperature on the bridge spiked.

"Getting a little toasty in here," Ty said.

"Not to mention tight. This ship was designed for humans." Cal eased forward in his chair as Doc ran a scanner over the Kever and Dania.

It had seemed like she may have been coming out of her deranged stupor, but Geron was putting her right back into general-zone. Cal wanted to shove the Kever off her, to tell him that she was a better person free, but that would have been selfish. The galaxy needed her now more than he did.

Ty spun the *Star Renegade* again, wiping the sweat from his brow. "Okay, this was fun for a while, but the excitement is kind of wearing off."

Geron released Dania and she stepped away from him. Her hands formed fists as she faced the window.

In the distance, three larger, pyramid-shaped Cartek ships drifted into the fray, dwarfing the skippers. Where the hell had they come from?

Two more friendly ships exploded outside.

Ty banked up.

Cal tapped the comm to Engineering. "Ethan? How are the shields doing?"

Rachel's voice answered. "Um, Ethan says he's a little busy." Max barked twice somewhere behind her. "But he's keeping ahead of it. I'm not sure what *it* is, but he says he's on it."

That didn't make Cal feel as good as he would have hoped.

An enforcer ship took a hit to the wing and started spinning, venting gas crystals into space. They needed to do something, or they were all going to die out there.

Dania growled, her hands pulsing open and closed.

"What's wrong?" Geron hissed. "Get them back in line."

Dania sneered at the screen. "They aren't complying. They aren't even answering me. Their minds are firing flight neurons. Why won't they listen?"

Doc ran a scanner over her. "Maybe they can't hear you."

Dania turned to him. "What?"

"Your pathogen load is pretty high, but it's lessening by

the second. I think your natural pathogens are too busy to give you the magic mojo you need."

"What does that mean?" Geron asked.

Doc flinched. "Promise not to kill me?"

The king's expression darkened. "Tell me what's wrong!"

"I think the synthetic pathogens are tracking down and killing off the real ones. They're acting like white blood cells, fighting off an infection."

His eyes narrowed. "Primordial energy is not an infection."

Another ship exploded. Pieces of metal slammed against the screen, screeching as it scraped along the ship before floating off into space.

"The Cartek ships have breached the Earthan defense line," Alanna said.

"Good," Ty said. "That means the stationary cannons on the surface will be able to give us a hand."

"Yeah." Alanna held the edge of her station as the ship shook. "But it also means the larger Cartek ships can start firing on the planet."

Cal slowly turned to the screen, a chill settling over his skin despite the heat still coming off the Kever. Throughout the battle, small groups of ships seemed to create their own attack patterns.

From the outside looking in, Cal could easily see the Cartek ships sectioning off the Human and Kever forces into smaller groups.

Cal understood Geron and Dania's concern. This was how the Banes had failed the last time. They needed to keep a united front, but any front they'd had had disintegrated once the fighters had seen the true number of Carteks they were up against.

"Comm coming through," Alanna said.

Alexander's voice came over the line. "Ada, what's going on? Why have you left the cruiser?"

"Dania lost her link to the enforcers. I tried feeding her, but it hasn't helped."

"It's the artificial treatments." Alexander's comm fizzled when another ship exploded. "I'd feared they might cause a complication, but when she took such fast control, I thought I'd been wrong."

"Is there anything we can do?" Geron asked.

"I have an idea, but I don't want either of you expelling any more power unnecessarily. Meet me in the *Star Renegade*'s med bay."

"We're on our way."

Interesting that they both seemed ready to obey the commands of their healer. They really must have believed that Dania was the key to winning the war. With the way their people were panicking, it seemed they might be right.

Another explosion flashed outside, and the bridge shook.

Cal stood as Dania, Doc, and Geron headed for the door. "What do you want me to do?"

Dania shouted from the hall. "Get the ship out of harm's way, you fool! You're carrying your king!"

"There's no such thing as *out of harm's way*." Geron walked through the door. "Don't concern yourself with my safety. Do what you can to save Earth."

CAL TOOK a deep breath and released it slowly. *Don't worry about saving the king.* No problem. But if anything happened to Geron, and Cal managed to live to tell about it, every enforcer still breathing would be chasing him down, vying for the honor of spreading Cal's guts from one end of the galaxy to another.

Nothing new. Just an average day for the captain of the *Star Renegade*.

Ty sent the ship right, probably looking for a better vantage point. The explosions glimmered like star flies flashing behind a ship throttling at full burn, eating up the gas emissions.

Alanna wiped tears from her eyes. "They were following orders. They were fine." She wiped her nose. "Then all of a sudden, Dania wasn't there anymore." She looked out at the stars, like she could see the people dying inside those ships. "Without Dania controlling them, they all woke up like they'd been dreaming. Half of them didn't even remember the battle starting. They're lost and confused and just fighting to stay alive."

"You can feel them?" Cal asked.

"No, but Alexander can."

Cal didn't need to have a magical link to an enforcer to see that the pilots were a mess. Their problem was plain and simple: mind control.

Human soldiers learned to deal with their emotions. If they got cut off from their commander, they still had their wits and training. Yes, human pilots got scared, but they could use that fear to their advantage. The damn Kevers had to see now that having total control of another being was not the answer to all their problems.

Cal massaged his temples, warding off the dull ache threatening to take hold. "I get that they're scared. I just don't know what to do about it."

Alanna frowned at him. "You're a captain. Giving orders is your job. Just do it."

"*You* all barely listen to me, and I'm your actual captain."

"Yes, we do. When it counts, at least." She held on to the edges of her console as the ship shook. "Dania would have wanted you to help."

Yeah, the *old Dania* would have wanted him to help. The new Dania would probably filet him alive for the impertinence, despite Geron's orders to save Earth.

Still, Alanna had a point. He needed to channel authority, just like Dania had. New Dania was too strung up on the idea of using them like puppets. Cal's Dania understood the importance of her voice—how people simply needed authority and direction, not fear or mind control.

Alanna looked at her screen. "Another heartbeat just appeared in the med bay. I guess that means Alexander is here."

Good. If they really needed Dania to rein in all these Bane pilots, he genuinely hoped Alex could fix her. They'd all work on bringing both her and Alexander back from the abyss, if it were possible, when they weren't in danger of extinction anymore.

"Give me the comm to all ships," Cal said.

"All yours, boss."

"This is Calvin Espinoza on the *Star Renegade*. Dania DuBane is..." He looked at the door Dania, Doc and the Kever had left through. "Dania DuBane and King Geron are in my med bay. The king instructed me to protect Earth." Hey, look at that... It wasn't even a lie. "I need all of you to fall in line. We need to coordinate this attack and stop scattering like stardust."

"Comm coming in," Alanna announced.

"This is Shivana, Captain. I have a fleet of forty ships following me. Awaiting orders."

"Shiv!" Ethan called from Engineering.

Cal smiled. "Nice to have you, Shivana. Cluster about the *Star Renegade*. I'd like to give your sponsor a little cushion."

The comm pinged again and Orion's voice came through. "I will be the one protecting the *Star Renegade*. Our king deserves a commander, not a..."

"Yo!" Cal shook his head.

The last thing he needed was Orion offending the woman who'd won the shooting competition. Still, he never thought he'd see the day when enforcers would lobby for the honor of protecting a smuggling ship.

"No point in fighting over me. It looks like Orion has fewer ships. Let's let him form a little wall while everyone regroups. Shivana, I need you to help lasso in anyone else flying on their own. You're the most talented pilot out there. We can really use your expertise."

"Understood, Captain."

Cal repeated his orders to fall in, and Shivana grouped as many stragglers as she could, but most of the ships flew in haphazard rings, looking more like they were trying to keep themselves from getting killed than fighting a battle.

The larger Cartek ships moved forward, firing massive cannons that shot right past the fighters and into Earth's atmosphere. Planetary defenses engaged, and bright flashes lit up the stratosphere.

Skies, Cal hoped none of those shots were getting through to the surface.

Either way, though, Earth's defenders were still outnumbered. They may only have been buying Earth some time, and it didn't look like anyone on Earth was evacuating. Probably because they had nowhere else left to go.

Cal's stomach clenched. The smart thing to do would be to run. All of his crew was onboard. Even Dania and Alexander. Geron would be pissed at Cal, but at least they'd all be safe.

Cal blinked and shook away the thought. Despite the reality that the king would probably kill them all, the fight was here. Geron, for all his annoying, pompous, self-centered rhetoric, had been right. Running was foolish. The Carteks would simply claim Earth and then track down and kill everyone else. This insanity had to stop.

Cal flicked a glance at the door again. He'd half-wished that Doc hadn't gone to the med bay to meet Alexander. Peter had no battle training, but he always managed to keep a clear head. He could figure out anything.

"Cal." Alanna watched him from the nav station. "You once told me that I could do anything, that I was stronger than the rest of you. I appreciated the vote of confidence, but

I always knew that wasn't true. Any strength I had came from you—from your love of this ship and everyone on it. I trust you, Cal. And everyone out there will, too."

Ty sniffed, pretending to wipe tears from his eye. "That was beautiful." He placed his hands on the controls and propelled the *Star Renegade* up and over another scan beam. "Ditto what Alanna said, boss. How about you stop over-thinking things and kick some alien ass?"

That actually sounded like a really good plan.

A flash of light lit up the screen, held, and then winked out.

Cal rubbed the spots from his eyes. "What in Jupiter's moons was that?"

"A scan hit us." Alanna typed on her console. "I can't tell if it did anything."

Outside, the three larger, pyramid-shaped ships were all but ignoring the fighters and seemed to be focused on round after round of shots directed at the planet. They dwarfed the *Star Renegade*, though, and everything else out there.

They'd have to worry about the scan later.

"Patch me through to the *Oliganton*."

"You're on," Alanna said.

"This is Calvin Espinoza on the *Star Renegade*. I trust you know Geron and Dania are both onboard my ship?"

"Affirmative," a woman's voice said. "You will back away from the fighting and get the king a safe distance from the battle."

Ty huffed a laugh. "Sounds like they're more worried about coming out of this with their precious last Bane than actually winning the battle."

"Well, then, they're in for a rude awakening." Cal tapped

the comm. "Negative, *Oliganton*. I have direct orders from Geron to save Earth. Who am I speaking with?"

There was a slight pause. "Commander Katana."

"Fine, Commander. If you'd like me to patch you through to our med bay to confirm that order with your king, I'd be happy to do so."

Another pause. "Negative. What are you proposing, Mr. Espinoza?"

"Those three larger ships are targeting the planet. Do you think you can take them out?"

Another bomber fired before Commander Katana answered. "If all three of those Cartek bombers change their focus to us, that could be problematic. Not insurmountable, but problematic."

Two massive bolts of light shot from the center of the three Cartek pyramids. Each bolt blotted out the smaller ships that moved out of the way of the blasts.

"The heat reading from those shots is off the charts," Alanna said. "Anyone who gets in the way of those bolts will be incinerated."

Planetary defenses met the bolts, exploding them over the atmosphere. Cal didn't know much about Earth's defenses, but he hoped they had enough tech to continue stopping the barrage.

Cal tapped the comm again. "What are your orders from Dania, *Oliganton*?"

"To hold back in reserves until needed."

And Dania was otherwise occupied in the med bay, unable to retract that order.

Cal took a deep breath. The enforcers' totalitarian need to follow orders to the minutia simply wouldn't work if their leadership faltered. This was probably one of the big reasons the Carteks had nearly wiped them out this time. Why in the name of the stars hadn't the enforcers owned up to that reality?

"I know you want to follow orders, but Geron basically put me in charge. Are you ready to accept that?"

"Within reason, Mr. Espinoza."

"Do you agree that you are the best one to engage those ships?"

"Of course."

Then blast it, take some initiative! "The Carteks seem to be pretty interested in the *Star Renegade*. I'm going to fly close to take some of their fire. That should give you room to swoop in and give them hell."

"Negative, Mr. Espinoza. Protect the king."

"*Negative* back atcha. We're going in. If you want to protect your king, then take out one of those ships." Cal severed the comm.

Ty snickered. "Are we about to do something Kile would call *reprehensibly foolish*?"

"You bet your ass we are. Are you feeling up to it?"

"I haven't gotten a chance to be tired yet."

But they *would* get tired eventually. Too bad Cal couldn't offer them time to sleep.

Rachel's voice came over the comm. "Oh! Tiredness is something I can help with. Coffee, anyone?"

"Yes!" Cal and Ty shouted.

"I'd like a hot cocoa," Alanna said. "Extra on the cocoa."

"You got it! Did I ever tell you guys I used to be a barista?"

Of course she'd been a barista. And a hundred other things that Cal never would have thought would be useful.

"Feel free to use my kitchen. Remember to use the stabilization table so you don't burn yourself."

"Geez, Cally. You act like I've never been in a battle before."

The comm flicked off.

Ty rolled his shoulders. "I don't know what I'm more excited about: fresh coffee or making fools out of these Carteks."

Cal stretched his back. "Let's do both."

"Roger that." Ty turned and fired right at one of the larger Carteks ships.

In the distance, an explosion lit up space before getting extinguished from lack of air. Cal couldn't tell if that had been a friendly or a Cartek. There were just too many ships and countless individual battles going on out there.

They moved closer to a pyramid and Cal shot off a battery of laser fire. Lasers wouldn't do much against anything that big, but all they were doing was trying to get their attention. If they were firing on the *Renegade*, Katana would have the best chance of getting the better of one of the bombers.

A shot cut right over their bow, rumbling the *Renegade*.

Ty flinched. "That was a little close. Sorry about that."

"Close is fine. Just don't let them hit us."

The Cartek behemoth on the far right cut away from the others and headed straight for them.

Ty punched his fist in the air. "It worked!"

Alanna adjusted her earpiece. "Yeah, but now they're firing those big guns on us, too."

"Keep a step ahead of them." Cal knew that was a foolish thing to say, but Ty didn't come back with a quip. There wasn't much to say when they'd just purposely placed themselves in a situation where they'd be the primary target of a monstrosity probably built to destroy worlds.

CHAPTER 38
DANIA

DANIA GROWLED, grinding her teeth as the walls of the med bay shook around her. "This is foolish! I need to be in the battle."

Alexander pulled a treatment bag to the side of her bed. "I do believe you were the one complaining you'd lost the link to our soldiers."

"They should listen, anyway," Geron said. "They are trained to comply."

"The enforcers are, but not the humans." Peter attached a tube to the treatment bag. "Fear is an unfortunate thing. People want to live. It's a natural instinct."

Geron's lips thinned. "That does not apply to enforcers."

"Well, from what I saw, the enforcers want to comply. The problem is that they're not getting the commands fast enough to follow your orders before the next threat hits them."

"Which is why they need to be controlled," Dania said.

Peter shrugged. "There are other alternatives."

"There are not," Geron said. "Disjointed troops are why my father's empire failed. We need unification."

"That's what we're doing." Alexander placed a needle in Dania's arm.

She winced, gritting her teeth. "I don't need artificial treatments. You said the human amalgamation was the problem."

"We can't get the artificial pathogens out of your system," Peter said. "So, my boy Alex came up with a brilliant idea."

Alexander started the treatment. "The last set of artificial pathogens took root in your bloodstream and then fought off Geron's real primordial energy. Our hypothesis is that a full feeding, while at the same time giving you a treatment, will make them both equal, and they'll work together, rather than fighting each other."

Geron looked at Dania, then Alexander. "Are you sure this is safe?"

Alexander grimaced. "For you, yes. There is no reason to think that the treatment would affect you while feeding. For Dania..." He shook his head. "I simply don't know, but it's all we could come up with, and we're out of time."

Dania's chest fluttered. This might not be safe for *her*? What did that mean? Could she die? Or worse, could she degrade back toward humanity again? Neither were acceptable.

Those thoughts were weak, though. They were the result of the artificial amalgamation fighting the natural, life-giving energy of her sponsor. Alexander was right. Geron was the important person in this equation. Dania was simply a tool, and she had been created to serve, no matter what might come of her.

Geron sighed. "Fine." He stroked Dania's cheek with his fingertips. "Are you ready?"

"Always." But the trepidation still fluttered over her chest.

She'd always been prepared to do her duty, but this newfound fear, these odd thoughts of self-preservation, were things she was more than ready to leave behind.

Geron pulled her into his arms while Alexander adjusted the tubes leading to Dania's veins. Sweet heat poured over her, and her head lolled back as her body opened, accepting all Geron offered.

Deep inside, something within cried out, clawing and screaming, begging him to stop.

She set her jaw, forcing the specter of weakness down. She was Dania DuBane. She was beyond humanity, and she refused to succumb.

THE *STAR RENEGADE* shook as a blast grazed them, then another blast sliced through space just on their port side.

Maybe drawing the larger ship's attention hadn't been the best idea.

"Oh, boy." Alanna adjusted her headset again.

"What is it?" Cal asked.

"Ships. Lots and lots of ships. They're all throwing Cartek signatures. They're advancing from deep space on multiple sides." A map appeared on Cal's side of the main viewing screen. "They're coming from all angles. We're getting sandwiched in."

The interior comm pinged and Rachel's voice filled the bridge. "Cally, I can't find the grinder for the coffee beans."

Seriously?

Cal tapped the comm. "Not a good time, Rachel."

"Okay, geez, I'll keep looking."

Cal gritted his teeth as the massive number of dots started to blend and melt together, almost like they were creating a cloud of their own. The new ships were creating a box, and most of Geron's forces, including the *Star Renegade*, were trapped inside.

"They have us surrounded."

Cal was supposed to save Earth, but he couldn't do that if they were dead. He needed to get to the sidelines to get a better view, not stay trapped in the middle of a bloodbath. "Shivana. Target those oncoming ships. We're going to try to get Geron out of here."

"Affirmative. Save the king. Orion, keep…"

The commander's voice filled the comm. "Do not assume I would not protect my king, Lieutenant."

Shivana laughed.

Yes…that was *definitely* a laugh.

"I wouldn't think of it, Commander, but understand if that ship takes a single hit, I will personally take retribution out of your hide."

Out of his hide? Where had she even heard that? Could she be snapping out of it like Dania had?

Ethan snickered over the comm. "That's my kind of woman."

"Priority one text coming in from the incoming ships on the starboard front," Alanna said.

Cal frowned. It was his private channel. How'd they get that?

The text read:

Don't start shooting
until you see the
whites of their eyes.
Or the french fries
dangling from their fingers.

French fries? What did that mean?

Unless…

Cal snorted, grabbing his temples. He chuckled, then coughed, chuckling again.

"Don't lose it, boss," Ty said. "We kinda need you right now."

"I'm good." Cal hit the comm. "Shivana. Call off the attack on the ships on our starboard side."

"Why?"

"I'll explain later. Make a defensive line and get ready to hit the ships advancing from sector seven."

"Yes, sir."

Did she just call him *sir*?

Orion cut in. "I refuse to break off the attack on the imminent threat. Those ships are unidentified, and they look heavily armored."

"I get that," Cal said. "Consider it intuition. Give me a moment to confirm."

"A moment? How dare—" His voice scratched into a blast of static.

"That was me," Alanna said. "He wasn't being constructive. And I also don't really like him."

Cal flicked a glance in her direction. Coming from Alanna, that might as well have been a curse. Maybe Rachel was rubbing off on her.

Her eyes widened. "A new comm is coming in from our starboard." Alanna sat straighter in her seat. "Here it comes."

The screen split in two and Glenn's rosy cheeks and balding head appeared. "Cal, Cal, Cal! Exciting stuff going on out there. You have me all in a tither!"

Glenn was one of the most notorious traders in the

galaxy. He was based out of Walker Station and had his hands in everything from pirated goods to high-stakes gambling. The last time they'd had seen Glenn in person, Cal had traded a dangerous piece of tech for several cases of oranges to bring to the colony of Kirato.

"Glenn, where the hell are you?"

"Safe and sound, watching all the excitement from about ten lightyears away. I have to say the odds are twenty-six to one against you. But my money is always on the *Star Renegade*."

"You're running bets on the war?"

"Don't be mad. It's just good business." He waved a french fry at the screen. "But I also like to protect my assets, so to speak." He took a bite of the french fry. "There are a little over three hundred heavily armored *stingray* sniper ships headed your way. Don't let their size fool you. They are piloted by ex-military. All dishonorably discharged and have been working for me for years, but they still have family on Earth. The Carteks won't know what hit them. Good luck, Cal, my friend."

The screen winked out.

"Whoa." Alanna looked closer at the screen. "That's a lot of ships, and he wasn't kidding. They're packing some heavy and very illegal artillery."

Yeah, that was good, but with the numbers still spewing out of the Cartek cloud, it probably wasn't enough.

The stingrays shot past the *Star Renegade* and engaged the closest bomber. The pyramid stopped firing on Earth and the *Star Renegade* and refocused its weapons on defending itself from the fast-moving ships...missing every stingray and nearly hitting the *Star Renegade* in the process.

"Back us off!" Cal said. "We're not the target anymore, but that doesn't mean those bolts won't fry us!"

"Backing up." Ty waved his hands over the controls. "Do we engage or watch from the outside?"

The *Oliganton* spiraled, showering one of the bombers with orange sprays of light. The bomber Glenn's stingrays were attacking spewed ships of its own into the fray.

"Fabulous," Cal whispered. "Just freaking fabulous."

The ex-military pilots flew like a unified front, which was exactly what Dania had tried to accomplish with her mind control. Maybe that kind of military formation would help the rest of their ships to see what they were doing wrong until Dania could bring them back in line.

The third bomber edged around the battlefield and looked like it had a free run to Earth.

Cal tapped the comm. "Shivana. One of those pyramid-shaped ships is moving on Earth behind you."

"I see it. Turning to engage, but the incoming ships from deep space number more than a thousand. I suggest splitting our forces."

A thousand?

"Confirmed," Alanna said. "They're in two waves. The first set is nearly four hundred ships, coming from Earth's southeastern periphery."

Cal squinted toward Earth. Sparkles of light shone in space, approaching fast. *Dammit!*

Alanna continued. "The second wave is just behind them, coming from the direction of Z8."

Cal looked over his shoulder at her. "Z8?"

"Yeah. It's a massive block of cloaked ships. Cal, I think it's the Cartek blockade. Scans are inconclusive, but with the size and formation I'm seeing, it looks like at least twelve hundred more ships flying tight and unified."

Cal's breath hitched, and his eyes started to burn.

How could they possibly defend Earth against that many ships?

He took a deep breath and released it. Panicking wasn't going to do them any good. "ETA?"

"It looks like less than two hours. Holy heck, they're burning hot and fast."

"I guess they heard about the party and want to join the fun," Ty said.

The bomber fired five consecutive shots at the planet.

Cal hit the comm. "Shivana, engage the bomber."

With any luck, Glenn's hired guns would make short work of their initial target and then help eradicate the rest. Destroying the bombers would at least give them a chance.

In the distance, Shivana's fighters changed course. "What about the incoming Cartek reinforcements?"

"Alanna says they're two hours out. Those bombers can decimate Earth in that time. Let's deal with who's here now. We still have Geron's cruiser and fresh pilots when the next wave gets here."

"Confirmed," Shivana said. "We are targeting the bomber. Orion, stay with the king."

"How dare you even insinuate I wouldn't..." Orion faded to static again.

"Oops." Alanna twisted controls on her panel. "I really don't like that guy."

Flashes of light and explosions lit up the main screen as Cal looked to his left. "Ready?"

"Do I have a choice?" Ty burned the engines, swirling in and out of smaller ships engaged in dog fights.

"Orion wants to talk to you," Alanna said.

Cal bet he did. "Let it through."

A small image of the commander appeared on the screen. "I feel compelled to remind you that the king is still aboard your ship. He gave you an order, but he must be protected. Fall back."

Easier said than done, when it seemed like the entire Cartek fleet was pointed right at them.

CHAPTER 40
DANIA

DANIA GROANED, her body shaking as Geron eased her back to the bed. The room spun and Dania rubbed her eyes. Her fingers tingled, but was the odd sensation ghosting over her skin primordial energy, ready to be unleashed, or a new weakness they'd have to deal with?

Peter ran a scan over Geron's forehead. "You look good, Your Highness-ness. Everything feel like it normally would?"

"I'm fine. How is my Dania?"

Alexander waved his palms over her, and a cool rush of air floated across her skin. Her heart, then her stomach, pricked like tiny sparks igniting within.

"She's fine. I see no rejection or sign of one pathogen trying to dominate another." Alexander removed the tubing and placed a bandage on her arm. "I'd be cautious, though. Don't throw commands unnecessarily. Test for control and then use your powers in moderation."

Dania closed her eyes and reached out. She could sense the pilots in their ships, feel their fear. Most of their hearts beat erratically and their breathing was unsteady. No wonder so many had broken ranks.

She sought out Kile and found jumbled, lost thoughts. "Kile is still unconscious?"

Alexander nodded. "He's safe. I treated him, but he's severely weakened. He'll need a feeding before he returns to service."

Unfortunate. She now had other new commanders in her service, but none she trusted like Kile. Sending herself, Kile, and Alexander out as bait along with the *Star Renegade* had scattered the cloud, as she'd hoped, but she'd feel the sting of losing Kile, even temporarily.

She searched through the ships battling around her and found Shivana.

A *whoosh* of relief reached through the connection.

"General! We're working in small units, bringing down the Cartek ships, but they just keep coming. It's like there's no end to their numbers."

Dania could sense movement, probably Shivana engaging in battle.

"We have new targets arriving on every front, General, as well as a small, unified force following the *Star Renegade*'s direction. Other than that, Orion and I have been scrambling to bring order."

They were struggling. Her weakness had caused this, but no longer.

Dania's hands formed fists. "I'm going to pull you back together. You need to be made an army again."

"That would be preferable. You are a better leader."

Dania scanned the area about her lieutenant. Shivana had the largest number of ships fighting alongside her. More so than even Orion. "You've done a good job, Shivana. You do your sponsor proud."

Another swirl of emotion. "Thank you, General."

Interesting that so much emotion—possibly pride—came through. It was as if there were something more in Shivana's life than had been there before. A sense of singularity.

Dania would concern herself with this later. Anything that drained her lieutenant's focus was a problem, but it was not an immediate concern if the emotion made her stronger.

Dania steadied her breathing and reached for the fresh power swirling through her cells. One mind blended with hers and then the next. She called to the enforcers on the outer edges of the fray and drew back those who'd fled. Cowardice would not be rewarded. She rearranged the ships, placing those who'd run at the front of the battle.

"Do you have control?" Geron asked.

A smile crossed her lips. "Yes."

Finally, she'd be able to draw blood.

The ship about them rocked.

"Have we been hit?" Geron asked.

"Just a graze," the doctor said. "Don't worry. The *Star Renegade* is tougher than she looks."

Geron turned to Alexander. "We're returning to my cruiser. This craft has become too much of a target."

Geron wrapped his arms around Dania and the wide eyes of the doctor disappeared in a flash of white light before Geron's command deck appeared around her.

In the distance, the *Oliganton* bore down on one of the bombers, while the *Star Renegade* whisked up and over a set of skippers firing on them. It was possible the Carteks thought Dania and Geron were still on board. She could use that to their advantage.

Dania moved to the center of the deck.

It was time to end this.

THE *STAR RENEGADE* rumbled as a ship exploded just off their port bow. Cal ran a quick scan. So far, they were holding together.

"We have about ninety minutes until the first wave of Cartek reinforcements show up," Alanna said.

Ty cursed under his breath.

Cal didn't blame him. They were barely holding their own with this batch, and the new reinforcements wouldn't be tired.

Around them, the Bane ships stopped firing. They seemed to freeze in space, gliding like all of their pilots had passed out at the same time.

Cal leaned closer to the screen. "What the hell?"

The door opened and Doc stepped onto the bridge. "Geron and Alexander took Dania back to his cruiser." He stepped over to the Engineering station and tapped on the panel.

"How's Dania?" Cal asked.

"Her hair is floating and she looked like she was excited to start killing people." He grimaced. "Sorry, Cal."

Cal lowered his eyes. It wasn't all that unexpected, but he'd dared to hope that she'd keep a few molecules of her humanity.

"If she's okay, what's that all about?" Cal pointed to the frozen ships. One exploded as the Carteks, it seemed, figured out something was wrong.

Glenn's ex-military stingrays whipped around the free-standing skippers, pulling away from the farthest pyramid-shaped bomber they'd been attacking. They formed a sharp, triangular formation and headed in Shivana's direction as the first bomber they'd been attacking exploded in a blinding blast before space snuffed the fire.

"Yes!" Ty stood, punching his fist in the air. He high-fived Cal before taking to the controls again, ducking below two Cartek ships.

Cal turned back to the screen. "But what about...?"

Around them, every enforcer-manned ship woke up and turned, throttling at full power and aimed at the center bomber. The non-enforcer Bane ships followed in close formation.

"Holy stars over Jupiter." Alanna held her hand over her mouth. "Are those ships flying as close as they look?"

Doc cursed. "They sure are. My readings are showing less than a foot away from each other. That kind of tactical flying at those speeds is suicidal."

It wasn't suicidal if they were all being flown by the same pilot.

"It's Dania, isn't it?" Alanna said. "Can she do that? I mean, control them all like that?"

Doc adjusted a dial on his screen. "Apparently, she can."

The ships flew like a single unit, swirling around the

bomber and narrowly missing the scores of ships trying to defend.

"What's going on?" Ethan asked from Engineering.

"Too much," Cal said. "Just keep those engines humming."

The engineer most likely wanted intel on his favorite enforcer. But Cal honestly wouldn't have been able to pick Shivana's ship from any of the others. It was like someone had woven a blanket out of Bane fighters and threw it at the bomber.

"Hold on," Doc said. "I've got your girl, Ethan. She's still out there with about twenty Bane ships and Glenn's reinforcements. I guess Dania left them to slow the third ship down while she hit the center one."

The enforcer ships fired, igniting the stars with an array of artillery that shone like a sun, before cutting hard angles and flying away.

Cal patted Ty's back. "I'm thinking we should back off."

"I'm on it, boss."

They arced left and space erupted in flames as the second bomber exploded.

"Whoa!" Ty shielded his eyes. "We almost got toasted."

Three of the stingrays popped out of the blast zone, two with scorch marks on their tails.

Cal gritted his teeth. They were fighting for the same side. It would have been nice if Dania or Alexander had warned them that the bomber had been about to blow.

Then again, she probably couldn't care less about the ex-military pilots, and the *Star Renegade* had probably outlasted its usefulness. She'd claimed she'd wanted to command from Cal's bridge to have more maneuverability, but maybe all she'd wanted was to use them as part of her plan to get the cloud to dissipate.

Ty banked around two friendly ships as the fleet cut back and headed for the last bomber. The scattered Cartek ships swarmed around them, but the Bane ships seemed to ignore the smaller vessels. Several friendly skippers exploded, but Dania seemed to aim dozens of them at their target, not worrying about casualties.

Another friendly ship exploded. Then another.

"Can't she see she's losing ships?" Alanna asked.

"Casualties aren't a concern for enforcers," Cal whispered.

"Cal's right," Doc said. "Geron wants this war won. She'll do anything it takes to get that done."

All the Bane ships shot at once, including Shivana's ships, who now seemed to be locked in with the others. The ex-military shot a few seconds later and then cut away. Like an automated video game, all the Bane ships cut right angles up or down at the same moment, and the last bomber erupted in flames.

Doc and Alanna *whooped*, hugging, while Ty cut around a Cartek ship. Cal fired, taking one more out.

"That's it, right?" Ty asked. "They're beat."

Cal pursed his lips. "There's still a ridiculous amount of ships out here. They just aren't as big."

"They're pulling back a bit, though," Doc said. "It looks to me like losing the bigger ships spooked them."

Cal tapped into the comm. "If anyone out there is still willing to talk to me, can I get a casualty report?"

A ping sounded.

"It's one of the ships Glenn sent," Alanna said.

"Put it through."

A small square appeared on the lower left of the screen and the face of a man with graying hair and kind eyes appeared. "Apologies, Captain Espinoza. This is Captain Tillan of the United Traders Defense League. Glenn said you were our point person, but we saw the bogies and laid in."

Cal smiled. The man's voice was curt and no-nonsense, a direct contradiction to his grandfatherly face.

"That's all right, Tillan. We appreciate the help." It wasn't like Cal would have told ex-military guys to do anything differently.

"We've lost one ship," Tillan said. "Coby. Good man. I'll contact his family once we make the rest of these squids pay for it. Can I take it we should engage the stragglers?" One of the military ships fired, snapping the wings off a Cartek skipper making a run on the *Star Renegade*.

Dania's ships finished their straight runs and cut a hard turn toward the remaining Cartek ships in a single, unified movement. *Creepy*.

"Yeah, let's clean things up here." Cal adjusted the sensitivity settings on his panel.

Doc rubbed his chin. "This was the biggest battle we've ever been in, but did it really feel like thousands of ships to you?"

"It did to me," Ty said.

Cal eased back in his chair. "We could only see part of the battle. There were plenty of explosions in the distance."

Doc continued to rub his chin. "Yeah, I guess. But I never felt as overwhelmed as I expected."

"Speak for yourself," Ty said. "You weren't flying through them all."

Captain Tillan's stingrays cut back and took out five more skippers before Dania's ships engaged. When the last ship exploded, whoops and hollers sounded off from the ex-military pilots.

Dania's ships drew back and formed a perfect square, hanging in space.

Cal shivered. They were no better than robots. Even the non-enforcer Kever ships hung in close formation off the *Star Renegade*'s starboard bow, probably scared to death what Dania might do to them if they didn't comply.

Ty swiped back his sweaty bangs. "I can't believe it's over." He ran his fingers affectionately over the edge of the control panel. "You scraped by again, old girl. Mel always said you were a tough cookie."

Across the room, Alanna massaged her temples, taking slow, steady breaths.

Cal stood and placed his hand on her shoulder. "Are you okay?"

"Something's not right. These readings..." She shivered. "Something's just *off*."

Ty spun in his chair. "What do you mean? We won. Earth is saved."

"For now, it is." Cal crouched beside her so he could look up into her eyes. "Is it the ships you saw before? The ones coming from Z8?"

"No. They're still pretty far out but burning hard."

Ty cursed under his breath. "I thought we'd already fought those guys."

Cal stood and inched toward the main screen. Beyond Dania's freaky square of ships that hung in space like an empty picture frame, the stars shifted.

Cal squinted. He had to be seeing that wrong.

The yellow light on Ty's dashboard flashed three times. Ty tapped it, and it flashed again.

"Weird," Ty said.

"Another malfunction?" Cal asked.

"I don't know. I mean, of course there's a proximity alarm with all those ships out there, but we're still on red alert, so it should be ignoring the friendlies. It's almost acting like there's something bigger that we need to be aware of."

"Guys?" Alanna rubbed her shoulders. "I think there *is* something bigger."

THE STARS WAVERED in the distance, flaring like they'd become comets, and then they melted into another yellow-hulled bomber, this one dwarfing the others ten times over. Six massive, black openings appeared, and six new bombers spewed into space. Four fired on the Bane ships while the rest shot toward Earth.

Ty cursed, taking the controls again and backing off, bringing the *Star Renegade* far from firing distance. "What do we do, boss? That's a ridiculous amount of artillery."

One might say a *planet-killing* amount of artillery.

"The more important question is: where the hell did that giant ship come from? It seemed to just appear out of nowhere."

"I see no sign of a cloak or remnants of a cloud." Alanna looked out the main viewscreen. "But space looks strange. Something is wrong out there."

"I agree." Cal checked their shield ratings. "Can you get me a comm to Dania?"

Alanna's hands moved over her console. "I'm trying, but she's not responding."

Of course she wasn't. The *Star Renegade* was a single ship, one she was willing to sacrifice to lure the Carteks out of the cloud. They weren't part of her robotic army, so she probably had no need for them anymore.

Ty kept his attention on the screen. "What's the verdict, boss?"

What Cal really wanted to do was take the secret stairs down to his quarters and crawl into bed until this nightmare was over.

Ty's eyes were red.

Alanna's skin was puffy and pale.

Doc looked drawn.

How long had they all been out there? It seemed like an eternity, rather than a little over a day, but how many days had they been awake before that? They were all running on empty, which was not a good way to be when the enemy had just spewed out a slew of fresh ships.

"We need to rest," Cal said.

Doc rubbed his eyes. "It doesn't look like the Carteks have that problem."

Cal rubbed his own eyes. "They hit us hard with what looked like an unstoppable force, and we gave it our all trying to stop them. They kept their true numbers hidden—letting us waste our resources and tire out."

Doc nodded. "It's the same thing they did to the former king, just on a larger scale."

"And we fell for it again, even though we thought we were ready for it."

On the screen in the distance, Dania's ships cut into four units and each attacked a bomber. Glenn's ex-military guys in their stingrays had already homed in on the ship closest to the *Star Renegade*.

A deep numbness settled over Cal, like this was a bad dream that he hoped to wake up from. But if he stayed here much longer without making a decision, none of them would wake up.

He tapped the internal comm. "It's going to be close quarters, but I need everyone on the bridge."

The doors opened and Rachel walked in with Max in her arms. "I know, I know… I was supposed to bring coffee, but it took me forever to find the coffeemaker. And then all I could find were coffee beans…and you hid the grinder for some reason." She leaned against the wall. "You sure don't make it easy on a girl, Cally."

Ethan entered behind her and closed the door. "She's not lying. I found both her and Max with their heads inside the cabinets in your kitchen."

Cal spun his chair toward them. "How did you get here so fast?"

Ethan shrugged. "I know you, boss. This is the kind of thing that needs a meeting, so I stopped by the kitchen to grab Rachel and Max before I came up."

Was Cal really that predictable?

Of course he was, or the three of them wouldn't be there already.

Cal scanned their tired, pale faces. "You all know what we're up against."

"I'm staying." Alanna stood. "I don't know where my family is. They could be dead. They could be on Earth. I don't know, but it doesn't matter. There are people down there with no choice but to look up at the stars and hope someone out there is brave enough to save them." She wiped tears from her eyes. "Well, I may not be all that brave, but I'm going to fight for them."

"Then I guess you'll need a crack-shot pilot, ma'am." Ty gave her a fist pump.

"And an engineer." Ethan stuck out his fist and they both just looked at him. Ethan tilted his head. "Aww, come on. Don't leave me hanging."

Ty raised his fist. "Just messing with you, my friend."

Alanna skipped the fist bump and gave him a hug.

Rachel put Max on the floor then looked at Ethan. "Of course they want you. My Big Guy always said they'd all be dead without you." She folded her arms and looked at the battle in the distance. "This is going to call for lots of coffee. Which I can do—now that I've found all the supplies." She pointed at Alanna. "And cocoa. I got you, girl." She headed for the door. "I guess I better get on that."

Max garbled something, saluted Cal, and scurried out the door behind her.

Doc watched him leave. "I don't have anywhere else I have to be, so I guess I'm in."

Ty stretched his neck. "I don't know why you always ask us this question, boss. You know we're always with you."

Cal shook his head. "I didn't expect a different response, but I still didn't want to take anything for granted. You've all gone above and beyond anything you've signed up for."

Alanna eased back into her seat. "If we leave, and the Carteks take Earth, I'll never be able to forgive myself. This is humanity's fight. Everyone has a stake in this."

Doc nudged her. "Look at you getting all philosophical." He looked at Cal. "What's the game plan to, you know, not die?"

Cal turned back to the screen. "Let's be smart and take stock first."

More skippers burst from the smaller bombers, and the space around Earth again became alight with artillery.

"It's like we're starting all over again," Ty said.

Doc stood behind Cal and looked through the screen. "Not that I want to get back into the middle of all that right away, but what are we looking for?"

"I don't know. An opening? A place we can make a difference? There's no use flying in there and getting killed for nothing."

Doc tapped Cal's shoulder. "You've become wise in your old age, my friend."

Space became a blur as more ships shot out of the bombers. "How could they possibly have this many ships in reserve?"

"I bet they're drones," Doc said. "Look at the way they're flying. They aren't as precise as Dania's attacks, but they're not hesitating. There's no sign of fear. I don't think they're manned."

Which meant they probably analyzed movements like machines. They'd quickly pick up on the fact that all the Bane ships were being controlled by one person.

"Alanna, I need to talk to Dania."

She slipped into her seat. "I'll try. I may have a better chance if I just try to tap into someone else's computer on her bridge."

"Do what you need to do."

Ty glanced at her. "If you need help, let me know. I'll work my magic to get you through."

"I might need to take you up on that. My pings are reflecting right back at me."

"How rude," Ethan said.

Cal doubted Dania was even capable of understanding the concept of rudeness anymore. "Alanna, tape my voice so you'll have it when you get a comm through."

"Recording. Go ahead."

"Dania, it's Cal. Doc figures that most of the Cartek skippers are drones. They may even be AI piloted. I know you have control of your own enforcers, and they're lethal, but I think it might be best to randomize them, if you can."

"Is that even a thing?" Ethan asked.

Cal honestly wasn't sure. "If you can't randomize, I'd suggest setting Shivana and her team loose and letting her do some target practice. She may be able to do more damage that way than she would if she stayed under your control."

Cal wasn't sure how Dania would feel about that, but no matter how much of her memory had been erased, she would probably remember what a good pilot Shivana had been on her own.

"Got it," Alanna said.

Good. Now they had to find a way to get that message to Dania.

Cal switched helm control to his dashboard. "I'll fly for a bit. You help Alanna."

"You got it, boss." Ty left his seat and moved to Alanna's station. "Are you okay if I do my magic over here?"

She stood. "Be my guest." Alanna sat in the pilot seat next to Cal and rubbed his arm. "She's probably still under there, you know. Alexander, too."

Cal wanted to think the woman he loved still existed, but he knew the chances were slim. Especially after she'd thrown the *Star Renegade* right at the enemy with no way to escape.

"She came back to us," Alanna said. "I know it was only

for a few minutes, but she still came back. Something inside her remembered that this was home."

Maybe. Or it was another tactical enforcer reason they hadn't figured out yet. Cal wasn't sure he could stand another person he loved being murdered by the power of the Banes. He didn't want to give in to hope, only to find himself mourning her all over again.

"I'm in!" Ty tapped the edge of Alanna's console. "And message sent. She might be pissed at us, but Cal's voice is about to play on every speaker on that ship."

"Every speaker?" Cal banked down, taking the *Star Renegade* on the opposite side of the battle from Geron's cruiser.

Ty stumbled back to the pilot's station. "What are you doing, boss?"

"If Dania gets pissed, we don't want to be within range of her superior weapons systems."

Ty sat in his chair. "Good call."

"You're rubbing off on me."

Alanna replaced her earpiece. "Lots of chatter out there. Mostly the human pilots. Those bombers are getting too close to Earth. And…" She held her hand over her ear. "What in the name of Jupiter's moons is that?"

Cal groaned. "Please don't tell me there's something worse out here."

"I don't know what this is. It's just…strange."

"Define *strange*."

"Another big, funny-looking thing behind the remnants of the cloud. But it's not moving or anything. It might just be interference, or space dust from the battle." She swiped back her hair. "Sorry, I can't tell. I've never been in this big of a fight before. There's so much going on."

"Whatever it is, keep an eye on it and let me know if it moves."

"Roger that."

The last thing Cal needed was more surprises, but he knew they hadn't seen everything the Carteks had planned to throw at them, yet.

Alanna tapped on her screens. "Remember the Carteks still have those reserves heading toward the dark side of the planet."

Cal cursed, then steadied himself. "Try to get through to Dania again."

"I can try. Go ahead and talk. Maybe she'll listen this time."

"Dania, we have Cartek reserves coming in from behind Earth. If I understand how your power works, you need to be able to see what's coming. Please break off some of your ships and let them follow me to join Earth's defenses or the other side of the planet is going to be wiped out."

If there was any shred of the real Dania left, she'd send help. Stars, even General Dania should see the value in not letting the enemy swoop in on the other side of the planet!

"No answer," Alanna said.

"Dammit!" Cal shot a flair of old-fashioned metal shells over a pack of three attackers, and all three started drifting.

"Nice shooting, boss!" Ty flew between the two ships on the right.

"Yeah. It doesn't look like they're prepared for older artillery. Maybe they've never had anyone shoot bullets at them."

"The damage caused by metal shell munitions is very different from what's caused by lasers and plasma blasts," Doc said. "You may be onto something there."

"Too bad we don't have more." Cal tensed. They didn't have a ton of old munitions on board, but they were flying over the planet that had invented the stuff. "Alanna, send that little tidbit of info to Earth. They may have stockpiles of old ammunition down there that might be a game changer if they can get it loaded on ships in time."

"Roger that. Calling it in."

More and more vessels filled the viewscreen. It was getting harder to tell the difference between friend and foe with all the different kinds of ships. This wasn't his part of the problem, though. Dania, somehow, was doing a good job of sorting all this out. Cal needed to help the people on the other side of the world.

Cal flipped on the comm. "Shivana, are you able to answer?"

Outside, artillery flared, and needle-like shots sliced through space, nearly blinding him.

The comm engaged. "I'm here."

Thank the stars! "Are you and all your pilots unlinked from Dania, or whatever you call it?"

"We are in reserve, but we're currently autonomous, if that's what you're asking."

"We're heading to the other side of Earth. We have maybe forty-five minutes before the next wave of Carteks hit the dark side of the planet." Cal called up a visual of Earth's blue oceans and the edge of a place labeled *California* below them. "If my map skills are correct, Europe and Africa are going to get hit head-on by those fresh forces. We needed to give their defenses as much help as possible."

"Agreed," Shivana said. "We're heading there now."

Ethan leaned over Alanna's shoulder. "Shiv?"

"Shivana." The enforcer sounded slightly annoyed.

"Yeah, whatever. Listen, Shiv. Be careful out there, okay?"

Her ships shot away from the battle and formed a circle.

"Why should I be careful? I should be tactical. Pointed. Strong."

"Well, yeah, you could be all that. I know you're badass, but, you know, I want to make sure you come back."

Static crackled on the line. "Why?"

"Because I care."

Her ships formed a triangle formation.

"I..." The ships halted, drifting before Shivana's voice returned. "You be careful, too."

Shivana's ships turned, their engines flashing with yellow light as they headed for the other side of the planet. Dozens of Cartek skippers followed her.

Cal tapped the comm. "Shivana, you have incoming."

Her ships flipped up and over, engaging the Carteks.

That was a small force to send after her, though. Shivana could have taken that many on her own, without the squadron backing her up. The drones started exploding as Shivana's ships engaged.

"Boss?" Ty pointed to the screen. "Do you see what I'm seeing?"

Past the myriad of firing ships, one of the pyramid-shaped bombers picked up speed, steering around the battle.

"All those drones were a decoy so the real threat could get a head start. Dammit!" Cal pointed to the left. "Head around the other side of the battle. Let's see if he can get ahead of that bomber and slow them down."

Ty's eyes were wide. "By ourselves?"

He was right. They'd be severely outgunned.

"I know. It's crazy. But we have to try." Cal looked to the nav station. "Alanna, tap me into the defense network in

Africa or Europe or whoever on that side of the world will answer."

Below them, the blue ocean turned dark, and lights twinkled in the distance.

Ice flooded Cal's veins. All those lights were like a giant target to the Carteks screaming, *'Here are the people! Come drop a bomb on me!'*

"I have someone called Eurasia. I don't know who that is, but I'm putting it through."

"Perfect. Send Dania's royal codes so they know we're legit."

"On it." Alanna tapped a few keys on her dashboard. "Okay, go."

Cal tapped the comm. "Eurasia, this is Captain Calvin Espinoza on the *Star Renegade*. You have a massive attack heading in your direction. One bomber for now, but there may be more, and there is a fleet of ships coming from deep space. That is your immediate threat, but the Earth's normal rotation is going to spin you into something even worse in the next twelve hours or so. We are on our way with a battalion of enforcer and Bane ships, but it won't be enough. What kind of defenses can you get into the air?"

A woman with warm skin and straight, black hair, wearing a black uniform with a red-and-white stripe on her shoulder appeared on the lower left of Cal's screen. "Thank you for your assistance, *Star Renegade*. I am Comm Officer Skirika. We were monitoring the attack up until the Excelsior space station was destroyed."

Cal glanced at Ty. Excelsior had housed a ton of weapons meant to defend against this sort of attack. Then again, no one had ever dreamed of being hit with this much.

Skirika leaned closer to the screen. "I have been instructed to ask for terms of surrender."

"What?" Ty, Cal, Ethan, and Alanna said at the same time.

"The National Convention is monitoring the situation. They have switched their goal to saving as many lives as possible."

Cal gritted his teeth. What fantasy world were they living in? "Are they in assembly now?"

"Yes."

"I know this is irregular, but patch me in. Screw any protocols. They need to know what's going on up here."

"I-I can't do that."

"Did you get the codes we sent? We are speaking for Dania DuBane, the general out here trying to save all your hides. Do you think we're risking our lives out here for the fun of it?"

She straightened, taking a deep breath. "Give me a moment."

The screen blinked out.

Alanna swiped back her hair. "We're going to be close enough to engage that bomber in seven minutes."

Cal leaned closer to the glass. "Where's Shivana?"

"Still fighting the skippers."

Dammit!

Alanna touched the transmitter in her ear. "We just got a transmission from Captain Tillan. He's coming with a squadron of stingrays, but they're fifteen minutes out."

Cal looked out at the pyramid in the distance. "That's not going to be fast enough."

The screen came to life, showing a miniaturized hall filled

with seats arranged in a "U" pattern. Cal imagined his image was being shown on the main screen.

A man in the center stood. "You are now addressing…"

"Cut the crap," Cal said. "We don't have time for it. You have a planet-crushing force headed your way. Forget about surrender or any other foolishness going through your minds. Keveron is gone. Wiped out. Their entire race is clustered in a small number of ships in a secure location. No one else is coming but us."

The man in the center looked right at the screen. "Who is in charge out there?"

"For your immediate future? Me. In the next twelve hours or so, the Earth's rotation will turn you into the thick of the battle, where there are more ships and even more bombers to deal with. Then your lives will be in the hands of our new king, Geron Bane, and a host of enforcers larger than I've ever imagined could exist." Cal took a deep breath as they all paled. "Do not make the mistake of thinking surrender is an option. The Carteks decimated Keveron. They are out to destroy, plain and simple. They have no interest in survivors."

The man on the screen gulped. "Certainly they would want to avoid casualties on their own side. There must be a way to…"

"Get it out of your head that there is any humanity in the Cartek ranks. They're pissed that the king drove them out the first time. Do you remember what they did to our colonies all those years ago? What they did to the planets they've already decimated?"

The shadows of the dignitaries shifted nervously.

"Let me tell you, those were just appetizers for them. Keveron and Earth are the grand prize, and Keveron is already gone. Every single Cartek ship is now pointed at you."

The man on the screen and the shadows behind him flinched as Cal pointed at the screen.

Good. Cal had their attention. "I need every ship you have. I need every pilot. And if you can load them up with ancient artillery, that will be even better. If enemy skippers end up in the atmosphere, fight them with planes. Pull jets out of museums if you have to. Make no mistake, this is a fight for survival. They don't plan on leaving anyone alive."

A woman in the back part of the "U" stood and the camera zoomed in on her location. Her long, gold gown shimmered in the overhead lighting. "I am Becana Aratu, the President of the African Union. We have already scrambled our ships, and I just sent a transmission to get them loaded with any and all munitions." She turned to the others. "Now is not the time to think of ourselves. Any ships that you have been hiding from each other, any weapons you've been developing to gain advantage over your neighbors, must be pointed at our skies."

Cal had never heard of the African Union, but he already liked this lady.

A man stood three chairs to her right. "Have you offered the ships you have poised at our borders?"

Aratu lifted her chin. "Those were the first in the skies. They are space-worthy and already in our atmosphere."

The man gaped at her.

"Umm, Cal?" Alanna said. "We've got about three minutes."

"Listen, people," Cal said. "You need to get over your differences. Kill each other later, if you want to. Right now, we need to make sure we have a planet to fight over." The bomber grew larger on the viewscreen. "We'll be fighting up here for your right to live. I'd really appreciate it if you joined us." He tapped the comm, ending the transmission.

"Didn't you want to hear their answer?" Ty asked.

"It doesn't matter. We don't need the distraction."

A red circle appeared on the screen, marking off dozens of red lights leaving Earth's atmosphere. "It looks like those are the ships from the African Union. Do you want to talk to them?"

"No. Tell them to fight like their lives depend on it." There really wasn't anything else left to say. Cal looked over his shoulder. "Ethan, as much as I enjoy your company…"

Ethan tapped on his screen. "Yeah, already with you, boss. I'm opening a comm to Engineering so I can hear everything down there. So don't say anything mean about me."

Ty laughed. "We say mean things about you even when you *are* here."

"But only because you love me like a brother." Ethan smacked Ty on the head. "Fly like you mean it."

"I always do."

Ethan winked at Alanna before disappearing through the door.

Cal turned to Doc. "Do you want to get somewhere with a seat? It's going to get bumpy."

"And miss all the action? Nah. Anyway, I have more access up here than I do in the med bay. I'd rather be where I can do more damage."

"As long as it's damage to the Carteks."

Cal flinched. It wasn't all that long ago that Doc, manning the same station, had gotten thrown across the bridge. The crew had said he'd broken his neck. He'd been dead.

At the time, they'd thought Dania had saved him, but they'd later found out that it had been Alanna and her unknown Bane power that had brought him back.

Alanna was still on the bridge, but he'd rather not be faced with losing another member of the crew. Still, it was Doc's choice, and Cal would be a fool to think that the man's big brain wasn't an asset.

The door opened again, and Rachel stepped in with a tray of covered mugs. "Java orders are up." She seemed oddly calm for a woman delivering caffeine right before a space battle. She handed Ty and Cal each a mug with a straw sticking out of the top. "Be careful. You don't want to spill and short out any circuits or anything."

Ty accepted the drink. "Straws?"

"Yeah, well, I figured you two might be super busy with pilot stuff. Don't you need to keep your hands on the wheel and all that stuff?"

Ty held up his mug. "Well, that's actually super intuitive of you."

"Of course it is. I think a lot. I even let it cool a bit so no one got burned." She turned to Alanna. "And cocoa for my favorite girl. Not too hot, not too cold."

Alanna grabbed the mug, taking a sip. "Mmm, perfect. Bless your heart."

"I know. I'm very blessable." She handed one to Doc. "I gave Ethan his mug in the hallway. Are you going to be okay without a cup holder?"

A bark filled the bridge and Max appeared. He reached for the mug, opening and closing his front paws.

"Okay, then." Rachel handed Max the mug. "Instant coffee holder." She turned to Cal. Her hair was sticking out in a few places and her eyes were puffy. Lack of sleep, it seemed, was getting to all of them. "I'm going to head down to help Ethan. If you need anything, holler."

Ethan's voice came over the comm. "Rachel, this coffee is amazing!"

"I know!" she said, walking out the door.

Cal smiled. He loved his crew's ability to add a little levity, even with the bomber getting larger and larger in the screen. Dania and Orion—and probably Kile, even in his more human state—wouldn't stand for it. But this friendship…this *camaraderie* was what made them human. This was what they were fighting for. This crew deserved their moments of fun, after all they'd been through this year.

"One minute to being in range of their guns." Alanna slipped her mug into the holder on her dashboard.

"Aren't we well within range of their big cannons?" Ty asked.

"Yeah," Doc said, "but we're little stars in a big galaxy. They probably don't see us as a threat, so why waste the artillery when the goal is a bigger, easier-to-hit target?" He took the mug from Max. "I appreciate the enthusiasm, but there are more important things you can do rather than hold my coffee."

Max chittered something at him.

Doc nodded. "Yeah, I'm sure. Why don't you go help Ethan and Rachel in Engineering?"

Max shook his head and reached for the cup again.

"Well, okay," Doc said. "But be ready to make a break for Engineering if anything happens, okay?"

Max saluted before holding the cup again.

Outside, the African Union ships engaged the rogue bomber. The massive ship seemed to ignore them. They looked like fleas jumping around on a dog.

They were going to need a hell of a lot more ships.

Alanna rolled her shoulders and stretched her arms. "I love you guys. You know that, right?"

Ethan's voice came over the comm. "It wouldn't be a battle without Alanna telling us she loves us."

"Well, it's true." She adjusted her earpiece.

"What's going on?" Rachel's voice joined Ethan's.

"Alanna loves us."

"Love you, too, babe!" Rachel called over the speaker.

Max barked, waving Doc's coffee.

"Max is right," Cal said. "It's time to get serious."

"We're always serious!" Ethan said, but he still turned down his comm from the Engineering side.

A long, straight beam of light shone from the side of the bomber.

Ty banked the ship up. "Looks like they're about to start shooting!"

"Get in front of those targeting rays." Cal looked at Alanna. "Tell the AU ships to do the same. We need to distract them as much as possible until Earth sends more help."

Ty glanced at him. "You really want me to get in front of the big ship with the big guns?"

"Got any better ideas?"

"Not really."

"Just be ready for some fancy piloting if they shoot."

Ty leaned over and sipped his coffee through the straw. "Whew! That's a hearty brew." He clapped his hands. "Okay, let's go!"

Explosions lit up the bomber from the other side.

"Shivana is here!" Ty threw his fist in the air and *whooped*. "Glad to see you, girl!"

Cal didn't expect Shivana to answer, but he could just imagine what was going through the enforcer's mind.

"The cavalry has arrived," Doc said.

Alanna squinted at her screen. "She's lost a lot of ships."

Cal checked the screen. Alanna was right. Nearly half of Shivana's ships were missing.

"They're still enforcers," Cal said.

But that might not be enough.

DANIA GRITTED her teeth as another one of her ships exploded. Her people were doing significant damage, but the bombers seemed to open a few times an hour, spewing fresh ships into the stars.

"Should we call the *Oliganton* back into combat?" Orion asked.

An interesting question. Calvin Espinoza had ordered the former king's cruiser into battle without her permission. It had done its part to weaken the enemy, but she'd called it back into reserves. The remaining ships had easily destroyed the bomber the *Oliganton* had been targeting, though. Maybe cycling the cruiser in and out of the battle would be a good idea.

The doors behind her opened, and she sensed Geron before he actually entered.

He moved to her side. "This is taking longer than I hoped."

"These things take time, Ada."

He glanced at her, and her chest thickened.

She felt...*small*. She'd never felt small beside him. She'd always been his equal. Of course, that was before she'd been weakened by the human doctor's heinous amalgamation. It might take years for those pollutants to cycle out of her blood.

Once this battle was won, she'd get their top scientists working on a way to purge her of these foreign contaminants. She needed Geron to believe in her again.

Another ship exploded. Then another.

Geron flicked a glance at her. "Are you growing weary?"

"No." She reset her footing. "Their numbers never seem to wane. I need to concentrate."

And, possibly, consider the smuggler's suggestion to randomize her attack patterns. She'd discounted the idea, furious that his voice had echoed from speakers all over her command deck, but her normal, full-on attack strategies didn't seem to be working.

She took the ships on her right and coordinated their movements before gritting her teeth and sending each pilot separate orders. They swirled in an erratic pattern, and explosions lit up the stars, littering space with Cartek skippers. The crew jumped to their feet, cheering.

Dania resisted the urge to turn and look at her sponsor, but she could feel a wave of warmth spread through her bond. It was familiar and achingly *right*. She needed to get back to a place where he always felt that way around her.

The communications officer stood. "General, we have a communication coming in from Shivana on the other side of the planet. She is asking for an additional squadron of ships. Do we comply?"

Another Kever ship exploded. Dania channeled her power and took out seven Cartek skippers before the embers of her lost ship winked out.

Her nostrils flared. She'd sent Shivana to the dark side of the planet so Dania wouldn't have to be distracted. Her lieutenant was more than capable of winning such a small battle.

"We will not comply. She is only dealing with one bomber. We are dealing with five. She should be coordinating with Earth's defenses."

The comm officer's brow pinched, and she looked at Geron. "Is that the message I should relay?"

Heat coursed through Dania's veins, and Geron stepped between her and the officer. He met her gaze, and a shimmering sound barrier wrapped around them.

"I remind you, my Dania, that we need all of our best people. We will deal with any insolence later."

She took a cleansing breath to try to calm herself, but it didn't work as well as a clean execution would have to ease her anger. Ada was right, though. The officer was usually competent. Their crew may have simply been getting tired.

The shimmering wall around them vanished, and Dania addressed the comm officer. "Relay the message as I said. Shivana is more than capable of…"

"Her numbers are dwindling," Orion said, looking up from a screen. "If we don't send help, we risk losing all her pilots." He straightened, his eyes fixing on Dania. "That could mean the *Star Renegade* would also be destroyed."

Was that a challenge? If he was testing her, he was in for disappointment.

Dania held his gaze. "Victory is the goal. All pilots, all *ships* are expendable if our sponsor's goals are obtained."

Orion flicked a questioning glance at Geron.

"I concur." Geron stared into the chaotic array of ships outside. "Shivana and the *Star Renegade* both have their orders. Leave them to fulfill them."

CAL SCRATCHED the back of his neck. They seriously weren't going to send them help?

"Looks like they're in trouble over there themselves." Doc turned to him. "Things aren't going well for any of us."

Shivana's voice filled the room. "Captain, we're going to make another run on the rear lower quadrant of the bomber. The main weapons port is showing signs of internal fires."

"Do you have the people to do that?"

"I have five ships left."

Just five? "Where are the United Traders Defense ships?"

"They are engaging the smaller ships coming from the bomber. Captain Tillan and his eight remaining ships are engaging the forward weapons with two of my enforcers."

They were? Cal squinted through the debris, then blinked, rubbing his eyes. He could barely see straight.

A light flashed, making a ring around the bomber.

"They just fired again." Alanna gasped. "No. They didn't fire. They dropped something!"

"It's a bomb!" Doc tapped manically on his panel. "A

massive, fifty-four kilotons falling fast. The gravity is making it pick up speed!"

"Shivana, can you stop that bomb?"

The enforcer ship seemed to hang in space. Were they just going to watch?

"Shivana!"

When she didn't answer, Cal slammed his fist on the interplanetary comm. "Planetary defenses. You have a bogey coming in hot."

"We see it."

The light sunk into the atmosphere.

Cal held his breath, and deep silence hung on the bridge. The flashing of skippers in battle swirled in their periphery, before a huge, bright circle appeared, igniting the pre-dawn darkness.

Cal's chest thickened. "Comm Officer Skirika, please tell me you shot that thing down."

Static coated the line. "Negative. We—" She sobbed into the comm. "We have impact. We-We're trying to ascertain how bad, but...my God, did you see that mushroom cloud?"

Was that the blast they'd seen?

Cal tapped the comm. "Yeah. I'd just hoped."

Her voice broke apart. "Please...Please stop them. Stars... All those people..."

Cal turned off the comm.

Ty glanced at the comm button. "Did you do that on purpose?"

Cal grimaced. "I wasn't sure what I'd say to her, anyway. I can't lie and tell her everything's under control. It's not. We're dying out here."

Alanna wiped tears from her eyes. "Cal... It... They." She shook her head. "I don't even want to tell you." She hit the comm. "Dammit, Dania. We need help! What the hell is wrong with you? We're out of ships and…and…" She banged her fist on the comm, turning it off. "Dammit!"

Doc hugged her from behind. "Hey, girl. It's okay."

She shoved him away. "No. No, it's not."

Doc frowned at Cal.

Cal got it. He wanted to try to console her, too.

He'd never seen Alanna lose it like that. She shouldn't be here, seeing this kind of destruction. None of them should. Yet here they were, trying to save a planet.

All the while, billions of people beneath them were waking up to war, counting on the ships in space to save them.

Two bursts of light left the surface and barreled toward them.

"Interplanetary defenses, coming in." Alanna tapped on her panel. "They're targeting the bomber."

"The bomber is shifting." Ty pulled back, giving them a better view as both sprays of artillery shot right past the floating death machine and into deep space.

Cal punched the edge of his console. "Why can't we get a break?"

On the surface of the planet, the bright cloud had turned an ashy gray. How large a swath of Earth had been destroyed? How many people had been incinerated in their sleep?

Ty glanced at Cal, then back to Alanna before spiraling the ship up and over the bomber. Everyone remained oddly silent. A few sniffs came over the comm, possibly Rachel in Engineering, or maybe Ethan. Hell, Cal was barely holding it together. A low, whining sound came from the corner, where

Max sat, still clinging to Doc's coffee, looking just as down and beat as the rest of them.

The enforcer ships started to move again.

The screen pinged, and Shivana appeared in the lower corner.

She panted like she'd been running. "I'm sorry, sir. I tried."

"Did you just go down to the planet?"

She nodded. "I couldn't get to the bomb on time. I failed them."

Cal sighed. "We all did."

Captain Tillan appeared in a small box beside her. "We got about seven ships left. Anyone got a plan? That bomber is just getting started."

Shivana's face grew stony. "We saw signs of internal fires before they dropped the bomb. If the lower ship is compromised, we could ram the ports they dropped the bomb from. If they're already damaged, this may render them useless."

Cal zoomed in on the feed of the bomber. "That thing is basically a pyramid. It could have bomb turrets on all sides, for all we know."

Shivana shook her head. "Negative. The scans show a single lineup of multiple bombs feeding four release points, all on the lower level facing the planet."

"When did you have time to scan it?" Doc asked.

"We're enforcers."

"How did I know she'd say that?" Ty cut around a friendly ship, keeping back from the bomber.

Cal checked the readings on the hull of the pyramid. "That thing is too tough. Ramming it is out of the question."

"Our weapons are barely getting through their defenses."

Shivana's picture flickered on the screen. "Ramming them has a higher statistical rate of success."

"And a higher death count."

She seemed to take a deep breath. "If we time it correctly, we can project ourselves from our ships."

"Can you project yourselves far enough away to be protected from the blast?"

She grimaced. "It is a risk we are willing to take."

"So, you want to sacrifice yourselves on a slim chance of success?"

"To stop billions from dying on the surface? Yes."

Ethan's voice filled the bridge. "Shiv! No!"

Her lips thinned. "Helping my sponsor achieve his goals will be a noble death."

She appeared to take a steadying breath. Was she having second thoughts?

Shivana collected herself. "Please tell Geron that I did what I could to save the planet. The rest will be up to you."

"No!" Ethan called from Engineering. "There's got to be another way. There's always another way!"

Shivana lowered her eyes. "Goodbye, Ethan." Her face faded from the screen.

"Dammit, Cal!" Ethan screamed. "Stop her!"

"What's he supposed to do?" Rachel told him. "She's being super brave. You should be proud." The comm clicked off from the Engineering side.

The enforcers probably weren't the best choice for a kamikaze mission. But Shivana probably knew that human pilots might change their minds at the last minute, whereas enforcers—at least the ones jacked up on Geron's authentic pathogens—would follow orders.

"Enforcers can't kill themselves," Alanna said. "How can she even consider this?"

"It's not killing themselves," Doc said. "They're in battle, and they have to take out a ship to defend the innocent. She's already devised that there's no other way to take down that bomber with the manpower we have."

Cal focused on Tillan. "What kind of backup can we give her?"

"We can clear the road, I guess. There's too few of us to do much else."

"Cal?" Alanna wiped her eyes. "The first wave of Cartek reinforcements is almost here. We have two flights coming in hot. The first will be here in thirty seconds."

"Dammit!" Cal hit the comm. "Shivana, we've got fresh Cartek bogeys coming in hot in less than twenty seconds."

"Give me cover. We'll try to take out those cannons before they get here."

Cal gripped Ty's shoulder. "Give her all you got."

"Roger that."

Cal rubbed his eyes again. When the Cartek numbers had started to decline, he'd thought they'd had a chance. With a new wave coming in, everything rode on Shivana succeeding. If they got lucky and destroying the weapons also destroyed the bomber, then that would leave Tillan, his seven ships, and the *Star Renegade* to face the reinforcements.

How many incoming had Alanna said there were? A hundred? A thousand? Not that it mattered. They all knew the chances of getting out of this alive had been slim.

The *Star Renegade* rolled, taking out two skippers before raining fire down on the bomber.

"It's working," Alanna said. "All those remaining Cartek ships are turning toward us."

Cal checked the power reading coming from the engines. "How are our shields holding up?"

"About seventy-five percent."

Cal tapped Ty's shoulder again. "Then let's not get hit."

"That's the plan."

Ty rolled around the attackers. In the distance, Shivana's ships moved below the bomber and fired their engines, heading straight for the bottom of the ship.

"Good luck," Cal whispered.

Earth spun below, moving the blast zone farther away but placing a new, pristine continent right in the path of the bomber.

"They're getting ready to shoot again!" Alanna turned, facing the main screen. "And here comes the first round of fresh Cartek fighters." Alanna pressed the receiver tight to her ear. "Five. Four. Three. Two. One."

"Hold on, everybody!" Cal grabbed the edge of his console and fired with his right hand, taking out a Cartek skipper while the massive new cloud of ships fell over them like a swarm of locusts ready to devour everything in their path.

DANIA CLENCHED and unclenched her fists as one of the human pilots darted away from the battle, fleeing like a coward. She homed in on the nearest enforcer ship, aimed, and fired. The human craft ignited in a flash of light, leaving only dust behind.

Cowardice would not be tolerated. She needed to rely on every ship under her command.

"We can't be turning on our own people," Alexander reminded her.

"I'm not turning on them. I'm giving the loyal pilots a reminder of what happens if they disappoint their new king."

Alexander turned toward the screen, but the slight flutter in their connection told her he didn't agree. If he were anyone else, she might have been concerned. Alexander would follow orders, though, no matter what he thought about them.

Across the room, Orion inclined his head to her, maybe for the first time agreeing with one of her decisions. He, like any properly trained commander, understood the importance of keeping control.

Outside, a burst of fire shot from the bottom of one of the bombers before snuffing out in the oxygen-less cold of space.

"Was that a hit, or did something inside it rupture?" Alexander asked.

"Inconclusive." Captain Quaren tapped on his screen.

Alexander narrowed his eyes. "That kind of damage from an internal explosion means…"

"Internal bleeding." She glanced at Alexander. "Can I assume a full strike would…"

"Cause a chain reaction through the entire ship." Alexander turned back to the screen, smiling.

Dania slipped her fingers into his. He closed his eyes as she drew on his power. Outside, three squadrons spun and shot at exactly the same moment, meters away from their target. She cut them upward, steering her pilots away as the bomber disappeared in a mass of billowing flame before the fire dissipated, leaving a blackened, metal core floating lifeless in space.

The Bane crew cheered, and Geron smiled at her.

That was only one, though. There were four more to be dealt with.

"Did we acquire any data showing what had weakened that ship's hull?" Alexander asked.

"We're reviewing data," Quaren said. "We'll relay anything that looks promising."

Dania released Alexander's hand. If they had done something to weaken the first ship, they would quickly use it to exploit the others. But they couldn't wait to discover that weakness.

She linked with the pilot of the *Oliganton* and sent the former king's cruiser after the two bombers on the right, while focusing her fighters on the two ships on the left.

Hopefully, the attack would stop them from firing on the planet below. If she could make them waste their firepower on her ships, that might be enough time for them to find the weakness that had caused the explosion within the previous ship and exploit it.

"What is that?" Captain Quaren ran to the communications station and pointed at the screen. "Expand that part of the image and analyze."

"What is it?" Dania asked.

Quaren frowned, standing and facing her. "Two more bombers are advancing from deep within the area where the cloud was."

"*What?*" Orion charged at him. "That's impossible! The cloud has already dissipated. There's nothing else out there!"

Two specks of light in the distance grew larger and brighter. It may have been impossible, yet there they were.

Orion turned to her. "We're running low on ships. We cannot take on two more." He looked at Geron. "Ada, we need to get you to a secure location."

"And go where?" Geron stared at the screen, his eyes more focused than Dania had ever seen. "If we flee and regroup with our people, we will be tracked down and slaughtered." He seemed to watch the two new enemy ships advance. "If we fight them now, or we fight them ten days from now, our chances will be no better." He turned from the screen. "We fight to our last ship. There is nowhere else to go."

CHAPTER 46
CAL

TY CURSED, gritting his teeth as the massive ambush of Cartek reinforcements breached the surrounding space. The *Star Renegade* rumbled from the sheer number of ships roaring over them until the last of them flew past.

Cal blinked. "Did those ships all fly right by us?"

"They're..." Alanna covered her lips with her fingers. "They're all attacking the bomber!"

"What?"

The comm pinged. "Hey there, buddy! Glad to see you made it this far!" Chris Columbus's face appeared on the screen. "Looks like you all could use some help."

Cal gaped. "What...? How...?"

"Good, old-fashioned pirate ingenuity, my friend. And maybe a decent amount of stolen Cartek parts." A light flashed on Chris's face on the screen. "Sorry we're late. It took me a little time to convince everyone that if Earth fell, they'd have no one to sell our spoils to."

Cal shook his head, snapping out of it. "You're-You're here to fight? On our side?"

"Well, hell yeah! We certainly aren't siding with the squids. Well, not this time, at least."

Now the defenders had *ships*. Lots and lots of heavily armored ships! "Shivana! Abort! Abort, abort, abort!"

"It's too late," Alanna said. "Two of the enforcers' ships already exploded."

"What's going on?" Chris asked.

"Those enforcers are ramming the bomb ports to try to stop them from firing again."

"The enforcers rammed the ship?" Chris looked down, as if checking his instruments. "Damn. I didn't know they had it in them."

They certainly had more moxie than Cal had expected, but those enforcers had seen the same horrors Cal had. "That bomber already launched on Earth and… Chris…we can't let them fire again. The casualties must be in the millions."

The pirate gave a curt nod. "Well, then, let's stop talking and start kicking some ass."

Three explosions lit up the front of the bomber.

"It looks like one of the main weapons ports are down," Alanna said. "One is still semi-operational. Two more are fine."

"Was it the enforcers?" Ethan called over the comm. "Is Shiv still out there?"

"I don't know, Ethan. I'm sorry. There's too much static and debris to see much."

The new ships swirled toward the bomber in a corkscrew pattern, avoiding both the bomber's weapons and the drones flying around it. Ty flew inside one of the spirals as Cal shot straight ahead, hitting the bomber with a double volley of pointed munitions.

Ty swiped his hands over the controls. "We're hitting

them with everything we have, but it's not doing enough damage."

"Hold on a minute." Alanna tapped on her screen. "Something's happening."

Cal flinched as a nearby ship exploded. "Please tell me it's something good!"

"The rate of drones leaving the ship has slowed…a lot. Look!" She pointed out the viewscreen.

Five ships flew out of the aperture, then three, then one. Chris and his buddies swirled around the new drones, destroying all but one before the hole in the side of the bomber closed.

"Looks like they stopped having babies," Ty said. "That means we can take on the mama."

"Let's bring her down," Cal said. "Chris, you with me?"

"You know it! Let's have some fun!"

Chris's skipper throttled toward the bomber and sprays of fire littered the Cartek ship's hull. Ty made a firing run right behind him, but half the weapons' blasts bounced right back.

Small licks of flame still flickered within the damaged weapons port on the bottom of the bomber. That had to be eating up a lot of oxygen. Maybe with a little bit of good, old-fashioned human ingenuity, they could find a way to rip that hole open a little wider without breaking the air shield and accidentally putting out the fire.

Cal hit the comm. "Chris, how many of your ships are armed with traditional artillery?"

"That depends on what you mean by *traditional*?"

"Really old-school. I'm talking bullets."

"Most of us."

"Perfect! See that bleeding hole in the bomber's belly?" Cal pointed, but he knew Chris couldn't see him.

"Yeah."

"Their internal defenses can't handle old-Earth muni-tions. As long as there's a hole in their shields, older artillery will do more damage than modern weapons. Let's hit that with everything we have."

Chris's voice crackled on the line. "Sounds like fun. I'll spread the news."

Cal glanced at Ty. "Ready for a round of good, old-fash-ioned target practice?"

"Sounds like a party. Let's do it." Ty banked them down, heading straight for the hole in the lower quadrant of the ship. "Here we go!"

Sparkles shot out of the front-right gun turrets, the ancient metal glinting in the rays of the rising sun. Without gravity, the shots would be just as deadly when they hit a target miles away as they'd been when they were first fired.

The sparkles raced for the bomber but bounced back, hitting the shield just to the right of the target.

Ty cursed. "Sorry, boss."

Cal tapped his shoulder. "No worries. Just remember we'll run out of bullets real fast."

"On it."

Chris and two other ships flipped in space, approaching the bomber in what appeared to be an upside-down position from the *Star Renegade*'s perspective. Bullets sprayed out of the pirates' forward turrets, hitting the target head-on and disappearing within the flames.

"Can we tell if that did any good?" Cal asked.

Alanna tapped on her keyboard. "Not yet. No scans are getting through that shield. I think we'll see it before our instruments do if we're making any progress."

The few Cartek skippers still in the air spun and headed

straight for them. Half aimed at the *Star Renegade*, the other half going after Chris and his merry band of marauders.

Ty banked right. "Looks like we ticked them off. They're ignoring the others."

Cal tapped the comm. "Chris, it looks like we got their attention."

"Yeah, buddy, I see it. We must be onto something."

Cal nodded. "Let's hit them with everything we got."

The next wave of pirates shot past them. Five ships targeted the hole and then pulled up and away. The Cartek skippers tried to fend off the next set of five pirates, shooting down one, but the remaining four made it past them to hit their mark.

Cal took the *Star Renegade*'s controls. "I'll pilot." He glanced at Ty. "You hit the target this time."

Ty's gaze fixed on the burning hole on the bottom of the bomber. "A little less sarcasm would be appreciated."

"You'll get less sarcasm when you hit the big, flaming, hard-to-miss target."

"Such sass! I think I'll have to take this up with the union."

"The union agrees with the boss," Alanna said. "Don't miss this time."

The flames grew larger in Cal's window. "You gonna fire?"

"Get me closer."

Ty's eyes were wildly intent, but Cal wasn't about to crash his ship.

"I'm pulling up!"

Ty fired twice as Cal cut the ship up and away from crashing.

"That volley definitely went in," Alanna said.

"Roger that." Cal turned for another run, getting ready behind several other rows of pirates ready to do the same.

Above them and below them, dozens of pirate ships fended off and destroyed the remaining skipper crafts. Five explosions lit up the stars before winking out.

"It looks like that was the last of their defenses." Alanna tapped the comm. "Fire at will! Fire at will! Fire at will!"

Cal glanced over at her.

She shrugged. "Hey, you were going to say it, anyway. I want to say some fun stuff once in a while."

Cal tapped Ty's shoulder. "You heard the lady, but let's stay in formation. We don't want to accidently hit or run into each other with us all targeting the same point.

"Whoa!" Alanna stood. "Hold on. Something's happening."

A fireball shot out from the hole in the bomber, and the flames weren't consumed by space.

"What in all the stars is the galaxy...?" Alanna gaped at the screen.

"It's eating all the oxygen inside," Doc said. "That's the only thing I can think of."

The plume grew larger, and Cal's stomach sank.

He hit the comm. "Chris, I think we've outstayed our welcome!"

"I was thinking the same thing. Abort! Abort! Abort!" Chris's voice cut out in a spray of static.

Cal banked down while most of the pirates banked up, probably out of habit from fighting low over planets. Above them, the plume enveloped the bomber and then billowed out, flashing yellow light over them. The *Star Renegade* shook. The bridge heated.

"Report!" Cal called.

"It's hot!" Alanna said. "But I think we're okay. It's actually cooling."

Ty stood, staring at the plume as it shrank around a much smaller, melted hunk of metal. "I…I don't believe it."

Doc typed on the panel on the wall. "It's like a thousand-megaton bomb went off inside that thing. It's impossible."

Outside, the pirates shot off flares, casting green, red, and yellow bursts of light in the sky. Cal let out a deep breath, crossing his arms and laying his forehead on the edge of his panel.

Ty patted him on the back. "It's okay, boss. We won, and we're still in one piece."

Cal rubbed his stinging eyes. When was the last time he'd slept for more than a few hours? Before the *Oliganton* had shown up? He couldn't recall.

"Incoming transmission from Dania." Alanna held her earpiece tight to her ear. Her eyes widened before she turned to Cal. "There are six bombers targeting the day side of the planet. They've taken heavy casualties. She's calling all ships back to make one last stand."

Cal's face fell into his palms. It had taken all of them to bring down this one ship, and it had been bleeding. How were they supposed to survive six?

DANIA STUMBLED as Geron's cruiser shook around her. They were losing too many pilots and not doing enough damage. She narrowed her eyes and homed-in on several attackers. The enemy ships' navigations systems froze, and they cascaded off course, colliding in a flash of light that winked out instantly. She eased off on the stream of primordial energy, drawing it back into herself.

She'd destroy every one of them out this way if she needed to.

Alexander's hand appeared on her arm. "No, you won't. You're expelling far too much power."

"This is not a time for caution."

"No, but consider it is a time for prudence. All of my energy is at your disposal, but we will both need feeding eventually." He glanced at Geron. "And I don't think stopping in the middle of a battle would be wise."

"Noted." She strode to Captain Quaren's station. "Have we confirmed that the explosion on the other side of the planet was the bomber?"

He stood at attention. "Yes, General. Captain Espinoza

and a small fleet of ships from Earth and the pirate sector will be rendezvousing with us within fifteen minutes."

She frowned at him. "Did you say, *the pirate sector?*"

"Yes. Apparently, Captain Espinoza has managed to rally a significant number of lawbreakers to our cause."

Pirates. Interesting. At least that gave her more trash to put on the front lines while they worked out how to get through the Carteks' shields.

"We do have another problem, though, General."

"A worse problem than six bombers with seemingly impenetrable shields?"

His lips thinned. "Possibly. We have a significant number of ships traveling at high speed from the direction of the last confirmed location of the Cartek blockade in the Z8 sector."

"Could it be more pirates?"

"We don't believe so."

"Contact Espinoza and find out. If the blockade has dismantled to join this fight..." She frowned, not even sure how to complete that sentence.

She looked back to her sponsor as he glared at the broken ships and bodies floating in space. She hated to admit it, but Alexander was right. As formidable as their joined primordial energy was, it wouldn't last forever.

And as distasteful as it was to agree with those contradicting Geron's orders, they might have been right. There was no way to win this battle. However, now, with more enemy ships on their way, it was far too late to run.

CAL TAPPED THE COMM. "Chris, Alanna has been tracking a large group of ships coming from Z8. Please tell me you're expecting more friends."

"No. Everybody I know is already here." Chris's voice sounded rattled, although they probably all did.

"I was afraid you were going to say that." Cal sighed. "This could be bad."

"That could be very bad. Has anyone tried pinging them?"

"Through all this war chatter? We're lucky we can talk to each other without trying to get a transmission outside Earth's space."

"I can go and visually check, but I'm not sure what kind of good it would do."

"Getting yourself blown up is not going to help anyone. Where's Tillan and his stingrays?"

"I saw them flying shotgun with a couple enforcers."

Ethan's voice came over the comm. "Was it Shivana?"

"Who?" Chris asked.

"We're still keeping our eyes out for her, Ethan." Cal doubted Chris knew or cared if any enforcer had a name. But at least they knew now that at least a few of the enforcers had survived. "Chris, do you have any ships that have taken damage? Anyone too weak to fight?"

"Well, yeah, but we're pirates. We all took an oath before joining this mission to go all in. No one's gonna leave. I guarantee it."

"I don't want them to leave. I want to give them the most dangerous mission."

Chris seemed to pause. "What's that?"

"Meet those ships head-on. Let us know their real numbers."

"With the size of the armada heading for us, they'll be obliterated on site."

"Yeah. I know."

Another voice broke in. "I'll do it."

Chris answered. "Victor? How the hell did you get into a secure comm?"

"Oh, please, a ten-year-old could get past that encryption, and I hate being left out in the cold. I'll lead the five ships in the worst shape."

Chris's ship slowed slightly. "But your ship is fine."

"I know, but two of my guys are part of the damaged five. I may be an asshole, but I won't send them to die on their own. And I kinda feel like I owe the galaxy a solid. Ain't that right, Espinoza?"

Cal gripped the edges of his console. The last time he'd seen Victor, Rachel had hit the pirate over the head with a frying pan after he'd tried to hijack the *Star Renegade*. He was supposed to be on Themyscira.

Cal tapped the comm. "I thought you'd be in prison."

"The lovely ladies had a change of heart after they saw

how much me and my guys could eat. I have to admit, their prisoners eat better than pirate royalty!"

Cal highly doubted it had anything to do with how much they ate. More likely they set anyone free who could pilot a ship.

Static sizzled across the line before Victor's voice returned. "I know I got a lot to atone for. If I live, great. If I don't, at least I died doing the right thing for once in my life."

Cal switched off the comm. "I call bullshit."

Ty shrugged. "I admit he'll probably use this as a way to get out of whatever pirate oath he took, but there's also a chance, however slight, that he's being sincere."

It was unlikely, but Cal had to hope it was the latter.

He tapped the comm. "Okay, Victor. Good luck. All we need to know is the numbers—and what kind of artillery they're packing—if it's possible to tell."

"I'll give you everything I can for as long as I can. It's the least I can do."

Outside, six ships spun from Earth and shot back toward the dark side of the planet.

"Good luck, guys." Alanna wiped tears from her lashes, then scoffed at her damp fingers. "I think I'm getting tired. I'm actually worried about pirates."

Cal wanted to tell her that the pirates weren't all bad people, just people in bad circumstances. But he wasn't really sure even he believed that.

Even now, the pirates were there to defend the planet that they did the most trading with, and also the planet that they probably stole the most from. He doubted most of them were there out of any sense of honor.

Alanna wiped her palms on her knees. "We're about to be in range of the bright side of the planet."

Cal engaged the sun shield. "Watch your eyes, people."

A dark film glazed over the view screen as the sun blasted them. Ty brought them up and around so the sun was behind them and cursed once the glare had abated, allowing them to see again.

Alanna stood, covering her mouth with her hand. "Oh, my gosh!"

Doc moved beside her, his face pale and his lips parted as a body in a shimmering, white uniform floated past the screen. The enforcer's face came into view, his eyes crystalized and his lips frozen in an expression of shock.

Doc sighed, looking away. "I think that's Bleven."

"No." Alanna shook her head, still covering her mouth. "No, no, no."

Bleven had barely survived the loss of his sponsor and had been the first enforcer Geron had absorbed into his fold. Geron had brought him back to life, only to send him to his death—and he wasn't the only one.

Cal gulped, taking in the graveyard of hundreds of broken, burnt-out ships hanging in space. More bodies floated among the destroyed spacecrafts, some in shimmering, white uniforms, like Bleven's, but others in dark Earthan Union uniforms, and others in plain clothing...the civilians who had answered the call to protect their home.

On the planet below, three blackened scorch marks marred the surface beneath a massive, smoky cloud cover. Cal couldn't tell which continents had been hit, but if those were heavily populated areas, the devastation would be unthinkable.

Beyond the graveyard, the *Oliganton* lumbered around a

bomber, firing its weapons before turning its attention on a second bomber. A mass of mismatched ships from Earth engaged a third bomber. In the distance, Geron's cruiser and a mass of enforcer ships engaged a fourth bomber. If there were an additional two more out there, Cal couldn't see them from this vantage point.

Chris's ship pulled up alongside them. Cal looked at him through the viewscreen, seeing him in-person—rather than through a staticky transmission—for the first time since he'd escaped Geron's cruiser. His beard was thicker, and his hair wasn't neatly swept back as he normally kept it. Cal supposed he and his crew looked equally rattled.

"What do you think?" Chris asked.

"The only reason we were able to destroy our bomber was because it was already damaged. We need to help Dania's people cut holes in those ships. Even if we can only make little holes, we should have enough enforcers left to exploit any break in the bomber's exteriors."

"I agree, but we need more bullets."

"Let's see what we can wrangle up." Cal tapped the comm. "This is Calvin Espinoza of the *Star Renegade* coming to you from the edge of the dark side of the planet. We need every ship carrying outdated artillery to meet us now. Bonus points if you look like you're running for your lives so the Carteks don't chase you."

His screen cut out, blinking into a picture of Dania's command deck.

She stormed toward the screen until her face took up most of the space. "How dare you convey orders to my people?"

"I'm not ordering your people. I'm ordering *my* people. We're here to save the planet."

"This is my command."

"Yes, yes, it is. I have no problem with you taking on those bombers with magic and modern weaponry. Let me play my useless human games and see if maybe I'm able to make a bit of a difference. If I can't, then I'm more than happy to help you exhaust all your weaponry into those impenetrable shields."

She glared at him. "You have thirty minutes, Captain Espinoza. Then I want those ships back." Her command deck winked out and Cal looked at Chris through the simulated glass.

"She's such a charmer," Chris said. "I can see what you saw in her."

"Eat stardust."

"We have forty-six ships approaching to rendezvous," Alanna said. "All of them showing older weapons arrays."

"Good." He looked back to Chris. "You take half, and I'll take half. Let's see what kind of damage we could do working old school."

They split off into groups, each targeting the two closest bombers. The king's cruiser backed off, engaging a different target, while a small group of enforcer ships gave them cover from the incessant barrage of Cartek skippers still filing out of the massive pyramids.

After ten minutes of focused fire, a small, burning hole appeared on the top of the bomber farthest from Earth.

"Success!" Doc punched his fist in the air. "Now let's take this thing out!"

"No," Cal said. "Let's move on to the next one." He tapped the comm. "Dania, we've just cut a hole in the side of the bomber farthest from you. We discovered on the dark side of the planet that their shields don't work in the places where you've cut through. We're gonna hit the next ship and see if we can do the same."

A skipper exploded, flooding the bridge with yellow light.

Cal shielded his eyes before he continued. "With your permission, General, I'd love to have some of your enforcers throw everything they've got at that hole and see if you have the same luck that we did with the last bomber."

"I'm sending three ships. You will continue this interesting assault on the next bomber." The comm cut out.

Ty snickered. "Isn't that what you said?"

"Far be it for an enforcer to admit that someone else had a good idea." Doc looked at Alanna's screen from over her shoulder.

Not too long ago, none of them would have called Dania *an enforcer*. It seemed like they'd accepted that the woman they knew was gone.

Cal pushed away the incessant pain lodged in his chest. When this was all over, they'd have time to grieve for the loved ones they'd lost.

A battered skipper floated past with the top portion of the craft missing. The pilot's seat was empty, and warning lights still signaled on the dashboard.

He scanned the bodies floating in space. From the looks of it, the *Star Renegade* crew wouldn't be alone in mourning their dead.

The new enforcer ships flew in and focused their targeting on the hole in the bomber. Hopefully, one of them would get the glory of destroying that monstrosity.

"Let's go get the next one."

As they headed toward the bomber to the right, the hull of the Cartek ship seemed to crack open, and a dark cloud spewed into space.

"What in Jupiter's moons is that?" Ty asked.

Alanna gasped. "It's ships. Really small ships. Hundreds of them! And they're shooting in constant succession."

An Earthan ship exploded. Then another.

"Give our people cover fire!" Cal shouted.

Ty rolled the *Star Renegade*, raining munitions down on the enemy ships. Dozens of the small vessels seemed to choke, then stop shooting.

"It looks like they're shooting blind," Ty said.

"With that many of them, it's all they have to do." Cal checked readings on the crafts. "It's like they're mines, but you don't have to hit them. They just shoot at anything that moves."

"Well, these mines move," Alanna said. "They seem to be attracted to any ship that's not a Cartek."

Another aperture opened in the bomber and more tiny ships spewed into space like a swarm of star flies so thick, they seemed to block out any starlight.

"They just keep coming!" Ty swirled again, taking out a handful of the mines in the process.

The bomber behind them opened as well. More tiny ships dropped into space.

They were being overrun. There were just too many.

Several of the mines slammed against their hull and bounced off their shields.

Alanna held on to her console as the *Star Renegade* started to shake. "Each hit knocks something out of our shields. We can't stay out here much longer."

Ty spun the ship again as a mass of the tiny, hungry demon ships flew in haphazard circles around them. "What do we do, boss?"

Cal gaped as another ship exploded in the distance. How

in the name of all that was good and right in the galaxy could they fight *this*?

"We're coming! We're coming!" a voice called over the comm.

"Was that Victor?" Ty asked.

Alanna frowned at her screen. "Confirmed. It's Victor and… Omigosh! Cal!"

Doc cursed, looking into his screen.

A blanket of long-range munitions rained down on them, encasing the Cartek drones with bright-yellow light. Ten exploded, then thirty, maybe a hundred.

Ty jumped to his feet and *whooped* as three black-and-red Themysciran razor fighters skimmed over top of them, raining death on anything that even remotely looked like a squid.

Ty waved out the window. "Hello, ladies! Welcome to the party!"

Alanna collected herself. "They're shielding their numbers, but the incoming wave has to be thousands of ships. Where did they all come from?"

"We're talking about Themyscira. They've probably been stockpiling ships for the inevitability of a Bane invasion." Doc laughed. "I told you that Geron disabling those few ships around their home world would barely make them blink. They probably went back and used the data to make their ships stronger."

Either that or they were as smart as the Carteks and knew that swarming an enemy would make their attack unstoppable. If this many Themysciran ships had faced Geron's cruiser, there would have been a much different outcome.

Behind them, a bright flash lit up space. The first bomber

they'd cut a hole into exploded in a billowing cloud. Alanna and Ty jumped up, hugging each other.

Cal tapped the comm. "Themyscira, this is the *Star Renegade*. We've found a way to cut through the Cartek defenses, but we don't have a lot of ships that can pull it off. We'd appreciate it if you could keep those drones off the older ships."

"Affirmative, *Star Renegade*," a woman's voice said. "If a ship is not throwing a human or a Kever signature, it will be eliminated."

"Let's target the next bomber." Cal took a deep breath, then released it. "We might actually make it out of this alive."

"Wait." Alanna sat back. "Something looks wrong."

"No more wrong!" Cal slumped slightly in his seat. "Things were finally going right."

She shook her head. "There are seven more bombers heading out of deep space."

"*Seven*? How is that possible?"

"Hold on." Doc tapped on his keypad in the wall. "It's not deep space. It just looks like it." He moved behind Alanna and pointed at her screen. "Scan here. The stars don't look right."

Alanna pressed several keys, then her eyes widened. "You're right. It's a cloak. A massive cloak."

"What's out there?" Ty asked.

Cal wasn't sure he wanted to know. He reached for his mug but found it dry. "Does anyone have more coffee?"

A high-pitched bark filled the room, and Max held up the mug he'd been holding for Doc.

Doc pointed his thumb at Max. "Be my guest, boss."

Cal took the mug. "Thanks, buddy."

Alanna held her forehead. "I saw signs of a cloak earlier, but I thought it had turned into the first round of bombers. Shoot! I'm sorry I didn't realize it was still there!"

Cal took another drink of the now-cold coffee, emptying the cup before he handed it back to Max. "Maybe you better go tell Rachel we're going to need another round."

Max barked, ran in a circle, then disappeared. The bridge door opened and closed as their furry, little friend left.

"What's the plan, boss?" Ty asked.

"We're going to go find out what's behind that cloak."

CHAPTER 49
CAL

THE BATTLE RAGED on in the distance as Rachel stood in the center of the bridge and handed Cal a fresh coffee. "Okay, I get what you're telling me. It's important to see what the bad guys are hiding behind the cloak, but do we have to go alone?"

"If we take a lot of ships, we'll be noticed. We'll probably have to deal with a bomber." Cal took a sip of his coffee. Liquid gold rolled over his tongue before he swallowed, licking his lips. "That's good. Really good."

Rachel folded her arms. "Of course it is. *I* made it."

"Cal's right." Doc held up his mug. "About the coffee... and also that the Themyscirans are beating the crap out of anything out there with more than two legs. The Carteks are currently otherwise occupied."

"Dani must be pissed that the Themyscirans are kicking ass," Ethan said. "That can't do much for her enforcer ego."

"Egos aside, we still need to help." Cal set his cup down. "If there are a thousand bombers behind that curtain, we'll double back and regroup with everyone involved and come up with a game plan. Right now, they keep surprising us and throwing us off guard."

Doc nodded. "They've learned surprises are the best way to break a king."

"Yeah, well, I'd rather not be broken." Cal stood and stretched. "You all said you're all in. I'm hoping we don't need a vote on this. I want to get this done sooner rather than later."

Ty chugged his coffee, then slammed his cup down. "Whew! I am all caffeinated and ready to make some noise!"

"No noise." Cal pointed at him. "This is a stealth mission. We peek inside the curtain, and we get out. This is all about information gathering."

Ty took his seat at the co-pilot's station and rolled his shoulders. "I can be stealthy."

Ethan tapped mugs with Doc in a 'cheers' move, then headed for the door. "I'll be in the back doing my thing. Rachel, will you be my assistant again? You did a great job last time."

"Oh, really? Sure!" She rubbed her palms together, beaming.

Max barked.

"Come on, little buddy. You can help, too."

After Ethan, Rachel, and Max left, Cal scanned the room. Alanna looked pale. Doc had circles under his eyes, and Ty's overly caffeinated hands were already shaking on his knees. Cal wished he could have given them more time to rest, but their ten-minute reprieve had already been too long.

Ty maneuvered them around the outskirts of the battle.

The red-and-black Themysciran razors swooped in and out of the other ships like needles of death. Either they had been training since Geron's enforcers had sliced through their ships, or they really were using their numbers as an undeniable strength.

A bright flash lit up space before dissipating in an instant.

"There goes another bomber," Alanna said.

"Perfect." Cal switched his instruments to point at the cloak. "I think that leaves only ten more."

"Only ten?" Doc chugged the last of his coffee and set the mug in the corner. "Sounds like child's play."

"I wish." Cal refocused his instruments. "But we also have to worry about those two bigger ones that they came out of."

"I don't even see them anymore," Alanna said. "Where could they have gone?"

"Hopefully, Dania has her eyes on them. We need to focus on whatever's hiding."

They shot out into deep space, and then Ty turned, facing the odd sheen over the stars that almost seemed right if you weren't paying attention, but the constellations were just slightly off.

Ty gave a soft whistle then licked his lips. "How do you want to play this, boss?"

Cal looked past him. "Alanna, can the alien tech give us a solid boost to drive us into that cloak without our engines?"

She raised her brow like she was thinking, then nodded. "Yeah, with the way we rigged it to our engines, I think that could work. We could do a five-second burst, then shut everything down. That should give us enough momentum to slip right in."

"Would we need to shut off life support?" Ty asked. "Because I really hate it when it gets cold in here, and I don't want my hands cramping in case we need to make a quick getaway."

"We should be good with heat," Doc said. "But we should probably shut off anything that might have a hum, like the air, unfortunately, and the lights."

"We can live without air and lights for a few minutes." Cal glanced at the comm. "Ethan, are you listening? There won't be any issue with getting the air back on, right?"

"No, boss. We refurbished all those systems when we were on our little vacation in Geron's cargo hold. If we're going to do anything foolish, now's the time, because we're in the best shape ever."

"Okay. Give me that boost, and we'll slide right in."

Alanna tapped on her keys. "Ethan, I'm sending you a command sequence for the alien hardware."

"Got it." He hummed on the other end of the comm. "Okay. We're all set. The tech is at your disposal, milady."

Alanna looked at Cal. "Ready?"

Cal turned back to the front window. "Let's do this."

"Turning off lights and most non-essential systems," Doc said.

"Here comes the boost," Alanna said.

There was a jolt, and Alanna counted back from five. Then there was nothing…a long incessant pause. Absolute silence.

The only way Cal knew they were moving was because the veil over the stars was getting closer and closer on the screen.

"We're here," Alanna said.

"I guess we're not expecting a shield?" Ty said.

"Don't you think I would have mentioned a shield before I sent us hurtling into a solid wall?" Alanna asked.

"Sorry. I was just checking. Better safe than sorry."

A wave of black fell around them, very much like passing through a million curtains hung one after another.

"This is so freaky," Ty whispered.

"Shhh. Quiet." Cal wasn't sure why he wanted him to be quiet. The *Star Renegade* didn't have the capability to hide itself like the Carteks could. If the squids were looking, they'd definitely see them.

The last curtain swept away, and Alanna gasped before Cal could process the massive wall of black metal hanging in space on the other side. Lights flashed across it, twinkling very much like stars, which would have been great camouflage in and of itself, but behind those odd curtains, the ship, or spaceport—whatever the heck was hanging before them— was all but invisible.

Alanna shifted nervously in her seat. "I think we just figured out where those larger ships went."

A slit appeared in the side of the megalith and then widened. Once it had reached the point of being a rectangle, a bomber emerged, looking no larger than a skipper craft next to the monster floating fortress.

Alanna wiped the sweat from her brow. "I'm running estimations on the size of that bomber and the size of the mother ship. That thing could be holding a thousand or more bombers and who knows what else." She squinted at the screen. "It looks like there are a hundred and thirty-two places on the visible side that can open like the one we just saw."

Cal gulped. That meant a hundred and thirty-two bombers may be prepped and ready, with an unthinkable number of reserves. If this was what they'd hit Keveron with, no wonder the planet had fallen.

"Let's get out of here." Cal looked behind him. "Doc, you're being pretty quiet back there. Did you get all the information you need from that behemoth?"

"Yeah, I got all that I'm going to be able to get without going inside that thing." Doc grimaced at the screen. "Cal, this isn't good."

"That, I could tell without any of your fancy scans." Cal tapped Ty's shoulder. "Let's very slowly back out of here."

"Roger that." Ty waved his hands over the controls and the *Star Renegade* started to ease back into the curtains behind them.

If that colossal ship really was filled with bombers, they didn't have the people or supplies to stop this invasion. Their only hope may be that Earth had been holding out, or that the civilians, if faced with fighting or certain death, could come out in large enough numbers that they could swarm the Carteks.

With a target as enormous as this Cartek floating metropolis, though, being able to amass a strike force big enough was doubtful. That thing could just keep vomiting bombers until Earth's forces were depleted trying to protect the planet.

"Hold on." Alanna tapped on her panel. "Cal, the bomber that just launched is almost twice the size of the others."

"What?"

"You heard me. It's a beast and it's..." Her eyes widened. "It's targeting us!"

Alanna stood and faced the main viewscreen. She gaped, and a purple circle of swirling gears appeared at the edges of her fingers.

"They just fired!" Doc shouted.

A flash of white-blue light surrounded them.

Alanna cried out and lowered her hand as the magical gears disintegrated.

"So much for a stealthy retreat!" Ty called up the manual controls and grabbed on, arching them up as a projectile sped past them.

Alanna fell back into her seat. "I-I can't jump us. I'm sorry!"

"What happened?" Cal asked.

"That light. It stung." She looked at her fingers. "Now everything tingles."

"Don't worry, I got this." Ty brought the ship about and throttled toward the curtain. The soft waves of black coated them before the ship jolted to a stop, tossing them forward and then back like they'd hit something.

Cal blinked until his vision cleared. "Everyone okay?"

Ethan called from Engineering. "Rachel, Max, and I are okay. Just some bumps and bruises."

Doc pulled himself up off the floor, holding his head. "Once we get out of this, I'd like to requisition a fourth chair for me."

It wasn't a bad idea. Doc had gotten hurt on the bridge too many times.

Ty tugged on the controls. "I'm okay, but we're not moving anymore."

Cal leaned closer to the glass, but all he could see were the flowing waves of curtains. "What do you mean, we're not moving?"

Ty swiped back his hair. "They have us in some sort of... I don't know... It feels like a tractor beam."

"Like in the movies?" Ethan called over the comm.

"There's no such thing that can hold anything bigger than an orange."

Maybe, maybe not. There were far too many things the Carteks had figured out that humanity had deemed impossible.

Alanna tapped on her screen. "Well, whatever they've caught us in, we're losing ground. They're drawing us in."

Cal flipped through statistics on his dashboard. They were still burning engines, trying to get away, but instead of moving through the curtains, the *Star Renegade* was moving closer and closer to the floating metropolis behind them.

Alanna tapped on her keypad. "They're opening up another port in their ship."

"Another bomber?" Cal asked.

"Nope. It looks like we're heading right into it. At this rate, they'll pull us inside within twenty-eight minutes."

Great. "Where's the bomber that shot at us?"

"It's moving through the curtain toward Earth," Alanna said. "I guess they figured we're not a concern anymore."

Too bad they were probably right.

The Carteks hadn't shown mercy to any other ships. He didn't know why they wouldn't have let the bomber destroy the *Star Renegade*, but it probably had everything to do with the not-so-little deal that Cal had made with them, and then broken.

Cal didn't have any enforcers on his ship to pay Rgrythei off with, so they probably intended to take out their anger on Cal's crew. Or possibly hold the crew until Cal did something to make Dania back off and sacrifice Earth.

Even thinking that General Dania DuBane would actually comply made Cal want to laugh.

Not that it mattered. Either way, he refused to be a victim again. If the *Star Renegade* couldn't break free, they'd just have to use their own technology against them.

He hit the comm. "Ethan, I need you to get more power to the engines. See if we can either break free or…"

"Boss, we can't…"

"Don't give me *can't*, Ethan. You're wasting time."

Time that they didn't have.

"Doc, I want a full analysis of the portions of that Cartek ship that are nearest the hangar we're being drawn into."

"What are you thinking?"

"I don't know yet, but we only have twenty-seven minutes left."

"Twenty-six," Alanna corrected. "But who's counting?"

Ty glanced at him. "Should I keep burning engines, boss?"

"Definitely. We need more time to think." Cal looked past Ty to Alanna. "How's the alien tech looking?"

She tapped on her panel. "Looks good. It's the only thing on the ship not feeling the stress."

"Good. Be ready to use it."

"For what?"

"I'll let you know when I figure it out."

The comm pinged. "All right," Ethan said. "Rachel helped me enhance the rear imaging array with the alien tech. I did some scans on bio and artificial heat signatures. It's not much, but it's all I could get. That hull is heavily shielded."

"And?"

"It looks like the hull is so tough because the shields are not on the outside. They're actually running through the walls of the ship. It's like veins or arteries or something."

Cal looked at Doc. "You get all that?"

"Yeah." Doc tapped on a panel in the wall. "Ethan, send the details to my bridge station."

"You got it."

Doc pressed his palms to his temples, like he was trying to keep that big brain of his from swelling as Ethan's scans scrolled by on the screen. He tapped the panel, stopping at what appeared to be a weather map with red rivers and blood-red ponds running through black goo.

Doc cursed under his breath. "No wonder we've had so much trouble fighting them."

"Care to elucidate?" Cal asked.

"Ethan was spot on when he said they were like veins." He pointed to the screen. "These little rivers are bringing energy everywhere. It's like old-fashioned wiring in the walls of houses, but having the wires reach every square inch of the wall. The energy output is phenomenal." He tapped a few places on the screen. "Ethan, keep running scans as deep as you can get and feed that data to my computers in the med bay."

"Why?"

"So I can study it all if we live through this."

"Can we worry about studying it later?" Cal asked.

"Yes, but it can't hurt to think ahead." Doc took in a deep breath and released it. "The red areas all around the hangar they're pulling us into are getting redder and redder. They're sending tons of power there."

Cal left his station and looked over Doc's shoulders. "I see it. What are those duller lines?"

"I think it's just like veins. The heart pumps oxygen-rich red blood throughout the body. It sends used blood back to the heart to get more oxygen."

"Or in this case, power."

"Exactly."

"Can we tell what they're using as a conduit?"

"Running scans to see if I can recognize it." Doc wiped his forehead. "This thing is tougher than tough."

It certainly was, but everything was impenetrable until someone ingenious, or desperate, found its fatal flaw.

"You're not going to believe this," Ethan said. "It's a polymer. A *liquid* polymer. Metallic in base." He cursed. "Cal, it's the same freaking polymer I bought on Triton."

Cal stared at the screen. Ethan had bought the drum on a whim. Months later, when the rest of the crew had been knocked out, and the *Star Renegade* had been hurdling toward a massive piece of space junk, Cal had found a way to heat up and melt the hardened material in order to use it like glue to plug a hole in the ship. It wasn't until later that Cal had found out how dangerous that stuff was.

The darker lines blurred, swirling through the floating metropolis and disappearing into a dark void in the center of the monstrosity.

"What is that?" Cal pointed to the void on the screen.

"I'd guess that's the heart."

"And all these gray lines are carrying used polymer back to the heart?"

"I see those wheels turning, boss. I can't wait to see where they land."

Cal moved back to his chair and sat. "Cut the engines."

"What?" Ty said. "They'll pull us inside."

"Exactly." Cal leaned back to see Alanna. "When we were preparing to blast a hole in Geron's hull to get out, you said when we turned on the engines and shot simultaneously, that the result might be a bigger explosion than we expected. How big?"

She grimaced. "Lotsa big. I was kinda glad we didn't have to use it."

"Yeah, well, we're going to use it now."

"What?" They all shouted at the same time.

Cal slammed his fist on the edge of the console. "Cut the damn engines! Now!"

Ty held up his hands. "All right, all right." He tapped on his panel. "They're cut."

"We're being drawn back faster!" Alanna said.

"Good." Cal turned to her. "The plan to blast out of Geron's cruiser was to turn on the engines at the same time and shoot the new aft cannons."

Cal called up the aft cameras showing the floating Cartek city coming closer and closer on the screen. "We do the same thing here. We let them suck in our back end, and then we hit the engines and fire the cannons."

Ethan's voice came over the comm. "That ship is too big. It will only damage the hangar, and it might not even affect whatever technology they're using to draw us in."

Doc's eyes widened. "Oh, boss, I want to be you when I grow up." He turned back to his screen and zoomed in on the red and gray lines around the hangar. "That polymer is highly unstable. The landing bay interior looks like it's reinforced in case of a crash landing or other mishap, but they'll need to lower their shielding to pull us in. A blast that size inside their perimeter shielding will light up that polymer like Freedom Day on Teson Minor." He turned away from the screen, beaming. "That polymer will carry the explosion from the hangar straight to the heart of the ship."

"Boom!" Ethan said.

"You bet your ass, boom," Cal said. "How much time do we have?"

"Two minutes."

"We have one chance at this, people. Let's give it all we got." Cal slipped into his seat.

"I'm going down to the med bay so I don't become a projectile." Doc headed for the door.

"You have a minute and a half." Alanna looked over her shoulder at him. "Better sprint."

Doc's boots were pounding down the hallway before the door even closed.

Ty shifted in his seat. "How do we know we're going to have enough time to get away when this thing blows up?"

"We don't."

Ty and Alanna both gaped at him.

Cal sighed. "I'm not letting the squids take the *Renegade* so they can torture you all just to get back at me for breaking the deal they forced me into." He looked at each of them, hopefully not for the last time. "If we don't make it out, it will be a far less painful death for all of us than the squids have planned. I guarantee it."

He turned back to the screen as the *Star Renegade* started to hum from the strain. In the distance, the curtains waved like a breeze hit them in space, still covering the battle beyond. Hopefully, the extra super-bomber the Carteks had set free wouldn't be too much for Dania, Themyscira, Chris, and everyone else out there to handle.

The walls started to rumble around them.

"Sounds like we're here," Ty said.

Sweat ran down Cal's brow. "Once we confirm our back end is in their ship, we ignite the engines and fire. Everyone ready?"

Alanna straightened. "Counting down from twelve, eleven, ten…"

Cal's gut twisted. If the *Star Renegade* did explode, no one would know why or how.

"Six, five…"

It would have been some consolation to his mother, both having her son exonerated of murder charges and being the savior of the planet. But the latter might never make it to the history recordings.

"Two, one. Here we go!" Alanna shouted.

Ty grabbed the manual controls and pushed them forward. The *Star Renegade* roared to life.

"I'm shooting off the rear cannons," Alanna said. "But I can't tell if anything is happening!"

The comm broke over the commotion. "We are definitely shooting!" Ethan called. "It sounds like a war zone back here!"

The shaking intensified and Cal closed his eyes as his head started to ring. He choked down the bile building in his throat.

Now was not the time to get a migraine!

Something screeched and cracked above Cal's head. "What the hell was that?"

"We just lost our grappling hooks." Alanna's face looked yellow in the light of her screen. "Everything else looks okay."

There were far worse things you could lose in a fight than grappling hooks.

The shaking intensified. Cal pressed his eyes closed, again. He needed to keep things together. If he started puking he'd be no help to anyone.

The ship jolted, and Cal lurched forward, grabbing his console.

"We're free!" Alanna said.

Cal took a deep breath. "Punch it!"

"Punching it!" Ty pressed on the controls.

The *Renegade* continued to shake.

"Are we moving?" Cal asked.

Ty's knuckles whitened on the manual levers. "Just barely."

Cal tapped the comm. "Doc, can you see anything down there?"

"Yeah. Readings are showing a massive explosion in the Cartek hangar. It's churning like it's drawing oxygen out of the ship, but it's not...wait a minute... There it is! A massive infusion of heat surging through those veins. Ty, get us out of here!"

"This is all I got!" Ty said.

"Hold on!" Alanna stood and stumbled to the engineer's station behind her seat. She tapped a few times on the keypad. "I just switched the alien tech from the weapons to the engines." She held on to the wall as she returned to her seat. "Here comes your power, Ty!"

A *whomp* noise echoed through the ship and the *Star Renegade* stopped shaking.

Doc's voice came over the comm. "That thing is going to blow in five, four, three, two..."

A wave of yellow light engulfed them.

Cal covered his eyes as the *Renegade* started to shake again.

Ty growled like he was flying with all his might.

The walls creaked as the heat jumped ten degrees, then twenty.

Ty's growling filled the bridge, almost as loud as the rattling.

Despite their odds, Cal had hoped to survive this. He'd still had a fleeting dream of finding a nice, quiet place nestled in nature, just like the colony he'd grown up in. He'd hoped to live out his days with grass under his feet and Dania at his side.

Mostly, though, he'd wanted to see his crew safe.

The rattling deepened. The room got even hotter.

This wasn't fair. They all deserved to live long, happy lives doing whatever made them happy.

"No!" Ty cried out as lights started flashing over both their dashboards. "Come on!"

Sweat ran into Cal's eyes. He should have known all those dreams were just fantasies. He gripped the arms of his chair as his chest thickened, realizing how badly he'd failed his crew.

The massive curtain in front of them winked out, and Earth appeared with several bombers being circled by small skippers and Themysciran razors.

"Wahoo!" Ty punched his fist in the air. "The *Star Renegade* slips through their fingers again!"

Cal leaned back, wiping the sweat from his face. The hot air burned his lungs, but every breath seemed like a gift. Was this real? Were they actually alive?

Orion appeared on the screen. "What's going on? Where have you been?"

Cal leaned forward in his chair. "The Carteks are hiding a massive attack force behind that curtain."

"*Were* hiding!" Doc shouted over the comm. "Alanna, you did it! It's gone. The whole damn space station is nothing but scattered garbage!"

Orion's nose crinkled. "We are reading signs of a massive debris field."

Cal moved closer to the screen. "The words you're looking for are: *thank you.*"

The commander grimaced. "Indeed." The screen winked out and the battle returned.

"You're welcome, jerk." Ty leaned his elbows on his dashboard. "Now what? Do we rejoin the fight?"

Cal rubbed his temples as the temperature on the bridge leveled out. "I don't think we have a choice."

THE BOMBER farthest from the *Star Renegade* exploded. One of the remaining two moved away from the planet, and the red-and-black Themysciran razors swooped down on them, coordinating the effort until a small hole appeared in the fleeing bomber's hull.

"Let's help them out," Cal said.

Ty spun the *Star Renegade* through some of the friendly ships and fired on the opening. The gap widened, fire swirling within the depths of the Cartek ship.

"Where've you been, buddy?" Christopher Columbus sped past with two wingmen. All three fired into the aperture, and a fluffy, yellow, orange, and purple plume shot out from the ship before consuming all the oxygen and then winking out. The bomber drifted, its gun turrets silent.

"Lucky shot," Cal said. "You always were the type to swoop in and steal the glory."

"Nah, I have a feeling whatever happened while you all disappeared is going to be the stuff of legends. I can't wait to hear about it."

"A story for another day, my friend. We've got one more ship to take down."

The remaining Cartek ships flew toward the last bomber. Ty maneuvered the *Star Renegade* around dozens of broken skippers.

Alanna stood and approached the screen. "There's so many broken ships."

Her eyes widened and she backed away as a body drifted past. Then another. One wore an opal-white enforcer uniform with the arms burned off. The other appeared to be a civilian pilot in khaki pants and a black shirt that made his torso fade in and out of existence in the blackness of space.

The enforcer's body shifted, showing his face.

Cal's stomach sank.

"That's Bob." Ty shook his head and cursed under his breath.

Cal sighed. Bob had lost his memory and led them all to Trellis to save the Kever princess Kalina. Now he was another casualty of a war none of them had asked for.

"Will they just float around like this forever?" Alanna asked.

"Some will fall to Earth and burn up in the atmosphere," Doc said. "But yeah, most will be out here until Earth can come out and clean up space."

But after several bombs had dropped on the surface, it would be months or years before anyone came out to claim the bodies. The governments would have to work on saving the living before they could worry about burying the dead.

The Cartek ships flying toward the bomber circled up and over them and started attacking the razors. On the side facing Earth, the bomber's weapon-portal opened.

Cal wiped the sweat from his brow as he stood and hit the universal comm. "They're going to drop another bomb!"

CHAPTER 51
DANIA

DANIA POINTED at an enemy skipper in the distance, and it exploded. She flexed her fingers and ships sped through space, firing on her command. A sneer played at the edges of her lips. She was walking death, but more and more Cartek ships seemed to line up for execution.

"You need to pace yourself." Alexander placed his palm on the back of her neck, sending a slight healing stroke through her.

She flicked him a glance, siphoning more energy from his touch. "So do you. I need you strong."

"I'm fine."

It wasn't a lie, or even a light misrepresentation of the truth. He was their strongest. He should have been out there, fighting.

Her hands fisted. She hated that the artificial amalgamation the humans had injected into her had weakened her so much. She didn't like being forced to rely on her friend for strength.

Geron's palm replaced Alexander's. "Do you need a feeding, my Dania?"

She shook her head. "No. I don't want you weakened. I'll see this through, Ada."

"As you wish."

Her sponsor sauntered to a tactical console and looked over the crewperson's shoulder. He appeared far too calm for a king lording over the massive battle still raging outside the ship. Dania knew better, though.

Geron pointed at the screen. "It appears the onslaught of Cartek reinforcements has diminished." He looked back into the stars. "Could this finally be the end of their numbers?"

Dania narrowed her eyes as the Themysciran and pirate ships seemed to congregate. "What's going on?"

Captain Quaren walked over to the navigation station. "Give us a clear line of sight."

The comm officer stood. "The smuggling ship has returned."

Dania scanned the stars, searching for the troublesome ship. She'd figured they'd run from the battle like so many other cowards had, until Orion had informed her that they'd destroyed some sort of cloaked Cartek base.

"We have line of sight," the nav officer announced. "The new bomber's weapon's port has opened."

Geron walked to the center of the room. "That bomber is larger than the previous ones. How many bombs could they be housing in that ship?"

Too many.

The nav officer tapped on his screen. "The smuggling ship is coordinating a centered attack on the weapons port."

Dania turned back to her own line of ships. "Keep an eye on their progress. I'll finish off these remaining Carteks then assist if needed."

She took Alexander's hand, drawing more of his energy.

She hated depending on the commoners, the most annoying of all being the smuggling ship. She still wanted them to pay for what they'd done to her. If that bomb fell, it would be their fault for disabling her. If she'd been at full strength, she would have ended this battle hours ago.

Alexander's voice exploded in her mind. *Don't let your ego get ahead of you.*

Dania gritted her teeth. *Keep out of my thoughts.*

Impossible when we're making contact. He glanced at her before returning his attention to the battle beyond. *You are an unconscionable terror, but even at full strength, this attack would have been too much for you to overcome on your own.*

Possibly. But she'd certainly be closer to victory than she was now.

The navigation officer shot to his feet. "The bomb is dropped!"

"Estimated time of impact?" Captain Quaren asked.

"Fifteen minutes."

Geron's face twisted in an unfamiliar furrow of concern. "Where will it fall?"

The officer lowered their eyes. "An area near the eastern shore of the North American continent."

Their sponsor grimaced. "Population?"

"An estimated twenty-nine million."

Geron's lips twisted. "I can't allow this to happen again."

A pull centered in Dania's stomach before she slid across the floor with every other enforcer on the bridge. "Ada, what are you doing?"

"Everything I can."

The air about them vibrated before the room heated.

Alexander placed both of his hands on Geron's back. "I'm here, Ada."

Outside, the remaining Cartek ships started attacking the common vessels fighting over Earth, forcing them away from the falling bomb.

One of the larger Earthan ships sped in front of the missile, then the pilot ejected in an escape pod. The bomb sliced through the sacrificed ship, undeterred.

"The bomb's heading has changed by a hundredth of a degree," the nav officer announced. "It will fall slightly farther north, but the decrease in death toll is negligible."

"It appears they are sending out another ship to intervene," the comm officer said.

The humans had hundreds of ships to sacrifice, but trying to shove the bomb off course was a foolish endeavor. They were sacrificing ships with little hope of success.

Their losses were not her concern, though. She placed her hand on Geron's arm, ready for him to siphon what strength might be needed.

"Stand in reserve, Dania," Geron said.

She lowered her hand. "Yes, Ada."

Several of her enforcers, new men and women Geron had added into his fold since his return, leaned back and moaned. One woman fell to her knees, then slid to the floor.

Alexander glanced at the woman but kept his hands steady.

Dania did the same. She'd been physically moved to her sponsor's side. He needed her. For what, she didn't know, but none of them would move until given permission otherwise.

The temperature in the room increased, and a rush of tingling heat swept over them. Outside, a burst of white energy exploded like a miniature sun, then raced toward the planet like a massive comet. Dania closed her eyes, her subconscious riding the wave of that storm as her sponsor's energy rolled and churned through space, forming swirling tendrils racing for the planet.

The bomb came into view, an oblong, semi-rounded cylinder with a point at the front and back—falling, using the Earth's gravity against them.

Geron's energy turned into a five-fingered phantom hand, not unlike the hand that had tried to grab the *Star Renegade* out of space seconds before they had been sucked into a black hole. If he'd only succeeded that day, Dania would never have fallen into the downward spiral that had left her a shell of her former self.

She pushed away the thought. She was here now, making things right, and she'd never forsake her sponsor again.

Geron's spirit hand widened and closed down on the bomb. A flash shot from the Cartek pyramid, and Ada cried out and dropped to his knees.

"What was that?" Captain Quaren shouted.

"We're trying to figure that out, sir," someone answered.

The bomb drove through the energy field and Geron's apparition dissipated and winked out as if it had never been there.

Geron held his own hand like he'd been stabbed. Dania steadied herself from falling beside him as the sting burned through her as much as if she had been hit herself.

Alexander crouched beside Geron and a flash of light erupted around them as Alexander drove healing energy into their sponsor.

"Stop!" Geron cried, pushing up to one knee. "You need your energy." He grabbed Dania's collar. "Stop that bomb. Nothing else matters. Do you understand? Nothing."

Nothing? She gulped but nodded.

She closed her eyes, called on all her strength, and took hold of eight of the strongest enforcers she could find on the ship. Their minds buckled under her power as she fed them their orders.

Alexander moved beside her. "You do realize most of them won't survive."

"We need to slow that bomb down." Dania met Geron's gaze. "Nothing else matters."

She wished Kile weren't still in the infirmary. She needed his strength, and a commander whom she trusted. But she had no time to worry about her recent personnel change.

"Alexander. Orion. Come with me."

Dania focused on the alien energy throttling toward the planet and projected herself into space.

CHAPTER 52
CAL

CAL HELD his head as the giant phantom hand dissolved to nothing. "What the hell just happened?"

Alanna shivered. "I'm all tingly again. I think that flash was the same thing they did to me to stop us from jumping."

"It was a full spectrum blast." Doc called up a map of the battle on the screen. "Multiple entry points. Once from the bomber, and then the energy was somehow enhanced here." A red circle appeared on the screen. "And here." Another circle appeared over a Cartek ship that had been hanging back from the battle.

Doc rubbed his mouth with his palm. "I can't even fathom how they did that. They somehow just dissipated Bane energy."

Cal took a deep breath. "This is probably why they kept attacking the royal family one at a time. They were perfecting this weapon."

"And then they turned it on the king and Keveron."

"But why wait until so late in this battle to unleash it?"

"Because His Highness had been lying low. They probably weren't even sure which ship he was on."

But now they knew.

"Is there any sign that the ships are turning on Geron's cruiser?"

"No. They're all still here, protecting that bomber."

Cal glanced at Doc. "They didn't need that weapon because they were winning. Now they're down to this one oversized bomber."

Alanna wiped her eyes. "The bomb the Carteks just dropped is going to hit the northern part of the New Jersey sector in ten minutes."

"How bad is that?" Cal asked.

"That region is the most densely populated part of North America. It's just north of the seat of the planet's international government." Doc pursed his lips. "That's not a random drop. They had to have been waiting for the planet to rotate and bring them the biggest prize they could annihilate."

"No, no, no, no, no!" Alanna clawed at her hair as she gazed into her screen.

"What is it?" Cal looked over her shoulder.

"The bomber is repositioning itself. If it stays on its current course, it will end up over the North China Plane."

"That's bad?"

"Four hundred and nine million people bad."

Cal tapped the comm. "Chris, I'm sure you're tapped into our data feeds."

"You know me too well." A low hiss sounded behind Chris's voice. "The death tolls coming in from the first three bombs are astronomical. We can't help the people below us, but we may be able to stop this thing from getting to China."

"How?"

"We just need to break a hole through this bomber's hide.

It's bigger than the others, but it looks like the same design. Once we break the skin, we can bring it down."

"Yeah, but the last ones were already burning. I don't think we have enough munitions left to cut a hole in anything this big."

"You still got that massive cruiser?"

"The *Oliganton*?" Cal glanced at Doc, then back at the comm. "Yeah."

"I'm thinking maybe we evacuate it as soon as possible."

Cal massaged his temples as his head started to throb. "You want to ram a cruiser into the bomber?"

"You got any other ideas?"

Cal sighed. Unfortunately, he'd run out of ideas hours ago.

He looked at Alanna. "Ask the cruiser if they would consider it."

She drew her gaze from the screen. Her eyes were glassy and red. "What about the bomb they just dropped?"

"There's nothing more we can do. We already tried sacrificing ships. It didn't even slow it down."

"So, we're just giving up on the people down there?"

"Maybe not." Doc tapped on his screen. "Eleven very hot human signatures just materialized in the air just to the south of a long island called..." His eyes narrowed on the screen. "Okay, the island is actually called Long Island. How original."

"Human signatures?" Cal asked.

Doc met his gaze. "My guess would be enforcers."

Cal gripped the arms of his chair, gaping at the planet below them. Dania would be among them, and if Geron had ordered it, she'd die to stop that bomb.

A FLOOD of cool air whipped at Dania's face as she materialized above a large body of water. The continent she supposed was North America sprawled to her left, a combination of high-rise buildings and long masses of trees. North of her, an elongated island filled with tall buildings bustled with lines of small, terrestrial vehicles filling the bridges heading toward the mainland, while hundreds of small passenger ships took flight.

Orion appeared at her left, while Fallon and Alexander appeared at her right.

North of them, well past the shoreline and higher than the clouds, the remaining eight enforcers began to glow, throwing all their energy at the falling needle of death. Their task was simple: to slow it down and stop it.

"It's not slowing," Fallon said.

Unfortunately, his analysis was correct.

Dania pointed to the sky. "Join them. Throw all your strength at that bomb. Do you understand?"

His lips thinned slightly. "I do."

He began to glow before shooting up into the sky, disappearing into the clouds.

Car horns honked on the primitive Earthan roadways as more ships took flight, fleeing the impending destruction.

Dania cringed, feeling Alexander's desire to try to save the innocents stuck in the land-locked vessels.

"They aren't our concern." She scanned the clouds, looking for her other enforcers. "We need to stop the bomb. Nothing else matters."

Luckily, he didn't object. Alexander knew the only way to save those people was by focusing on Geron's orders.

"Follow me."

Dania's primordial energy swirled through the air as they drifted over the water, past a green statue of a human in loose robes holding a book in one hand and a torch in the other.

She slowed near the shoreline below the glowing enforcers in the sky as Orion and Alexander drifted to her right and left.

It was unlikely that those eight enforcers would be able to stop the bomb, even with Fallon's additional assistance, but they'd die trying. That was why Dania was below them as the planet's last line of defense.

Captain Quaren's voice sounded in her earpiece. "The Earthan forces are engaging the bomber. The Carteks are positioning themselves over another planetary target."

A problem for another time.

She had her orders.

Stop the bomb. Nothing else mattered.

Nothing else mattered.

Nothing else mattered.

Sunlight glinted off an opalescent enforcer uniform falling from the sky. Long, silvery-white hair flapped in the breeze as Fallon's unconscious body passed them.

Alexander thrust out his fist and the enforcer slowed.

"Leave him! Save your strength for the bomb."

Alexander yanked his fist back as if he held a rope in his hands. The enforcer flew toward him.

"Alexander!"

He glared at her and held his fist tight a few seconds longer than necessary before releasing his grip.

Fallon splashed into the river beside a boat filled with people fleeing the city.

Above, the flashing of primordial energy increased, drifting farther over the more populated area. Dania grimaced. She'd hoped to drag the bomb toward the water, but the chances of that working had always been slim.

Another unconscious enforcer fell from the sky as the bomb billowed in flames on entry into the atmosphere. The heat rolled over Dania's skin, even from this distance.

"This is it." Dania held up her palms, drawing on her power. "That bomb does not explode. Is that understood?"

Orion's power flexed, and then Alexander's. Orion shot first, hitting the falling object and engulfing it in primordial energy. Dania could sense him push while the enforcers above pulled, still trying to slow the missile's fall.

Alexander's power shot into Dania, adding his strength to her own. She channeled and cycled his warmth, combining their strength and then throwing everything they both had at the falling monolith.

The bomb's descent slowed.

Perfect. Now they just needed to find a way to...

Her power jolted, like she'd been holding fifty pounds, but now held eighty. Orion groaned. His skin grew pale before his head lolled back and he fell.

Alexander punched his power out to slow Orion's fall.

The weight of the bomb doubled.

"Stop!" Dania called. "The bomb is our priority!"

Alexander punched once again and Orion's limp form flew toward a grassy area between the buildings.

Heat flooded Dania again, but the weight pressed down on her.

Below, thousands of people still lined the bridges and streets, trying to flee the city.

They were all about to die. Them, and the millions of others that she couldn't see.

Alexander's voice exploded in Dania's mind. "Save them."

She startled, turning toward him. "What?"

Her friend punched both fists at her, and her veins ignited with his power—far more primordial energy than Alexander should have had, let alone offered to another.

"Stop!" she screamed, but it was too late. He grew pale.

Save them, he repeated in her mind before he started to fall.

Her heart broke as her only friend's unconscious body raced toward the surface, but her sponsor's orders were clear.

Nothing else mattered.

She looked up and threw all her power at the falling bomb. The megalith shook and slowed.

Dania's breathing grew shallow. She screamed under the weight as the obelisk-shaped projectile rattled, the tension shaking through her skin.

Primordial energy surged through her veins.

Heat coursed through her core, burning her from within.

She screamed under the pressure, gnashing her teeth until the bomb stopped and hovered a few hundred feet above the city.

Below, people ran and cars lined the streets.

She'd saved them, but that salvation would be short-lived if Dania were to lose her grip.

Panting, she swirled the power around the bomb. Her energy weave began to falter, and her sight blurred. She needed to finish this before she weakened any further.

Her arms shook as she eased the weapon down slowly.

She held the monstrosity above the street as long as she could to give the people time to escape before laying the obelisk down, crushing countless cars and destroying the edges of the buildings. But it was far less damage than if the bomb had made contact and exploded.

Her eyes grew weary, and she closed them, remotely aware that she'd started to fall.

———

Dania woke as the ground raced toward her. She gasped, stopping her fall just in time to roll through the momentum and land on her knees. She dropped her hands to the ground, weaving her fingers into the thick blades of grass...grass that would have been incinerated if the bomb had fallen.

She looked at the canopy of trees around her and the tall buildings reaching into the sky beyond the trees on all sides.

The city was fine. She'd fulfilled her sponsor's command.

But at what cost?

"Alexander?" She tried to get up but fell. The trees spun around her.

"Ma'am?" A boy of about twelve years inched toward her holding a board with four wheels on the bottom. "Are you okay?"

"Tommy, get back!" a woman with similar features and identical hair color said to him.

The boy—Tommy, Dania assumed—held out his hand to Dania. "Can I help you?"

Did she need help? Her vision came in and out of focus.

She shook her head until her sight cleared. "There was another enforcer. A man. Did you see him?"

The boy pointed to his right. "A big guy fell over there." Then he pointed left. "A guy with really long hair fell over there."

Dania pushed herself to her feet. "Show me."

She stumbled after the boy and found Alexander lying on the ground with a woman trying to give him water.

Dania scrambled toward him. "Alexander!"

The woman backed away. "He groaned a few times. I was trying to get him to drink." The woman's eyes widened. "You're the one who saved us."

A ridiculous statement. "You were saved by King Geron of Keveron."

The woman grabbed her hand. "Thank you."

The woman's expression was warm. Kind.

Warmth spread through Dania's chest. She gaped, confused.

"Yeah. Thank you." The boy looked at Alexander. "I hope your friend is okay."

A man in a shiny, yellow hard hat and a belt filled with

tools approached. "The other one may have a broken leg and a broken arm. He's yelling at anyone who tries to help."

Orion. Typical.

Dania closed her eyes and reached out to Geron.

A trickle of power ghosted over her skin before his voice entered her mind. *My Dania. I take it you've been successful.*

Yes, Ada. Alexander and Orion are injured in the green area in the center of the city. I'm not sure where the others are.

I've already sent a ship. It should arrive momentarily.

A medical cruiser appeared in the sky and sunk into the thick grass a few yards away. Two enforcers emerged and checked Alexander. Orion shouted from somewhere behind the trees as humans gathered, not to gawk or watch an execution, but to help the enforcers load Alexander and Orion more gently onto gurneys than she'd seen any enforcer accomplish, including Alexander.

The humans backed away as the enforcers steered the gurneys into the medical cruiser. The adolescent boy returned, holding out his hand to Dania. "Can I help you get onto your ship?"

Ridiculous! She didn't need help from a child!

The boy smiled at her, his large, brown eyes filled with hope and gratitude.

Dania's own eyes burned slightly as she placed her hand into the child's. "Thank you."

As they walked toward the ship, the adult who'd cautioned him earlier wiped tears from her eyes and clapped her hands. Then the man in the yellow hat joined her. Soon all the humans gathered around the ship applauded, some whistling and yelling, but not in disdain, as she was used to.

They were...*happy.*

The boy smiled up at her as she stepped onto the entrance ramp. "Thanks for saving us."

She opened her lips to correct him, but as the crowd grew louder and the smiles grew wider, she found the correction unnecessary. Enforcers had saved them—*Geron*'s enforcers. She'd pass their praise on to her sponsor.

Dania smiled at the boy. "Step back from the ship. Keep a safe distance."

The boy saluted her, backing into the woman's arms. The crowd continued to cheer as the doors closed.

An interesting tingle filled her as she walked toward the beds. Her steps felt lighter as a sense of accomplishment swelled in her chest. She pushed it aside. Emotions only got in the way of doing her duty.

She passed three beds with sheets covering the patients.

Dania pulled back a sheet and placed her hand over Fallon's damp chest. "Dead?"

"Yes, General." The med tech replaced the sheet. "The first three we found were already gone. We were pleased to find you and the rest of your team alive."

But Orion and Alexander hadn't been her entire team. She'd sent these three enforcers to slow the bomb from above, along with five more. "Where are the others?"

"As of now, unaccounted for. There is another ship searching."

An unnecessary use of resources, but she didn't reprimand them as she reached the side of Alexander's bed. "How is he?"

The enforcer scanning him didn't look up. "I'm still running tests."

Dania smoothed back Alexander's hair as the small cruiser took flight.

His lashes fluttered. "Did we succeed?"

Dania kissed his forehead. "Yes. The people are safe."

His eyes rolled back in his head.

"Alexander?" She shook him. "Alexander!"

The med tech waved an instrument over him again. "He's just exhausted. He has a few broken bones from the fall, but he's already healing himself. He'll be fine."

"He doesn't look fine."

The med-tech pursed her lips. "General, you've all been through a lot. To be honest, I'm surprised you're still standing."

She was standing because Alexander had given her all his strength. She placed her hand on his neck and willed the strength back, but the room started to spin.

"General, stop!" The med tech drew her back. "You need sleep as well. Geron is feeding Kile so he can take command while you're recuperating. He wants you rested so you can be debriefed and fed when you return."

This was good news. Kile had his weaknesses, but she'd felt his absence. Drawing on Geron's healing strength may not have been the best idea, though.

"We need to discover what kind of weapon the Carteks used against Geron. He needs to conserve his strength."

The med tech helped her lie on the empty gurney next to Alexander. "We have people studying the pulse that hit him. They've discovered the source and are working on a solution. Trust me, Geron was most perturbed. Most of our analytical resources have been rerouted to the project. Even the medical staff."

"As it should be. We cannot allow another attack on our king."

The med tech ran a scanner over Dania. "You need to rest,

General. You need to heal so you are ready for what is to come."

Sleep seemed like a dangerous luxury, but she closed her eyes, doing her best to comply. This fight was far from over, and she refused to be the weak link. She'd made a promise to Geron to stand by his side and win this war, and she intended to keep that promise.

THE BOMBER LOOMED IN SPACE, mocking Cal as it moved undeterred toward the continent of Asia. They'd taken out every other ship in the Cartek fleet, but this one made him feel more and more helpless by the minute.

A quartet of Themysciran Razors spiraled down on the bomber, artillery fire glowing in a cascade of red and yellow.

Sparks rolled over the hull and then faded into space, but the bomber still hovered as the Earth turned below, bringing them closer to the most populated part of the planet.

Cal rubbed his face. "We have to keep trying. Eventually, one of us will get a lucky shot."

Alanna tapped on her screen. "Cal, the bomb on the North American continent's eastern shoreline… It didn't go off."

"What?"

"It hit the ground on an island called Manhattan, but it didn't explode. They're reporting crushed automobiles and damaged buildings, but no explosions."

Cal took in the clouds billowing over the planet below. "Was it Dania?"

"Most likely," Doc said. "There were eleven of them. With the battle mostly won up here, they would have sent their strongest."

Cal pressed his palms against his temples as an exhausted chuckle slipped from his lips.

"Boss, are you okay?" Doc asked.

"Oh, I'm better than okay. Millions of people just got a chance to see another sunset. You can't get much more okay than that." Cal reclined and looked at the ceiling. "Dania, I love you. Even when you're a psychotic monster." He sat up and hit the comm. "Do you hear that, Dania? I stinking love you!"

Cal turned off the comm. His head throbbed, the pain dull and drumming from the stress of having a front-row seat to millions of people being incinerated. He'd tried to blot it out, numbing himself to the pending horror on the planet below so he could try to stop the bomber from inflicting any more carnage.

He took slow, steady breaths, trying to process that those people had survived. His temples still throbbed, though.

"We're getting a response from Geron's cruiser," Alanna said. "Dania was medevacked from the surface and is being treated in Geron's infirmary with Alexander, Orion, and a few other enforcers and is unable to respond." She giggled. "No comment about you saying that you love her." She wiped tears from her eyes. "It looks like they both made it back alive."

Cal nodded. "Good. That's good."

Dania really wasn't the woman he'd fallen in love with anymore. To him, she was already dead, but that didn't mean that he wanted General Dania DuBane dead. Her face, even twisted in anger, evoked fond memories of the time they'd shared, even if it did hurt, knowing he'd never see her smile or laugh again.

Cal held his head and sighed.

"Do you have a headache again, boss?" Doc pulled something out of his pocket. "Why didn't you tell me?"

"We've been a little busy."

Doc shined a pen light in his eyes.

Cal flinched. "Ouch. You already saw I had a headache."

"Just making sure what kind." He grabbed a cylinder from inside the cabinet and placed the tip against Cal's shoulder. "This is going to pinch. Remember, I have these rescue shots hidden all over the ship. Don't be a hero."

Cal rubbed his eyes.

"Maybe you should lie down for a few minutes until this takes effect?"

"It's not that bad. It's getting better already." Cal rolled his shoulder and winced.

"Are you lying to me?"

"Doc, we have another bomb to stop. My headache can wait."

"I'm just saying it works better if you rest." Peter shook his head and returned to his station. "Stubbornness only gets you so far."

Cal continued to rub his eyes. "My stubbornness has kept us all alive." He looked through the viewscreen at the massive pyramid looming in space. "Anything new to report?"

Alanna gave Cal a worried glance before pointing at the giant pyramid suspended in space. "The last three runs of ships did zero damage to the bomber."

Doc tapped on his screen. "I've run every analysis I can

think of, but I can't figure out why this one's hide is so much tougher."

Cal turned his chair forward. "How much longer until it reaches the heaviest populated area?"

"Sixty-three minutes."

A set of pirates and Earthan defense ships made another run, trying to break through the bomber's exterior. Once again, the artillery bounced off the pyramid's glossy surface.

"Dammit!" Cal punched the edge of his dashboard. "This is just one bomber. Why can't we crack it?"

The comm speaker scratched and a deep hissing, followed by an all-too-familiar voice, filled the room. "Because I learn from others' mistakes, Calvin Espinoza."

Ice flooded Cal's veins. "Rgrythei?"

Doc frowned. "Friend of yours?"

"Hardly."

The comm crackled again. "If you had simply paid your debt to me, Mr. Espinoza, you could have gone free."

"*Debt?* You blackmailed me. That was a bad deal with no good options and you know it."

"Yet you took the deal. You agreed to give me three high-level enforcers."

"To save my crew!"

"Inconsequential, Mr. Espinoza."

"So, what? You're here now to get payback? The enforcers you wanted aren't on board my ship anymore."

"No, they are not. The most interesting of the three were on the surface, exhausting themselves. We were surprised it took them so long. We expected them to project to the surface to stop the first three bombs. They let far more humans die than we anticipated."

A chill ran up Cal's back. "Wait. You *wanted them* on the surface?"

The Cartek's snicker sounded like walking on broken glass. "You have played your part well, Mr. Espinoza. The last living Bane's strongest enforcers have exhausted themselves. The Cartek Empire thanks you for your service."

The comm sizzled before the transmission ended.

"I don't like the sound of that," Ty said.

"Neither do I. Be ready for anything."

Doc rubbed his face. "Cal, all this isn't a coincidence. This Rgrythei-guy is a Cartek general. Geron told us that this guy wants revenge for crimes against the Cartek people."

"Crimes against his people? They started all this years ago attacking Earth's colonies without provocation."

"Yeah, but after the Kevers drove them out of our space, the high prince obliterated entire Cartek planets without mercy. Once the dust settled, Rgrythei vowed to destroy anything ever touched by a Bane."

Cal rubbed his face with his palms. "Well, that's just freaking fabulous. So, this was all caused by the Banes?"

"Let's figure this all out later, boys." Alanna pointed at the main screen. "There's a projectile heading our way from the bomber!"

A glistening metal needle spiraled toward them.

"Adjusting," Ty said. "Let me know if it follows."

"It's definitely following."

"Can we take it out?" Cal asked.

Ty banked the ship down. "I could, if I could see it."

Two Themysciran razors swooped past, guns blazing.

Cal looked through the viewscreen, hoping to see an explosion. "Did they get it?"

"No!" Alanna tapped on her screen. "It's still following and picking up speed."

The space to their right wavered, and a huge cruiser warped into view.

"Whoa!" Ty grabbed the manual control and pulled up.

"It's the *Oliganton*," Alanna said. "And they're firing."

A yellow glow formed outside the cruiser's aft gun turrets and then fired directly at the *Star Renegade*.

"What the hell?" Cal said.

Alanna stood. "Ty. Don't touch the controls at all."

Ty lifted his hands in the air. "Not touching—but not liking the not touching."

Had they all gone mad? Cal reached for his manual override, then drew his hand back.

He held his breath. Alanna was rarely wrong.

The glowing artillery passed inches from the viewscreen and over their heads.

Alanna sat back down and tapped on her screens. "Got 'em!" She turned to Cal. "Target neutralized."

"I'm seeing another big anomaly," Doc said.

"Yeah, it's coming up on my thermal readings, too." She pointed at the main viewscreen. "It's Geron's cruiser."

"Dania?" Cal swiveled back to his console.

The comm pinged, and a small box appeared at the bottom of Cal's screen. The transmission blurred and stretched before Kile's stern expression appeared.

"You are welcome, Mr. Espinoza."

Seriously? He was calling to gloat?

Cal tapped the comm. "Kile, you need to hit that bomber with everything you have. They're headed to the most populated portion of Earth."

A large, black form moved behind Kile before Geron leaned into view. "We are aware of that, Mr. Espinoza."

"Well, if you are aware of it, why aren't you doing more to try to stop it?"

"How dare you?" Kile spat. "You will address your king with the respect he deserves."

"Yeah, well, I'm prepared to give him the same amount of respect that he gave me." Which was none, in most cases.

Geron's eyes bore into him. "I think this is not the time for childish bickering. Now is the time to..."

"Cal!" Alanna jumped from her seat. "The bomber just unleashed over a hundred of those needles at Geron's ship."

Dammit! "Kile, get your cruiser out of there!"

The small square on the screen seemed to rattle, and Geron stumbled back.

"That was a direct hit," Alanna said. "And more incoming."

"The *Oliganton* is firing on the bomber," Doc said. "The Carteks have launched at least fifty small attack ships, but they're all targeting Geron."

The communication square winked out. No doubt Kile figured he had more important things to worry about.

"Geron's cruiser just took another direct hit," Alanna said. "It looks like it's on fire."

Chris's face appeared on Cal's screen. "I'm not liking the readings on princey-poo's ship."

Cal scanned the energy fluctuations. "Me, neither."

Kile appeared in the square beside Chris. "*Star Renegade.* You are to re-assign all available ships to protect Geron's cruiser. I repeat...all ships."

How was he supposed to do that? "What about Earth?"

Kile moved closer to the screen. "You heard me. Defend your king's ship like your life depends on it, because it does."

The comm winked out.

Another round of Cartek ships shot out from the bomber, surrounding Geron's cruiser like a swarm. The *Oliganton* moved between the bomber and the cruiser, and Cartek ships started exploding, lighting up space like fireflies.

The *Oliganton* wasn't taking them out fast enough, though.

Doc cursed. "They just took out Geron's engines. They're dead in space."

Alanna stood again. "The bomber's main door is opening!"

A massive needle shot from the ship, but this time, it didn't use the planet's gravity to drag it to Earth. This one shot at Geron's cruiser.

"We have to do something!" Alanna called.

Cal hit the comm. "Everyone, fire on that needle. We need to stop its momentum."

The enforcer ships were already on their way. Half the pirates followed. The Themyscirans stayed back.

Laser fire and miniature explosions lit up space as artillery bombarded the space needle.

"It's barely slowing down!" Alanna said.

"Two enforcers just projected themselves into space," Doc said.

"Dania and Alexander?" Cal asked.

"I don't think so. Neither of the enforcers out there have long hair."

The two shimmering uniforms appeared a few yards out from the needle and shot energy toward the massive bomb, but it sliced right past them.

A glow appeared around Geron's ship.

"It looks like he's going to jump the cruiser," Alanna said.

Cal gripped the arms of his chair. "He better hurry up."

The enforcers winked out and reappeared in front of the needle, throwing glowing energy balls, but the missile barely slowed down.

"It's going to hit," Doc whispered.

The glow around the cruiser fizzled.

Doc cursed. "He must be too weak to jump his ship."

Alanna's fingers trembled on her lips, reminding Cal that he wasn't the only one in the crew with someone they loved on that cruiser.

Cal slammed his dashboard again. "There has to be something we can do! Keep hitting it!"

Two of Glenn's stingrays descended, shooting waves of sonic blast fire as Geron's cruiser slowly veered to the left.

"They're not moving fast enough," Doc said.

Alanna sank back into her seat. "Impact in nine, eight, seven…"

Ty swirled his hands over the controls. "I'm getting out of here."

"Wait." Cal held up his hand.

Ty only glanced at him as he continued to move the *Star Renegade* back.

A glow appeared around Geron's cruiser as the impact shielding kicked in.

Alanna stood, gaping. "There's no change in the weapon's velocity!"

The needle sliced right through the swirling, green armor as if it weren't even there.

"No!" Alanna screamed.

A flash lit up space and became a huge circle as bright as

the sun. A jolt slammed into them, like they'd been hit with a giant propulsion wrench. The *Star Renegade* spun as several smaller ships spiraled out of control alongside them and exploded, colliding with each other.

A roar rolled over them, like a million lions screaming, before silence overtook them once more.

Cal, Alanna, and Ty stared at the dark space where the cruiser had been, while Doc tapped manically on the panel on the wall.

Doc cursed. "No signs of any escape pods." He lowered his eyes. "They're gone."

"No." Alanna covered her mouth with her hands. "No!"

She started to sob, and Cal pulled her into his arms. A chill settled over him. A numbness that he welcomed.

Dania had died beside her sponsor, where she'd wanted to be. Whether that desire had been real or programmed didn't matter anymore. Still, a deep ache settled in his chest as the finality sunk in.

She wasn't coming back… Neither of them were.

Alanna wailed, clutching his chest. Cal's hands shook.

It wasn't supposed to end like this.

Ty glanced at them before he sighed and turned back to the controls. The air in the bridge felt heavy as Ty flew the *Star Renegade* around a stream of swirling drones, taking out three as they passed.

Outside, the two enforcers who'd tried to stop the needle lowered glowing shields that were probably protecting themselves from the debris. They hung in space, staring at the void where the cruiser had been.

Alanna sniffed, easing Cal away and wiping her nose. She opened her mouth to say something, but instead patted Cal's chest three times and then returned to her seat.

Cal slumped into the command chair and tried to block out the droning hum that made him feel like he was in a hollow void. Somehow, everything seemed smaller than it had a few moments ago.

Alanna sniffed again. "Why did they only send two enforcers to protect the ship?" She wiped her nose again. "They sent eleven enforcers to stop the needle headed for Earth."

"Maybe there weren't any more to send." Doc grimaced. "Like Cal's Cartek friend said, he wanted them all tuckered out."

The bomber shifted, their main gun turrets opening, pointing right at the *Oliganton*.

The first enforcer shimmered, then disappeared. Then the next did the same.

Alanna tapped her instrument panel. "They must have projected themselves into the *Oliganton*."

"Wait. What?" Cal turned toward the viewscreen. "Why didn't they fall into a floundering mess when Geron died?"

The former king's massive cruiser faded from space like it had never been there and then re-materialized, guns blazing, pointed directly at the bomber.

Doc gaped. "How'd they do that without a Bane on board?"

The *Oliganton* started to glow, and a massive, ghostly, bolt-like apparition jutted out like a fist and punched directly into the weapons aperture of the bomber.

Ty cursed. "That doesn't look like a dead Bane to me!"

No, it certainly didn't.

Cal laughed, tears skewing his vision.

Alanna choked out a sob, then covered her mouth. "I'm fine. I'm fine. I'm sorry."

"It's okay," Doc said. "We're all relieved." He tapped on his screen. "The *Oliganton* is fully loaded with people. It looks like they transported Geron's entire crew there."

"That was one hell of a bait and switch," Ty said.

Five flashes lit up space around the top of the bomber, then eight more as enforcers surrounded the tip of the pyramid and shot long lines of primordial flame at the apex of the ship.

"Dania?" Cal zoomed the camera in.

His lips thinned, realizing they were all men.

"I'm reading a massive wave of energy swirling just under the top of the pyramid," Doc said. "It looks like some sort of disruption field." He turned to Cal. "I bet that's the weapon they used to suck away Alanna's and Geron's power."

"That would explain the number of enforcers they're throwing at it." Cal gripped the arms of his chair. "I sure hope they found a way to fight it."

The enforcers continued to barrage the apex of the bomber as Geron's ghostly fist wedged farther into the lower half of the ship.

In the center of the attacking enforcers, Corin's face came into focus in the camera lens, his expression as terrifying as it had been when he'd stood over Cal's father's body all those years ago. Blast after blast of yellow-white energy shot from the enforcer's fists. Thank goodness he'd found a way to use his power for good, rather than executing the innocent.

Cal moved the camera down the side of the pyramid. The doors of the ship bounced against Geron's ghost-like arm, trying to close.

"Geron is stopping them from closing the weapons port!" Cal leaned forward. "That's it. That's our way through their tough hide." Cal hit the comm. "Aim at the weapon's port! Hit it with everything you've got!"

The remaining Earthan security ships, the Themysciran razors, Glenn's mercenaries, and the pirates fired on the aperture as dozens of enforcers appeared in space, flooding the dark with swirling, magical energy.

Long, shimmering silver hair floated about an enforcer punching swirls of energy at the oncoming Cartek ships returning from destroying Geron's cruiser. The enforcer shifted and Cal gasped like he'd been punched in the chest, seeing Dania's beautiful face twisted into a sneer as she annihilated everything in her path.

She really *was* alive. Part of him had been too afraid to believe it could be true.

Doc pointed over Cal's shoulder. "There's Alexander behind her." He looked back to Alanna. "Your boy is fine."

Alanna wiped her eyes. "Okay. Okay. Good. We're good."

Were they?

Chaos ensued around them as wave after wave of ships circled each other. The cruiser and the Earthan ships blasted the hole Geron was holding open, but nothing seemed to get through.

Cal hit the comm. "Chris, are you still out there, buddy?"

Chris appeared on the screen. "I'm here. Just barely, but I'm here." He flinched as a bright light flashed in his face.

"Do you have any more ships with ancient munitions?"

"I have a ship with a torpedo, but they move too slow to hit modern ships."

"Not if the ship is being held still by a pissed-off Bane."

Chris's grin lit up the small screen. "I love the way you think. I'll see you when this is all over, my friend." The square faded off the screen

"I certainly hope so," Cal whispered to the blank space where Chris's face had been.

The apex of the pyramid exploded, leaving a blunt nub where the pointed tip used to be. The enforcers winked out one after another.

Cal adjusted the shields. "Hopefully, we just took out their ace in the hole."

Ty twirled under a set of Cartek ships and cut over a Themysciran razor. "These Cartek skippers are flying pissed."

"Wouldn't you be, if you thought you'd won but just got tricked by a figurehead royal with no tactical training?" Doc said.

Cal fired a spray of artillery over a pack of five enemy skippers, exploding one and sending a second veering toward the right and out of view as a large, beat-up hauler with some very illegal hardware mounted to its hull moved closer to the bomber. The smaller pirate ships circled them, creating a buffer between the Carteks and the huge, slow hauler, while the Themyscirans swirled around the outside, picking off the Carteks.

"There are more than five enemy ships exploding per minute," Alanna said, "but they're still pouring out of that bomber."

"There are no life signs on those smaller ships," Doc said. "They probably had a stockpile of drones at the ready."

The other bomber captains had utilized those drones earlier. Rgrythei had held his back, probably to save his own cephalopod hide, if needed.

The hauler moved into position and the drones clustered in front of the laser cannons. But they obviously had no concept of what the business end of a late-twenty-first-century munitions port looked like.

The hauler fired, the missile shooting right over the cluster of drones. After a slight delay, the drones followed, but the enforcers and the razors rained hell on the unmanned crafts. When the last explosion winked out, the missile slid right between Geron's ghostly energy hands and disappeared inside the bomber.

Cal held his breath until the port ignited in flames.

Ty jumped to his feet and thrust his fist in the air. "We got them!" He hugged Alanna and shook Doc's hands.

Flames flickered in the depths of the bomber.

Cal's cheek ticked. "Why didn't it explode?"

"What's that?" Ty returned to the viewscreen.

"The bomber. It didn't explode."

Hundreds of drones and a few larger Cartek ships swooped in, concentrating on the *Oliganton*. The ghostly hands seemed to shake, struggling to keep the aperture open as the enforcers kept firing on the hole Geron struggled to keep open in the bomber.

"The missile wasn't enough," Alanna said. "It looks like there's extensive damage, but the explosion isn't spreading past the impact site."

"Why the hell not?" Cal punched the arm of his chair. "It worked with all the others!"

"It looks like the crew of this pyramid was paying attention to how we destroyed their predecessors." Doc pointed at the screen. "The dark area around the weapons appears to be a recently added liquid amalgamation. It looks like some sort of insulation." He rubbed his face. "Which means even if we crashed a ship in there, it still wouldn't be enough."

Cal leaned his elbow on the dashboard. "So we need a bigger boom."

Doc turned to them. "What are you thinking, boss?"

Cal tapped on the internal comm. "Ethan, how many of those large citrus containers do we have downstairs?"

"Umm, three, I think. No. Make that two."

"And how much of that unknown polymer is left?"

"A lot. Alex kinda scared me into not using it anymore. I was too afraid I'd blow myself up."

"Can we load all of it into those citrus containers and seal them shut?"

"Umm, yeah. But why would we do that?"

Doc cursed under his breath. "You're going to give the Carteks a present, aren't you?"

"It's certainly worth a shot." He looked back at the comm. "Ethan, get on it immediately. Drop everything else. Get Rachel and Max to help."

"I'll go, too." Alanna stood and headed for the door.

"Hold on," Cal said. "Let's make sure our plan is solid, then we'll all go down and help." He turned to Ty. "If we load the citrus containers into the garbage chutes, can we shoot them right into that hole?"

Ty reclined in his seat, tugging at his hair. "Whew, that will be some fancy flying. I mean, we shot Bessie the cadaver out a garbage chute, but I wasn't really aiming at the time."

"I didn't ask if it would be hard. I asked if you can do it."

A star-eating grin spread across Ty's lips. "You bet your ass I can, boss."

"Getting the polymer into the ship will be the easy part," Doc said. "We'll have to get at least a dozen ships close enough to ignite it."

Cal looked at the viewscreen. The ships were getting close, but the drones were doing a good job of fending off the pirates and mercenaries before they got too close to that opening.

"Enforcers," Cal whispered. "Enforcers can hang back and then project themselves right in front of that ship and light the polymer up."

"The cruiser has gone dark, though," Alanna said. "They must be concentrating on coordinating their own attack."

"Probably leaving the rest of us to be slaughtered." Cal rubbed his chin. "How close is that bomber to another drop point?"

"Half an hour, maybe?" Alanna said. "But that's only if Geron keeps holding them still. Right now, the spin of the planet is fighting against us."

"A half hour will be cutting it close," Doc said.

"Not if we work smart." Cal turned to Alanna. "Can you call Alexander like Dania does?"

Her eyes widened. "I-I don't know. I never tried. I wouldn't even know how."

"Maybe just think his name?"

"Okay." She closed her eyes and bit her lower lip before she frowned. "I don't think this is working."

"Try demanding. Push from the inside. Call him like you mean it."

She closed her eyes again and gritted her teeth. "Alexander, I'm calling you. Come here. Right now!"

The center of the room wavered, and Doc stepped back as Alexander appeared.

The enforcer glared at Alanna. "You. How dare you?"

"Hold on there." Doc inched closer. "Yes, Alanna called you. No one else could do that. You have a link to her. You can feel it, can't you?"

"My bond is to my general and my sponsor. No one else."

"Yet you can still feel her, right? You're brilliant, Alexander. You may be hyped up on pure Bane pathogens, but you still need to be intrigued by her calling you."

Alexander kept staring at Alanna. "What do you want?"

Alanna pointed at Cal. "My captain wants to talk to you."

He turned to Cal. "We are in the middle of a battle. I do not have time for your games."

"No games. Your cruiser has gone dark on comms. It's a good call. The Carteks have found a way to monitor any outside line we leave open. That's why we brought you here."

"Fine. I am listening."

"When you were on board this ship, you let us know the polymer we were using was highly explosive. Do you remember?"

"Of course. My memory is impeccable."

"Good. We're loading all of that polymer into citrus containers. Ty is going to shoot them into the hole Geron is so graciously holding open for us."

Alexander frowned, tilting his head. "You are going to shoot a cargo container from your ship? How?"

"From the trash chute."

"You are a fool if you think that will work."

"Well, my pilot is exceptional, but just in case he misses, I'd love a little enforcer intervention to give it a boost."

Alexander glanced at Ty, then returned his attention to Cal. "The polymer will not ignite on contact, especially in insulated citrus containers."

"True, but they're all we have that will fit in the trash chutes." He pointed out the window. "Our ships aren't getting close enough to light the containers up once they're inside. But enforcers could project themselves close enough to send fireballs right into the hole. I've seen primordial fire up close when Kile got pissed off at the men who held you captive. My understanding is Kile is nowhere near as strong as you or Dania or even Orion."

"You would be correct."

"I'm guessing that the enforcer fire wouldn't be enough to damage that ship, or you would have used it already. But the fire that Kile conjured melted stone in that castle. It would easily eat right through those containers and ignite the polymer."

Alexander's expression remained stony. "Your idea has merit."

"So, you'll help us?"

The air about Alexander shimmered, and he disappeared.

"I guess we need to take that as a *yes*," Ty said.

"I certainly hope so." Cal tapped Ty on the back. "You keep us alive. The rest of you, come with me. We have some polymer to load."

CAL TAPPED his fingers nervously on the edge of his console. Loading the polymer had been harder than he'd anticipated. Ethan and Doc had flinched far too many times, like they'd both expected the container to explode every time they accidentally banged it into something. Luckily, they'd been wrong.

Each passing moment, though, gave him more time to think about how lucky they'd been so far, and how many things *could* go wrong with this plan. As usual, far too much was at stake, and the plan was laser-thin at best.

"Relax, boss." Ty sat with his eyes focused on the viewscreen. "I got this. You just sit back and enjoy the ride."

Sure. Enjoy the ride when they were about to shoot two containers of highly flammable polymer out a trash chute with hundreds of ships firing at each other.

What could possibly go wrong?

"Any news from Dania or Alexander?" Cal asked.

"None," Alanna said. "Geron's ship is still in a complete communication blackout."

"He's focusing all his efforts on keeping that aperture open," Doc said. "If I were him, I would have given up by now. That's got to be a positive sign that they're on board with our plan."

"They're with us," Alanna said.

Cal leaned back to see past Ty. "How do you know?"

"I just had a flood of warmth run through me." She smiled, wrapping her arms around her shoulders. "It... This may sound crazy, but it feels like a hug."

Ethan's voice came over the comm. "I kinda feel that way when I eat expired ration packets. What did you have for lunch?"

"Focus, people." Cal gripped Ty's shoulder. "Ready to do your magic?"

"You know me, boss. I'm always ready."

Cal tapped the external comm. "Chris, you with us?"

"Yeah. What's up?"

"Remember that time we watched the Europa team races?"

"Yeah. I spent too much time explaining the rules and missed placing my bet."

"It was a darn good race, though. Interesting tactics. Especially that blue team."

Static crackled on the line. By now, Chris had to have figured out that the comms were being tapped. Hopefully, he'd think over that race and understand what Cal wanted.

"That *was* a great race," Chris's voice said. "One for the history books."

"Definitely one for the history books."

The comm cut off on Chris's end, and Cal closed off the external comms.

Ty started picking up speed. "Europa team races are known for being dirty. Only one ship in a team of five needs to cross the finish line first."

Cal nodded. "So the others stay back and shower all the competition with artillery, keeping all possible threats from reaching the finish line." He patted Ty on the back. "They'll keep you clear. You just have to hit the target."

Ty rolled his shoulders. "This is going to be fun!"

Cal certainly hoped so. "Don't have *too much* fun. Those people on the planet are out of time."

Ty wove the *Star Renegade* through friendly and unfriendly ships crossing in front of them.

"This is nuts." Ty ducked as the pirates and Glenn's mercenaries swooped over them, spraying the drones with munitions.

Closer to the giant pyramid of death, the Themysciran razors engaged new drones entering space.

This was as close to chaos as Cal had ever seen.

"Here we go." Ty spun the *Star Renegade*, aiming the trash chute at the glowing hands holding the bomber steady.

"Ethan, you ready?" Cal asked.

"You tell me to punch it, and I punch it."

Ty's eyes narrowed as the bomber became larger in the view screen. "All right. Three. Two. One. Punch it!"

An odd rumble and a *whoot whoot* sounded below their feet, before the two citrus containers shot out into space.

"Dead on target," Alanna said. "Nice work, Ty."

"Thank you, thank you. Yes, I know I'm the best."

A Cartek drone darted through the pirate skippers and slammed into the first container.

"No!" Ty stood, leaning on his dashboard.

Cal shot and the drone exploded. Three more got past.

Cal volleyed them with artillery and the first two started to drift, motionless, but the third got through and rammed the second container.

"They aren't going to make it," Alanna said. "They're too far off course now."

"Dammit!" Cal punched his console. He'd dared to hope something could be easy for once.

The stars wavered to the right of the containers, and Alexander appeared suspended in space. His long, silver-blonde hair billowed about him as he raised his palms and a swirling cascade of nearly invisible energy shot from his hands, shoving the containers.

"Yes!" Ty punched his fist in the air again.

"Both containers back on course," Alanna said.

A new set of drones appeared, racing toward the containers. Cal shot three out of the stars. Alexander flicked his fingers and another careened off course. The drones then descended on Alexander, swarming him like Reglian army maggots on a carcass.

Geron's ghostly hands seemed to shake as they tried to make the hole in the side of the bomber larger.

"Hold on, Your Highness," Cal whispered. "Just a few more minutes."

Alanna walked toward the main screen. "What about Alexander?"

The glow of Alexander's primordial energy was barely visible beneath the myriad of drones slamming into his air shield. Lights flashed inside like Alex was fighting, but the glow of his shield began to dim.

"We can't fire on them. We might hit Alex." Cal turned to Doc. "Any ideas?"

"Other than using enforcer energy, which he's already doing? No."

The first case of polymer slipped through the hole in the side of the bomber.

"One down!" Ty said.

"That should be all we need." Cal looked back to Alexander. "But our hired muscle is too occupied to light it on fire."

Doc shook his head. "It doesn't make sense. We've all seen what enforcers can do. Alexander should have melted all those drones down to nothing already."

"Could he be tired?" Alanna's eyes were red and puffy as the bright explosions within the bubble around Alexander became less constant.

Cal sighed. "More likely, Rgrythei figured a way around that."

"Typical Cartek game plan," Doc said. "Overwhelm with numbers."

The second case slipped inside the hole, and a staticky box appeared on the screen as a transmission came through.

A dark, barely discernible shadow moved within the square.

"Did you think you could destroy us with your trash?" Rgrythei's voice rasped. "This is a highly-tuned vessel. The small amount of heat in your weapons will cool in space and be useless by the time it reaches us. You'll never be able to ignite the *shouina* oil with your small, insignificant smuggling ship." The figure's form seemed to shake, and a screeching sound filled the comm as the Cartek chortled. "We are centering our weapons over Earth's largest population center, and your pet Bane prince's grip on my ship is failing by the second. We will deal a devastating blow to Earth and then destroy the last Bane. You've lost, Mr. Espinoza."

Ty grabbed Cal's shoulder and pointed at the viewscreen. "Look!"

The stars began to waver around the hole in the bomber's hide. First in one place, then a second, until dozens of flashes appeared around the stars.

Enforcers. Dozens and dozens of enforcers!

Cal smirked, flipping on the comm. "I don't think we're quite done yet, Rgrythei. Give my regards to the Cartek Empire."

The enforcers punched their fists toward the hole in the bomber.

The drones around Alexander exploded all at once, creating a halo around him. He looked like an avenging angel as fire spewed from his hands into the pyramid.

"He was faking it!" Alanna said.

Doc swiped his fingers over his panel. "Our boy was making it look like they'd been beat. Ingenious!"

Orion appeared at Alexander's side, then Kile. A third, larger flash lit up the darkness, and Dania blinked into existence, balls of fiery purple energy blasting out of her hands.

Corin appeared beside her, white fire shooting from his palms. The hole in the bomber widened, and Geron's ghostly hands relaxed and faded, as if he'd finally passed out under the pressure.

"The hole is closing!" Alanna said. She closed her eyes and gritted her teeth. "Alexander, the hole is closing. You need to give it everything you have. Now!"

Ty cursed under his breath as the enforcers lit up like demonic torches. Their otherworldly glow switched to fire-like orange and yellow. Cal shielded his eyes as the heat permeated the hull of the ship.

"Ty! Get us out of here!" Cal shouted.

"On it!"

The hull started to rumble.

"We're not moving!" Ty cursed. "I got no controls!"

"Ethan!" Cal called.

"I got nothing!" Ethan shouted over the comm. "Everything is fried from the heat!"

That ship was about to go super nova, and they were way too close.

Unless…

Cal spun his chair, but Alanna was already on her feet, purple dials spinning in alternating directions at the ends of her fingertips.

"I'm not sure if this will work, but here we go. Hang on, everyone!" She pressed the center of the phantom dial, and the world became purple and pink. Air whisked out of the room, and damp heat pressed in on all sides before they rematerialized behind the Themysciran razors scouting the perimeter of the battle. Ten of the red-and-black ships veered left or right so they didn't crash into them.

In the distance, a huge, orange circle lit up space like a sun, then disappeared, as if it had never been there.

Cal flopped back in his chair. "Goodbye, Rgrythei."

"Yes!" Ty jumped from his seat. "Yes! We did it!"

Doc started laughing. "*Give my regards to the Cartek Empire?* I can't believe you said something that cheesy. I mean, funny, but cheesy."

Cal smiled. "Yeah, well, that was the best I could come up with at the moment."

"No!" Alanna held her head and fell to her knees. "No, no, no!"

"No?" Cal knelt beside her.

"I tried. I couldn't get them. They were too far away." She started to sway like she might pass out.

Doc tapped on the screen in the wall. "The *Oliganton* is right beside us, plus about fifty friendly ships." He gaped, looking at her. "She jumped all of us."

"Who'd she miss?" Ty asked.

Alanna's eyes rolled back and closed. "The enforcers."

CHAPTER 56
ALEXANDER

ALEXANDER MARVELED AT THE MASSIVE, shimmering hands of his sponsor holding the doors of the Cartek bomber open. The apparition shook as Geron struggled to keep hold of the large ship, while the erratic pulses of primordial energy fluxing through space betrayed that it wouldn't be long before the king would be forced to let go.

One storage case, hopefully filled with flammable cargo, passed through the Cartek weapons' portal, and the second followed. The enemy ships swirled erratically, turning from the cases to the human ships as a swirl of energy ghosted over Alexander.

Dania's voice exploded in his mind. *"It's time!"*

Alexander followed her energy patterns and projected himself to the aperture. He called fiery heat into his hands as more enforcers followed, creating a wall between the battle beyond and the bomber.

"Now!" Dania raised her hands.

Alexander and all the enforcers punched their fiery fists

as one. Red, swirling heat cut through the cold of space, lancing the Cartek pyramid from forty-seven directions before Geron's hold lapsed, and the weapons port started to close.

The cold of space ignited with primordial energy as Dania doubled the draw on the enforcers' power.

The soldier on Alexander's left started to shake, but the enforcer continued to send lances of blue fire into the aperture.

Alexander found the tendril of power leading back to Dania. *"Some of them are weakening. We need to cut the weaker enforcers free."*

Silence answered him. Dania increased the heat, and more enforcers started to sway, as if losing their grip on their power. One enforcer fell unconscious, exhausted, then another. But she drew more energy from them, forcing them to draw on the last of their strength to light up the final Cartek bomber.

A drone darted close to Alexander, then exploded as a human ship flew over the enforcers, providing cover fire.

Dania loomed higher than the rest, her hair dancing in the glow of primordial energy around her. She was every bit the horror of legend, ready to prove, without a doubt, that Keveron was still the ultimate power in the galaxy.

Geron's power wavered before the ghostly hands disappeared. Dania howled, pulling harder on her people. Two more enforcers fell adrift before fire erupted within the weapons' port and the large, metal doors of the ship closed.

Dania released her enforcers as three more passed out and started floating in space.

The side of the bomber where the portal had been began to glow a deep, swirling orange. Veins of light shot across the exterior of the ship, as if the craft's flesh had caught a swift-moving disease.

"*It's going to explode!*" Alexander shot his power out in a net, pulling the unconscious enforcers to him.

The *Oliganton* reversed its engines.

The human ships spun and bolted toward the stars as Alexander drew the web together and pulled the wounded toward the cruiser.

"*Help me!*" Alexander grimaced, struggling under the weight of so many unconscious enforcers.

"*Leave them!*" Dania drifted closer with Kile and Miguel at her side.

One of the enforcers behind them fended off an attacking drone.

Was she paying attention? "*That ship is going to explode. They'll all die!*"

Kile drifted lower, expanding his air shield around Alexander and Dania so they could speak. "He's right. If all the lucid enforcers take one or two with them, we can project everyone into the cruiser."

Heat swept over Alexander's face, despite the chill of space. They were running out of time. The bomber was getting too hot, too fast, and the *Oliganton*, despite its slow retreat, was far too close to the pending detonation.

Dania's annoyance ran across their bond before she shouted, "Fine."

Kile pulled two unconscious enforcers together. "Miguel!"

Miguel winked out and reappeared next to Kile. He pulled the two enforcers to his chest, and all three of them disappeared.

The rest of the enforcers reached for the wounded as a

bright blue-and-purple haze of primordial energy settled over the *Oliganton*'s hull.

The fluxing waves of power were foreign, yet also familiar. Those colors were warm, sweet, and unforgettable.

Alanna's strength...but that was more primordial energy than Alexander had ever felt her draw.

The purple-and-pink haze brightened, encompassing the smaller ships.

"Go now!" Kile grabbed two enforcers and winked out as the cruiser disappeared in a flash of purple light.

The closed weapons port on the bomber glowed brighter as the *Oliganton* rematerialized in the distance, too far away for any of them to make it back carrying those who'd exhausted themselves.

Dania glanced at Orion and the seventeen other enforcers still awake. "Return to Geron."

Seventeen bubbles of primordial energy winked out. Orion leered at Alexander before the commander complied, leaving Alexander still struggling to keep the remaining twenty-one alive as a deep-yellow glow covered the bomber.

Dania held her hand out to him. *"We need to get out of here!"*

She knew better than to think he'd just abandon them.

Alexander thickened the shield around the unconscious enforcers.

The energy around Dania flared as her hair swirled in mad fury. *"Stop this. That weave is meant to support one person in space, not so many. You'll exhaust yourself!"*

"Then help me!"

Light engulfed the bomber, like it had become a sun. Dania held up her hands and threw a glowing, blue shield over Alexander. The bubble tried to encase him, pinching down on the weave holding the enforcers.

A roar filled space. Alexander growled as the flash burned his eyes, and the heat from the explosion throttled his shield.

A dull roar filled his ears, even though he knew no sound could carry in space. His energy warbled and he screamed in defiance, squeezing his fists to hold the tendrils of primordial energy, refusing to let the enforcers go as heat and metal shrapnel pummeled his shielding.

The explosion abated, and stars sparkled around them again. The edge of the Earth's moon peeked out from the side of the planet, looking peaceful despite the graveyard floating in the planet's gravitational orbit.

A few meters away, Dania's weave of primordial energy dulled. If she was weakening, maybe he could find a way to tap into her humanity.

"Can you sense Kile? There's no way he made it onto that cruiser before it skipped space."

Dania's brow furrowed, before she shook her head as if trying to defuse an irrelevant thought. *"He can take care of himself. You're growing pale."* She condensed her power into knives that started slicing through his weave. *"Let go of them. You need to save enough power to return to Geron."*

"No! I won't leave them!"

Dania punched out more energy. She paled slightly as she created an orb around both herself and Alexander. She clenched her fists and the sphere started to close, cutting off the others.

Alexander fought against her formidable strength. He knew the other enforcers' lives were meaningless to her, but she would fight for Alexander. He needed to hold out until she came to her senses.

He growled, shoving more energy at her orb, blocking the

sphere from closing. *"Stop trying to fight me and help me save them."*

"We don't have enough strength to project them all to the ship." She caught his gaze. *"Alexander, you have to let them go. There is no use in you dying, too."*

"I will not let them go while I still have energy left to keep them alive."

"If you pass out, they will still die. There is no reason to risk yourself."

She called up two balls of ethereal flames, and Alexander doubled down on his shield.

They were about to find out which of them truly *was* the strongest.

CHAPTER 57

CAL

DOC TAPPED the comm on the wall. "Rachel, prep a bed in the med bay. Alanna just passed out."

"Again? Geez! Okay, I'm on it!"

Cal eased Alanna to the floor.

"I got her." Doc placed his hand under her head and took her pulse.

Cal stood and looked past the graveyard of ships only partially illuminated by the Earth's sun. It was all so...*quiet*.

He reached over his chair and hit the comm. "Chris! Chris, report."

Still...the silence.

"Chris!"

Cal's stomach sank. There were so many gutted ships out there. So many bodies floating in space.

"I think I have a fix on his ship." Ty placed a red square on the screen and zoomed in.

The pirate fighter hung in space, the cockpit blown open and the pilot's seat empty. One of the wings was missing, and ice crystals floated behind the charred engine like it had been leaking fuel into space.

Ty paled, then looked down. "Sorry, Cal."

Cal's stomach tightened. "Could he have survived that?"

But he knew the answer.

He hit the comm again. "Chris! Chris, come on, buddy. Answer me!"

Ty moved to Alanna's station and placed her earpiece in his ear. "There's zero chatter out there. Not even anything from Earth."

"Can you tell why?" Cal took a deep breath and released it slowly, but it did nothing to quell the empty churning in his gut.

"I'm not sure. Maybe the explosion did something?"

"It could be an EMP from the blast," Doc said. "That could easily cause outages or complete systems failures."

That didn't sound good, but if Chris had survived, he couldn't answer. It at least gave Cal hope.

He gulped, taking in the jagged shards of polyglass and the blast marks on the ship. *Was there* any way to survive that?

Doc appeared behind him and squeezed his shoulder. "I know he was your friend. I'm sorry."

Cal pressed his lips together. "Yeah. I'm sorry, too." He tapped the internal comm. "Ethan, do we have engines?"

"Yeah, it looks like it. I don't think we should be firing up the long-distance fuel system yet, but we have cooled down enough to maneuver."

Cal sat and took the controls. "Let's go take a look."

They slipped past broken-open and listing ships, both friendly and Cartek. He zoomed in on bodies, but none of them was Chris. It might take weeks or months to identify them all.

Cal maneuvered the ship around a dense patch of

mangled ships. "It's going to be years before they get this debris field cleaned up."

Doc leaned on the back of his chair. "Probably. But at least they'll have the opportunity to clean it up."

Cal nodded. They'd won. He needed to focus on that.

Those who'd lost their lives were heroes. It wouldn't make their loss any easier on the survivors, though.

Earth shone like a beacon in the dark, lighting up the endless night.

Somewhere down there, Cal's mother was probably looking up at the sky as the people of Earth celebrated. Would she have any idea that Cal had been out there, fighting for humanity's right to exist?

Ty left Alanna's station and eased back into his own seat. "Looks like we're approaching ground zero."

The body of an enforcer floated past, their entire left side incinerated, and their expression frozen forever in time in a wide-eyed gaze of shock.

The door slid open, and Ethan and Rachel entered the bridge.

"What are you all doing here?" Cal asked.

Ethan looked through the screen. "Any sign of Shivana?"

"And my Big Guy?" Rachel peeked around him.

"Not in a long time. And you two should stay at your posts. It's already tight in here."

"Well, you need me." Rachel knelt beside Alanna. "We have a medical emergency."

"I got this." Doc returned to Alanna. "I want to run a few more scans and then we'll let her sleep it off in the med bay."

Rachel slapped his shoulder. "Shush. Don't act like you don't need me. I'm tired of being downstairs when everyone else is up here."

A growl filled the bridge, and Max materialized beside her with his paws on his hips and his chin lifted defiantly.

"I guess the gang is all here, then." Ty turned back to the screen. "Just don't move around too much or we'll all trip on each other."

"Oh! Even better!" Rachel sat in Alanna's seat. "If our girl is out, I can take over on nav and comm. She trained me, remember? I can be useful."

"Good point," Cal said. "Keep pinging other ships. I'm willing to talk to anyone at this point."

"I'm on it."

Cal slowly pushed the *Star Renegade* forward. A white-uniformed arm floated past, the edges of the fabric at the elbow singed and black.

"Gross," Rachel whispered. "That arm is too thick to be Alex or Dani, and it's too thin to be my Big Guy."

"It's not Shivana, either." Ethan's lips thinned. "She's fine. She's badass."

Normally, the team would have consoled him, saying they were sure she *was* fine, but silence filled the bridge, over-shadowing even the dull hum of the life support systems running through the floor.

"Ewe." Rachel crinkled her nose. "There's the rest of the missing arm."

Yet another body floated past, and Cal's breath hitched.

The frozen, lifeless eyes of Corin, the man who'd haunted Cal's dreams for years, drifted into view. The enforcer's one-armed body bumped into the glass before drifting over them.

Cal gritted his teeth. The enforcer had gotten what he deserved after killing Cal's dad and ruining his life forever.

His stomach clenched, and a shiver ran over him.

When he'd met Corin, the enforcer had seemed remorseful. He'd admitted that he, and all enforcers, had trouble dealing with the memories of those they'd executed. Cal certainly hadn't held Dania accountable for all those she'd passed judgment on.

Cal rubbed his hands together, his stomach churning.

He hadn't wanted Corin dead. Not really. Cal had left their chance encounter off-balance and feeling sorry for the enforcer. Which was ridiculous.

But was it?

His stomach twisted and bile rose in his throat. Cal had been too self-righteous and angry to admit that Corin had never had a choice in who he'd executed. None of them did.

Cal had one chance to be the better man, and he hadn't taken it.

He should have forgiven Corin. It would have been the best thing for both of them.

Now, he never could.

He took a deep breath as tears welled in his eyes—tears for his dad, Corin, and everyone else who'd died without reason.

"What's that?" Ty pointed to the right, where a faint glow lit up the black of space.

"More importantly, what's *that*?" Doc stood and pointed to the left, where another enforcer floated upright in space, holding their midriff.

"It's my Big Guy!" Rachel sprang from the nav station and lunged for the screen.

Cal grabbed her. "Stop. It's not like you can run to him."

He wiped his eyes, tapped on the camera controls, and zoomed in on that section of the screen.

Kile's eyes were dark, like he'd been sucker-punched, and

blood droplets hung in space around his nose. Two more white-uniformed bodies drifted a short distance away.

A slight glow hung about the commander...the bubble of energy that allowed enforcers to breathe was usually bright and pulsing, but Kile's was waning.

Rachel hugged herself. "He looks bad. Really bad."

"He must not have enough energy to project himself to safety," Doc said. "Is there any way we can pull him into the ship?"

Cal sighed. They'd pulled Dania's unconscious body onto the ship once, but they'd had grappling hooks at the time. Those were now drifting in space somewhere between here and Jupiter.

Ty dragged his fingers through his hair. "I've seen Kever skippers do it, but they had specialized instruments. I'd be afraid I'd crush him using anything we have."

"My baby!" Rachel reached for the polyglass.

My baby, my commander, my cold-blooded death machine... All valid titles for the huge mass of a man hanging in space, probably taking his final breaths.

Kile would have gladly sent any person on this crew to their deaths, but that didn't mean Cal could sit there and watch him die.

"Get closer," Cal said.

"Yes, yes! Get closer!" Rachel held her hands at the base of her throat. "We have to help him."

"You got an idea?" Ty asked.

"Maybe, but it will only work if he remembers us." Or trusted them, which may have been a much harder ask.

Kile became bigger on the screen as they came closer. The glow about him was almost gone.

"How close should I get?" Ty asked.

Cal's lips thinned. "Hit him."

"Hey!" Rachel shouted.

"Not hard. Just get him right up against the glass, if you can."

Kile neared the viewscreen.

"If I get any closer, I might bump him and push him away," Ty said.

"Good point."

The lights of a million stars twinkled behind the commander as his gaze lanced Cal through the screen. Kile's lips moved, probably cursing Cal and using his last bits of air to tell him how incompetent he was.

"You need to project yourself into the ship." Cal leaned over his console toward the enforcer. "Go right to the infirmary, and we'll treat you."

Kile's eyes narrowed.

Dammit!

Cal held out his hand to Rachel. "Come here."

She moved closer. "Can we save him?"

"That's up to him. You better say goodbye, just in case."

She placed her hand on the polyglass. "Come on, Big Guy. I'll take care of you. Just come on board."

Kile blinked twice, then reached out to Rachel, touching the glass near her face.

"That's it," Rachel said. "It's me. Remember?"

His face went lax. He grabbed his throat.

Rachel pounded on the polyglass with the side of her fist. "There's air in here you big, over-pretentious, self-centered jerk. Just swallow that over-inflated ego and admit you need help!"

His face turned into a sneer again.

"Looks like he made his decision," Ty said.

The bubble around Kile winked out.

"No!" Rachel punched the glass again. "Stop being self-righteous for once in your life and live!"

The commander's eyes widened, holding her gaze.

Tears streamed down Rachel's cheeks. "Kile, *please!*"

She gasped as the Big Guy winked out and rematerialized on the inside of the screen and dropped onto Ty's dashboard.

"Aww, come on, Big Guy!" Ty pushed his chair back as Kile's unconscious body fell in his lap. "We said send yourself to the med bay!"

Rachel grabbed Kile's shoulders and tried to pull. "Don't just stand there. Help me!"

Cal grabbed one arm and Ty grabbed the other. Doc pulled Alanna up against the door, making room so they could flop Kile on the floor.

Ty wiped his brow. "I'm not dragging that beast back to the med bay."

Rachel fell to her knees and kissed the enforcer, cupping his face in her hands. "Big Guy? Big Guy, talk to me."

Alanna eased up to a sitting position, holding her head.

"Ouch." Her eyes widened, seeing Kile. "Okay, it looks like I missed a few things."

Doc grabbed a water ration from the wall pocket and handed it to her. "You just sit and rest. Drink this."

She took the water. "You don't have to ask me twice."

"Getting a little tight in here." Ethan sidled past Kile and Rachel and slipped into Alanna's seat. "Any sign of Dania and Alexander?"

Ty returned to his station. "I'm heading over to that glowy area. It doesn't look like anything normal for this close to an inhabited planet."

Cal frowned as the glow grew closer. "That glow is too big to be an enforcer."

"You're right," Ethan said. "Because it's not. It's a *whole slew* of enforcers."

As the glow started to fill the screen, the glistening, white bubble took on an hourglass shape. The shimmering form of a man and a woman, both with long, silver-blonde hair, hung within the bubble on the right. The glow pinched, then expanded to the left around several dozen more.

"What's going on?" Cal asked.

Ethan shook his head. "Well, in my very uneducated opinion, and looking at the colors of their air-bubble thingies, it looks like Alexander lassoed all those enforcers, and then Dania lassoed him, but not the rest of them."

Doc ran a medical instrument over Kile. "Ethan, match the intensity of the light bubble around them to the glow that was around Kile just before he jumped onto the ship."

"Heck, I don't need instruments to do that. The enforcers Alex is holding are as dim as or duller than Big Guy was. Dani's and Alex's bubbles are only slightly brighter."

Doc looked at Cal. "When the enforcers first popped into space, they were as bright as an exam light. If they're almost as dull as Kile was, that probably means they're still out here because they don't have enough energy to get back to the *Oliganton*."

Alanna clung to the wall as she stood. "That makes no sense. Let me look." She took one step, then grabbed on to the wall again. "Ow."

Doc stood from treating Kile. "I told you to sit tight."

"Sit tight and trust Ethan with readings that might mean life or death for Alexander and Dania? No, thank you."

"Hey!" Ethan said. "I *kinda* know how to use these computers."

Alanna held her temple as she stepped over Doc and Kile. "Get up."

Ethan stood. "Okay, okay. But could you do me a favor and see if you can find Shiv?"

"If I see anything, I'll let you know." She eased into her chair.

Doc wiped his brow with his shirtsleeve. "How about you and Rachel get a gurney from the med bay and try to jerry-rig a way to get Big Guy onto it without any of us throwing our backs out?"

"Why is it always me?" Ethan asked.

"Because I'm treating him, and you are the best person I know for coming up with brilliant ways to do things."

Ethan stood taller. "That's because I'm the competent one."

"Yeah, yeah, whatever." Rachel slapped him on the chest with the back of her hand. "Let's see what we can figure out. My Big Guy needs more space and there isn't enough air in here for all of us."

They slipped out the door.

Cal smiled at Doc. "Thanks."

"Don't thank me yet. It's still close quarters in here."

"Okay." Alanna swiped back her damp hair. "I hate to say it, but Ethan was right. It looks like Alexander is holding on to a bunch of unconscious enforcers. Half of them have no shield of their own, so Alex is the only reason they're still alive." She pointed at the screen. "That little pinch in the bubble is coming from Dania. The best I can tell, she's trying to get Alexander to let them go."

"That's strange." Doc tapped the panel on the wall and

his fingers danced over the screen. "Wow. If my measurements on the intensity of the glow around her are right, Dania has barely enough strength to take her and Alexander back to the *Oliganton*. She's probably trying to force him to give up on the others."

"He's in agony." Alanna held her chest. "He doesn't want to let them die."

"Sounds like our boy," Ty said.

The bubble around Dania pulsed. Her shoulders were hunched, and her arms seemed to shake. She glared at Alexander, her teeth bared, as she hovered closer to him.

Cal could just imagine the heated conversation going on between them. "Do either one of them have enough strength to zap those unconscious enforcers onboard?"

Alanna took slow, steady breaths. "Alexander is barely keeping it together. He's basically holding the enforcers with one hand and fighting off Dania with the other."

So Dania really *had* turned back into a heartless automaton. The only person in the galaxy who she'd seemed to care about outside of her sponsor had been Alexander. She probably couldn't care less about the other lives under her command.

Maybe Geron could strike some sense into her. "Try calling the *Oliganton*. Tell them their enforcers are in trouble."

"No reply," Alanna said. "It's like dead air out there."

It was worth a try.

Once again, it was up to the *Star Renegade* to save a bunch of people who probably wanted them dead.

"Get closer," Cal said. "Is there anything we can do to make her let go of Alex?"

Ty shook his head. "I can't see how."

Cal called up the weapons controls and fired a spray of lasers through the pinched part of the bubble.

"Are you crazy?" Ty asked.

Dania turned away from Alexander and gaped at them.

"I'm not lying," Ty said. "I'm really glad her hands are already full because she looks pretty pissed at us."

"Did the lasers do anything?" Cal asked.

"She reacted like it hurt a bit, but she's still holding strong," Alanna said.

Kile grunted from the floor and slowly sat, holding his stomach. "She is an enforcer, you fools. Lasers will only anger her further."

Cal glanced down at him. "You can tell that she's mad?"

"Yes, but now her anger is split equally between you and Alexander." Kile grumbled and held his head. "Where is Ms. Quirky?"

"She's getting you a bed, Big Guy. You should relax a little," Doc said.

"I do not need to relax." He stood slowly, his gaze fixed on the glowing auras outside.

Cal turned toward him. "Is there any way for all of them to hop onto the *Star Renegade*, just like you did?"

"If there were, my general would have commandeered your vessel the second it arrived." His nose flared. "It appears Alexander is being obstinate, as usual."

"With good cause," Alanna said. "He's trying to save lives."

"Dying while trying to save those who cannot be saved is foolhardy."

Alanna shot to her feet. "Shut up." She grabbed her console with one hand and her head with the other. "Everything is impossible until it's done the first time." She blinked like she was trying to clear her vision. "Rachel is right. You need to get over that annoying ego and be some help, or just walk your oversized tushy down the hall to sick bay and stop taking up space here."

His eyes narrowed.

"Oh, don't give me that death stare. I'm over all this enforcer foolishness." She grabbed the console to steady herself, took a deep breath, then held her chin high again. "Give us an idea how to help Alex without hurting Dani or get out." Alanna pointed at the door, swaying slightly.

"You certainly have come out of your shell, little one." Kile's left brow rose slowly. "The cruiser and several ships skipped space to avoid the blast. Geron had already weakened, so I take for granted that was your doing."

Alanna held his gaze without blanching. "Yeah."

Kile massaged his temple as he looked to the viewscreen. "Can you do the same now? Can you put a bubble around this ship, and the enforcers, and skip us back to the *Oliganton*?"

"Don't you dare try it, girl," Doc said.

"Unfortunately, Doc is right." She flopped into her seat. "I can barely stand." Alanna sighed. "But if there are no other options, I'll at least try."

Like hell, she would.

"How do the small Kever ships drag unconscious enforcers to safety?" Cal asked.

"They have apparatuses akin to the nets used to scoop refuse floating in space." Kile winced, stretching his shoulder. "Or many times enforcers will simply grab on to bars outside the ship and allow themselves to be pulled to safety rather than facing the humiliation of being netted like trash."

The hourglass glow about the enforcers glinted in the darkness.

Cal rubbed his fingers together. "Could it be that easy?"

"What are you thinking, boss?" Ty looked from the enforcers, to him, to the enforcers, again.

Cal looked back to Kile. "Can Dania grab on to the *Star Renegade*, and we pull her back to the cruiser?"

"If she were to agree, possibly."

"Will she agree?"

"Doubtful."

"Why?"

"Because she probably gave Alexander an order, and he is defying her. Doing something to help him would contradict her order, and she is unlikely to backtrack on an order she has already given."

"Damn enforcers and their senseless sensibility." Cal turned back to the viewscreen. Dania was now close enough that he could see her head bob slightly with each breath. "She's struggling."

"Obviously." Kile folded his arms, then winced and let his arms fall to his sides.

Cal resisted the urge to punch the guy. "Do you want to help her or not?"

"Of course I do. She is like a daught..." His eyes widened before he looked back out the window.

Had he almost said she was like a daughter to him?

Cal lowered his voice. "I want to try to save her." To save them all, but the Big Guy didn't need to know that. "Will you help me?"

"She will not let go of Alexander, even if it means her own death."

"I thought enforcers couldn't knowingly hurt themselves?"

"They can die doing their duty." Kile pointed at the screen. "Alexander is following his programming to save everyone he can. Dania is acting on her programming to make the best possible tactical decision. Of all the enforcers out there, Alexander is the only one with enough value to fight for."

"Enforcers are all insane," Ty whispered.

Dania's gaze locked with Cal's. Her lips twisted in a sneer, marring her beauty.

Cal placed his palm on the viewscreen. "Please let us help you."

She stared at him through the glass, her expression unchanged.

"Cal." Alanna stepped closer. "She can't hear you."

"Dammit!" Cal rubbed his face. "Can you translate for me? Can you send the thoughts to Alex so he can send them to her?"

Alanna puffed out a breath. "I can try."

Cal placed his hand on the glass again. "Dania, we can pull you to the cruiser. Once they see you, they'll send out ships to help."

Her eyes narrowed, and her breaths grew more shallow.

"Come on, Dania. Please, let me help."

Her lips formed a very clear word: *Alexander*.

"If we pull you slowly, and you keep holding him, he'll drift along with you."

"Alex is worried." Alanna rubbed her chest. "I can actually feel it. I think he's afraid he'll drop the others."

The light brightened around Alexander and then around the enforcers.

"He'll burn himself out," Kile said. "But if he loses consciousness, he'll drop the wounded and Dania may still be able to bring him back."

She'd save Alexander, but not the others.

"Well, then let's get them all out of here before he burns himself out." Ty reached for the controls.

"Hold on." Cal pressed his palm on the polyglass again. "Grab the ship, Dania. Show everyone what a strong leader you are. Stronger than anyone."

She grimaced, then glanced at Alexander.

"He's stubborn," Cal said. "Maybe more stubborn than you. Think it over. This is the only way to save him."

She turned back to Cal, and her eyes softened, looking more like those of the woman he knew, before the stark coldness returned.

"Alex looks like hell." Ty grabbed the controls. "If she won't accept a ride, maybe he will." Ty tilted the ship, moving the outer maintenance ladders toward them.

Dania skated across the glass and disappeared from the viewscreen.

Cal dropped back into his chair. "Give me eyes on the side of the ship."

The screen faded and turned into a blurry image of the maintenance ladder outside.

Dania drifted into view and Cal could almost imagine hearing her growl as her hand shot past the camera and grabbed the ladder.

"Yes!" Ty punched his fist in the air.

Cal placed his hand on Ty's shoulder. "Now pull them back really slow."

The glow around Alexander abated.

"Not too slow." Alanna hugged herself. "He's getting tired."

"Tell him to hold on," Cal said. "If we work together, we'll get everyone to safety."

Alanna nodded and closed her eyes, looking like she was thinking the words as hard as she could.

They glided through space, parts of ships and the occasional body part bouncing off the bubble around the enforcers until they neared the cruiser.

"Call Geron's ship," Cal said. "Let them know we have wounded."

"The skippers are already en route." Alanna tapped on her keypad. "It looks like they saw us coming." She grabbed the transponder in her ear. "Looks like we're finally getting a transmission from the *Oliganton*."

A square popped up on the lower left of the viewscreen, and a blue-skinned Kever man in a soiled uniform appeared on the screen. "Commander."

Kile straightened, wincing slightly. "Captain Quaren."

The captain cocked his head slightly. "King Geron relays his appreciation for your quick thinking in procuring the use of the smuggling ship to bring home our injured."

His lips parted slightly. "I..."

Cal stood. "Yes, the commander really took charge of the situation. Came up with the idea all on his own."

"Of course he did. He's an enforcer." Captain Quaren looked past Cal to Kile. "The king expects you will help with the injured on your return."

Kile raised his chin. "Of course."

The square winked off the screen.

Kile closed his eyes and massaged the bridge on his nose.

Cal reached up and tapped him on the shoulder. "You're welcome, Big Guy."

The door opened.

"We're here!" Rachel announced, pulling in a stretcher.

She gaped at Kile, then placed her hands on her hips. "Someone could have told us!"

Ethan leaned on the stretcher and tapped a metal apparatus attached to the side of the mattress. "Well, at least we have a working enforcer-hoister for the next time someone passes out on the bridge."

"I'm sure we'll get a chance to use it again." Cal turned back to the stars, where new enforcers were popping into space, helping to place air bubbles around their unconscious counterparts.

Rachel pushed up on her tiptoes and hugged Kile. "I'm glad you are up and about, though. I was worried."

Kile eased away from her. "I will accept your offer of transportation." He looked at Doc. "I still will not allow your artificial amalgamations, but I would appreciate some electrolytes before I return to my sponsor."

Doc placed his palm on the commander's back, leading him to the gurney. "You got it, Big Guy."

Outside, Alexander handed off the last of the unconscious enforcers to a waiting skipper and then turned toward his general floating near him.

Dania's lips thinned to a harsh frown. She raised her hands and a blue hue surrounded them both before they disappeared.

"She sure looked pissed," Ty said.

"She certainly did." Cal turned from the screen. "Good luck, Alex."

CAL HEADED to the med bay after a hot shower and a good amount of time trying to sort through everything that had happened. The deep ache behind his eyes continued despite the soothing water, forcing him to shut down and simply not think anymore.

It was probably better that way. The risk of this headache getting any worse simply wasn't worth it when he still had to deal with a homicidal enforcer onboard who'd spent considerable time telling Cal how much he hated him.

Cal placed his palm on the access panel beside the med bay door. The brighter light within stung like lances straight through his brain. He held his hand over his brow to shield his eyes from the onslaught.

Inside, Kile sat on the edge of a gurney as Rachel removed a line of thin tubing from his arm.

"Don't worry." She placed a bandage on the injection site. "I watched the whole time. He didn't give you anything but fluids and electrolytes." She sat on the gurney beside him. "But would it really be bad to try some? They did wonders for Dani."

"They did *not do wonders* for Dania. They made her weak."

"But... But we all kinda liked her like that." She sat beside him and hugged his arm. "I mean, I think even she liked herself like that."

"I assure you; she would no longer agree."

Cal's chest tightened. He hadn't had much time to think about Dania, even when he'd been staring into her angry glare.

A deep heaviness weighed his chest, making his next breath shallow and painful. That enforcer hanging in space hadn't been the woman he'd spent so many days laughing with and teaching how to cook. Seeing her face on another person hurt far worse than he ever could have imagined.

Rachel inched a little closer to Kile. "But you remember me now, right?"

"I remember you being on this ship, but not much more." Kile's gaze remained forward, as if purposely not looking at her.

She lowered her gaze and tears formed in her eyes.

Kile watched a tear fall down her face before lifting her chin carefully, like he was afraid he might break her with his large hands.

"I may not remember you, but the previous version of me *wanted* to remember. I left myself messages all over this decrepit, heinous ship. Pictures. Stories. Memories lost forever."

Rachel looked up, hope in her eyes.

Kile turned away from her. "I wanted to remember, even though I knew I wouldn't."

"You-You could stay. Maybe make new memories?"

Kile shook his head. "My sponsor has called me home. I need to do my duty."

She leaned down to look up into his eyes. "And *after* you do your duty?"

He turned away from her again. "I can promise nothing." He stood and took a few steps toward the exit.

Cal remained in the doorway, blocking his way. "Any news from the *Oliganton*? Apparently, we don't rate high enough for updates."

"Of course you wouldn't." Kile crinkled his nose. "You're a former smuggler."

A former smuggler whose ship and crew took out the Cartek space port and turned the tide of the war. But apparently, that wasn't enough to impress the Kevers.

Cal held Kile's gaze. "Care to share what you *do* know?"

The Big Guy sighed. "The few remaining Cartek ships have scattered, but they are being hunted down. Geron has sent three complements of ships and the least-weakened enforcers to eradicate any remaining Cartek threats in the colonies that were overrun."

"He's not worried about the Carteks fighting back?" Cal leaned against the doorframe. "I didn't see any ships in our fleet that hadn't taken a lot of damage."

"They've been directed to fall back and call for reinforcements if they experience any resistance. My general is not a fool. She will not chance losing more ships. However, Geron has chosen to honor the covenants of his father, so we must risk taking further losses. Our sponsor is resolved that he will take back the lost planets in the Earthan Cradle."

Cal wasn't sure how to feel about that. He appreciated the help, but would that place Earth and all its colonies back under the control of a Bane again? Was humanity stuck under the thumb of yet another totalitarian king who couldn't fathom the idea that not all crimes deserved death?

He closed his eyes as the ever-present ache behind his brow deepened. He needed to think about what he *could* control, or maybe what he *might be able* to control. Anything else would land him on one of these gurneys.

Kile's gaze remained leveled on him. "Step aside."

Cal refused to be intimidated by enforcers anymore. "I happened to notice that you haven't threatened to kill any of us today."

"My sponsor has exonerated you of all your crimes." Kile's eyes darkened. "Believe me, the moment you break the law again, there will be a lineup of enforcers ready to pass judgment on you."

"And I suppose you'd be at the start of that line."

"Of course."

Cal was beyond expecting friendship or loyalty from any of them at this point. "May I ask you a personal question?"

"Would that expedite you stepping out of my way?"

"Maybe."

"Then proceed."

"You left yourself messages all over this ship. The old version of Kile knew Geron would erase Rachel, but he wanted to remember her. Doesn't that drive you crazy?"

Kile blinked, then looked to the side. "It does make me contemplate the reasoning behind my actions."

"The reasoning behind those actions was because you loved her. I mean, all of us thought it was crazy, but you never found her annoying."

"Hey!" Rachel leapt from the table and put her hands on her hips.

"It's true, Rachel." Cal turned back to Kile. "You seemed to find her quirkiness endearing."

"I doubt that," Kile said.

"Come on. That's bordering on a lie. All those messages you left behind had to make you wonder."

Kile looked down and grimaced.

"Right now, you aren't being a complete asshole. That tells me you probably need to be fed."

"Yes, but there are those in far worse condition, and my sponsor cannot be asked to overexert himself."

Cal held up his pointer finger. "Hold that thought." He took a breath, hoping to quell the pain in his temple telling him this was a bad idea. "You are completely lethal at this moment. You could filet me alive if I committed a crime and not even break a sweat, right?"

A wry grin spread across Kile's face. "Easily. Why? Are you considering a crime?"

"No. What I'm thinking is…why do you need to be fully charged? Couldn't you live your life fine, serving your king, without being an automaton?"

"Being fully charged leaves us less dependent on our sponsor for energy. We don't need to inconvenience the king with additional feedings."

"But keeping you partially charged is not as hard for him, right? Can't he give you a partial charge just by touching you? Alanna sent primordial energy to Dania and Alexander by accident, just being in the same room with them. Someone with Geron's power could probably keep a whole army alive just by walking through a room."

"If we were at war and needed to battle like we did through the past few days, we would need to be at our strongest."

"Yeah, I get that. But we aren't at war anymore. On Earth, they used to have what they called the *army reserves*. They kept people trained, but not on full active duty, just in case there was a war. Those people stayed home. They had families. They had lives of their own. But they knew that if war happened, they'd be called to serve."

"Impossible." He growled through clenched teeth. "Families are a weakness."

"No. Not at all. Families are a reason to fight. Those soldiers weren't forced to serve. They volunteered. And if they were called to protect their countries, they weren't just fighting for a government or a flag. They were fighting to protect the people they loved."

"Galactic politics are nothing like petty Earthan squabbles."

"I disagree. Did you see how some of those small class freighters and civilian ships fought? Those pilots were not trained military. They were civilians. They were fighting for their families' right to survive. That's what made them voracious." Cal squinted as the bright light increased the ache behind his eyes. "They were risking their lives because if one of those bombs dropped, their families, friends, and neighbors could die in an instant. That kind of commitment makes the fiercest fighters imaginable."

Kile puffed out a breath and folded his arms. "What is your point, Mr. Espinoza?"

"My point is that you can remain as you are and be lethal enough to protect your sponsor and uphold the law. But at the same time, when you are not on active duty, you could spend time with Rachel and find out what it was about her that made you plant so many reminders on this ship to make sure you knew that she had been something special to you."

Kile looked at Rachel. Her eyes were filled with tears again. She smiled and waved her fingers at him. Max materialized at her side and waved at him, too.

Kile turned back to the door. "An impossible dream." He started walking again. "Let me pass."

Cal grabbed his arm. The enforcer could have easily ripped Cal's shoulder from its socket, but the commander stopped.

"It doesn't have to be a dream." Cal met his angered gaze. "The old king is gone. Geron is the new power in the galaxy. You were there when he admitted in front of everyone that his father was an asshole. If Geron is the great leader you all claim him to be, he'll make changes now that he's king. This could be one of those changes."

"He would never sacrifice his enforcers."

"This wouldn't mean sacrificing them. It will make them stronger."

"I doubt he would agree."

"Well, then maybe you should change his mind."

Kile shook his head.

"Think of it... How many kids on Earth saw enforcers flying in the sky without ships and using magical powers to stop that bomb from falling? Don't think that the news feeds didn't broadcast that play-by-play all over the world."

"Your point?"

"My point is... I guarantee you millions of kids are play-acting today, pretending to be enforcers. In one heroic show of power, enforcers went from being hated and feared, to being superheroes."

"I still don't understand whatever minimal point it is that you are wasting my time with."

"If you stop and think for a minute, you'll realize what this means. The Banes have been scanning medical records and finding children who match whatever the qualifications are that they need to make them enforcers. Then they'd go to those planets and take those kids."

Kile's ears reddened. "Those children were surrendered by their parents and the parents were compensated."

"But they still didn't have a choice. I'm sure some families broke the law and refused—and probably didn't live to tell anyone."

Kile's face was stony, but he didn't reply.

"Imagine if people *volunteered* to be tested. Imagine if being selected as an enforcer was a privilege?"

"That would not happen on Earth."

"It would, if enforcers were on reserve, and if their families and their histories weren't erased. You know your parents, right?"

"I am of royal lineage."

If what Doc had found out was true, Kile's royal lineage was partial, like Alanna's. It was the human side of him that gave him the genetics that allowed him to be taken as an enforcer.

"They didn't make you forget your parents, but Dania and Alexander were forced to forget. Have you ever considered why?"

Kile blinked twice. "No."

"I'm going to guess it was because your Kever family was excited to hand you over. Being an enforcer was an honor for your people, especially since it didn't happen often."

"Yes."

"But Dania and Alexander were ripped from their human homes. So instead of dealing with trauma-inducing memories, the Banes erased their pasts."

"Most likely, yes."

"If the people of Earth were given a choice, after seeing

the enforcers do good, I guarantee you people would line up for the privilege. Geron would never have to steal another child from their bed."

Kile backed up a step. His eyes scanned the floor, focusing on nothing. "I can see where your ideas have merit; however, you are taking for granted that Geron would be willing to share his enforcers with their families."

So, it all came back to the king…

"Then I guess we're all about to find out whether or not Geron is as much of an asshole as his father was."

Kile's lips thinned as his eyes darkened. "Do not speak ill of your new king."

"I did nothing of the sort. I said we're going to find out who he is. Personally, I'm hoping he surprises us all."

Kile pushed Cal out of the way. "I would not stake my life on that."

THE AIR in the lounge seemed heavier than usual as Alanna shifted her weight and sat on her foot. It had been three days since they'd heard anything from the *Oliganton*.

Information coming from Earth had been spotty. From what she could tell, the area that Cal's mother had relocated to hadn't been hit by the Carteks, but Cal hadn't been able to contact her to confirm she was okay.

Alanna hadn't been able to find any information as to where her own family had evacuated to, so the crew was all in an odd state of limbo.

Ty had his arms folded on the far end of the table, rather than having his feet up as he normally did. Cal sat at the other end of the table, drumming his fingers on his armrests.

Alanna and Doc sat on Cal's right and Rachel and Ethan sat on Cal's left. The center chair beside Alanna and the chair immediately to Cal's left remained ominously empty.

The door opened, then closed, and Max appeared on Rachel's lap. She stroked his fur, staring at the tabletop.

Cal finally stopped tapping his fingers. "I guess we have

some decisions to make. There's really no reason to stay here."

Alanna balked. "Aren't you going to try to find your mom?"

"Yes, but I'm not comfortable enough to put a target on her head. There's still a lot of bad blood in the enforcer ranks, even with the reprieve."

Alanna lowered her eyes. That was a good point. Maybe she should have been worried about her own family, too.

"What are you thinking?" Ty asked.

"I was considering gathering as many supplies as we can —legally, of course—and heading to Kirato. I'm sure they would appreciate the help."

Not to mention it was the only place any of them had really felt at home in years. Alanna would normally have been excited about a trip to Kirato. Things were different now, though.

She shifted her weight again. "Are we giving up on Dani and Alexander?"

"And my Big Guy?" Rachel clutched Max to her chest, stroking his fur.

"I think our boy Kile made things perfectly clear." Cal sat back. "Even though he's intrigued by the idea, I don't think he's capable of seeking out anything having to do with his humanity."

Rachel lowered her eyes. "But he did before."

"The only reason you were able to break through his defenses the first time was because he was basically trapped on this ship." Cal looked down at his hands. "The longer he was away from Geron, the more human he became. Just like Dania and Alex." Cal pursed his lips. "I hate to say it, but they're gone."

Alanna's gut clenched. She hadn't expected a different answer, but the finality of his words, and the truth behind them, cut her to the core.

Ty unfolded his arms and tapped his hands on his lap. "I guess I could stand a trip home. I wouldn't say *no* to some of Mel's homecooked meals."

Ethan wiped his face. "I just wish I knew what happened to Shiv. I mean, I guess we weren't as involved as the rest of you were, but I would at least think she'd want me to know if she was okay."

"She would if she were capable, I'm sure. But there's nothing to stop them from being close to Geron now, so they're all going to be unresponsive, just like Kile." Cal swallowed hard, like a ball had been lodged in his throat. "We all need to move on."

The temperature in the lounge increased before a flash of light lit up the room. Alanna blinked, covering her eyes, then jumped as Kile appeared behind Ty.

The commander walked past Ethan and Rachel. "I presumed you'd be here, having one of your sickening group discussions."

"How could you possibly know that?" Cal asked.

"Simple. Alexander appeared unnecessarily anxious. Several times over, I've linked this anomaly back to your navigator being distressed."

Alanna glanced around the room. Alex could feel her emotions?

Kile paused behind the empty seat Dania used to sit in. Rachel's eyes lit up...then saddened when he didn't even seem to notice her.

The Big Guy looked across the table at Doc. "I destroyed

the weapon you threatened Geron with. Have you created another?"

Doc quirked a brow. "Of course. I'm not a fool."

"*Doc!*" Cal said.

Alanna gripped the edge of her chair. Was he insane? Why would he admit that?

Doc glanced at Cal with a bored expression on his face before turning back to Kile. "There would be no point in lying. He'd be able to tell, and he knows that I'm smart enough to try to gain any tactical advantage I can, especially with this many enforcers around."

Kile grabbed the back of the empty chair. "You have proven yourself capable, despite your insidious experimentation."

Doc smiled wryly. "From you, I'll take that as a compliment."

"I will also trust that you have those weapons dispersed throughout the ship."

"Yeah. So?"

"Is one immediately available?"

Doc stared at him for a moment before he sighed, stood, and opened the compartment in the wall where they kept the extra silverware. He reached deeper than he normally would have and drew out a small revolver.

Wait. What? Since when did they stash weapons with the knives and forks?

"May I see it?" Kile asked.

Doc tossed the weapon to him.

The commander flipped the gun over in his hand. "This weapon is not capable of dealing a fatal blow, as I'm sure you expected."

"Then why did you melt that last one?"

"Because you used it to threaten my sponsor. Moreover, this could have caused a temporary, unpleasant annoyance to my kind."

Doc stood a little straighter. "So, it *would* work to disable an enforcer."

Kile held the gun up to the light. "If you were angry, the sting of a bee would annoy you, but not stop you from doing your duty." He lowered the weapon. "Unless…"

Doc lifted his chin. "Okay, I'm intrigued. Unless what?"

Kile walked behind Cal's chair as he addressed Alanna. "My research on this ship told me that you are the crewmember they all consider to be, as some of them recorded in their journals, a *crack shot*."

Alanna gaped. "I guess. I mean, I tend to hit my target, but they never let me get in the crosshairs because they say I forget to duck when people shoot at me."

Doc made a *pft* sound. "Because you *do* forget to duck, girlfriend. That's why I'm always stitching you up."

Alanna hunched her shoulders as her cheeks burned slightly.

Kile handed the gun to her.

The metal was cold in her palm and a chill raced up her spine.

"I want you to shoot Alexander."

Her eyes widened. "What? Why?"

"Because I intend to make him very angry with me. I believe I can stave off his power long enough for him to drain himself, but I'm not strong enough to stop him from executing me."

"What are you talking about?" Cal asked.

"After I found several messages, I unloaded a considerable amount of energy into this titanium-plated wall." He pointed to the shiny space Ethan had repaired. "I weakened myself enough to *feel* again."

Alanna's lips parted. "You want to do the same thing for Alexander? Is that even possible?"

"When Geron fed Alexander, he asked him to execute you. I believe he saw something in Alexander's mind that made him question whether or not you'd been completely erased."

Cal's cheek ticked, and he shifted his weight from one foot to another. "Do you think he saw that she'd been feeding him?"

"Possibly, although I doubt he would have recognized it for what it was. Their connection is unheard of."

The overhead lighting glinted off the gun in Alanna's hand. "You think Alex is still in there?"

"It's a possibility. I am interested in testing the hypothesis, but I need to drain him in a place where he cannot run right to Geron to obtain a feeding. I also need him to be somewhere he would find himself remembering what may be buried deep in his psyche."

"So why the gun, Big Guy?" Ethan asked.

"Because Alexander, even in his current encumbered strength, is capable of overpowering me in a short time." He looked at Alanna. "I will take the chance of weakening him, if I have your word you will shoot him to save my life."

"You can't ask her to do that." Cal stood and took the gun from her shaking hand. "*I'll* shoot him."

Kile grabbed the weapon from Cal. "You would happily see me dead. You'd wait for Alexander to kill me and then shoot."

Cal shook his head and sighed. "What if I gave you my word?"

"You are a former smuggler. Your word is worth nothing." He handed the gun back to Alanna. "You, however, are known to be the one person on the crew who always keeps her word, no matter what."

Alanna's bottom lip quivered as the gun trembled in her palm.

Ethan raised his hand. "I'd be happy to shoot him."

Kile scoffed. "While I do trust you, in general, you are also the worst marksman on the ship. If you miss the target, Alexander will kill you and then kill me. That is an outcome neither of us would enjoy." Kile turned back to Alanna. "We're almost out of time. Will you do it?"

Rachel stood, clutching Max like he was a lifeline. "You can't ask her to do that. Alanna is the sweetest person I know. Unlike you, you big, annoyingly handsome jerk!"

"Thanks, Rachel." Alanna gulped, staring at the gun before she looked at Kile. "You want me to shoot the man I love to give us a chance to save him?"

"You must shoot him squarely on the back of the neck. Here." He pointed to the base of his own neck. "The pulse to his spine will send a flush of energy to that point to protect himself from injury. My postulation is that if I can weaken him enough first, that will be the last expulsion of energy needed to allow him to feel emotion again."

"It's just a postulation?" Cal asked.

Ethan raised his hand. "What's a postulation?"

"It means he's guessing." Cal moved between Alanna and Kile. "And if he's wrong, he'll kill her first, and then him."

"Not to mention the rest of us as accomplices," Doc pointed out.

Max jumped out of Rachel's arms and sat on the table in front of Doc. He yipped twice, then disappeared.

Alanna couldn't blame him. This may go down in history as the most reckless idea of all time...if any of them lived through it to tell anyone.

She gripped the weapon to her chest. "Maybe the rest of you should leave?"

"No way." Cal placed his hand on her shoulder. "I'm here with you."

"Me too," Doc said.

"You know I've always got your back, beautiful," Ethan said.

The gun warmed slightly in her hands. She loved them all so much, but she didn't want them in the room if she couldn't do this. If she failed, and Alexander got mad enough to kill them all, she wouldn't be able to live with herself. Not that she'd live all that long if Alex started spraying them all with molten primordial energy.

Rachel got out of her seat and shoved Kile. "Why are you doing this? Alex could kill you."

He cupped her cheek with his huge hand. "I believe I loved you once. If Alexander has any memory of his relationship with the navigator, he could be a definitive ally."

"Ally in what?" Cal asked.

Kile lowered his hand. "I've been considering your over-ambitious hopes for the future, Mr. Espinoza. The galaxy has changed, and if we could show Geron that allowing his enforcers outside interests may be a boon rather than an inconvenience, I believe we have a chance to realign his thinking."

The room heated again before a flash of white light morphed into Alexander. His golden-white hair floated about him like he was underwater. Alanna stood and backed to the wall, pressing the gun behind her back.

She could do this. For Alexander. For her friends.

Alex's ice-blue eyes seemed lifeless as he glanced around the room. "More trouble with the former smugglers?"

Kile walked past him. "On the contrary. I've been having an interesting conversation with the captain."

Alex smirked at Cal. "I highly doubt that."

Alanna gritted her teeth, praying Cal didn't tell him off. What was it about enforcers that made them all act like such jerks?

Kile folded his arms. "We believe that Geron needs a realignment of thinking."

"*We* believe? Have you called me here to bring you back for a feeding?"

"No. I called you back here to convince you to help me discuss the point with our sponsor."

"You obviously need a feeding." He held out a hand to Kile. "Come. I'll bring you right to Geron."

"No. I don't need a feeding."

"Yes, you do."

"No, I don't."

A ball of purple-blue flames appeared in Alexander's palm. "Yes, you do."

Sweat beaded on Alanna's brow.

This was it. But when should she shoot?

Kile flexed his fingers and his own fist started to glow.

Alexander's head tilted slightly. "Are you threatening me, Commander?"

"I believe you threatened me first."

The fire in Alexander's hand churned. "Stand down."

Ethan slowly got out of his chair and moved toward the wall with Ty.

Kile glanced at Alanna standing behind Alexander. She

nodded, her hand shaking on the gun concealed behind her back.

Kile ignited the purple flames in his other hand.

"Do not test me," Alexander said. "You will not enjoy the outcome."

"You may be stronger than I am, but I think you underestimate the power of experience."

Alexander reset his footing. "Stand down."

The glow in both Kile's hands increased. "I am your commander."

"That is in rank only, and you know it."

"I think your ego is getting the better of you, boy."

The lights in Alexander's fists flashed. "You are coming back with me. Now."

"No. I'm not."

Kile raised his fists, but the fire erupted from Alexander first. The blast of light slammed into Kile, spreading over him as if he held a large, medieval shield.

Alanna raised the gun, her hands shaking.

Could she really do this? Could she shoot Alexander?

Cal placed his hand on her arm and mouthed the word "wait."

Her breath hitched. Her lower lip trembled.

As badly as she wanted to get this over with, they needed to give Kile enough time to drain Alexander's energy.

She needed to be cool. Calm… Easy to say when you weren't about to shoot the man you loved.

Alex growled at Kile, the light around them intensifying. "Stand down, Commander. We both know how this will end."

Kile's gaze remained stony and defiant through the swirling flames.

Sweat dampened Alanna's palms as the heat filled the room. She gripped the gun tighter as her finger slipped onto the trigger.

Kile fell to one knee. A beam of flames broke through his defenses, singeing his shoulder.

"Stand down!" Alex repeated. "Let me take you back. Geron can fix this."

Another swath of flame broke through, scorching the other shoulder.

Alanna raised the gun.

"Not yet!" Kile cried.

Alex cocked his head again. *"Not yet?"*

Kile's shield dissipated, becoming a sheer ball. Flames engulfed him.

The commander screamed. His cry echoed off the walls.

That was it. She couldn't take it anymore. Alanna focused on the back of Alexander's neck and fired.

Flamed still circled Kile, and Alexander didn't even flinch. Had she missed?

Alanna stood frozen as Alexander touched the back of his neck and turned toward her.

Her stomach roiled as she met eyes filled with stark fury.

What did she do? Should she shoot again?

The flames winked out as Alexander blinked, shifting slightly like his vision had begun to spin. He grunted, grabbing his temples before he fell to his knees.

Doc ran to Kile lying on the floor behind Alex. "Big Guy, are you okay?"

The commander pushed Doc away, staring at Alex kneeling on the floor, holding his head. "Don't fight it, Alexander! Let it in."

Alex turned to him. "What are you talking about?"

"Look around you. Remember."

Alexander closed his eyes instead. "I need to be fed. I need to…"

Alex started to glow, like he was about to project himself off the ship.

"No!" Alanna dropped the gun and scrambled to him, grabbing his face. "Take what you need from me."

Alex blinked, looking at her. "What?"

"I'm here, Alex. I haven't given up on you."

His breathing slowed as a coolness ghosted over her skin.

"That's it," she said. "I'm here."

He stared into her eyes. "How-How are you doing this?"

"I don't really know. But you figured it all out, remember? I was feeding you for months. I became your sponsor."

"You're not strong enough."

"Maybe not as strong as Geron, but I am strong enough. You never got tired or lost your strength like the others, remember?"

He placed his hands over hers. "Alanna?"

She burst into tears. "Yes."

She hugged him, and he reluctantly returned the embrace.

Alex eased her away. "Everything is strange. Like a dream."

Kile pulled himself over. His face and hands were red, like he had a severe sunburn. Parts of his uniform were blackened and charred.

He winced with each movement. "Give it time. It will come back."

"It didn't come back for you." Rachel hugged herself. "You said you didn't remember."

Kile's lips thinned. "I didn't forget everything. I only lost bits and pieces."

"You mean all the times we were alone."

He didn't meet her gaze. "Those times, and others. Geron was efficient, leaving anything of tactical value and erasing the rest."

The question was: Had he done the same thing to Alexander?

"Are you okay?" Alanna reached for Alex. "Are you *you* again?"

He rubbed his temples, his brow furrowed like it hurt. "You shot me."

"Yes, but only because I thought it would help." She laughed. "Stars, that sounded like something Ethan would say." She ran her fingers through Alex's hair. "Do you remember me?"

He pressed his palms against the sides of his head. "Yes, but no. Things are surfacing, but it's skewed. It doesn't make sense."

Kile panted beside him. "Don't fight it. Those are memories stolen from you."

Alexander blinked, looking at Kile. "I hurt you." He reached for Kile and the air in the room heated. A soft, barely discernible shimmer of light hovered over them before the burns on Kile's skin started to fade.

"Amazing," Doc whispered.

Kile's eyes remained on Alex. "All you were capable of was defending your sponsor and following your programming to heal the wounded. In my case, you knew I needed feeding to heal what you thought was an ailment."

Alexander blinked, shaking his head like trying to clear a fog. "Is this what Dania went through?"

"Yes, but probably slower," Doc said. "She had all the symptoms, but over time. The artificial pathogens helped."

"You don't need those monstrosities in your system," Kile said.

Alex's lips thinned. "I need Geron."

"No!" Alanna grabbed Alex's face again.

He placed one palm over hers. "I know I need him, but I don't want to go. I feel…" He took two deep breaths.

"Free?" Kile asked.

Alex lowered his gaze. "Yes."

Alanna covered her mouth to hold the sob back in. She'd done it! Alex was back!

Kile grunted, pulling himself to his feet. "You should rest. Here, on this ship. And then we need to talk." He glanced around at the crew. "I fear waking Alexander was the easiest part of this plan."

CAL PACED the bridge as Ty maneuvered the *Star Renegade* through the *Oliganton*'s massive air shield and into their docking port.

"This isn't a spaceship," Alanna said. "It's like a moving city."

"You gotta admit it's pretty cool." Ty maneuvered them toward a glowing landing platform. "I hope some of the Kever engineers survived so they can build some more of these things...you know...as long as they're not filled with homicidal enforcers chasing us down."

Alexander and Kile waited on the platform below and started walking to the ship as soon as Ty had turned off the engines.

Alanna stood and walked toward the exit. "I'm going down there."

"Hold on." Ty spun his chair, but she was already out the door. "Somebody's excited."

"Hopefully, she won't be disappointed." Cal tapped the button sequence to lower the cargo ramp and headed for the door.

Ty followed him down the hallway. "You're not afraid they aren't going to let us leave?"

"I asked Kile point blank if we were considered criminals, and he said *no*. One thing that never faded with any of them was their inability to lie."

"But they all figured out how to dance around the truth, though."

"That's why I asked him the same question five different ways until he got mad and told me this wasn't a trap."

They stepped off the ladder onto the lower level just as Alexander and Kile stepped on board. Alanna ran to Alexander and stopped a few feet from him. "Do you still remember me?"

He held open his arms. "I will do everything in my power never to forget you again."

Rachel ran down the upper ramp from the other side of the ship and stopped near Kile. "Do you remember me yet?"

Kile's lips thinned, and he shook his head.

Rachel stomped her foot, looking at Alexander and Alanna embracing. "This isn't fair."

She turned and ran back up the ramp.

"Ms. Quirky!" Kile reached for her but didn't follow.

Obviously, he had orders he needed to complete before talking to her.

"Do you know what Geron wants to speak to me about?" Cal asked.

"He didn't elaborate. However, he didn't force me or Alexander to feed, either." He grimaced. "Then again, I took Dania's lead from when she was in our situation and made sure we talked to him when he was exhausted from feeding those who *were* in desperate need."

"Alanna might be able to help you if you're getting a little shaky." Cal smirked. "She might make you say *pretty please*, though."

"I may consider that, unless things change faster than I anticipate. Right now, only Alexander, Hendry, and I are lobbying for *free enforcer reserves*, as we are calling it. Geron only seemed to listen because he understood that none of us wanted to leave him. He still wants control, though. I sense he's annoyed by the whole idea."

"It's a new way of thinking. I don't doubt it."

Ethan jumped down the last few steps of the ladder. "I'm here, Big Guy."

"What are you doing here?" Cal asked.

"I just got a high-priority communication." Ethan stuck out his chest. "Our newly crowned king asked for me personally."

Cal looked at Kile. "Really?"

"Indeed. Apparently, our king finds him just as capable as I do."

"You know it!" Ethan tried to put his arm around Kile's shoulder but only managed to get his arm halfway up his torso.

Kile's lips thinned. "Your enthusiasm is unnecessary."

Ethan elbowed him in the side. "Aww, you're just say'n that, Big Guy. I know you love it." He started walking toward the exit.

Kile turned to the ramp that led to the second level of the *Star Renegade*, and the doorway Rachel had disappeared through.

"You okay, Big Guy?" Cal asked.

The commander turned to the exit. "I find it most unpleasant when she cries."

Cal looked up at the second level. "You can hear her?"

"I'm an…"

"Enforcer. I know, I know. I shouldn't have asked."

Kile took one last glance at the upper level, then followed Ethan down the cargo ramp.

Alexander gave Alanna a kiss before he and Cal strode onto the *Oliganton*.

How much Alex remembered was still a mystery, but Alanna seemed happy. For now, that was the biggest plus in all of this.

That, and the galaxy being saved. But that already felt like years ago, rather than just a few days.

The *Oliganton* was bustling with Kevers and a few humans racing through the halls like they were on high alert. Most of them were probably getting used to their new home, after they'd sacrificed Geron's original cruiser in the bait-and-switch operation.

Which was, Cal had to admit, brilliant on Geron's part. Or maybe it had been Dania's plan.

Not that it really mattered. Earth had been saved. That had been the goal. How it had happened was something to probably be contested in history books. For now, he was just happy they were all still alive.

Kile and Alex led them to a massive set of doors that parted as they approached.

Geron sat at the other side of the room at a round table that hovered about five feet off the floor. Geron's translator and the Kever princess stood beside him. The red crystals running down the front of Kalina's dark-blue gown glinted in the overhead lighting.

As Cal, Alex, Kile, and Ethan stepped inside, four chairs detached from the walls and slid at places equidistant from each other around the table.

It was an interesting setup for a Kever vessel, leaving no one at the proverbial 'head' of the table.

Geron glanced at the princess. Kever words warbled from his lips before the translation exploded in Cal's mind.

"Kalina, return to your rooms."

She bowed. "As you wish." She wrinkled her nose at Cal as she scurried past and exited.

Ethan walked toward Geron and waved. "Hey, Your Highness-ness. Looking good. I guess kingliness suits you."

Geron tilted his head. "I no doubt look no different than I did the last time I saw you. But your human pleasantries are expected and understood."

"Yeah. Um, you're welcome." Ethan pulled out the seat to Geron's left and sat.

Kile gaped at him.

Cal had to admit that was a little presumptuous, even for Ethan.

Alex seemed to bite back a grin before taking the seat next to Ethan. Kile took the seat to Geron's right and Cal took the last seat between Alex and Kile.

Ethan folded his hands on the table. "So, nice place you got here."

The air behind Geron wavered and Dania stepped out of the shadows. "This human's mockery is unacceptable."

Cal jumped. He hadn't even seen her there. Her hair floated high above her head, a striking white rather than beautiful dark blonde, and her brown eyes had regained the color of blue ice as she scowled at them.

Cal shivered. She seemed even more lost than she'd been when he'd first dragged her onto the *Star Renegade* in handcuffs.

Geron held up his hand. "Be at ease, Dania. I have nothing to fear from these humans."

"They waste your time, Ada."

"Allow me to be the judge of that."

She narrowed her eyes on Ethan, then turned that steely gaze on Cal. There was no longer the desire to kill in those eyes, but there was a deadliness there, as well as a complete lack of compassion. The being standing behind Geron was no longer Dania. It was a specter—something evil living in her body, looming behind her king with a deadly, fluid grace.

It was interesting that she didn't call up a chair for herself. It was probably so she could be ready to defend Geron, executing anyone with the flick of her wrist.

The new king kept his attention on Cal. "My commander tells me that you have delusions of free enforcers protecting the galaxy."

Cal met his gaze, careful not to flinch from the heated focus of a being with what seemed like nearly limitless power, and the ghoul standing behind him, ready to end Cal's life should he say anything she considered illegal.

"I'm guessing, since Kile and Alexander still have their free will, that you don't necessarily consider it a delusion."

Geron's expression remained stony. "Kile, Alexander… stand."

They both stood without hesitation, almost like it had been rehearsed.

Geron pointed to his left. "Left."

They both winked out and reappeared at his side.

The king pointed to his right. "Right."

They disappeared again and reappeared on his right.

He pointed to their seats, and they both walked over and pulled out their chairs.

"Sit," Geron said.

They sat at exactly the same moment, almost like they'd been shoved down from a force above them.

Geron leaned toward Cal. "Do not misconstrue independent thought with what it is to be an enforcer."

Cal did his best not to cringe at the disgusting display of what any human would call slavery. "But you didn't erase their feelings when they asked to remain free."

"A mistake," Dania said.

"I don't think so, Dani," Ethan said. "I mean, I kinda like these guys now. Heck, I even used to like *you* when you didn't have a pile converter shoved up your butt."

Blue flames appeared in Dania's hand.

Geron lifted his finger, and Dania's fire winked out. She still glared at Ethan, though.

The king's expression remained placid. "My commander and my healer requested that they be last on the list to be fed. I am still in complete control, so I see no issue in granting that request."

"They are weak in their condition, Ada," Dania said.

"At this moment, few of my enforcers are at full strength. Luckily, we are currently at peace and our only enemy is on the run. Orion is doing a fine job in Kile's stead."

Kile flinched. Cal supposed he wouldn't be too happy, either, if someone else was gunning for his job.

"So, why did you ask me here?" Cal asked.

"Because you are the captain, and I respect a chain of command. I require the assistance of your engineer."

Cal startled. "What for?"

"Because your engineer has a penchant for extreme, unfettered honesty." Geron turned to Ethan beside him. "I am interested in your opinion."

Ethan straightened. "You got it. I'm always filled with opinions."

"Indeed." Geron's irises seemed to glow in the odd alien lighting. "My commander tells me that due to recent events, humans may be willing to be tested for the honor of being an enforcer."

Ethan rubbed his chin. "Well, not everyone, but yeah, I think that people probably would see that enforcers could use all that scary power for good, but I think you need more than that."

"Elucidate."

Ethan frowned. "Eluci-who?"

Dania reset her footing. "It means *clarify,* you fool."

"Ah, yeah. Thanks for the info, Dani. Always a pleasure." Ethan batted his lashes at her. "And my, what *big, scary, blue eyes* you have."

He was going to get his face burned off if he wasn't careful.

Geron held his forehead. "Would you please clarify?"

Ethan nodded. "Okay. You remember your father, the asshole?"

The king visibly tensed. "He is a being hard to forget."

"Okay. Well, let's focus on that asshole-ness. What made him an asshole to you?"

Dania's hair swirled wildly. "We are not here to speak ill of our past king."

"It's all right, Dania. You know I detested my father." Geron turned back to Ethan. "My father was of one mind. He refused to listen to others."

"Okay. Hold that thought." Ethan pointed at Dania. "Can I be frank without her burning my face off?"

Geron raised a brow. "Dania, you will not dole out punishment today for anyone for any reason."

She gasped. "Ada!"

He waved his hand, not even looking at her. "Continue."

Ethan winked at Dania. He was definitely pressing his luck.

"So," Ethan continued, "you don't want to be like your dad, right?"

"Of course not."

"Okay, then, maybe you should stop being an asshole."

Dania's hands erupted in flames. She snarled, probably realizing she was physically incapable of burning Ethan to a crisp.

Geron laughed. It was an odd, metallic sound. "You are nothing if not entertaining." He leaned on the table. "How, exactly, am I an *ass-hole*?"

"Well, you are of one mind, and you refuse to listen to others."

"I am not."

"Oh, heck, yeah, you are."

Dania clenched her hands into fists. "Ada, allow me to remove this useless human."

Geron turned and faced her for the first time. "You will no longer speak unless I give you permission to do so."

She gaped before she closed her mouth and looked down.

If that had been his Dania, Cal would have felt sorry for her. No thinking, feeling being should be mentally controlled like that. If his Dania were in there, could she see through the general's eyes?

Cal wanted to smile at her and give her some sense of comfort that he was still there, fighting for her, but that would only anger Dania DuBane further.

Geron's lips were thin as he turned back to Ethan, but Cal wasn't sure if he was angry with Dania, or with Ethan's Ethan-ness.

"I do not refuse to listen to others. I am seeking counsel right now."

"Maybe, but you've already decided that you're going to erase Kile and Alex as soon as their number is up. Right?"

Geron's reptilian eyes narrowed. "Correct."

"Well, a short stay of execution is still an execution. If you had listened to them, you would have realized that the whole idea has merit."

"Explain."

"You just said that we're at peace. You have time to build up your enforcers. You can do that easily if people volunteer. People *will* volunteer if they are guaranteed that you won't erase who they are, and if you stop killing people for no reason."

"Enforcers only execute the guilty."

"But the whole idea of executions for every crime is ridiculous. I mean, did you always follow the rules when you were a kid?"

"Of course not. I was learning."

"Right. But enforcers kill kids all the time for breaking the law. You can't tell me that a kid who does something by mistake will end up a hardened criminal, or that someone who steals some fruit to feed his kids is really a danger to society."

"You want to go back to the prison systems of your ancient past? That rarely worked and was an excessive drain on public resources."

"I'm not saying I have the answers." Ethan blushed as he scratched the back of his neck. "But what I *am* saying is that you have a chance to make a fresh start. Show people that you intend to be an even better king. Show them you have mercy."

"You want me to have mercy for the guilty?"

"Not for everyone, but you could maybe have mercy for those who deserve a second chance."

Geron drummed his fingers on the table. "You are saying that there should be different levels of crime?"

"Exactly. And believe me, with some of the freaky stuff enforcers can do as punishments, people will be scared enough not to commit crimes, even without the threat of death."

Geron's lips parted. "Are you suggesting public maiming?"

"Well, no—at least, I don't think so." Ethan looked down before waving his hand in front of his face. "I'm not smart enough for that, but I'm saying you can create a new galactic law. Make enforcers a true police force. Make people love them, rather than running whenever they see them. You have the unique opportunity to make the galaxy an even better place. The people will love you, rather than curse your name in dark corners like they used to do with your dad."

"My father was celebrated for saving the Earthan Cradle."

"Yeah, for a few weeks after the Carteks were gone. Then the enforcers started enforcing. Believe me, opinions changed quickly." Ethan leaned his elbow on the table. "Dude, make a difference. You can be the cool king people are excited about and would flock to have their picture taken with. They wouldn't be burning you in effigy behind closed doors."

Geron grimaced, staring at the table.

Kile and Alexander passed glances at each other, their eyes wide. Had Ethan actually gotten through to Geron?

Would he be willing to watch over Earth as a benevolent king, rather than a totalitarian overlord?

Geron stood suddenly, and Cal and Ethan both startled as his bulk suddenly encompassed the room..

The Kever placed his hands on the table, still staring at the glossy surface before he turned to Kile. "If you are not fully fed, you will be encumbered by the stressors of the things you've done."

Kile seemed to consider his response. "Frankly, Ada, I've been shielding myself for years, making you believe I needed less of a feeding than I actually did. I always enjoyed a certain amount of autonomy. I found emotional thought grounding."

"Emotions are counterproductive."

"I disagree, Ada. I focused my emotions into art."

Geron narrowed his eyes. "Art?"

"Yes. I found solace in the ancient Earthan practice of drawing. Paper and pencil." He lowered his eyes. "I drew the faces of those I'd passed judgment on and asked for forgiveness."

Dania growled behind Geron, her eyes flaring in anger.

"This didn't weaken you?"

"I always did my duty, Ada. Part of me wanted to stay..." He frowned, as if rethinking his words.

"Continue," Geron said.

"Keeping my own thoughts made me feel more *real*. I didn't want to lose myself." He looked at Geron. "Have you ever been unhappy with my performance, Ada?"

"Never. You are one of my more trusted enforcers."

"Then I would hope, Ada, that your own words will give you your answer."

Dania growled again. She shook like she might light herself on fire with her own angry pathogens.

Geron turned to Alexander. "And you…part of your energy has molded to the resonance of the human female. I find this troubling."

"It shouldn't trouble you, Ada. She makes me stronger."

"This connection puts her in a position to take you from me."

"She is in a position to *keep me strong* while I am away from you. She has significant primordial energy, but it's nothing like yours. Even when I was the most comfortable with her power, I was always drawn back to you."

"So, you would serve me, even if I allow you to be with her?"

"I would, Ada."

Geron's attention turned back to that blank space on the table. Could he actually be considering this?

Ethan clapped his hands and sat back. "See? This could be the answer to everything."

The king's face remained emotionless. "I highly doubt that is an accurate assumption."

"But it *is* a possibility. You have to admit, the idea has merit."

Geron's chest puffed out, and he slowly released a breath.

"You don't have to do it all at once," Ethan said. "You can maybe do a trial run. You can let Alexander, Kile, and Dania free and see how you like it."

The temperature in the room spiked. Fire erupted around Dania, casting a halo around her.

"You may speak, Dania." Geron's gaze remained centered on the table.

"I will have nothing to do with this lunacy. My place is at your side, Ada." Her gaze latched on Cal. "You weakened me with Palian steel, then you poisoned me, purging my blood of everything that made me strong." Her eyes darkened. "You will never have that opportunity again."

Cal's chest tightened. Every time she opened her mouth, he had less hope that any part of the woman he loved had survived.

Geron held up his hand and the fire around Dania winked out.

The king looked at Cal. "It seems we have three different opinions on the situation."

Cal gripped the edge of the table. "The single negative vote is coming from the only enforcer in this room who is so hyped up on your primordial energy that she's incapable of thinking for herself."

Flames appeared in Dania's hands again. "Insolent, narrow-minded fool."

Cal didn't flinch. If he were going to die today, he'd rather have it be at the hands of the woman he loved.

"You're calling me *narrow-minded*? Think about it, Dania. Your most trusted commander and your best friend are both lobbying for freedom. You are the only one here with an overload of Geron's power. You're incapable of channeling anything but exactly what Geron wants you to think."

"As it should be."

Alexander leaned on the table. "It doesn't have to be that way."

"Yes, it does." Dania took a step toward him but still remained behind Geron. "I will take great pride in bringing you back to your full strength, Alexander, and then we will be able to speak about this more rationally."

"When you're both back under Geron's total control, mentally and physically?" Cal asked.

"Yes."

"Can you even hear yourself?" Cal stood. "You used to love long conversations at night. You used to love learning new recipes and blending spices together. You loved to play games in the lounge and learn about all the things you missed in life because you were trapped in indominable servitude of a prince."

"Those were all useless, unhelpful things."

"You were happy, Dania. Are you happy now? Can you honestly say that you are happier now than you were on the *Star Renegade?*"

Her nose twitched. Her lips thinned.

Geron looked over his shoulder at her. "Answer."

She blinked twice. "Those things had no meaning. There was no value to them. They did nothing to serve my sponsor."

"That's not what I asked you," Cal said.

Geron stood and faced her. "Answer the question."

Cal clawed at his seat as Geron cupped her cheek. Ethan shook his head at Cal, a gentle reminder that none of them wanted to die today.

Dania lowered her eyes. "I cannot answer the question, Ada, because I am incapable of lying. I do not know the answer, because those memories are foreign to me." She raised her gaze. "But I cannot fathom a life where I would not want to be at your side. The smuggler's disgusting excuse for a doctor poisoned me. I would never leave you." She sneered at Alexander and Kile. "No enforcer in their right mind would ever leave their sponsor."

Cal cringed. Those were almost the exact words that Kile had said to her when he'd been fully charged. How deep in their psyche did this programming go? And was it possible to erase the damage already done? Would Kile ever remember his time with Rachel? Would Dania ever remember Cal?

Geron held her face between his large, green-blue hands and leaned down, kissing her forehead. Her lips parted and she sighed.

Cal gritted his teeth. Every moment she was near him, she absorbed more and more of that blasted power. She was slowly slipping further and further into the abyss, and she had no idea that she was losing herself.

Geron turned back to them. "I will allow Alexander and Kile to live at their current energy levels." He looked at each of them. "You will return to me weekly to make sure your primordial energy is stabilized. I will not allow you to suffer or begin to drain." He grimaced. "This experiment is over if you become sick, or if this arrangement becomes inconvenient in any way. You will be expected to serve like any other."

"Does that mean you are going to give all of your enforcers the choice to be free?" Cal asked.

"That remains to be seen." Geron turned to Ethan. "This is, as you suggest, a trial run."

"That sounds fair. Totally fair." Ethan beamed. "Right, Cal?"

Maybe, if the Kever could be trusted. "How do we know that when they come back in a week, you won't change your mind and erase their memories of this conversation?"

"Because I am giving you my word. Even better..." He looked at Kile, then Alexander. "I am giving you both my word that I will allow this trial to go on. The outcome of this experiment is up to you. If I see or feel any lack of dedication, the experiment is over."

They both lowered their heads and said in tandem, "Thank you, Ada."

The level of control that Geron had, even with them both thinking clearly, made Cal's skin crawl. Still, this was a step in the right direction.

"What about Dania?" Cal asked.

"Never," she hissed.

Geron held up his hand, silencing her again. "You are correct that Dania is linked to me, and her thoughts and desires are very much my own. This is as it has to be. She is my general, and I need her to link my enforcers if needed."

"We aren't at war anymore," Cal said. "You don't need that much control over her."

"No, but I can't take the chance of losing her again. I need her at my side."

Alexander stood slowly. "May I speak, Ada?"

"Of course."

"I was meant to be your general. I would be willing to be reprogrammed to take on the role of second general for you."

Geron stared at him, gaping. "You ask me this, yet you also ask for less power coursing through your veins? Those requests are in direct conflict with each other."

"Not necessarily, Ada. When this trial is over, and you see that the commander and I are still loyal, and you expand the program, I believe you'll see that you can easily cycle enforcers in and out of service as we've been lobbying for. Dania and I can share the role, giving each of us time for *personal pursuits*."

Dania's nose flared. "I do not want personal pursuits."

Geron sat back in his chair. "Let us not, as the humans like to say, *get ahead of ourselves*. We shall monitor this experiment for five weeks and then discuss how we will proceed."

Alexander bowed. "A wise course of action, Ada."

"You are only being appeased." Dania folded her arms. "You'll soon be begging for forgiveness."

She turned and her eyes bored into Cal like she was counting down the days before he committed a crime, and she could wipe his existence from the galaxy forever.

Cal sucked in a breath. He needed to get it into his head that she may be beyond saving, but he'd still fight like hell until he knew for sure.

CHAPTER 61
CAL

DUST KICKED up around Cal's ankles. Real dust—made from dirt, rather than years of metallic particles built up on the surface of a starship. He left the Naples space port and walked into the villages, following a handheld GPS. The buildings rose several stories on either side of the street, and people mulled about, most on the right side of the street heading away from the space port, and most on the left heading toward it.

In many ways, Naples looked like any other colony, but the skies on Earth were a richer blue than Cal had ever seen. And the soft tufts of clouds drifting above looked like you could reach out and touch them.

With most of Earth still reeling from the bombs and the effects of the EMP destroying a large portion of the anti-quated communications network, it had taken him far longer than he'd hoped to pinpoint the location of his ancestors' family home. Now that he was here, his palms sweated, and his heart raced. He had no idea what he'd find when he made it to the address flashing on the small screen, or if he'd even make it there before the small, damaged satellite above moved out of range.

The GPS led him deeper into the city, where the crowds abated, revealing the deep, ancient paving stones beneath his feet. He smiled at the impracticality of a street more concerned with beauty than a smooth, traversable surface, but this place seemed frozen in time, and there was a sense of peace in that.

The buildings seemed older the farther he got from the space port, and fewer people passed on the street. Those who did bowed their heads slightly and said, *"Buongiorno."*

Cal tried to repeat the word, but he was sure he was butchering the pronunciation. No one seemed to mind, though.

While the pavers completely covered the areas between the buildings, each home had a planter box at the front door, and many had long boxes streaming with greenery hanging from the windows as well. It was like bringing the country into the city, and the smells of slow-cooked sauces drifting from the open windows reminded him of simpler days.

Two women entered the street from an alley, laughing while carrying bags. As Cal neared them, one stopped short. The woman dropped her bag and gasped, covering her mouth.

"Luis?" She grew pale, her hand shaking.

Cal froze, shocked to hear someone call him by his father's name, until his gaze locked on to eyes he was incapable of forgetting.

His mother's hair was grayer than Cal had expected. Deep lines had set in around her lips, but her eyes were as brown and beautiful as he remembered.

He took a tentative step toward her. "Mom, it's me."

"C-Calvin?" Her bottom lip trembled.

Cal choked down the sob building in his throat. "Yeah, it's me." He held out his hands. "Surprise."

She cried out and ran to him. Cal met her halfway and pulled her into his arms. She smelled like basil, rosemary, and mint. She smelled like home.

He held her tightly, afraid that if he let go, she'd disappear like a dream. "I didn't think I'd ever see you again."

She leaned back and wiped his cheeks with her fingers. "Nonsense. I knew you'd make it home eventually."

Cal looked up at the tightly-placed buildings. "This is a little far from the farms of Gratuga."

She placed her hand on his chest. "Home is where your family is." She turned to the woman she'd been walking with. "Regina, this is your nephew, Calvin."

Regina smiled. She had his mother's eyes. "I figured. Welcome home, Calvin."

He reached out to shake her hand. "Pleased to meet you. You can call me *Cal*."

She glanced at his hand. "So formal." She held out her arms. "Give your aunt a hug."

Cal laughed. "Okay."

She hugged him, rocking him from side to side. "My sister has been talking about you nonstop. Her boy, out there taking on the galaxy." She picked up the bag that his mother had dropped and handed it to him. "Were you out there fighting the invasion?"

They started walking in the direction they had come from.

"I was one of a lot of ships."

His mother wrapped her hands around his arm. "I bet you have lots of great stories."

"Yeah. I'm still trying to wrap my head around it. Some of it seems hard to believe, and I lived through it."

His mother squeezed his arm. "My son, the hero."

Cal shook his head. "I don't know about that. I'm just one of many people who were out there."

She tapped his biceps. "But a hero all the same."

They steered him to one of the doorways with planters teeming with fresh herbs on either side of a six-paneled wooden entryway.

Regina opened the door. "My home is your home."

Wooden floors lined a small foyer with a set of stairs to the side. Vines grew from pots on the floor, trailing up the railings. Sunlight from a second-floor window illuminated a small patch of fruit clinging to the vine.

They walked into the kitchen, and Regina pointed to the table. "Have a seat. Your mother and I will get to work on dinner."

Cal scanned the rows of pots, cutlery, and gadgets he hadn't seen since leaving Gratuga. "I'd like to help."

"Do you still cook?" his mother asked.

"Of course! I always made meals for my crew whenever we could find real food." He smiled. "If they were here, I think they'd thank you for teaching me. They all seemed to enjoy it."

Regina drew a handful of carrots and celery from the refrigerator. "It sounds like my nephew became an important man. Captain of your own ship? It sounds like a dream."

Cal took the carrots and placed them on a cutting board. "I don't really know if it was a dream, or a calling made out of necessity. A trader was nice enough to hide me for a while. Then he gave me a ship when I was ready to leave." Cal started slicing the carrots. "I used that ship to pay back his kindness."

His mother rubbed his back. "That sounds noble."

Cal piled up his sliced carrots. "I guess. It just seemed like the right thing to do. You and Dad always taught me to stick up for those who can't stick up for themselves." Of course, that was how he'd gotten himself slapped with a murder charge, taking the blame for a child who would have never lived to be an adult if they'd caught him.

That murder charge had set Cal on the run, though. If he hadn't smuggled himself out of a bad situation in a cargo container, he never would have ended up on Kirato. Then Stanley never would have given him the *Star Renegade*, so Cal never would have helped feed that colony. And he wouldn't have built a crew that had become an instrumental part in the war.

'*All things happen for a reason*,' that enforcer had told him.

Maybe that was true.

"Is there anyone special in your life?" his mother asked.

Cal lowered his gaze, staring at the pile of carrots.

She put her arm around his shoulder. "I'm sorry, sweetheart. Did something happen?"

Cal sighed. "It's complicated."

"It always is. Did you love her?"

"Yeah. I think I did. And I think she loved me, too. But that wasn't enough."

"It's always enough," Regina said. "It doesn't mean it will be easy, but it's always enough."

Cal pushed the carrots into a bowl and grabbed the celery. "In this case, it wasn't." He shook his head. "I can't even be mad at her. She made the right decision for the greater good. She's one of the big reasons Earth survived."

His mother frowned. "Did she die up there?"

"No." He rubbed his eyes. "Like I said, it's really complicated."

His mother took the knife from him and grabbed his hands. "If it was meant to be, it will happen. If it wasn't meant to be, then it was a great adventure that made you the man you are today."

Cal laughed. "Dad used to always say that."

"Which makes it all the more true." She released his hands. "Do you regret knowing her?"

"No. Not at all." He frowned, stunned by how quickly he'd answered.

"Then the only question left is: Was it a great adventure, or the start of your new life?"

"Can you call her?" Regina asked.

Cal leaned against the counter. "Not yet."

"Why not?" they both asked at the same time.

"This is where it gets complicated. I have to wait five weeks to see if it's even possible to get her back. It's too hard to explain, but I don't even know if she'll remember me."

"How could anyone forget my handsome son?"

"You're a little biased, Mom."

She tapped his cheek with her palm. "I'm your mother. I have the right to be biased." She picked up the knife and started chopping the celery. "So, is this *five weeks* starting now?"

"No. It took me some time to find you. I have three weeks and two days left."

She nodded. "Good. Then I look forward to meeting her in three weeks and four days." She nudged him with her elbow. "I'll give you two days to get reacquainted."

Cal huffed a small laugh, but tears formed in his eyes. "She told me once that she wanted to meet you."

"Why does that make you sad?"

Because there was a good chance Cal's version of Dania had been erased. Because the general who had taken over her body had no interest in humanity.

Cal rubbed his face. "I just can't even think about this anymore until I know if she's okay. It's driving me crazy."

His mother squeezed his shoulder. "So that gives you three weeks to spend with your mother. You'll relax while you're here and let me dote over you. We can cook together three times a day, just like we used to. You'll have no time to think about the world outside this village."

Cal smiled. "That sounds great."

She cupped his cheek with her palm. "You coming home is a reason to celebrate. There are so many members of our family who I'd love you to meet."

Cal pulled her into his arms. "I think I'd like that."

She squeezed him. "No matter what happens, I will always be here for you. If things don't go as planned, you always have family to come home to."

"When I was alone, lost, and running for my life, I dreamed of a home on Gratuga. A house in the middle of a field. Pastures. A little garden filled with herbs for cooking."

"A boy after my own heart." She smiled, wiping her hands on her apron. "All good things come in time."

Cal hoped so, because he was tired of running.

CHAPTER 62
DANIA

GERON STOOD in front of the windows in his father's old quarters. Outside, ships flew past in the distance, some grabbing wreckage from the battles. Scavengers usually annoyed her, but with so much debris circling Earth, the salvagers were a necessary component to bringing the Earthan Cradle back to its former beauty.

The rest of the room had been stripped of the opulent décor the former king had favored. The white, stark walls seemed a blank canvas, neutral and untested. She found the absence of pointed choices unnerving.

"So much has changed over the last five weeks." Geron turned from the stars that had always given him solace. "Only now have I been able to take it all in."

"You were victorious, Ada. The Kever people are safe, and you have kept your father's covenants."

"Yes, but now is the time to rebuild. This comes with even more challenging complications."

She was sure it would.

"Will you send the fleet back home to restore Keveron? My understanding is that it was desolated after the attack."

"Not yet. I've sent ships to assess the damage to the planet, but from those who witnessed the devastation, it will take decades to rebuild."

Although, with any luck, the line of ships they had patrolling space along the Cartek border would make sure Geron's engineers had the opportunity to replace critical infrastructures without the fear of another war tearing down what they'd built.

"You will see it done, Ada. I have no doubt."

"Thank you for your confidence."

That was an odd thing to say, when she was incapable of thinking him incompetent.

A swath of sadness overcame her, mixed with fear and the egotistical determination she was accustomed to in the presence of her sponsor.

"Are you okay, Ada?"

"As I said. It's difficult. Nothing is the same anymore. I'm being forced to make choices I don't want to make." He made a fist and held it tightly to his chest. "Choices that hurt me deeply."

"Then don't make those choices. You are the king. That's your right."

"But I do not want to be an *ass-hole*. I cannot make the same mistakes my father did." Geron rubbed his eyes. "My father always did what he wanted for the good of himself. He layered his poor decisions in pomp and pageantry, lauding how they helped Keveron, but in the end, most of those decisions only helped himself."

"I'm sure you will make good decisions, Ada."

"I'm trying. However, I'm unaccustomed to worrying about anyone but myself. I've never had to squelch my own desires for the greater good."

"We will persevere, Ada. There is nothing that we can't do."

His smile was uncharacteristically tender as he walked back to her and cupped her face with his hands. He stared into her eyes and kissed her. His power tingled on her lips, and she drank it in.

He leaned away, still holding her face. "You are aware of how much I love you."

"Of course, Ada. You love us all."

He stepped back. "Yes, I do." He looked back to the windows. "Alexander is on a mission that requires your assistance."

Dania frowned. She'd barely spoken to Alexander after reprimanding him for not following orders. She understood, though, that their programming was sometimes in direct opposition to each other. That didn't make things easier when he blatantly defied her, though.

She took a deep breath to steady herself. "Why was I not informed of this earlier?"

"Because it was unnecessary to concern you until now." He sat on the long, hard, shelf-like couch in front of the window. "Can you feel him?"

"Yes."

The air about him wavered slightly. "Go to him."

She straightened. "What are your orders once I get there?"

"No more questions. Go. Now."

She bowed. "Yes, Ada."

She called up her primordial energy and a thin veil of white light surrounded her. Geron covered his face with his palms, and she could sense an angry scream brewing in his lungs. Any other time, she would have stopped and consoled him, but she had a direct order to go to Alexander. She needed to comply.

The veil deepened and Geron disappeared. She concentrated on Alexander, their bond sliding her through the currents of energy until her feet settled on the ground and the light faded to an outcropping of thriving, green trees.

"Earth is beautiful, isn't it?" Alexander moved beside her and seemed to drink in the smell of the air.

That was an odd greeting, when she was here to assist with his mission. Still, the lush foliage was hard to ignore.

"The fauna is exemplary. I'm glad Geron was able to save the planet."

She and Alexander stood in a naturally clear area open to a blue sky dotted with soft, wispy clouds. Massive trunks surrounded them, lifting leaves high into the sky, while smaller saplings grew at their bases.

"Why are we here?" Dania asked.

Another presence pressed in on her, and Orion stepped out of the trees.

Had he been shielding himself from her?

She frowned. "What are you doing here?"

A wry grin appeared on his face. "I would not miss this opportunity—even if offered the chance to execute everyone who ever vexed my sponsor."

That was a lofty thing to say, especially for a man who was incapable of lying.

Kile stepped out of the trees several yards away. His breaths were shallow and his hands trembled. Fear was an inhibiting emotion that caused more harm than good. He would probably need a feeding sooner than any of them had anticipated.

She turned to Alexander. "Geron assigned you a mission?"

"He did." He stepped back. "Begin."

Heat flooded her from behind as a blast of primordial energy hit her between the shoulders.

She cried out. Alexander had been a distraction, causing her to let her guard down. Why would he not have warned her they were in danger?

Dania spun, her flaming hands raised, as Orion punched another bolt of light at her.

"Traitor!" She met his flames with her own.

How could this be happening? Had he devolved without Geron's knowledge? Had Ada forgotten to feed him, or possibly not properly recoded him?

She blasted through his flames, driving him to the ground. "What are you doing?"

"Putting you in your place." A wave of burning energy swept over her. Her skin tingled, but she swept the particles into a primordial ball and threw it back at him.

He stumbled back and fell, laughing. "That was far more satisfying than I ever could have imagined."

Madness was a possible consequence of war. They all knew this. She'd just never thought she'd have to deal with it in her own ranks.

"Stand down." Dania inched forward. "I will take you back to Geron to be fed."

Orion glared at her. "I assure you, I am fully fed."

He raised both his hands and the heat from this last attack devolved into ice. Her muscles ached as she swirled a shield in front of her. He gasped and a slight break formed in his energy weave. She centered her power on that flaw, and Orion lifted off his feet and slammed against a tree.

She stalked toward him. "Stop this. Whatever is wrong with you, we can fix it."

He punched his fists out. The trembling air tingled around her, landing needle-like holes into her shield. That blast of energy was meant to be a killing blow.

This was not a game, or even an exercise. One of her commanders was trying to murder her. How was this even possible?

If Geron were here, she'd ask for permission, but linking to her sponsor would take time she didn't have. The punishment for attacking your superior was death. She curled her fingers and channeled energy from her core. She drank in the power, delighting in the base energy of her sponsor, and then set it free.

Orion's eyes widened as his shield fell. He screamed, dropping to his knees.

"Enough!" A bolt of energy hit her shoulder, a pointed attack reducing the intensity of her power—a strike in a place only an enforcer would know where to hit her.

She spun, facing down Kile. "What are you doing?"

He raised both his hands and she left her feet, shooting through the air to land five-point-two-six yards from where Orion lay panting and staring at the sky.

Her head rang as she called on her power to hoist herself to her feet. "Have you all gone mad?"

Kile hit her again, sliding her back toward the trees.

She punched out a fist, dissipating his attack into a rain of useless sparks. "What's wrong with you?"

He raised both his hands and a swirl of energy started to form. Dania made a whip of primordial energy, holding him still.

She moved closer until she could see his eyes through the

weaves of air constricting him. "Don't you see what's happening? You let your power drain too far. You've lost your mind! This is why we must stay close to our sponsor. You need to abandon these ridiculous ideas of *reserve time* and re-devote yourself to your sponsor!"

That was the only explanation someone like Kile, whom she'd trust with her life, would turn on her. He was far too weak to even dream he could successfully attack her.

Although that didn't explain Orion, whose strength had been formidable. With that much power at his disposal, he should have been completely under Geron's control.

A thump pressed against her back. She spun to find Hendry with his hands raised. The stroke of his power had been nothing. He might as well have thrown a stone at her. She flicked her wrist, and he sailed into the trees.

Was there something in the air? Had the Earthan atmosphere done something to poison their minds?

Kile pressed his fists together, sending a bolt of energy into her chest despite the binding. She gasped, the wind knocking out of her lungs.

Dania's hands formed fists. "Don't make me hurt you."

His face showed none of the emotion she could see hiding behind his eyes. "I have no choice." A glow lighted about him as a storm of energy surged over her.

He'd obviously lost his mind. There was no other explanation.

His primordial energy kneaded her shield, searching for entry. If given the chance, Kile was experienced enough to find a way through. That, she could never allow.

She balled her power and a purple-green haze flowed over her. "I give you a last warning to stand down, Commander."

He sneered at her. "Never."

She let the bolt of energy free, and Kile screamed, yet somehow held the primordial energy still grappling at her shielding.

She increased the strength of her attack. He grimaced under the pressure before his gaze met hers. She'd looked into those eyes more times than she could remember.

He'd been there when she was a child. He'd trained her. He'd admonished her failures and celebrated her achievements. He was like family. Even in their disagreements, he'd been a solid force in her life, and now he'd left her with no choice but to end his life.

Tears welled in her lashes as she centered her power and darkened the swirling purple energy to black.

"Please stop," she whispered, pain building in her throat.

But his expression only hardened with a determination she'd learned could not be thwarted. He pressed his energy out and a knife of his power slashed through, slicing her thigh.

Whatever was wrong, he was past redemption. This was not her fault—it was his. The black cloud around her formed a spear and she flung it at his chest.

Her heartbeat drummed in her chest as the spear sliced through his shield and his eyes widened.

He'd been a nuisance…and a trusted friend, despite their differences. He was the last person she'd ever expected to turn on her. She felt his loss deepen with each microsecond. Her own heart tore open. His death was her fault.

This is not your fault. It's his fault. He gave you no choice.

She'd done the only thing she could think of to defend herself. So why did it hurt so much as his gaze latched on to hers as he took his last breath?

A blast of bright purple energy shot from her left,

throwing her lance off course and into the trees. Kile fell back, gasping for air and clutching his chest.

Alexander stood to his left, his hands alight and his hair whisking through the air.

"Not you, too." Dania's heart sank. "You have a mission. That mission should override any mental disease you've contracted."

Alexander eased to the left, maneuvering her focus from Kile. She could take a moment to throw a last killing blow, but that might give Alexander a chance to fling the considerable amount of energy dancing at his fingertips.

"You don't have to do this," she whispered. "Stand down. Geron can fix this."

A fireball screamed toward her from his left fist, then his right. She enhanced her shield to take the blow.

She'd given him a direct order. Even in his weakened state, he should have been compelled to comply.

They started to circle like two predators waiting to strike. As she and Alexander spun, she registered Kile lying on the ground, tendrils of smoke rising from his hair. Orion struggled to stand. Once she'd dealt with Alexander, she'd give them each a merciful death.

Her chest clenched.

Dealt with Alexander. How could she even think such a thing?

"Alexander, please think this through. This isn't you. You're my friend. My brother. You're my healer, sworn to protect me."

He punched and she ducked, the trees behind them igniting in yellow flame.

"This isn't possible!" she screamed at him.

His gaze remained determined. Focused. "It's completely

possible, Dania. An enforcer will follow their orders explicitly."

"You're insane. I am your general. Your orders come from me."

His eyes narrowed as another blast hit, then another. She pressed out her shield, spinning his energy back and throwing him to the ground.

She bore down on him, her fists in flames and tears blurring her vision. "You need to stop this."

"You know I can't." Alexander held up a palm swirling with blue light.

The blast of his power hit her jaw as hard as if he'd hit her with his fist.

She threw her power and he groaned as the blast exploded over him.

A mallet of energy slammed her from behind, hitting her between the shoulder blades with a *thump*. Dania turned, her power reflexively spiraling through the air.

Orion's eyes widened before the energy sliced through his chest, leaving a gaping hole where his heart had been. His lips formed an 'O' before he fell back, his corpse leaving a deep imprint in the grass.

Rage flooded her as she spun and sent the next blast squarely at Alexander's chest. He fended off the blow, the blast shooting over the trees.

His hands ignited again.

This outcome would be no different than the fight with Kile and Orion. This was a fight to the death. She just wished she understood what was wrong so she could try to fix it.

"Why, Alexander?"

"An enforcer is incapable of not following a direct order from their sponsor."

His power blasted at her shield, stabbing from all angles with a strength she'd never encountered before.

An enforcer is incapable of not following an order from their sponsor.

The words cut through her with the force of a million stars exploding.

He was following orders.

They had *all* been following orders.

She pressed power into her shield as Alexander's considerable strength blasted against her defenses.

Geron had given her a kiss. When she'd called up her power to project herself to the planet, he'd fallen into a chair and held his head. He'd screamed into his hands.

He knew what Alexander's mission was, because he had given the order.

Geron had sent her there to die.

But why? She'd been nothing but a faithful servant. She'd won a war for him.

She screamed, pressing all her strength into her shield. They may have been given an order to execute her, but he hadn't given her an order not to fight for her life.

Another power mixed with Alexander's. She blinked and gritted her teeth as Kile moved beside Alexander with flaming-blue hands.

A deep dread fell over her. She'd almost killed him, and he'd only been following orders. But how could she have known? Certainly, Geron hadn't expected her not to follow her coding to survive at all costs.

Her eyes grew heavy. The circle of energy around her grew thin. Alexander had always been stronger than her. She'd always wondered why. She never dreamed that his considerable strength would ever be aimed at her, nor that she'd be fighting against him for her right to live.

Her power flexed and she cringed, waiting for the burn of his energy to engulf her. As the heat touched her skin, it chilled, sinking into her and shooting through her veins. She fell to her knees as the pressure increased. She tried to take a breath, but it didn't come. She opened her mouth again, but it was like she was trapped in the vacuum of space. No air entered her lungs no matter how hard she tried.

Dania tried to cry out, but no sound came from her lips. Her lungs burned.

Dania looked up. Alexander's face was slightly warped from a shield of energy still holding her down.

She grabbed her throat. Did he hate her? Was he taking pleasure in watching her suffocate?

Alexander raised his hand. "Alanna! Now!"

The veil of energy around her dissipated. Tears filled Dania's eyes as her head started to pound.

A flare of purple erupted in front of her and Alanna appeared.

"I'm here!" Alanna grabbed Dania's face. "Dani! I'm here. Recharge yourself. Take my energy."

Dania sucked in a breath, and sweet, clean, glorious air filled her lungs. She sat and tried to push the woman away.

Alanna held firm. "Come on, Dani. You need to take the energy on your own. I don't know how to give it."

Dania started to sway. Sparkles of light flickered in her eyes.

Alexander's presence came closer, and Dania recoiled, awaiting the death blow.

He placed his hand on Alanna's back. "You need more contact."

The woman tucked Dania's head against her shoulder and clung to her. "Come on, Dani. You got this."

Dania's next breath cut her throat like shards of broken glass. "I don't need you," she rasped. "I need Geron."

"Well, tough." The woman gripped her tighter. "I'm not letting you go. I have no idea what I'm doing, but I sure as the stars am not giving up on my friend."

Dania willed her hands to push her away, but she could barely move. She took in another breath, then another.

The smuggler doctor appeared at her side. "She's breathing on her own. Keep doing what you're doing, girl."

"I don't know if this is helping," Alanna said.

Alexander placed his hand on Dania's forehead. "It's definitely helping."

Alexander stepped back, and the smuggler captain took his place. "Come on, Dania. Fight this."

Fight this? She was trying. She needed to get back to her sponsor. She was dying.

The doctor tapped a syringe, holding it up to the light. "This is the good stuff."

Dania flinched away, but that was the most she could do. The syringe sunk into her arm and a searing heat spread under her skin.

She scowled at him. "What have you done?"

"Just a little booster. You've had one before. Your body should remember in a minute."

Her breathing settled. The pain subsided. She tried to raise her hand, but the weight of her own arm seemed insurmountable. Why was she so...*weak?*

The navigator released her. "Are you okay?"

Dania blinked. A slight haze coated her eyes.

She looked past the woman to Alexander. "Geron wanted

me dead?" Dania dug her fingers into the silt, not sure if she wanted the answer.

"He didn't want you dead. He wanted you free to make your own choices."

Dania frowned. "I don't understand."

"Give yourself a few more minutes and I think you will."

Time was irrelevant. Alexander had crafted a pointed attack. Orion had thrown death blows, forcing her to expel a great deal of energy. Then Kile expounded on that.

Orion's shocked expression as he fell with a gaping hole in his chest flickered in her mind. Kile may have suffered the same fate had Alexander not taken his place, expelling the rest of Dania's strength.

She glared at her healer. "You're supposed to protect me."

"That's exactly what I've done."

The navigator touched Dania's cheek, smiling at her. "Do you remember me?"

The woman's eyes were kind, leaving Dania at ease.

But that was ridiculous. She was a smuggler. If Geron hadn't erased her past crimes, Dania would have executed her already.

A deep weight pressed on Dania's chest. She was glad that Geron had removed the woman's crimes. She didn't want to end her life.

But that was ridiculous. Why would she care? One criminal was the same as any other.

The woman slipped her hand into Dania's. "It's okay. I'm here. I'll stick with you just like I always have." She looked over her shoulder to the concerned faces around her. "We all will."

These faces were all familiar, but also had a slight haze around them. She remembered being handcuffed. She remembered being imprisoned in an energy shield. But there was something else…something slightly hidden under a veil. It was important. It gave context, but it was also slightly out of reach.

Dania closed her eyes, grabbed the edge of that veil…and lifted. She gasped as the woman's face flickered in her mind. Laughing. Crying. Staring at a hand of cards. Laughing again.

Dania blinked as the montage settled. "You showed me how to style my hair. You introduced me to games. You were my… You were my *friend*."

Dania held her head. That couldn't be right. The woman was a human. A crew member on a smuggling ship.

A man crouched beside her. A sadness filled his dark eyes, but also hope. "Do you remember me?"

"Calvin Espinoza." She sneered at him. "I suppose you're enjoying this."

He shook his head. "Not at all." He reached for her, then frowned, pulling his hand back. "Do you remember anything about me?"

"You are the captain of a smuggling ship. The man who dragged me into your cargo hold in Palian steel handcuffs."

Kile limped into view. "Geron erased anything about Calvin Espinoza that was inconvenient, just like he erased Rachel Quirky from my mind."

"What are you talking about?" Dania asked.

"You loved me once," Espinoza said.

A deep heat flooded through Dania's veins.

"Impossible. You are a former smuggler and a liar. You are lucky that the king has forgiven your past crimes."

Espinoza grabbed her hand. She tried to pull away, but he only gripped her tighter. "You love games. You love to cook.

You're kind and giving. You're not the monster you think you are."

"Who are you to tell me who I am?"

"I'm someone who loved you. Who *still* loves you."

"I would never love you."

"You did," Alexander said. "Geron stole your memories of him, and countless other memories he didn't want you to have."

"Can we get them back?" Alanna asked.

Dania held her head as their words swam in her mind. "My memories are fine."

The human captain sat on the ground beside her, his hands resting on his knees. A deep sadness resonated from his eyes...a loss he was having trouble dealing with.

Dania closed her own eyes and searched her senses. There was no possible way Geron would take her memories. Why would he do that? Memories made one stronger.

Unless he believed that a memory might make her weak.

A woman with auburn hair hung behind the others, holding herself. Rachel Quirky sniffed and wiped tears from her cheeks.

No doubt she was lamenting Kile. Their relationship had been so strange. Dania never would have expected her commander to fall for someone so different from him.

Geron had been right to erase her from his memory, though. Their relationship would have made him weak.

She gasped, covering her mouth.

Geron had erased Rachel Quirky from Kile's memory. She remembered that clearly. Geron had told Dania what he'd planned to do as soon as he'd found out Kile had been encumbered.

If he'd done that to Kile, he could have done that to any one of them.

She looked back at Calvin Espinoza, the notorious smuggler who had eluded so many enforcers throughout the years.

It was impossible that she would have developed a relationship with him. Wasn't it?

The smuggler moved closer. "Dani, are you okay?"

Her mind swirled. She searched her thoughts, finding wide gaps. But that was impossible. Her memory was flawless. She could recount missions from years ago. Why would a large swath of time simply be gone?

She looked back to Rachel, then to Kile, then back to the smuggler.

"Pasta," she whispered.

His face reddened. "What about pasta?"

"I don't know." She held her forehead. "Is that... Is that a food?"

Espinoza choked out a laugh that sounded more like a sob. "Yeah, it is. You liked it. We slow-simmered sauces together. You made a mistake once and added cinnamon, and it was delicious. Everyone loved it."

She tilted her head. "*Everyone?*"

"Yeah. Alexander, Alanna, Doc, Ethan, Ty, Rachel." He grabbed her hand. "And me."

She closed her eyes, looking down. "How could a mistake bring enjoyment?"

His grip on her hand tightened. "It was a good kind of mistake. Cinnamon is a flavor. It was different. You started experimenting after that and you enjoyed it."

"*Experimenting?*"

"Cooking. You loved to cook."

She shook her head. "I can't remember."

"You told me that cooking was like creating. It gave you joy because you'd spent so much of your life destroying things."

Stars! What else couldn't she remember?

She massaged her chest as a deep ache settled in. Geron had stolen part of her. How could she even be sure who she was anymore?

Kile crouched beside her on her left. "Our sponsor never meant to hurt either of us. He was simply…"

"Keeping his weapons sharp and at the ready." She pressed her lips together. "We are tools to him. Nothing more." She turned to the smuggler. "I don't remember you. Nothing outside of wanting you dead, at least."

The doctor ran an instrument over her. "I have an idea. It won't replace all of your memories, but it might replace some."

"What do you mean?"

"When you first agreed to take the artificial pathogens, I was afraid that something strange might happen and you might not remember that you trusted us." He held up both hands. "You gave me permission to take an imprint of your brain."

Dania gasped, covering her lips with her fingers. "That's illegal. I never would have agreed."

"Yeah, well, you gave some sort of odd reasoning that made the enforcer side of you think that it wasn't against the law. I honestly don't remember what it was, but I still have that engram. We could upload that to your brain and bring you back to the way you were."

Dania frowned. "But that would erase everything from that point, on. I would lose the memories of the war. I wouldn't know that Keveron had been destroyed, and all we'd done to save what's left of our people and Earth."

The doctor looked down. "Yeah, I guess that would be the downside."

Dania shook her head. "I think I've lost enough."

"Would you like to come back to the *Star Renegade*?" Espinoza asked. "I can show you your room. I can show you where we cooked together. Maybe it will jar a few memories."

"There will be few," Kile said. "She may have a haze or a feeling, but unless she left herself hints, any memories Geron deemed problematical are gone."

Her gut clenched. When she considered Kile and Rachel, erasing the commander's memory made perfect sense. Why did considering her own loss leave a deep emptiness inside her?

She held her stomach. "I feel violated."

Espinoza placed his hand over hers. It was oddly soothing. "You've said that before. He's stolen a lot from you."

She drew her hand away. "With reason. He never would have done so to hurt me." Her stomach clenched. He may not have done it to hurt her, but that didn't make it hurt any less.

How could she feel betrayed by her own sponsor?

"Geron was a good prince, and he'll be an even better king." She believed that. But at the same time, a deep dread settled over her. How could she adore someone and feel betrayed by him at the same time?

"I agree," Kile said. "That is why we proposed freeing the enforcers. Alexander and I have proven over the past weeks that we could be loyal while living our own lives."

"That's why he ordered us to work you to exhaustion. He

wanted to give you the same choice, and to get your counsel."

Dania covered her mouth with her hand. A few yards away, Orion's body lay in the grass...an empty shell. "I-I killed him. He was only following orders."

Alexander stepped between her and the body. "No. I killed him. I didn't stop you in time. His death is my fault. Not yours."

She closed her eyes. "No one should have died at all."

Dania had been sure they had all been wrong and acting impulsively. She'd been certain they'd all come slinking back to Geron. All that time, she'd believed herself aloof and above their desires to be free. She'd been the one who'd been corrupted, though. She'd been under control of another, incapable of her own thoughts.

"I was so hyper-focused on you all being weak and in need of feeding that I couldn't see what was happening." She looked back at Orion's body. "I didn't hesitate. I considered him a traitor and killed without hesitation."

She covered her face and choked back a sob. No wonder Geron took away their individuality. It made them more lethal.

Espinoza squeezed her arms and rubbed his thumb in a circular pattern on her biceps. It was calming and...*familiar*.

He leaned down to look into her eyes. "What are you thinking?"

"I'm not sure what to think. I feel betrayed, but I also understand why Geron did what he did. I want to hate him, but I don't."

"Neither do I," Kile said. "But I am looking to the future. Not just for me, but for all of us."

Dania tried to stand. "I'd like to go home. I need to rest."

Espinoza helped her to her feet. "I'll take you wherever you want to go."

The question was, then…where was *home*?

She clung to his arm. Her stomach quaked as her body leaned in to the familiarity of the former smuggler's touch.

He was a stranger. A criminal. But at the same time, her body responded, like her skin remembered his touch and yearned for more.

How much had been stolen from her, and was there any way to get it back?

THE HALLS of the smuggling ship were familiar, which made sense. She'd been held captive there for months. The pits and grooves, blast marks, and broken panels gave her an odd sense of comfort, though. Which was odd, since she'd never allow a ship under her control to fall to such disrepair.

She stared at the door to the *Star Renegade*'s Engineering area. She'd been inside there, helping with repairs, once. There'd been an issue with the machinery, filling the room with catastrophic heat. She'd saved the engineer—and herself. But had she saved the engineer on purpose, or had he simply been close enough to benefit from her power?

"Do you remember something?" Espinoza asked her.

"Yes."

The memory seemed all the more puzzling. She'd been incapacitated at the time. She shouldn't have been able to manifest that kind of power. Although they'd explained that the navigator had been unknowingly feeding Dania, keeping her strong.

If that hadn't been true, she may have died that day, along with the engineer.

She turned to her right and passed the door of the room where Alexander had stayed, then the room where Kile had cohabitated with Rachel, and then stopped in front of the next door.

"This was your room," Espinoza said.

"I know." But if she'd been a prisoner, why hadn't she been contained? She had been in a cell at one point, and in a containment field in the medical area. Those memories were at the top of her mind. This place, however, was one of the memories lightly coated in a veil.

"Would you like to go in?" Espinoza tapped a panel on the wall.

Dania didn't answer, but she stepped inside.

The walls were stark and the furnishings mostly bare—with the exception of a few folded shirts and pants on the dresser.

There was an old-fashioned book on the table beside the bed. She had no recollection of ever owning a paper book. Beside it was a deck of playing cards and a pencil drawing of a woman floating in space with her arms outstretched. The face looked remarkably like her own.

She remembered none of these things.

Dania held the drawing up to the light. Close up, it was just a mass of swirling lines, but farther away, the likeness was extraordinary.

"Did you draw this?" She showed it to Cal.

Cal laughed. "No. I have no artistic talent at all. You told me Kile drew it. Something about wanting to remember you how you used to be."

Dania shivered. The woman in the drawing looked... *angry.*

She puffed out a breath and placed the drawing back on the table.

The remainder of the room barely seemed touched, like she spent little time in her quarters.

"You said I liked to cook. Did I do that here?" she asked.

"No. The kitchen is up in the front of the ship, in my quarters below the bridge."

"May I see it? The kitchen, that is."

"Of course."

Espinoza walked her back past Alexander and Kile's rooms and they turned left toward the ladder that would bring them up to the bridge level or down to the cargo area where the entrance and exit to the ship were. They continued past the ladder to the end of the hall, where there were three doors. The captain's quarters, his office, and his private meeting room.

Espinoza opened the last door to the meeting room.

Dania entered and looked at the long table with eight chairs arranged around it. "I remember having meals here."

"Yes." Espinoza slipped into the room behind her. "I make as many meals for the crew as I can—if we have fresh food, that is."

"Some of that food was stolen."

"Maybe. I never ask where it came from. From my perspective, I paid for it."

A picture hung on the wall. A man and a woman with dark hair with their hands on the shoulders of a young boy of maybe twelve years. The woman had a round face and eyes similar to Espinoza's. The man was slightly shorter than the woman, with a familiar nose and mouth.

Dania turned to the smuggler. "Are these your parents?"

"Yeah." He pointed to the boy. "And that's me."

Cal seemed to sadden. There had been something about this photo that skidded along the edge of her memory. The sadness spread through her, and she tried to push it out. She didn't even know these people, so why should their photos evoke emotion?

She pushed through the door and into the kitchen. Rows of pans, pots, and assorted utensils lined the counters in neat rows. Dania stopped at a rack of small jars with white labels on them.

"Those are the spices." Espinoza picked up a jar with a brown powder inside. "This is cinnamon. Do you remember?"

She shook her head.

"Try this." He unscrewed the cap and handed it to her.

Dania quirked a brow before smelling the jar. A world of sensations exploded in her mind.

Laughter.

Joy.

Comradery.

Friendship.

Pride.

Accomplishment.

Bliss.

Family.

She held her hand to her chest.

Family. She'd had a family here. A real family...not one acting under the orders of their sponsor.

"Are you all right?" Espinoza asked.

"I don't know." She wiped tears from her eyes. "I really was happy here, wasn't I?"

"I'd like to think so."

She ran her fingers along the top of a green, deep, ceramic bowl. "This is familiar."

"Yeah. That's the slow cooker that we made sauce in over and over again." He laughed. "We were trying to make a meal together, but something kept happening to get in the way. We kept having to start over. I don't think we ever actually ate that meal." He frowned. "Wait a minute. We *never did* eat that meal."

"Never?"

He moved closer, placing his hand on her hip. "No. We never did. Geron showed up and everything kinda went to hell."

Dania ran her palm across the counter. The surface was cool, but the sensation felt right. Familiar. Comfortable. "I remember the word *pasta*."

He smiled. "You really enjoyed pasta."

Her breath hitched as she choked down pain building in her throat. "I think I'd still like to try it."

He placed both his hands on her hips, pulling her closer.

Everything inside her told her to push the criminal away, but the touch was so confoundingly familiar. Right... Like this kitchen.

"I'd love to show you how to cook." He blinked away partially shed tears. "We had lots of fun learning the first time. There's no reason we can't relive all those great memories again."

"But I don't remember."

He placed his hand on her cheek. "That's okay. You had some trouble with your memory before, and I'll tell you the same thing I told you then: I don't mind reliving memories with you. We can relive every moment on this ship, if you want. We're all rooting for you. We miss you." He gulped. "*I miss you.*"

Dania looked around the room again. "I think this is where I want to be."

Espinoza straightened. "Really?"

"I want to learn what I've forgotten. I want to know why the smell of a spice fills me with joy." She reached up and touched his face. "I want to know why standing beside a criminal makes me feel...*safe.*"

He placed his hand over hers. "Because I would do anything for you."

His temperature didn't fluctuate. That was the truth, and she'd never heard anyone speak with such conviction outside of an enforcer forced to defend their sponsor.

She eased away from him. "I need to tell Geron how I feel."

Espinoza tensed. "I don't want you going anywhere near him."

She had a feeling she'd heard him say that many times before.

"He ordered Alexander to make me expel enough energy that I'd be capable of making my own choices. He didn't have to do that."

"No, but that doesn't change the fact that he's used to getting what he wants. If you're in the room with him again, there'd be nothing stopping him from taking you back, whether you want it or not."

She placed her hand on his arm. "Come with me. You'll see how rational he can be."

He dragged his fingers through his hair. "I suppose we're going to have to face him one day or another."

CHAPTER 64
CAL

THE WALLS in the *Oliganton* smelled like tin. The *Star Renegade* was made of metal, too. Why his own ship smelled like home and this one smelled like it was freshly cut from a mill, Cal had no idea.

"Don't be nervous." Dania nudged him playfully as they walked. "He sounded excited that I wanted to see him."

"That's exactly what I'm worried about."

Kile called from over his shoulder ahead of them. "Our sponsor has not called any of us back to service. He's kept his word."

"But that's only because he's been busy and hasn't been annoyed by your lack of presence," Cal said. "You all need to remember that he could turn on a fleck of starlight and change his mind at any moment."

The translator-guy bowed to Dania as they approached. "The king has been waiting for you." He opened the door and watched as they passed through.

The meeting room presented more like a throne room, with a large, open space devoid of furniture and what looked like benches along the walls. Maybe the previous king had

523

preferred his subjects to be standing when he'd executed them.

Geron stood at the far side of the room with the Kever princess they'd saved from the bowels of Trellis. She wore a long, blue gown studded with beads that sparkled when she moved. She turned toward them, her gaze falling on Dania, searching her up and down before her nose wrinkled like she'd smelled spoiled fruit.

The king took a step away from her. "Kalina, you may leave."

The princess gaped, then turned to Dania again. Her lips thinned before she bowed to Geron. "Of course, sire."

She walked to the door, taking one last disgruntled glance at Dania before leaving.

Geron held out both his hands. "My Dania. I've missed you."

"I missed you too, Ada." She took a step toward him, but Cal grabbed her arm.

Geron lowered his hands. There was death in the Kever's eyes.

Not much had changed between him and Cal, apparently. Which was fine, as long as His Royal Highness-ness didn't have his slimy grip on the woman Cal loved.

"I'm glad you came back of your own accord, Dania." The new king perused his nails. "I trust you have reasoned with Alexander and Kile and we are done with all this foolishness."

"Hardly," Cal said.

Dania squeezed Cal's arm, stopping him from saying something that probably would have gotten him executed for impudence.

She turned back to Geron. "You sent enforcers to attack me."

"*Attack* is a misconstrued word. Their assignment was to force you to expel a great deal of your power."

"I was fighting for my life."

"As I expected you to. You needed to believe you were in danger to force yourself to expel enough power to engage in this experiment." Geron pursed his lips. "If I had ordered you to overexert yourself without reason, you would have stopped when you started to weaken and then returned to me to be fed before you lost your resolve."

"*Lost my resolve?* I thought they'd gone rogue. My programming kicked in to execute them."

"That's why Alexander's multifaceted approach to your realignment was brilliant. By the time he stepped in, you were exhausted enough that he could force out the rest of your power while still protecting himself."

Dania tilted her head. "But I killed Orion in the process."

"You killed him defending yourself. That was hardly murder, Dania."

"But he didn't have to die." She clutched her heart. "Don't you understand? Orion had many years of life ahead of him, and I snuffed that life out...for *nothing*."

"His loss is unfortunate." Geron checked the nails on his other hand. "He was a good soldier."

"You barely seem concerned, Ada."

"He wasn't one of my own. He was one that I saved."

Her eyes saddened. "But he was then *yours*, Ada. Surely, you don't think your new enforcers to be of any less value than those you raised."

The king stared at her like he was deciphering her words.

"I find these extraneous emotions inconvenient." His lips thinned before he turned to Alexander. "This started with you. When I sensed the resonance of the human female, I should have eradicated her and done everything in my power to sever those links. If I had, none of this would have happened."

Alex's eyes widened before his skin paled, and he looked down.

"I disagree." Kile stepped forward, his hands clasped behind his back. "You would have eliminated the memories, but there would be core feelings left behind, as I'm sure Dania is experiencing now." He took a deep breath, as if he were building courage. "I knew you would erase Rachel Quirky from my mind. I didn't want to forget, so I hid as many memories as I could in the smugglers' ship. Those memories are gone, but I could see that I'd been happy."

Geron folded his arms. "Your point?"

"My point is that I came back. I never lost devotion to you, even though I knew that returning would take away the one piece of me that made me feel alive." He pointed at Dania. "And when Dania started to become the happiest I've ever seen her, I still pressed her to return to you, even though I knew what you'd do to her."

"I made her strong again."

"Yes, you made her strong. But in doing so, you took away her humanity."

The deep blue patches on his cheeks darkened. "She is my general. I need her."

"No doubt. However, allowing her...allowing *all of us* to live our lives will only make us stronger. More devoted."

Geron gritted his teeth. "I do not trust your counsel on this matter, but your words are close to mimicking the counsel of someone I *do* trust."

"Who?" Cal asked.

"Your engineer."

"Ethan?"

"I've quickly realized that he is probably the reason your ship had been so hard to catch. He is wise beyond his limited years in existence."

"Ethan?" Cal pointed at his chest. "*My* Ethan?"

Dania elbowed him.

Cal continued to gape. *Ethan?* The galaxy got stranger and stranger every day.

"Your engineer is unafraid to speak what he considers the truth, even when it might anger those around him. I find that refreshing." Geron turned to the window. "I am willing to entertain expanding this *'enforcers in reserve'* program."

Dania gasped before covering her mouth with her fingers.

Geron continued looking out at the twinkling stars. "However, this program will not pertain to Dania."

Cal stepped forward. "Why the hell not?"

"Because she is my only general, and I need her."

What the blazes? "Then why allow them to drain her power? Why give her the chance to remember if you never intended to free her?"

"Because she is mine. She is who she is because I made it so. I never dreamed she'd want to belittle herself with a paltry human existence."

Dania shivered. "So, all of this was a ruse? Orion died for the simple reason that you wanted to appease Alexander and Kile?"

"Again, it was an unfortunate loss."

She dug her fingers into her hair. "It was not just an unfortunate loss. It was a grievous error in judgement."

The air about the Kever heated as his eyes narrowed. "I trust you don't think that error was mine."

"It certainly wasn't Alexander's or Kile's error. They both believed that you would set me free if I asked. To them, it was worth the risk."

Geron shook his head. "I simply wanted this foolishness to be done with so we could move on to more important things. These delusions are nothing but an annoyance."

Dania pointed at her sponsor. "The only one who is annoyed by them is you!"

Hol-ee-shit.

Cal could barely breathe as the heat in the room spiked.

Alexander's and Kile's eyes were wide. Neither of them moved.

Geron's eyes darkened as he stared Dania down. "You need to be fed."

She pulled her shoulder back. "No. I don't. I don't want this anymore. Don't you understand?"

Geron's nostrils flared. "You don't want what?"

"I don't want to be erased. I had a life on the *Star Renegade*, and you took it away. That was wrong of you."

"Taking away those memories made you stronger. It made you the general I needed you to be."

"The general you needed, or the general you wanted?"

"They are one and the same."

"No, they're not. Kile is right. He came back to you despite falling in love with a human. I did the same. I walked into your arms knowing what you'd do to me."

"You did the right thing."

"Yes. I did the right thing for the galaxy, but you took advantage of that."

Geron's eyes narrowed. "How? This makes no sense. I gave you the ability to command without reservation."

"But maybe those reservations would have made me a better general. You didn't need to erase Cal for me to command your enforcers."

"I disagree. You are what I want you to be."

"Can you even hear what you're saying?" Tears welled in her eyes. "You know if you ask me to come to you now, I will. I'd let you feed me and take away all memories of the *Star Renegade* and its crew. But I'm asking you not to."

"Why? This makes no sense." He held both his hands beside his face. "You are crying. You are weak."

"I'm crying because I'm disappointed."

Geron slowly lowered his hands. "*Disappointed?*"

"Yes. Because I believed you when you told me you didn't want to be an asshole. But now I see that you are no better than your father."

Alex and Kile glanced at each other. They both grew pale as the heat in the room spiked even higher. Dania hadn't said anything that wasn't true, but it didn't look like her sponsor was ready to hear the truth.

Dania gulped back her tears. "I had a room on that ship. My *own* room, not a prison cell." She took a step toward him. "I played games with the crew. We laughed and had fun together."

He grimaced, looking away. "Inconsequential and irrelevant."

"No. It's not. I enjoyed cooking. I learned how to blend spices to make new flavors. It gave me joy, and the crew—my *friends*—appreciated the meals I cooked."

"A waste of your valuable time."

"No, Ada. These things gave me pleasure. Can't you

understand that? I want to serve you. I want to stand by your side, but I want my own life, too. I want to go home to my family and friends. I want... No. I *need to* have a life beyond being your general."

Geron sneered, pointing at his chest. "You are my only general. I need you at my side at all times."

Cal gritted his teeth. Was the Kever even listening to a word she'd said? His hands started to shake before Alexander gripped his shoulder and drew him back.

"I was supposed to be your general." Alex placed himself between Geron and Cal. "I meant it when I said I'd be willing to be reprogrammed to act as her second."

"That will take time."

"But we are at peace. No doubt the Carteks will return, but it will be many years from now. By that time, you'll have built a new army of enforcers and added several more generals to your ranks."

Geron spun toward him. *"Several more?"*

"Your father and your siblings all had several generals. You can do something similar, by giving those with the strength of generals ranking order, so if the highest fell, the next in line would take control. It's an efficient system."

"Creating generals is a waste of time I no longer have. I cannot even remember the last time I did anything for pleasure."

"Neither can I." Dania held the Kever's gaze, unblinking.

Wow! Cal wished she'd been this bold before she'd lost her memories. Maybe they wouldn't be having this conversation.

Geron stared at her, gaping.

Dania took a deep breath and released it slowly. "Things are not as simple as they once were for us, Ada. Your enforcers are powerful, but we've all learned that our kind are not impervious to death or mishap." She raised her hand to Kile. "We already have a similar chain of command. Kile has always been fully capable of commanding in my stead. He just didn't have the power to control or feed the others. Think of how much more efficient he would have been in my absence if he'd had the same capabilities as I had."

Kile straightened slightly and a small smile played against his lips. Was that *pride*?

He'd alluded to thinking of Dania as a daughter, but maybe he craved recognition from her as well?

Geron pursed his lips and flicked a glance at Kile.

"Spreading your command capabilities is not a sign of weakness, Ada." Dania took another step toward her sponsor. "It's true that your father only had two generals, but you admitted yourself that he made decisions out of his own arrogance. He believed his enforcers were unstoppable. We discovered, at great consequence, that this was an erred way of thinking."

Cal circumvented Alexander. "Your father had a lot of erred ways of thinking. The people of Earth hated him. But they don't hate you. Not yet, at least."

Geron glared at him. "I suppose there is a point to you telling me what I already know?"

"You don't have enough enforcers left to enforce your father's law."

Geron's lips formed a sneer. "Again, you're telling me the obvious."

"What I'm saying is that this is a time of rebirth. For Keveron, for the colonies, for Earth...for everyone. Since you don't have the manpower to enforce law like your father did, this is the perfect time to reevaluate his edicts on right and wrong."

"There is right, and there is wrong. On that, my father and I agreed."

"But it's not so black and white. You can make degrees of crimes. Not everything deserves death. People can be rehabilitated, or sometimes they just make mistakes and didn't even intend to break a law. In those cases, a small punishment is in order. Hell, you can even let local law govern things like that." Cal inched closer. "Think about how much more good your enforcers could do in the galaxy if they weren't chasing petty criminals."

"Your thinking is flawed. Humanity will always hedge toward its darker nature."

"Not necessarily. Look at Themyscira. They have hardly any crime there. They have their own police force and their own laws. You could learn from them."

"While I agree," Kile said, "they are historically combative toward Keveron."

"Yet they fought beside you for the greater good. If you reached out to them in good faith, as part of the new, friendlier regime, I think they'd be willing to talk."

Geron growled. "You are asking for too much too soon. All this change will cause anarchy."

"You don't have to do it all overnight. I don't even suggest trying. But find more people smarter than you to advise you. I'd even suggest using your enforcers to tell you if your advisors are lying to you, or sense if they are not acting in good faith."

Dania nodded. "He's right, Ada. The important thing is you consider other opinions, think them over, and change the galaxy for the better. Be the king who people celebrate. Not the king that they fear." She took his hand. "Be the king I always believed you to be."

Geron nodded, then looked at Cal. "Perhaps your human captain has absorbed some of his engineer's wisdom."

"I'll take that as a compliment." Cal smiled.

The king still scowled at him, but with slightly less of a homicidal glare.

Geron looked to Alexander. "We will start sessions immediately to reprogram you. Dania will remain my primary general, but while she's taking time for...*human pursuits...*" He wrinkled his nose at Cal. "Alexander will take her place."

The king glared at Cal again, before looking away.

Cal didn't care if the guy blamed him for every last bit of insolence thrown at him today, as long as Dania remained free.

Alexander gave Cal an amused grin before he bowed. "I would be honored, Ada."

The king turned to Kile. "You will access the remaining enforcers and let me know if any others are viable candidates for command."

Kile's lips pursed before he also lowered his head. "Yes, Ada."

"Once Alexander is reprogrammed, you will start with two-hour sessions. I will reprogram you as well."

Kile's eyes widened before he lifted his chin. "I will serve you with honor as always, Ada."

Dania closed her eyes, but tears still ran down her cheeks.

Geron placed his palm on the side of her face. "Isn't this what you wanted?"

She choked back a sob. "Yes. Thank you for being the king I always knew you could be."

Geron frowned. "You've said that before, when I pardoned the crew."

She nodded. "Breaking with tradition suits you."

He smiled slightly, then leaned down and kissed her. Alex's fingers dug into Cal's shoulder, pulling him back again. Kissing your subordinates might have been normal in their culture, but that didn't mean that Cal had to like it.

Geron released Dania and turned to him. "I am also interested in something your engineer mentioned about humans possibly volunteering for the honor of being an enforcer. It would certainly be less bothersome if people volunteered to have their genetics tested, rather than scanning medical records."

"The pictures of your enforcers flying through the air and stopping the bomb from impacting in Manhattan are still trending in the news feeds." Cal looked at Dania and Alex. "The kids are looking up to you as heroes. If you make an open call, I guarantee you people will line up to be considered, but most are only going to be interested if you engage the reserve program permanently."

Geron nodded, looking at the floor. "Your engineer had similar thoughts."

He did? How many times had this guy been talking to Ethan?

Geron flexed and unflexed his hands, looking at his palms. "We will make these small changes, and I will meet with advisors on how to proceed." He turned to Cal. "I would like to offer you compensation for your engineer. I will continue to need his counsel."

Cal cocked his head to the right. "We are talking about the same Ethan, right?"

Dania elbowed him again.

Cal held up his hands. "Okay. I don't own Ethan. And even if I did, I wouldn't sell a member of my crew. You may ask him if he's interested. If he is, I'll be happy for him."

"But you will be without a vital member of your crew."

"Yeah, I will be. But that doesn't mean I'd stop any of them from an opportunity to do something greater. They're my family, and they'll continue to be my family, even if they're no longer on my ship."

"You have an interesting philosophy of command, Mr. Espinoza. Losing a member of your crew will lessen your strength."

"Maybe, for a short time. But we'll adapt. That's how we survive."

Geron's eyes scanned the room, finally resting on Dania. "Perhaps that's how we'll all survive."

CHAPTER 65
CAL

EIGHT MONTHS LATER

TY FLEW three circles over the clearing of trees and then gently set the *Star Renegade* down beside the large pond on the homestead Cal had purchased in a cozy, quiet valley with mountains rising over the tree line to the east and west.

You couldn't get much farther from outer space than this.

Ty placed his hands on his lap and gazed at the controls. "I guess that's it. Our last voyage together."

Cal tapped him on the shoulder. "It's been one heck of a ride."

"That's for sure." Ty rubbed his eyes. "I can't believe you signed the *Star Renegade* over to Glenn."

Cal ran his hands over the back of the dashboard. "Me, neither. But land is expensive on Earth. I really wanted to give Dania a quiet place she could come home to when she's off-duty."

"I get that. I know the *Renegade* is collateral on your loan, but why didn't Glenn let you keep her while you were paying him back?"

536

Cal lowered his gaze. "Yeah, I was a bit surprised as well, but his assistant said they needed the physical collateral to back up the cost of the land. I had to sign her over before they'd wire the funds."

There was so much about this ship that was home. Signing those contract feeds had been the hardest thing Cal had ever done, but the *Star Renegade* represented his past. He'd have no use for a freight hauler as he started his new life as the Second Reign Historical Documentation Advocate at the Galactic Academy on Earth.

Ty shook his head. "I can't believe he was such a stickler about it. I mean, it's not like the man hasn't broken rules before."

"I guess he had more important things to worry about. I never even spoke to him directly. He was too busy working on another deal. I guess Glenn will always be a businessman first and a friend second."

"That doesn't make it suck any less." Outside, four brown ducks flew in and landed on the pond. "I understand why you picked here to settle down, though. It's really beautiful. And so green! It's nothing like where I grew up."

"Yeah, well, like they say, for good or for bad, where you grew up is home."

"And sometimes you find home in the most unexpected of places."

"What do you mean?"

Ty's hands gripped the manual controls. "Nothing, I guess." His eyes reddened before he turned away. "We better get down there. I don't want to be late."

When their boots sank into the thick, lush grass, the back door to the house opened.

"My boys!" Mel ran toward them, her long skirts wafting

around her ankles. She looked out of place on green grass after spending so many years in her desert home on Kirato.

"Mel?" Ty ran to her and pulled his adoptive mother into his arms.

They both held on to each other as Mel whispered something into Ty's ear. Whatever it was made him cling to her harder.

Back at the house, Cal's mom stepped out the back door, wiping her hands on her apron. Seeing her like that brought back so many memories of homecooked dinners and games on the back porch.

She waved at him, then placed her finger over her lips, pointing at Ty and Mel.

"What are you doing here, Mel?" Ty sounded nearly smothered in Amelia's grip.

"Celebrating my Calvin's new appointment." Mel released Ty. "He's going to be documenting history for generations of students to learn from! I couldn't let just anyone cook for such a momentous occasion now, could I?" She gave Cal a hug. "I am very proud of you. I told my Stanley when you showed up in our back yard, that you had a bright future ahead of you."

"I was dehydrated and nearly dead when you found me in an interplanetary transport crate."

"It showed ingenuity. Not everyone would have the courage to smuggle themselves to another planet!" She turned back to the house waving her hands in the air. "Now I must get back to my cooking! You are both too skinny!"

Cal laughed. "Mel doesn't change."

Ty shook his head. "There are only a few constants in the galaxy, and Mel is one of them."

Cal's mom said a few words to Mel before walking to Cal. "Hello, sweetheart." She gave him a hug.

Cal held his hand out to Ty. "Mom, this is Ty. My first mate, a hell of a pilot, and an even better friend."

Ty tipped his head. "Nice to meet you, ma'am."

"Lisa!" Mel called from the house. "We need more rolls!"

Cal's mom called over her shoulder. "Coming, Amelia!" She smiled at Cal. "She's an interesting woman. Very much used to getting what she wants."

"We know that very well," Cal said.

His mom turned to Ty. "She thinks the world of you."

Ty's cheeks turned pink. "I'd like to think so. She and Stanley pretty much saved my life. I always wanted to make them proud."

"Oh, they are." She cupped his cheek. "They definitely are."

"Lisa!" Mel called from the house again.

Cal's mom laughed. "I guess I need to get back to work." She kissed Cal on the cheek. "I'll see you in a bit."

As his mom disappeared into the house, a skipper with royal insignias flew overhead and landed beside the *Star Renegade*. Ethan stepped out wearing a blue Kever uniform that clashed with his copper-colored hair.

"I got here on time, right?" Ethan shook both their hands. "I'd hate to think I missed a real homecooked meal."

Shivana exited the ship. She had to duck and turn sideways to fit through the door.

Ethan pointed his thumb over his shoulder. "You've all met my personal bodyguard, Shiv." He tugged his uniform collar. "You know, important advisors like me need all the protection."

Shivana quirked her brow. "As important as you are, our sponsor looks forward to quiet times where you are not available for constant counsel."

Ty snickered. "I guess Ethan still talks too much, huh?"

Shivana smiled. It actually made the massive woman look pretty. "He definitely still talks too much."

"I'm quiet when it counts, baby." Ethan nudged her with his shoulder.

Her smile widened. "Indeed."

"Too much information." Ty poked his fingers in his ears.

Stanley walked toward them from a small freight hauler. He scrolled through something on a data pad, probably checking business dealings back home. He paused, tapping on the screen, before tucking the device into a pocket in his billowing, striped robes and holding out his arms.

"Calvin Espinoza. I never thought I'd see that day when you'd retire." He embraced Cal, kissing both his cheeks. "I am so incredibly proud of you. Mel and I imagined you doing great things, and you far surpassed our expectations."

Ty shook his head and puffed out a breath, looking down with his hands in his pockets.

"And my Tyler." Stanley hugged him. "We never dared dream you'd be able to leave Kirato. And here you are, one of the heroes of the *War to End All Wars*."

He glanced back to the *Star Renegade*. "A lot of good it did me."

Cal's gut clenched. He understood. The thought of letting the *Star Renegade* fly away without Cal in the captain seat had left him with many sleepless nights.

In the end, though, he had to follow his dream.

The brush along the tree line separated, held back by

invisible hands as Dania, Alanna, and Alexander walked out carrying baskets. A smaller basket floated a few feet off the ground to Alanna's left before Max's legs, and only his legs, came into view, then blended with the grass again.

They exchanged greetings with Ty, Ethan, and Shivana before Dania gave Cal a kiss.

"What's this?" He pointed to the basket.

"Fresh berries from the bushes by the stream. Mel is going to be thrilled." Dania rooted through the basket. "Oh, and look at this." She pulled out a red tomato larger than her hand. "It ripened early. Won't your mother be excited?"

"Look at that beauty. My mom will be thrilled!" It was probably too late to add to a sauce, but the size of that fruit was bound to make his mom dream of culinary possibilities.

"I'm so excited to show her." There was a sparkle in her eyes. It was sweet, genuine, and so Dania.

Cal leaned down and gave her another kiss.

"What was that for?"

"Because I love you."

She slipped her hand around his neck and kissed him again. "Be careful, Mr. Espinoza. A girl could get used to being treated like this."

"Good. Because I intend to make you good and used to it."

"You two make me want to barf," Ty said.

Cal slipped his hand around Dania's waist. "Don't knock it until you try it, my friend." Cal reached past Ty and shook Alexander's hand. "How's the training going?"

"I'm getting used to my new skills, but it will be some time before I can adequately replace Dania."

Alanna jostled her basket from one arm to the other and

slipped her hand around Alex's biceps. "Meanwhile, we're looking for a nice place to settle down." Her eyes sparkled. "We're thinking of starting a family."

Dania gaped. "What does Geron think about that?"

"It's none of his business." Alex kissed Alanna's forehead. "I intend to do my tours of duty as required, but my personal time is my own."

Dania beamed. "Well, that sounds wonderful. I'm so happy for you."

"Not as happy as my mom." Alanna's smile was contagious. "She's so excited she's not even mad that she hasn't met Alex, yet."

Wait a minute… *Her mom?*

"So, she's okay then?" Cal asked. "You've talked to her?"

Alanna's eyes widened. "Oh! I forgot to tell you. Yes! They never left Europa. They're all fine. My little sister says 'Hi', by the way."

"That's great news." Cal gave her a hug, then turned to Alex. "You better go and make a good impression on her mother. That's important human stuff."

"She's going to love him as much as I do." Alanna hugged Alex's arm.

Mel walked out the door and pounded a metal spoon on the house's downspout. The *gong* noise echoed off the trees.

"Dinner!" Mel announced. "Don't make me wait. Food is to be enjoyed hot!"

Stanley patted Cal on the back. "She means that. We better get going."

When they entered, Doc and Cal's mother were placing plates on the table.

Cal shook Doc's hand. "I didn't realize you were already here."

"I was the first to arrive." Doc wiped his brow with this arm. "Mel put me to work. I thought *your* meals were elaborate, but they were nothing like this." Doc pulled him to the side. "I'd hoped to talk to you before everyone else got here. I have something for you."

He grabbed a metal box from the floor and opened it. A puff of cold air escaped as he pulled out a small cylinder.

"What's that?" Cal asked.

"It's a CGRP inhibitor."

"And what does a CGRP inhibitor do?"

"It cures migraines."

Cal gaped at him. "Seriously?"

"Yeah. It's not a hundred-percent cure, but it *can be* if you take it monthly. There's a year supply in this box." He popped the top off the syringe. "May I?"

"You sure as blazes can!" Cal rolled up his sleeve and tensed as the needle quickly pricked him.

Doc placed a tiny dot bandage on the site. "I hope this works as good as they say. Let me know, okay?"

Cal rolled his sleeve back down. "Thanks. This is amazing."

Doc tossed the used syringe into the side of the box. "It's the least I could do for putting up with me all these years."

Cal shook his hand. "The pleasure has been all mine."

On the other side of the room, Dania and Stanley laughed, arranging and rearranging the forks.

Ty stood off to the side staring at the floor. Cal had hoped seeing his parents would cheer him up.

"What's going on out there?" Mel called from the kitchen. "There is food to be served and no hands doing the serving!"

"Coming!" Doc headed into the kitchen.

"More! I need more hands!" Mel called.

Ethan clapped and rubbed his palms together. "Time to get to work. I've been looking forward to this for weeks."

Shivana ducked under the doorframe and entered the kitchen behind him. Everyone followed, each grabbing a serving dish or two and bringing it back to the table before they sat.

A stack of napkins hovered through the door, and one drifted off the pile and landed on each person's plate.

Cal reached into the air until he found fur and scratched behind Max's ears. "Thanks, buddy."

Cal's mother sat beside him. "Your invisible friend has been stealing my rolls. That's why I needed to make more."

"He has a habit of doing that. Always make double if Max is around."

"I'll remember that."

Dania passed the empty seat beside Cal and touched the back of the chair next to his mother. "Do you mind if I sit next to you, Lisa?"

Cal's mom beamed. "Of course! But please, call me *Mom*."

Dania's cheeks turned pink as she sat. Cal's mom leaned close and whispered something to Dania that made her laugh.

Cal closed his eyes and sighed. This day couldn't have been any more perfect.

Mel stood in the doorway and scanned the table, probably making sure nothing had been forgotten. "Good. Good. Now we can enjoy the fruits of our labors, yes?" She took the seat next to Stanley.

"Definitely yes!" Ethan said, reaching for a bowl of spiced mashed potatoes.

Stanley stood. "First, let's raise a glass." He picked up the cup of aged grape juice in front of his plate. "To kinship and comradery. May we all find the blessings of the stars."

"Hear, hear." Everyone raised their glasses, tapping each other's drinks. Shivana frowned, but after Ethan encouraged her, she did the same.

Across the table, Mel put a second helping of meat on Ty's plate. "You are too skinny. You need to eat more."

Ty gaped at his plate. "Mel, seriously? No one can eat that much!"

Beside them, Doc and Stanley discussed something about fusion reactors, while Max reached over and stole Doc's roll.

Farther down the table, Ethan placed a massive dollop of potatoes on his plate.

"What is that?" Shivana asked.

"When Mel is cooking, this is pure heaven." He reached for the butter. "You make a hole in the top and let the butter melt inside. Then you poke it in a few places and the butter runs down the side like a volcano."

She frowned, watching him mold his creation.

Alexander slid a glass of milk toward Alanna, and she smiled, placing her hand over his.

This was family. True family.

Cal had meant it when he'd said he wanted the best for his people. He hoped they all found their dreams, but even if their dreams took them far away, he hoped they'd still find a home here at his table.

The door burst open and slammed against the wall.

"Hey!" Rachel stepped inside. "You started eating without me?"

Cal nearly spit out his carrots as he stood. "You didn't tell me you were coming."

"Of course I'm coming. Why wouldn't I come? Sheesh, Cally, you should know me better by now." She looked over her shoulder. "Did you hear that? Cally thought we weren't coming."

Kile filled in the space behind her. "Then I'm sure this is a happy surprise."

Dania beamed, shaking his hand. "It's wonderful to see you, but who's in command?"

"Miguel asked for the honor. He's not as capable as you or Alexander, but he has the wherewithal to call for help." Kile pulled back his sleeve to reveal a communication band.

Mel stood, wiping her hands on her apron. "More mouths to feed means more happy bellies." She pointed around the table. "All you stand. Squeeze in. We will get more seats, yes?"

Doc stood and grabbed two more chairs. "Ask and you shall receive!"

Dania gave Rachel a hug and shook Kile's hand before handing each of them a plate. Mel followed on with silverware.

"Now sit. Eat!" Mel commanded, taking her place.

"How are things on Hitus?" Alanna asked Rachel.

"Amazing! We found a building right away. The ceilings are high enough that my Big Guy doesn't have to duck to get under the doors. I'm going to open my tour guide business as soon as I get final approval next week." She hugged Kile's arm. "We're so excited. Right, Big Guy?"

Kile nodded without expression. "Indeed."

Mel waved a spoon in the air. "Less talking. More eating. You are all too thin. The next breeze will blow you all over."

Both Shivana and Kile raised their brows, but they must

have been warned about Mel, because neither of them said anything. It was a good call, because magical powers or no magical powers, Mel was a force to be reckoned with.

A tone sounded on the wall screen.

"Who could that be?" Dania asked.

Cal stood. "I don't know. Everyone's here."

Cal tapped on the ID scanner. "It's coming from Walker Station." He clicked the *accept* button.

Glenn appeared on the monitor, his round, rosy cheeks taking up most of the screen. "Cal, Cal, Cal! Always a pleasure." He moved closer to the camera, like looking through a window. "And look at this! As they say back on Earth, 'The gang's all here!'" He raised a wineglass holding a reddish-colored liquid. "May I propose a toast to the people who made me a rich man?"

"You were already a rich man, Glenn." Cal took his place at the table.

"Yes, of course that's true, but now I'm an even richer man. Do you realize the odds that were stacked against you in that battle? And then when you went off half-cocked on your own? No one expected you to get out of that alive!" He moved closer to the glass again. "No one but me, that is." He reclined, and his whole body jiggled with mirth. "I could retire off the proceeds from that single bet alone. But I won't because what fun is there in that?"

Shivana scowled at the screen. "Did you call to gloat over gambling on a war while people were out there risking their lives?"

Glenn held up his hands. "Oh, no, my very large and very formidable-looking woman." He looked at Cal. "I called to tell my good friend Cal here, that the business deals I was working on have cleared, and I no longer need the collateral that we agreed to."

Cal dropped his fork. "You're kidding. Really?"

"I never kid when money is involved. Your property is cleared, and the deeds to your land and the house that you are sitting in have all been transferred into your name. I also took the liberty to overpay your taxes so much that you're probably covered for the next thirty years." He held out his hands again. "It was the least I could do. It was barely a fraction of my winnings, after all." He chortled again, slapping the table in front of him. "Congratulations, Cal. You're now a homeowner."

The table erupted in cheers.

Kile and Alexander quirked their brows, looking at each other. Shivana narrowed her eyes, glancing around at the merriment. They probably had no idea what a big deal this was. Owning land on Earth was an empty dream for most.

"Hold on, everyone." The room quieted as Cal turned back to the Glenn. "But what about the contingency clause?"

Glenn grinned in an almost fatherly way. "All taken care of. The *Star Renegade* is no longer under my name. Per our contract, I reregistered it under one Tyler Melrock-Stanley."

Ty coughed, spitting a piece of meat on his plate. "Say what?"

Cal leaned his arms on the table. "The *Renegade* is yours, Ty. I couldn't think of anyone else I could trust her with."

"Except for me," Glenn said.

"Yeah, I trusted you to promise to give her back."

"I do love that you trust me. I think you trust me more than I trust myself." Glenn snorted a laugh. "You know how many collectors offered me a small fortune for that old, beat-up ship?" He raised his glass again. "I wish you all well on your future endeavors." He placed the glass down. "In fact, instead of raising a glass to you all, I raise a carefully crafted french fry." He waved a fork filled with cut fried potatoes with a blend of brown spices on them. "Because, quite frankly, a carefully crafted french fry will beat wine in a taste-testing contest any day."

"Hear, hear." The room raised their glasses, and Glenn raised a french fry before stuffing it in his mouth with a wide, satisfied grin.

Glenn grabbed a few more french fries and saluted with them before closing out the comm.

Ty stared at his plate as his friends patted him on the back. He barely appeared to be breathing.

Cal waited for Mel to be looking in the other direction before he threw a roll at his former first mate.

The bread bounced off Ty's nose, floated across the table, and onto Max's plate before the furry stowaway rematerialized in his seat.

Cal returned his attention to Ty. "Are you okay?"

Ty's gaze rose from his plate. "You... You gave me the *Renegade*?"

"Yeah. I want you to have her." He held up his pointer finger. "With one caveat."

"You name it!"

"When Dania and I want to go anywhere, you'll come and get us. I hate public transportation."

Ty's face morphed into a red, teary mess before he stood and squeezed his way around the table to throw his arms around Cal. "I really thought you'd sold her."

"Well, I didn't want to get your hopes up in case Glenn didn't come through. I would have fought for her if it didn't work out, but I'm glad it did."

Doc raised his hands. "Excuse me, Captain Ty?"

Ty returned to his seat. "That sounds weird. I mean, I like it, but it's still weird."

"I'll call you whatever you want if I can still be your doctor. I kinda have nowhere else to live."

Ty reached across the table and shook Doc's hand. "That's good to know. Happy to have you."

Shivana raised her hand tentatively, looking almost meek despite her size. "If I may suggest, it would be prudent to keep a post open for an engineer as well."

Ethan straightened. "What do you mean?"

"While you are a trusted advisor, I am not sure how long King Geron will be able to stand your...*frankness* on a daily basis. I think he may be open to calling you through long-distance comms when he needs your consultation."

Ethan sat back. "Huh. That would actually be pretty cool. Maybe I'll pass that idea by my good friend the king and see what he thinks."

Shivana's eyes widened. "I guarantee you he will be quite open to the idea."

Ethan held out his hands. "Perfect. What do you say, Ty? Do you have room for me and Shiv?"

She frowned at him.

"Aww, come on, babe. You know you can't get enough of me, and I'd still be the king's advisor. I'll still need a body-guard. I'm sure His Highness-ness won't mind."

She sighed. "Indeed."

"I'd be happy to have both of you." Ty glanced around the table. "In fact, the *Star Renegade* will be open to any of you at any time." Ty tapped the edge of the table. "Wow. This day definitely didn't end up how I expected." He looked up. His eyes were red again. "Am I really the captain of my own ship?"

Mel shot to her feet, her eyes filled with tears. "Oh, my boy!" She hugged Ty. "I'm so proud of you!"

Ty folded into her arms. "Thanks, Mom." He flinched. "I mean, Mel. Thanks, Mel."

She smoothed back his hair with her palms. "No. I like the sound of *Mom*." She pulled him into her arms again.

Cal's own mother squeezed Cal's hand. Her smile didn't need words. Her other hand rested over Dania's, and Cal's chest ached like his heart might burst.

A few years ago, he'd thought he would die out in space, alone. Now here he was, surrounded by everyone he loved.

How had he gotten this lucky?

Stanley stood. "So, Captain Ty. How do you feel about taking your first commission? Do you think you could transport an old trader and his wife back to Kirato in a few days?"

Ty stood and saluted. "I'd be honored."

Stanley shook his hand. "No. It would be I who would be honored, my son."

Ty burst into tears again and hugged his adoptive parents before he turned, wiping his eyes. "Wow. Could you all promise to forget about all these tears? Because I'm sure Ethan is never going to let me live this down."

"Yes, I will," Ethan said. "It may take a few years, but eventually I'll find something else to ride you about."

Ty settled back into his chair and raised his glass. "How about we toast to old friends?"

Cal raised his mug. "And new beginnings."

They all raised their drinks. "To new beginnings."

———

Shoot! I'm crying more than Ty.
I'm a big, blubbering mess!

THANK YOU so much for taking this journey with me, Cal, Dania, and the whole crew of the Star Renegade.

We did it! It took six books and close to 600,000 words to save the Earthan Cradle. What a ride!

I'm not sure how long it took you to finish the series, but these six books took me over five years to write. (Six years if you include the planning stages.)

These characters are part of my family, and sending this final installment out into the world is both exhilarating and sad, because I'll no longer be spending time with this crew every day.

If you loved Star Bandits, it would mean so much to me if you told your friends or talked about the series on social media. Word of mouth is the best form of advertising, and every new reader spurs me on to write more books for you to enjoy.

Oh! And please tag me if you post about the series on social media so I don't miss it!

If you haven't read any of my other books, please check out my website at jennifermeaton.com to find your next epic adventure.

To be notified when my next book releases, follow me on Bookbub, Goodreads, or Amazon, (the details are on the "about the author" page) and if you'd like to be the first to hear about my next series or other news, please feel free to sign up for my newsletter by scanning the QR code below.

Thanks again for joining Cal, Dania, and all the Star Bandits on this incredible journey.

Happy smuggling!

—Jennifer M. Eaton

ACKNOWLEDGMENTS

The more books I put out, the harder/easier these acknowledgement sections are to write. Harder, because I like to make things sound fresh and new, and I'm usually thanking the same people. Easier, because, once again, I'm usually thanking the same people.

As always, I'd like to thank my husband and kids for being supportive. Having an author for a wife and mom isn't always easy, but at least I'm the "cool mom" with an interesting job. After all, I make stuff up for a living and get paid for it. Even though my kids are now adults, I'm reasonably sure they all think that's pretty cool.

Thanks to my beta readers and editing team—Emilee Thompson Harmon, Sharon Hughson, Shaila Patel, Eric, Amy McNulty, and Tandy Boese—for helping make me NOT look like a blithering fool. Every time I think I've mastered where to put that stinking comma, or the difference between lay and lie, I'm once again proven wrong.

And...not to sound like a broken engine manifold, but THANK YOU for reading. Without you enjoying these stories, they are just words on a page. You bring these characters to life in your own minds. Thank you for riding the *Star Renegade* with Cal, Dania and the crew.

ABOUT THE AUTHOR

Jennifer M. Eaton hails from the eastern shore of the North American Continent on planet Earth. Yes, regrettably, she is human, but please don't hold that against her.

While not traipsing through the galaxy looking for specimens for her space moth collection, she lives with her wonderfully supportive husband, three energetic offspring, and a duo of poodles who run the space-port when she's not around.

During infrequent excursions to her home planet of Earth, Jennifer enjoys long hikes in the woods, bicycling, swimming, snorkeling, and snuggling up by the fire with a great book; but great adventures are always a short shuttle ride away.

Read more from Jennifer M. Eaton

www.jennifereaton.com | Jennifermeaton.com

facebook.com/Jennifereaton.author

x.com/jennifermeaton

instagram.com/jennifermeaton

goodreads.com/Jennifermeaton

bookbub.com/profile/jennifer-m-eaton

amazon.com/stores/author/B00BEP9L1E

threads.com/@jennifermeaton

youtube.com/jennifereaton1011